About t

Pete Langman has tried to ensure that should he ever write an autobiography, he will not lack material to draw from. Accordingly, he worked as a painter and decorator, rock guitarist, theatre sound engineer and tour guide, amongst other things, before acquiring a PhD in early modern literature. He has lectured at several universities, including Oxford, Goldsmiths and Sussex, and was diagnosed with Parkinson's disease in 2008. He now works as a writer and editor specialising in seventeenth-century literature and history, fiction, Parkinson's and music.

KILLING BEAVTIES:

or

The CHRONICLE of

SUSAN *HYDE*

NEWLY WRITTEN BY THE
famous & *Esteemed* Pete Langman
Doctor of Philosophie

Authorised and Approved
By Miss Walsingham, *Invisible Agent*
& *his* Lordships *Mistress.*

INSPECTA EGO AVIS ENIM CANTANS

LONDON,
¶ Printed by *J. H.* for *Ulysses N. Bounderby* at the
Signe of the *Raven* in *Covent Garden.* 1656.

This edition first published in 2020

Unbound
6th Floor Mutual House, 70 Conduit Street, London W1S 2GF
www.unbound.com

ISBN (eBook): 978-1-78965-066-2
ISBN (Paperback): 978-1-78965-065-5

Cover design by Mecob

Printed and bound in Great Britain by Clays Ltd, Elcograf S.p.A.

MIX
Paper from responsible sources
FSC® C018072
FSC www.fsc.org

For the two most important women in my life, and my most faithful supporters, Michèle and Nadine.

Super Patrons

Nadine Akkerman
Mark Allison
Alison Andrews
Sandip Basu
Shelli Bell
Rory Birtwistle
Sara Bostel
Jay Bradley
Angela Brand
Birgitte Breemerkamp
Mark Brenner
Gilly Britton
Ed Clarke
Ian Cohen
Charlie Connelly
The Dangerous Creatures of D
Sally Davidge
Liz Davidson
Vicki Davis
Leanda de Lisle
Nikki Dearnley
Femke Deen
Lindsay Dennis
Kate Dennis
Janet Dickinson
Matthew Dimmock
Samuel Dodson
Allan Engel
Urban Evjen
Lotte Fikkers
John "Fingers" Fingleton
Naomi Foyle
Christiane Gerstetter
Rafi Gnirck
Andy Gordon
James Grime
Freya Gye
Jennifer Haddon
Gordon Hamme
Pat Heath
Derek Horsham
Chris Hunter
Ineke Huysman
Karin Jones
Claire Jones
Alex Jones
Sam Kaislaniemi
Anja Karl
David Katz
Calie Kelder
Dan Kieran
Harriet Knight
Simon Lamoon
Rosemary Langman
Michèle Langman
Ewan Lawrie
Geoff Lea
Jacqui Lofthouse
Anna McDuff
Eli Merchant

John Mitchinson
Michael Molcher
Carlo Navato
Jackie Neville
Lisa Overly
Oleksiy Petrov
Justin Pollard
J. Rhoads-Peterson
Vanessa Rigg
Lynn Robson
Mark Schofield
Astrid Schrader
William Scott
Wm. Scott Brown
Heather Sharman
Victoria Silberbauer
Paul 'Smudger' Smith
Jonathan Stamford
Tim Standish
Valorie Steinbeck
Alan Stewart
Martin Stiles
Dickon Tolson
Eleanor Updale
David van der Linden
Ruben Verwaal
Sarah Westbrooke
Lindsay Whitehurst
Shirley Whiteside
Simon Wilkinson
Margaret Wilkinson
Raymond Williams
Jenny Wilson
Rusty Wood
Kit Wright
Andrea Zuvich

Prologue

July 1655, London
John Thurloe receives a letter

John Thurloe did not so much as blink as the door behind him swung open, and the sound of heavy boots hitting thin floorboards filled the room. His eyes were fixed upon the man in front of him. Filthy, bloody, unconscious and with his clothes in tatters, he remained seated only on account of his having been tied to the chair. The palm of his right hand faced upwards, its three remaining digits curled and blackened. This was brutal work, not for the faint hearted nor the weak of stomach. But as brutal as it was, Thurloe knew it was necessary. Not to extract information from those he suspected, no. A man will say almost anything to make the pain stop, to be sent back to the relative comfort of his cell. Intact. But when a man stuck to his story in the midst of the most hellish of torments, then, and only then, might you begin to believe him. But the story must come first. And the stories continued.

'A letter for you, Master Secretary,' said the man with the boots. He was broad, muscular and stood with an assurance that bordered on arrogance.

'Thank you, Nathaniel,' said Thurloe. 'I wonder would you read it to me? My hands are a little, well, soiled.' This was true in more ways than Thurloe cared to admit, but now, as the light from the open door forced its way through the room's dismal atmosphere, he could see the truth all too clearly, etched into the face and body of the prisoner. Hobbes may have drawn the king as the body politic, but it was the one in front of him that truly represented the country. Ravaged, torn and bloodied, but hanging on for dear life.

The wars had begun as a reaction to tyranny, the king's arrogant disdain for parliament, and they had raged for the best part of a decade, during which time they had ripped the country apart. Even the execution of King Charles had not stemmed the slaughter, as the royalists fought on for another two years until, at Worcester, they were forced to acknowledge ultimate defeat. Thurloe had watched as many of his contemporaries threw their youth away on matters of principle that would never affect them. He was a pragmatist above all else, however, though his pragmatism was such that while he would not throw his hat into the ring until it was clear who the ringmaster was to be, when he did offer his services to the victor, they came with unquestioning loyalty. The victor was Oliver Cromwell. In such days as these, he was once told, both loyalty and ability are recognised quickly, and rewarded well. And so it was that Cromwell appointed Thurloe to be his Secretary of State, an office that encompassed the roles both of political advisor and head of intelligence. For all his power, his position demanded, on occasion, that he roll up his sleeves and get his hands dirty. Today was one such occasion.

Since Worcester an uneasy and fragile peace had settled on the country, like the ashes from a burning house when the thunderheads are climbing. Charles Stuart, son of the executed king, was in exile, his court riven with faction, his mother Henrietta Maria at odds with his most trusted advisor, Sir Edward Hyde. For all their bickering abroad, neither defeat nor exile were, it seemed, enough to fully quash their spirits, and still they raised their plots. But Thurloe, efficient and intellectually able, had spent the past two years recruiting spies all around England and on the continent, so while rebellion after rebellion was planned, each was, in its turn, betrayed, and then crushed. The latest, the so-called Penruddock rising, had been so well documented by his informers that it barely managed to break out. And yet here he was, months later, mopping up the last of the conspirators. How the country would ultimately respond to the newly imposed regimes of the major-generals, military men entrusted with the task of ensuring piety and obedience at a local level, was yet to be seen.

Behind him, Thurloe heard Nathaniel's knife separate the brittle wax seal from the thick and ragged paper, followed by the letter's unfolding.

Master Secretary,

I heare by one of creditte that within a sennight of the full moon two soldiers will make theyr waye to Queenborough by way of boat from Dunkirk. They are one Duggan, an Irish, and a Colonel Talbot, Scots. Theyr mission I knowe not but that they are sympathetick to the traitour's aunt.

I run short of coine as my purse is being run right ragged by my nurse here in Antwerp.

Your loyal servant,

H: Manning

'That Manning is an idiot,' said Thurloe. 'Too much so to lie with any conviction.' He slapped the face of the unconscious man in the chair. All that resulted was that his head moved from resting on his left shoulder to resting on his right. 'I detest the smell of betrayal, Nathaniel. Take this creature back to his cell. Let him sweat for another day and then remove him.' With this,

Thurloe stood, washed his hands in a pail of water, rolled down his sleeves and walked to the door, stopping briefly to allow Nathaniel to place a black cloak around his shoulders.

'Anything else, Master Secretary?' asked Nathaniel as he took Thurloe's hat and held it out for him.

'Yes,' said Thurloe, taking the hat and pressing it firmly onto his head. 'Ride to Queenborough tomorrow and wait for these men. Discover their intent. Pick a fight with them. If necessary, arrest them. I imagine they are mere adventurers, and the traitor's aunt has troubles enough with the Palatinate. Certainly too many to concern herself overmuch with us. Manning's information has been unreliable of late. I fear he may be lost. No matter. Perhaps these two in Kent may tell us.' And with this, he walked out of the room. As he traversed the corridor, he heard the sound of the prisoner being hit by a mass of water, and the initial shriek of surprise subsiding into a low sob. 'Good man,' he said to himself, and walked out into the street.

The evening felt fresh and cool, though it was anything but, as the breathless early August heat sat upon the city like a fever. But Thurloe had spent several hours in a small room breathing in nothing but the stench of burning flesh and the incontinence of a terrified man. Only this could render London's fetid air so much as tolerable.

Thurloe yearned for something new and fresh to purge him of the choler of this great but damned city.

I

I

Dunkirk, the Spanish Netherlands, August 1655
Diana Jennings takes a trip

Diana Jennings lifted the skirts of her dress and smiled at the sailor who stood in front of her, squinting slightly as the still weak morning sun groped at his face. She could see the waters of the English Channel lapping at his calves, and figured that exposing her rather unconventional footwear was preferable to allowing her already wet clothes to get even wetter. The prow of the two-masted vessel on which she had booked passage ground itself into the shingle of the beach beside her as its stern rocked gently on the swell. A light sea-fret drifted towards the shore, and had it not been for the chill of early morning Diana might have imagined the mist steam, and herself in one of the hot baths she'd heard were so popular in the Ottoman court. Sir Thomas Roe had been a friend of a friend and she had read third-hand versions of his reports of the Sultan's mores with relish, and no little envy. In truth, however, at this moment the opulence of the once mighty Byzantium seemed as distant as a child's fable.

She surveyed the small, natural harbour from where she was soon to set off for home, and shivered as the fret rolled over her. Home. Diana no longer knew where her home was. Certainly

Antwerp had become rather too dangerous since Henry Manning had appeared on the scene. She knew that she ought to have resisted the urge to fleece him as he slept off his evening's quota of wine, but Diana rarely did what she ought. It was a habit that always threatened to catch up with her, even if it never made good on its promises. But it wasn't Manning's coin that weighed down her skirts, nor was it her conscience. His coin merely weighed down her shoulder bag, and this was one burden she welcomed. Coin was always welcome. But the thick dew that still lay heavy in the air had soaked through each layer of her dress and was now cold against her skin.

'Have you no trunk, milady?' The sailor adjusted his cap as he spoke, and waded through the surf towards her.

Diana travelled light as a matter of course. She had learnt the hard way that a trunk of clothing rendered a dawn getaway virtually impossible. Anyway, coin and bare-faced lies smoothed the way into society better than any silk.

'Milady?' he enquired once more.

Diana held out the small satchel that was the full extent of her luggage. The sailor took it, hesitated for a moment as he felt its weight, and then threw it under the boat's canvas tilt. 'You'll do well to cover it, save it from the spray,' he said, looking Diana up and down. Diana was more than used to this. She knew that while at first glance she appeared much like all the others who sought his services as a ferryman, there was something about her that he could not put his finger on. Diana was just another woman in her mid-thirties, average height, moderately handsome, though not striking; dull from the felt hat that covered her light brown hair to her feet. Well, perhaps not to her feet. But it was her countenance that set her apart. Diana knew that ladies who used his services were generally forced to do so by the vicissitudes of fortune, and she imagined that they made no attempt to hide their distaste for either their situation or his appearance.

Diana was different. Trouble was Diana's primary currency: it was not something she ran from. Everything about her was conspicuously inconspicuous. She could melt into a crowd as easily as become the centre of its attention. Her dress was a case in point. It was embroidered silk, though not of the highest quality, and its initial impact dulled on closer inspection. It wasn't as expensive as it made itself out to be. In that sense, at least, the dress suited her perfectly.

'You have none more suitable clothing?' asked the sailor as he offered his assistance in boarding.

Diana shook her head almost imperceptibly, and a little disdainfully, before taking the sailor's hand and negotiating the gangplank. As he guided her steps onto her transport home, he held onto her hand for just a moment too long, and Diana knew that he was wondering how her skin might have felt on his were she not wearing soft leather gloves. But she could also see that he dismissed this as a fool's contemplation, and he was no fool. Once she was aboard, the sailor merely directed her to the position on the boat's two benches that offered most protection from the spray that would inevitably soak the passengers. She nodded her thanks and sat. He manhandled a piece of oiled cambric to wrap around her shoulders. Diana took the material and drew it close around her. The atmosphere was tense, and she sensed danger. It might just be time to try a new name.

As she hunkered down on the bench, Diana's attention was drawn by two men, both armed and of military bearing, who were approaching the boat at speed having appeared from an opening in the treeline. They threw their travel bags on board and leapt on after them without a moment's hesitation. They appeared a little nervous, and spoke in low voices to the sailor before one of them handed him a coin, then another. As they prepared to take their places another passenger appeared, a well-dressed gentleman in his mid-forties. He walked calmly towards the boat and boarded, his demeanour not the only part of him that was in stark contrast with his fellow passengers.

'Gentlemen, milady,' he said. 'Edward Skinner. Ned.' He handed another coin to the sailor. 'I believe you may cast off without further delay, my good man.'

'I have one more fare yet,' replied the sailor, slowly coiling up the hemps that lay loose on the deck.

'I travel alone, sir,' said Diana, conscious of where this placed her in the opinion of her fellow travellers. 'Other than my maidservant, who is currently inconvenienced.' No sooner had she spoken than a young woman, hardly more than a girl, appeared on shore, still adjusting her dress.

The sailor held out his hand. 'Come on, take it, jump. Then we can cast off.' The woman drew the air through her teeth and shook her head before launching into a tirade of invective so heavily accented that while not one of the words she used was recognisable, their meaning was perfectly clear. 'I don't reckon your maid much fancies the trip, milady,' he said, smiling at Diana.

'Well, I can't say I much care,' said Diana. 'She's a useless bloody girl anyway. Never hire a French maid from Antwerp.' She sank into her bench. 'More trouble than they're worth.' Diana allowed herself a little smile as the girl walked away from the shoreline. She'd accompanied Diana just as far as requested, and had terminated her contract likewise. Diana may have been travelling alone, but there was no need to look as though she was. An unaccompanied woman who was neither nurse nor midwife positively courted trouble, whereas one who had been abandoned by a servant might meet with a more sympathetic response. And sympathy, Diana well knew, came a close second to coin in terms of its utility.

'It seems we might set sail without further delay, brother?' said the taller of the two military men, the urgency in his words at odds with the soft Irish brogue in which they were delivered. The sailor looked at him, then his palm, and shrugged. There was a sigh, a sifting of more coin and a slightly shifty smile.

'Reckon we are fully loaded. Take to your seats and we'll cast off apace,' said the sailor as he retrieved his hemps, kicked at the gangplank, dug an oar into the shingle and pushed hard. The boat crunched its way off the shore, turning as it did so, and the sailor sat between the two masts and began to row in long, confident strokes, each one of which pushed them further away from the coast of the Spanish Netherlands, out of the shelter of the harbour and into open water. The further from dry land they travelled, the more relaxed the atmosphere on the boat. A shout went up from the shore.

'It appears someone is distraught at our progress,' said the Irishman to Diana, sitting on the bench next to her, so that they faced the other two passengers. 'Captain Duggan,' he said, and Diana held out her gloved hand. He took it in his and nodded. He was not only tall but thin, his face angular and long, almost equine, and lank, black hair sprouted from under his cap. A twist of hair, sealed at one end with wax and attached to a piece of ribbon, hung from his left ear.

'Aye, sir,' said the sailor, his arms straining to put more distance between the boat and shore. 'I see a man on horseback, but cannot hear him, alas.' He grunted with the effort. 'I served as gunner with Prince Rupert, in the Mediterranean and the Bahamas. Can barely hear a thing.'

Diana leant forward in order to get a better view of the apparently missing passenger. As she did so she saw a puff of smoke followed by a loud report. Then came a splash which was swallowed by their wake. 'Oh my,' she said, holding her right hand to her mouth in horror. It was Manning, there was no doubt about it. He'd made good time, too, considering the state she'd left him in. She was both impressed and a little flattered.

'Now that,' said the sailor, 'I both heard and saw.' He upped his tempo and rowed for another sixty yards before standing to unfurl one of the sails. 'He seems angry, gentlemen. I've had some rum customers but it's rare a late arrival feels the need to shoot at me.' The wind gripped the canvas and the boat leapt forward with a jolt. 'Will his anger run to pursuit now we are beyond his piece?'

'I very much doubt it,' said the well-dressed gentleman. 'And I very much doubt he was shooting at you.'

'Doubt is far more costly than certainty,' said the sailor, inspecting his sails. 'And anyone shooting at a passenger is shooting at both me and my craft.' He smiled and tugged at the rigging. 'I doubt not that my little boat might struggle to hold full canvas on such a day.'

'Really?' The gentleman shook his head in disbelief as he handed over yet another coin. 'Perhaps this may help cover any repairs that our unreasonable demand for expedition may render necessary, though it may seem prudent in this instance to withhold full payment from the ferryman until the destination is reached.' He turned from the sailor towards Diana. 'Enchanté,' he said.

'Lady Stanley,' said Diana. 'Widow of Sir Thomas.' She held out her hand once more but it was grasped instead by the second of the soldiers, who was shorter and fuller featured than Captain Duggan, and sported a beard in the Stuart style, his naturally curly hair crushed beneath a hat that sported a long feather. It took Diana a little longer to spot his hairlock earring, obscured as it was by his dark curls, but it was undoubtedly there.

'My condolences,' he said, his voice placing him on the East coast of Scotland. 'And allow me to introduce myself. Talbot. Colonel.'

'Lady Stanley,' repeated Diana, before turning to the gentleman Talbot had interrupted. 'And you?'

'Skinner,' he said. 'Edward Skinner. As I have already said.'

'Steady sou-sou-east,' said the ferryman as he finished with the rigging and sat down, grasping the tiller in one hand. The conversation between the passengers stopped as the small boat began pitching and rolling in the gentle swell, cutting through the waves with ease. The boat continued in silence for a quarter of an hour until the tall Irishman stood, without warning, and exited the canvas shelter under which he had been sitting with his fellow cargo.

'Hold on to the rope and not...' shouted the sailor as Duggan hung his head over the starboard side of the boat and vomited, '... into the wind.' His voice tailed off as the man retched again, as much because of the bile that had blown back over his face and mouth as because of the boat's motion.

'The good captain is no sailor,' said Edward to his companion on the bench.

'Indeed not,' said Colonel Talbot. 'But he is an honest man and a good subject.' The colonel turned to Diana. 'And to whom does your allegiance lie, given that you are bereft of a natural lord and master to direct your thoughts? Do you follow your late husband's support for the king or do you sway towards parliament now that you have some licence?'

Diana leant forward towards the two men and addressed them in as close to a whisper as she felt would be heard over the crash of the waves and the vomiting Duggan. 'My allegiance is my business, and I recognise no master. You would do well to keep yours to yourselves when in company you do not consider intimate.'

'So, we have a parliamentarian whore in our little boat,' said Talbot, smiling as he reached towards Diana with intent.

'Leave her be,' said the sailor, sternly.

'And what if I choose not to, man? I am Colonel of Horse in

the third Scots regiment of the Dutch army,' he said. 'I do what I choose, not what some blue powder monkey tells me.'

'Well, you may do as you wish, but good luck ordering the channel to bear you to safety rather than drag your miserable hide into the depths, which is what it will surely do after I throw you overboard,' said the sailor, adding 'sir' for good measure.

The colonel went for his sword, cursing, but the sailor pre-empted this movement, bringing a solid oak belaying pin down onto his hand before it had settled into the protective embrace of the sword's hilt. The colonel barked with pain, cursing his ferryman once more but now doing so as he grabbed at the stricken fingers, gripping them tightly to assuage the suffering.

'The next hand that reaches for its steel shall be left clutching a cracked head for its pains,' said the sailor. 'And you may be colonel on land, but on this boat you are but a piece of cargo. A right troublesome piece at that.' Diana quietly sheathed the stiletto she had half-drawn from her left sleeve. The sailor saw her motion, one that had gone unnoticed by the other passengers, and continued. 'You and your fellow passengers are under my care. No harm shall come to any one of you but by my hand.' He looked at Diana and winked.

'If you think...' began the colonel, still wincing with pain but now furious with thwarted desire, but the motion of his left arm to his pistol was stayed by Skinner.

'Peace, good colonel, peace,' he said. 'You have not only been bested in the fight but you are also outranked. The sailor here is right. This is his kingdom, however narrow of beam, however shallow of draft. And, what is more, if you shoot him you as good as drown us all, as I cannot handle this craft, Duggan certainly can't and I respectfully question your credentials for such a mission.' Skinner removed his hand from the colonel's arm and reached into his bag, from where he retrieved a small bottle. 'Cognac. You'll find the finest you've yet tasted cannot compare.' The colonel took the bottle and grudgingly swigged the spirit down while Skinner continued. 'If, of course, you suspect milady here of being a master mariner then by all means shoot the man.' He paused as if waiting for an answer. 'No? Well then, keep your hands from your weapons and we'll all arrive safe and sound at the landing ground of our choice, where you'd be advised to keep your weapon hidden.' Skinner looked at the sailor, who put his fingers to the brim of his cap and dipped his head in acknowledgement.

For the next few hours Diana kept both her counsel and her distance, sitting alone on her bench, cambric clasped tightly around her shoulders. Meanwhile, the Irishman retched and moaned, the colonel chuntered to himself and Skinner surveyed the horizon, keeping up a constant communication with their ferryman. She hoped there were to be no more surprises before they arrived at their destination.

The day had cleared considerably by the time they had a kenning of land, at which the sailor struck his sails, set about his oars and rowed the last mile or so until they made landfall.

The sailor jumped into the surf as the boat ran aground on the beach. He tied the painter to a wooden post and jumped back on board before looking at the gangplank and then the rake of the shore. 'My apologies, milady, but you must either walk the surf or I must carry you,' he said. Diana indicated that she favoured being carried, at which the sailor jumped into the shallow waters around the boat once more and, making her sit on the side of the craft where the sea was at its lowest, he took her in his arms and waded ashore. 'One of the gentlemen will like as not follow with your bag.'

'Thank you, for this and for earlier,' said Diana, as she was set down on dry land. 'I don't know what I would have done without you.'

The sailor smiled. 'You know exactly what you would have

done. A lady you may well be, but I'll warrant you're a dangerous one. I don't know what you have up your sleeve, but it would have surprised the colonel.'

'I find the element of surprise most advantageous,' said Diana, palming a coin that she then passed to the sailor undetected. 'But I think we have never met, nor have you heard of me.'

'I believe you're correct.'

'Which direction is Queenborough?' she asked.

'That way, through the narrow gate there,' said the sailor, indicating to their right.

'And the London road?'

'The track to the left,' said the sailor, indicating again. 'But you cannot mean to travel that way alone, milady?'

'Thank you,' was all Diana said, and watched as her three travelling companions leapt from the boat into the surf, wading the last few yards to dry land. The tall Irishman fell to his knees, grasping the soil in his hands with such joy it was almost as if it were from the foot of the cross rather than the coast of Kent. Skinner handed her bag to the sailor.

Duggan got to his feet and looked at the two tracks that they had to choose from. 'Which is for Queenborough?' he said, unhooking a water bottle, taking a swig and swirling it around his mouth before spitting it out into the sand.

'To the right,' said the sailor, taking the bag to Diana who stood to the left.

'She means to travel alone?' said Duggan.

'Indeed, sirs,' said the sailor. 'Can you blame her?'

'Well,' said the colonel. 'We are for Queenborough. I confess I care not for the so-called lady. The night may have her. Come, let us be on our way. I need some honest English ale to wash away this taste of parliament from my mouth.' At this, Colonel Talbot, Captain Duggan and Mr Skinner set off towards Queenborough, while Diana walked a few hundred yards along the London road, found a fallen tree to sit upon and waited.

After half an hour, she saw the form of Edward Skinner at the end of the track. She stood up as he approached her.

'You took your time, Edward.' Diana was glad to see her escort arrive, as she courted enough danger without travelling alone through the countryside.

'Oh, that bloody colonel. You really got under his hide,' he replied. 'I had to agree you were all sorts of slut before he would let it lie.'

'Now there's an irony,' said Diana. 'Let's get on. It'll be dusk soon and we've a couple of miles to make up.'

'It'll be good to see Susan again,' he said, and they began to walk.

Not for the first time, Diana was glad that the need to maintain a ladylike facade stopped at that, the facade. Beneath her silks she wore a pair of sturdy, bucket-top riding boots that rose to just below the knee. The weather had been clement for several weeks so the track was hard and stony, the grass worn away by the constant attention of travellers' feet and the hooves of their accompanying beasts of burden. While the track was wide enough to accommodate a small cart, Diana and Edward walked single file to avoid the blackthorn and blackberry bushes that reached their long, spiny fingers out into their path as if fishing for a silk dress.

Over the next three hours they barely spoke two words to one another. Diana was not sure what, exactly, it was that they were walking into, but it was unlikely to be entirely welcoming. They were tired, sore footed and thirsty when the track finally widened and fed into something approaching a road with a fingerpost showing the way to London. The King's Arms was a good half-mile further, but they had the fortune to be passed by a drover on his way home from market. He was more than happy to add the two dusty travellers to the goods he brought back home, not least as they promised to express thanks for their passage in the form of ale.

2

Diana makes her mark

It was almost dark when they reached the inn, and Diana knew that the laughter coming from within the King's Arms would stop the moment that she and Edward passed over the threshold, and so it was. As they entered, the evening's joviality vanished, revealing an underlying atmosphere of low menace that felt as if it was in the very smoke that seeped out of the great inglenook, the chimney not yet hot enough to draw the soot up and away from the customers. The menace was that born of fear, the fear of strangers, the fear of rumour, the fear of the unknown. It was the fear that had settled on much of the country in the few months that had passed since the failure of Penruddock's revolt, and the subsequent sequestration of local government by the major-generals. It was the fear that everyone was being watched just a little bit more closely than they had thought. Diana was also well aware that, at least so far as the inn's customers were concerned, she was out of her natural habitat. The innkeeper broke the silence.

'You folks looks a little fine for my humble establishment,' he said, spitting on the rag he was using to polish a pewter tankard. 'I'll hazard you are lost, milady, sir?' He doffed his cap. 'Not a good combination in these parts. Fine and lost.' Diana lowered her eyes as the innkeeper stared directly at her.

'I believe we are exactly where we want to be, my good man,' said Edward.

'Aye? And where might that be?' said the innkeeper.

'The King's Arms, Boxley. An honest inn honestly named where one might receive succour from the rigours of travel in return for coin.' And with this, Edward opened his purse and flipped some money at the innkeeper. 'We'd like a private dining room, three cots for the night, stabling for a horse yet to come, and two mounts ready for tomorrow morning.' Edward watched as the innkeeper bit into the metal and smiled. 'I am told the establishment is true to its name.'

'Indeed sir. We are loyal, though keep such loyalty to ourselves unless pressed.'

'And we have certainly pressed you hard,' said Edward, shaking his head. 'Do ensure that this good fellow is well furnished. His cart was a most welcome surprise on the road.'

'Certainly, sir,' said the innkeeper, the glow from the gold he had just held to his blackened teeth remaining in his countenance as he pocketed his bounty. He whistled and a young boy appeared. The innkeeper whispered something in his ear and the boy scampered off into the dusk.

'And his task?' said Edward, raising his eyebrows.

'To prevent any unwelcome surprises ruining your evening,' said the innkeeper. 'There are wandering groups of parliamentary soldiers - you know the sort I mean. Set by the major-generals to interfere with our lives and ensure we are pious, dull and obedient. They like to cause trouble, and they smell rebellion where others smell merely hard work and ale. And there is trouble in the air.'

'He is to be trusted?' asked Edward.

'He is my son, so I trust him about as much as I trust you. But this,' he said, tapping the coin beneath his shirt, 'this I trust. This my son trusts. Reputation is all. And reputation must be earnt.' He filled two tankards from the barrel, and handed one each to Edward and the drover. 'And for the lady?'

Diana took Edward's tankard, drained it, belched and placed it back on the table. 'I trust that answers your question,' she said. 'Where's your privy?'

'We men mostly use the indoor facility there,' said the innkeeper, pointing to a corner of the room where a bucket sat apart from the rest of the customers. 'We don't often entertain ladies of your class and elegance.' A smattering of laughter went up. The atmosphere was beginning to clear, from menace to something that Diana found a little more commonplace. 'You may wish to use our outdoor privy.' He leered at Diana a little longer than was comfortable. 'I'd be happy to hold a lantern for you so you know where you're pissing.'

Edward took a step forward but Diana held him back with a raised hand, and, without breaking eye contact, took the tankard from the table and slid it under her dress. The innkeeper was merely one in a seemingly infinite line of idiots who thought a lady incapable. She squatted and pissed loudly into it. He was also one of a similar group who mistook her for a lady. When the stream had abated she placed the now steaming tankard back onto the table. 'Now, see if this tastes any different from your ale.' She smiled. 'Wine. And make it your good stock. We may have coin aplenty, but we are short on patience.'

The innkeeper nodded as the silence that had fallen was broken by a cough, and then a snort as the other customers held back the next wave of laughter. He pointed to a door tucked away in a corner and Diana and Edward moved towards it. As they did so they heard the door slam shut and the hush return. A voice rang out. Clear, and confident. There would be no questioning the authority of this speaker.

'Susan,' said Diana.

3

Susan Hyde enters the inn

Susan Hyde, tall, dark haired and wrapped in a thick black cloak, stood in the doorway of the inn and summoned up every ounce of her conviction, every minute of her training. Where Diana had a certain attitude that could get things done, Susan had the easy, natural authority of a high-born gentleman, when she allowed herself to wield it. That it emanated from a female frame merely accentuated its affect. As she stood, feeling the collective gaze upon her, she realised that she needed to take control of what felt to her like an unnecessarily combative situation. It was at such times when she drew strength from the Sisterhood. Since their founding in the 1620s, Les Filles d'Ophélie, as they were known to those few aware of their existence, had expanded their remit from a single aim to something rather more noble. Those men who supported them did so willingly and yet unknowingly. But the sisters were more than capable of acting on their own. And now that was what Susan needed to do. Act. She touched the locket around her neck and whispered to herself: 'Moi, la différence.'

'My mount needs attention. See to it,' she said, before turning from the innkeeper and embracing Diana and Edward in turn. 'Sister. Brother.'

The innkeeper threw a cloth at a young man asleep by the fire. 'Horse,' he shouted. The young man fell off his stool and rushed out to see to Susan's mount.

'Have our needs been made clear, brother?' said Susan.

'We were just discussing more pressing arrangements, sister,' said Diana. 'But the answer is yes.'

Susan surveyed the ragtag band of customers slumped on tables or sat on stools by the fire, all silent, wondering what sort of trouble had just entered their world, before she turned to the innkeeper. 'Well?' she said. 'Are you going to keep us waiting in this fleapit or direct us to supper?'

The innkeeper pointed at a doorway, and ushered the three visitors towards it. As he did so, another man entered the inn. The innkeeper greeted him as he slapped the dust from his coat and turned to fetch him ale. 'All quiet on the roads?' he asked, as the man placed his money down.

'There's been trouble in Queenborough,' said the man, before taking a deep draught of his ale.

Susan stopped still at the mention of Queenborough. 'What trouble?' she asked.

The man raised his head, looked at Susan and then the innkeeper, who nodded. 'Two men, travellers,' he said. 'One Irish, one Scots. Detained after a fight down at the Cock, taken to Sittingbourne no doubt. Swore they were of the Swordsmen, and goodly blades they wielded too, I hear, but force of numbers saw them captured safely enough.'

'How came you by this information?' asked Susan. 'And tell me, did they continue to swear their allegiance to Prince Rupert once arrested or no?'

'From my cousin who rode through an hour ago,' said the man. 'And from what he said their belligerence faded as the ale wore off and their situation became rather more close.'

'Ha! These men are full of it until someone punctures their

pride,' said Susan with a snort. She shot Diana a look. 'I imagine they were alone?'

'So they said,' replied the man. 'They came from Dunkirk in a boat sailed by a local. He'll be questioned tomorrow, no doubt.' He faltered a little. 'But he's no telltale. They'll get nothing from him.'

'My thanks for that, good sir.' At this, Susan gestured at the innkeeper to refresh his tankard and then she, Diana and Edward walked into the private dining room. Before closing the door, she turned and spoke directly at the innkeeper. 'Knock and wait,' she said. And shut the door behind them.

The room was dominated by a heavy oak table. The three sat themselves around the end furthest from the door and were silent for a few moments, heads bowed in prayer. They then took each other's hands.

'Brother,' said Susan. 'You risk much in this dangerous passage to England. If you were to be caught, who knows what Thurloe's men might suffer you to endure?' As she spoke, she held her brother's hand tight. 'It would be no little victory were Cromwell's spymaster to capture the king's closest advisor, and in possession of cipher, no doubt. It is death now to one apprehended with such characters about their person.'

'Soft,' said Edward. 'I will not be apprehended. There are loyal subjects yet in this country of ours. Subjects who work to restore the anointed king.' He spoke quietly, as if he feared that there were still enough who supported the new regime for them to be surveiled unknown. 'I imagine that these two adventurers have done us a favour, so long as the ferryman does not tell of our accompanying them on the crossing.'

'A stroke of luck,' said Diana, smiling.

'Luck?' said Susan, 'I suppose you could call it that.'

'In what way was this not luck?' said Edward, looking from

Susan to Diana in quick succession, as if suspecting them of some involvement in the affair. 'Were they players?'

'Well,' said Diana. 'Duggan didn't play at sickness, nor the colonel at being so pugnacious, and they are both who they say they are.'

'To catch a spy you must set a well-baited trap,' said Susan. 'You taught me that when first you recruited me as a courier, brother. They will never suspect a woman, especially a lady, you said, and you were right.'

'We fed a suspected turncoat with the information that they were shortly to cross the channel,' said Diana.

'Manning?' said Edward.

'Manning,' replied Susan. 'And so we set no players.'

'An unnecessary risk,' said Edward. 'We would have uncovered him eventually. But to have their trip coincide with ours...' his voice tailed off as he contemplated the possibilities. 'It is as well I travelled under the name Skinner rather than Hyde.'

'You will note that I had no idea that either you or Diana were to visit until I received yesterday's message,' said Susan. 'What is the point of making me postmistress of the Knot and yet denying me such information?'

'Ah, the Knot,' said Edward. 'Does Penruddock not mark its end?'

'Even after the failure of Penruddock, the Knot is yet to unravel,' said Susan. 'And with Manning unmasked, its security seems assured.' As Susan spoke, she wondered which of them she was trying to convince. Since its creation, the Sealed Knot had remained a secret organisation, and yet still their every rebellion was thwarted almost before it began. It may not have been infiltrated, but it still appeared to leak rather badly. And yet Susan kept the organisation afloat, raising funds and coordinating lines of communication. Lines that Edward, in his infinite brotherly wisdom, ignored, putting them all in danger.

'And these men?'

'Safe, brother,' said Susan. 'Without doubt they carry nothing that links them to the Knot, nor will their behaviour seem anything other than that of two drunk and arrogant men. Of this you can be sure. They will make contrition in the morning, and be bound over or fined, then released. They played their part well.'

'And Manning? Is he aware he has been exposed?'

'He is aware he's been conned,' said Diana, smiling. 'He rather showed his hand as we left the coast behind. No doubt the opprobrium he feels towards me will keep his true fate unnoticed until we can have him dealt with.'

'This is all good news indeed,' said Susan. 'But brother, why we are here? Any business that demands such a perilous journey for one so important must be pressing.' Her brother's answer was interrupted by a knock at the door. Diana opened it carefully, and the innkeeper's daughter, a girl of no more than twelve, gaunt and thin, walked in bearing a large tray. She set the tray down on the table, turned and walked back towards the door. 'Girl!' said Susan. 'Have you no manners?' The girl stopped, turned and curtsied. 'Better.' Susan may have been in the back room of an inn, but manners were manners. 'So many in these straitened times have no respect for the natural order of things.'

As the girl took her leave of the party, Edward took a trencher from the tray and investigated it. 'No plate?' asked Edward. 'We must eat from the table like commoners?'

'Better live commoners than...' Susan checked herself and waited until the door was shut again. She took off her cloak to reveal her dress. She wore a thick petticoat, a linen shift and a woollen waistcoat with a kerchief around her shoulders. 'Don't laugh, brother,' she said, as she saw how he was looking at her now she wore the clothing of a commoner. 'We women sacrifice much in this age. If you think I keep the Knot's wheels turning from the salon you are much mistaken. I carry myself like antiquity and fame, with my head muffled from sight. As I am not even seen, I am hardly suspected.'

They ate as they talked, fatigue and hunger conquering their naturally formal selves. The meal was better than Susan expected. A venison pie was the centrepiece, the meat presumably easier to acquire than when all such beasts were technically property of the crown. It was hearty and plentiful. She resisted the temptation of asking her brother whether Charles Stuart's court in Paris ate quite so well. She doubted they drank so well, as while the inn and its inhabitants were of the rougher sort, it served quite excellent wine. There was a fair trade in contraband goods on this part of the Kent coast. Those government agents that did make the effort to discharge their office, carrying out regular and diligent checks on the goods coming into the country, soon found themselves with either rapidly failing health or, more commonly, a greatly enhanced lifestyle.

'This is surprisingly good,' said Edward, as he speared another slice of pie with his pocket knife and poked it into his mouth. As he swallowed, following it down with a great gulp of wine, he rifled through his bag. 'The truth is, I do not know the true intent of this trip's business. Other than that His Majesty insisted that I, personally, carry it out, and that I, personally, carry this to you.' He drew out a small, paper packet, sealed with a great globule of red sealing wax imprinted with the sign of the Knot. He handed it to Susan. 'I imagine it will explain more.'

Susan took the packet and inspected the seal. Then she slit it with a penknife and unfolded it, and as she did so a smaller packet dropped out. She read the main letter out loud.

Deare Sister

I haue receiued yours of the 15 of June wth the inclosed for wch I giue you many thankes and must intreate you to say all of kindesse from vs to mister Shaw. I am very glad our letters haue so good pasage and truly if thay did but know wth what inoscence wee write to each other, I am confident thay would not trouble them selues to open our letters, as yett none of yours to me haue bine tuched. Our freinde remembers him very affectionatly to you, god be thanked both he and all your freinds heare and at home are very well and all of vs much the better for the cordiall. I pray god continew the same blessing to you, and all wth you

Deare Sister

Your most affectionat
seruant Fran: Edwards

'And what of the enclosure?' asked Diana.

'Do you have some cordial?' asked Susan.

'Yes,' said Diana, passing a small glass bottle over the table. 'It's much better than the last batch. You need merely the faintest touch.'

Susan dabbed a tiny spot of the liquid onto a handkerchief and allowed the moistened material to glide over the package. As she did so, a series of letters became visible. Susan read them and immediately handed the smaller packet to Edward.

'Interesting,' said Edward, inspecting the packet carefully. 'Now this is a very, very special folding.' He turned the packet over in his hand and showed an edge to Susan and Diana. 'You see the locks here, here and here...' he pointed to a complex system of paper locks, seals and flosses while his audience remained unimpressed. 'This does not do what normal locks do. If this were intercepted, it would be obvious that there is no way of opening this letter without its being obvious. It simply cannot be reconstructed.'

'Edward,' said Susan, betraying her frustration by her tone. 'Do you forget who I am? This evening you talk not to your sister, but to the postmistress of the Sealed Knot. I do not need a lesson in the folding and interception of letters.'

'Charles says that no letters are being intercepted, but he cannot know that for certain,' continued Edward, ignoring Susan's complaints. 'And he cannot know that because his usual locks are not impervious to the attentions of a skilled technician. This one, however...'

'Came to us in a letter that wasn't even locked,' said Diana.

'Yes,' said Edward. 'But had it been intercepted then so would we. The message you revealed, "prey conveye the inclosed to the bearer", tells us everything we need to know.' At this he placed the tip of the blade of his pocket knife into one corner of the packet and sliced it horizontally. The letter unfolded almost by itself. 'You see this crease here?' he said, pointing at a slither of paper adjacent to two other slithers. 'If you were to open this in the obvious fashion, knowing that this would destroy the locks, this short area would be torn lengthways in four places. Even if you thought to do this,' he took Susan's handkerchief and wiped it along the crease. 'Then rebuilding this section would be nigh-on impossible.' He brought the letter closer to his face and went visibly pale.

'What is it, brother?' said Susan, now becoming fearful. 'What will the king have us do?'

Edward held up his hand, and Susan fell silent. She hated the way he thought to command her with such disdain, though she hated the way in which she was so easily commanded more. After what seemed like an age, he stood and tossed the enclosure into the fire. The flames flared red as the paper, and its message, were totally consumed. He kicked the chair and took another draught of his wine.

'Brother Edward, you're scaring me now,' said Susan. 'What is it we are to accomplish?'

'Susan,' said Edward. 'Sweet sister.' He paused. 'Know you of any suspicion that you are who you are, that your name and status have been uncovered?'

'None whatsoever,' replied Susan. 'Indeed, the last I heard, Thurloe was convinced that S.H. was Helen Sheldon. Mr D'Esmond of France is also suitably mysterious, and they make no connection with you.'

'Of this we must be thankful, and of the rest,' Edward hesitated.

'By the stars, will you just tell us what it is we are to do,' said Susan, now on the verge of shouting.

'Yes, yes,' said Edward. 'It is simple. You are to broker an exchange, that we may acquire knowledge.' He poured himself another cup of wine, splashing it on the table as he did so.

'An exchange?' said Susan, quietly.

'This is most distasteful,' said Edward. 'This will make you like to a common madame.'

'Time for a new code name? Rahab perhaps? Pandarus?' said Diana, laughing, and both Susan and Edward stared at her. 'What?' she asked, as she cleaned the last of the pie from her plate. 'You're surprised I know the Bible? And I can't believe you'd call Susan common, though I suppose she does a passable impression. And what common slut is she to employ, and in what scheme?'

'You, Diana,' said Edward. 'It is you who is to go to market. It is the word of the king. You are to be another Murray.'

'Diana is to try to seduce Cromwell?' said Susan. At this both she and Diana laughed out loud. Elizabeth Murray had long been accused of lying with Cromwell, but Susan knew full well this was nonsense, just the residual distrust of anyone Scottish.

'Well,' said Diana. 'I may be a trollop, but even I have my standards. Old Noll? Truly?'

'No, gentle sister,' said Edward. 'You are to become Thurloe's mistress. He ought not ask such a thing of me.'

'Very funny,' said Susan. 'You almost had me convinced there.

Seduce Thurloe? Diana is more like to join Abbess Mary Knatchbull in quiet religious contemplation.'

'It is all too serious,' replied Edward. 'The king fears Thurloe is winning the peace for parliament. He undermines us at every crossroads, he places agents in the highest places. He knows our every move - Penruddock is proof of that. Now we, or rather, you, are to wrest some control back for us. You, Diana, will seduce Thurloe, lay claim to his pillow, and from there you shall extract secrets from the devil who has himself penetrated so many men's hearts.'

'And you say he ought not ask such a thing of you?' said Susan, incredulous. She drained her cup. 'It is not you, brother, whose reputation will be torn to shreds.'

'And if it becomes known that I have instructed a married woman to share another man's bed, so that she is to be no more than a common slut?' said Edward.

'Because that's far worse than being the common slut in question, of course,' said Susan.

'I am Sir Edward Hyde,' said Edward. 'My name stands for something.'

'And her reputation counts for nothing?' asked Susan. 'And that notwithstanding, how exactly are we to engineer a meeting with parliament's spymaster?' Susan shook her head slowly, eyes towards the table, and then lifted her head and looked her brother directly in the eye. 'It is no wonder our every rebellion fails when this is the level of intelligence brought to bear on the situation. Perhaps we ought simply introduce ourselves to Thurloe and say we're bored of being told what to do by half-witted idiots with even lesser-witted schemes and would he be so very kind as to cease his meddling in our affairs? What say you, Sir Edward?' she said, enunciating his name and title slowly and precisely. Susan's faith in her brother was wearing as thin as the elbows of his coat sleeves, and Susan thought that he looked tired.

'This scheme is the king's own,' said Edward, his voice rising in volume. 'So it is to be carried out. I must not stay the night. I will take your horse, Susan, ride back to the boat and return to the continent on the first tide, so I bid you my leave.' He dropped three purses onto the table. 'This should help with your plans.'

'And what is the actual plan?' asked Diana.

'I have told it as I know it,' said Edward, 'and I am confident that between you a suitable course of action will be undertaken. I will have none of it. The fewer who know, the harder it will be to uncover. I merely await the results. I bid you both good night, and God speed.' He stood in the doorway. 'The king!' he said.

'The king!' replied the two women, by way of a salute. And Edward was gone.

Once their wine was replenished and the door was shut, Diana and Susan looked at each other.

'The cheeky bastard!' said Diana. 'And he has the gall to give us money. I wonder where he thinks it comes from.'

'Indeed, indeed,' said Susan. 'We are, as ever, on our own.'

'The king, his royal majesty, is as innocent as a bairn,' said Diana, 'unlike me. I suppose the Sisterhood must come to his rescue. As ever.' With this the two women raised their cups to the heavens and held their left hands over their hearts. 'The Sisterhood!' they said, in unison. And drained their cups.

4

Susan looks beyond

While Diana dealt with the mass of still damp layers that made up her clothing, Susan fretted and worried at the corner of a small folded packet, unsealed and long-ago read. The paper was old, with ragged edges and several instances of water damage, its exposed corners dark with the accumulation of eight years' worth of dirt. Susan knew every last mark, and where each had been acquired. It was at times such as these, uncertain times, dangerous times, that Susan turned to this relic from her past.

Eight years previously, Susan had been in Oxford, attending to her brother at court while the war waxed fatal all around. The king had been under effective house arrest for the best part of a year in various parts of the country, and all attempts to sign treaties with the Scots had come to naught. The atmosphere was close and oppressive but in amongst the suspicion and paranoia Susan had met a woman. She was Jane, Jane Whorwood, and she was as close to a she-intelligencer as Susan had ever known. Rumour had it that she was, or was to become, the king's mistress, but at that point she was merely the agent who smuggled gold in and out of the beleaguered city, thus keeping the war against the parliamentarian traitors alive. Jane, a few years older than Susan and much more experienced, took the younger woman under her wing, and introduced her to two names that would change the course of her life: Les Filles d'Ophélie and William Lilly. And this paper bore the fruit of her encounter with the latter, on one sunny day in May 1647. It was this encounter that drove her forward now.

'Remember how Constantine used to make such a fuss of pushing his way through the crowds of people to get Elizabeth's closet, loudly announcing his right to pass through each room in turn?' said Susan.

'And yet as secretary he had the keys to the back stairs?'

'Yes, exactly,' said Susan. 'But had he made use of them, no one would have known how important he was.'

'And of course, he wrote a poem about it, in case anybody had missed his daily performance.' Diana drew off some more wine and drank. 'What possible relevance has the affectation of an old Dutch poet to our present situation?'

'I feel as though we're being forced to be such a poet, and write about how we had a perfectly sensible way of operating in secret but decided to eschew it and use the entrance which demands that we state our purpose clearly.' Susan paused and shook her head. 'No matter. We must obey the king. He is, after all, our sovereign monarch. But how to engineer such a meeting?'

'We must work with what we have. We will send the Queen of Bohemia, our principal mother, a letter that accuses me of being an untrustworthy, greedy and unprincipled strumpet apt to grab fortune by the forelock,' said Diana. 'And we will send it by routes we know to be watched.'

'A little harsh, don't you think?' asked Susan, counting their store of coin.

'Thank you, sister,' said Diana. 'But it will work in our favour once we make known both my presence and my recent travails so that Thurloe can find me. He will figure me for a woman loose lipped and easily bought, so he will have me picked up and gently interrogated. Then I will get to work.'

'This is all too dangerous,' said Susan, suddenly fearful. 'The risk is too great. I will not allow it.' She shook her head. 'We must conjure another way. I will not allow you to court death so needlessly.'

'Susan,' said Diana. 'There is no danger. You know how they see us. Unless they've a blade covering their balls, of course.'

'There is some truth in that, sister,' said Susan, and the two women laughed.

'Until they bother to look, to see how we really are, we need not fear them. But they ought fear us. We will betray the few who need it, and I will be at the centre of things.'

'No. I will not allow it.'

'Come, Susan, he is but a man. No man can resist a woman for long,' said Diana. 'Especially one with my, well, my skills.'

'But one so precise, so clever. He would never submit to you, no matter what skills you may possess. I'd warrant he's impervious to witchcraft, even.'

'There will be a way. There's always a way. He is but a man.'

'No,' said Susan, summoning up some authority. 'I must perform this task. And I shall do so in secret.'

'You? You have no experience. You are postmistress and widow of many years standing. Who was the last man you lay with?'

'My husband. And many, many years since I grant you. But that, that and the fact I am barren, that is what will give me a chance.' Susan kissed Diana. 'You, Diana, have other work to do. This is not your place.'

'Sister,' began Diana, but Susan silenced her.

'Soft. We will use his pride and his arrogance against him.'

'How so?' asked Diana.

'Be it intellectual or spiritual,' said Susan, 'his pride will be his downfall, as it is with all men. I will treat him with disdain. Ignore the great man. Show no indication that I care either way for his reputation. Show that I have no fear. We merely need to engineer a meeting, and you have already indicated how we may do that. Speaking of meeting, what news from the Low Countries, sister? How are you back home? Is your husband ill?'

'Ill? No,' said Diana. 'The fool is merely inconvenienced.'

'Money?'

'Always money. It is but the folly of youth. William is in close confinement of the redeemable kind.'

'A debtor once more?' said Susan, filling up their cups again. 'This is more folly than simple youth might excuse, dearest Diana. I fear you have married a millstone rather than a mariner. And not even titled.'

'He is a good man.'

'He may be a goodly man, but he is hardly a good one,' replied Susan, reaching down to stoke the fire. At this Diana raised the skirts of her silk dress and exposed the still damp underwear to the heat. A good man, her William? Truth was he barely qualified as a man. When Diana had arrived in Antwerp she told everyone that the young lad she travelled with was her cousin. Only Susan knew the truth, that she'd eloped with the eighteen-year-old just a month previously. He was almost half her age, for shame. Yet, Susan had been a widow for almost as many years as he had seen summers. Sometimes she wondered if she wasn't the fool herself. Diana may have sailed close to the wind on more than one occasion, but at least she had felt it. Susan knew Diana was talking, but had no idea what she was saying.

'...it's one thing getting into a pissing contest with these men, but I'll be whipped till Michaelmas if I'll let any one of them view my undergarments,' she laughed, swishing them from side to side as she did so. 'Not unless he's a proper man.' She poured herself more wine and gulped some down. 'A sight better than his ale,' she said, looking at Susan with an air of resignation.

'You weren't expecting a mission such as this?' asked Susan.

'I had no idea what to expect when the call went out,' replied Diana.

'But you took it anyway?'

'I had very little choice,' said Diana, her face falling. 'I was practically chased out of Antwerp. My bounty is a letter of exoneration to Colonel Philips, the man who clapped my William in irons and told Henry Manning of my financial tendencies. Well, it was him and his irritatingly perfect wife. Manning found out this morning that the Colonel spoke the truth.' With this, Diana shook her bag. It jangled wealthily in the quiet of the room.

'For what sum was the ticket?' asked Susan as she took Diana's cup and emptied it.

'A mere £200 that we had borrowed from them to help settle some bills, the tailor, the butcher, the wine merchant. You know, the usual nonsense. And when I say borrowed...'

'You mean cheated,' said Susan. 'Will you ever learn, sister mine? You ought to have said. It's hardly a trifling sum, but I would have had John Shaw relieve you of your debts and furnish you with some ready cash besides.' Diana turned around and began to dry her arse in front of the fire. 'The Lord knows I send him enough.' There was a knock on the door. Susan answered it before Diana had resumed a seated position. The innkeeper spoke hurriedly, but in hushed tones.

'Milady,' he said, stumbling over the word. 'Milady, my boy here has returned. He says there is a group of parliamentary horse half an hour away. He says they speak of checking every inn between here and London. They search but they know not what for. You must be gone. And soon.'

'Tell me, innkeeper,' said Susan, her distrust of the man

dripping from every word. 'How can your boy see some horse, get back here and yet say they're half an hour away?'

'It does seem incredible, and he is quick,' replied the innkeeper. 'But in truth the road winds like a viper while my boy is small enough to slip through the hedges and trees as if a very crow.' The innkeeper's eyes strayed towards Diana once more.

Susan palmed the boy a penny before slapping the innkeeper around the face. 'Keep your eyes where they cannot conceive mischief and your mind on the task at hand. Can you hide the horses?'

'Of course, milady, but...'

'If they're not stabled there's no one expecting to travel tonight,' said Susan, interrupting. 'And we're not for London. Imagine it, two defenceless women on the road at night.'

'We cannot hide you, milady,' said the innkeeper, sounding a little scared. 'It is too dangerous.'

'I wouldn't ask you to,' said Susan. 'Hide the horses, and we'll disappear before your very eyes.'

'Milady?' The innkeeper betrayed his confusion in his voice.

'Fetch me a cauldron for the fire, some clean linen and a chicken,' said Susan.

'A chicken?' said the innkeeper, who was beginning to look scared.

'Don't ask questions, man,' said Susan, becoming mildly irritated. 'Do as I request.' She paused. 'And bring me an apron,' she added. 'We don't have long, so get your boy back out on watch. I need five minutes of warning before they arrive, and counsel the men not to look confused, whatever happens. You may direct the visitors here as soon as they enter, but have ale ready, too. On the house.'

'But milady,' the innkeeper protested. 'We never, we cannot, my reputation...'

'Will be enhanced tonight,' said Susan. 'As will your purse.

Now do as I say.' It always seemed to be the same with men such as the innkeeper. They were all bluff and swagger in front of the ladies, but show them a soldier and what little courage they had disappeared faster than a maid's virtue in a garrison town. And as for their wit...

'Did I hear you say chicken?' said Diana, turning her back on her partner. 'Would you mind?'

Susan shook her head free of disappointment, unlaced Diana's silks and pulled them carefully over her head. She rolled them up tightly before squeezing them into a dark oaken chest that squatted near the fireplace. She then placed her hat on top of the dress and closed the lid. She looked at Diana's bodice and frowned. 'There's no time to remove this,' she said, taking off her own waistcoat and pulling the sleeves down Diana's outstretched arms. 'And anyway, why did you choose the Philips to cozen? They are good, loyal subjects, devoted to the cause.'

'They are greedy, covetous and vain,' said Diana.

'They sound like your sort of people,' said Susan, and Diana simply stared at her. 'There. I've turned the lady into a trollop.' Not, she thought, a particularly onerous task.

Diana laughed. 'I've always found the trollop a far easier part to play. More fun, too.'

Susan simply raised an eyebrow and rolled up her sleeves. Thus reduced, the two women rearranged the room. The innkeeper returned with fresh linen, an apron and a chicken from the oven outside. And a man clutching a full cauldron of water.

'By the stars, you are an actual idiot,' said Susan, snatching the apron and the linen from him while shaking her head. 'Hot water so it's boiling when they arrive, and a live bloody chicken. Hooded. And dip it in the water, too, or the feathers go everywhere.' The men hurried off while Susan and Diana strewed the linen on the table and Diana lay on it, her legs apart and bent, facing the fire. When the men returned they hesitated for a minute before hanging the cauldron over the fire and handing Susan the wet chicken. The boy came running in, shouting wildly.

'They sped up. You got three minutes.'

'If you'd be so kind, sister,' she said, passing the chicken to Diana before turning on the dumbfounded men. 'Back into the bar with you!' She shut and bolted the door behind them, and Diana started moaning loudly. Three loud knocks at the door were followed by the sound of excited voices. 'You may commence operations if you wish.' With this, Diana let loose a scream that silenced the voices. There was another knock, followed by a heavy rattling after which the door flew open, ripping the bolt off the door frame. A soldier strode into the room.

'What is the meaning of this bolt, and who are you women?' he shouted, but stopped short when he saw the state of the room. 'For the love of-' he began, but Susan interrupted.

'What does it look like to you, sir?' said Susan, as sarcastically as she could manage. As she walked up to the soldier she wiped her hands on her apron, leaving great swashes of blood behind. Diana screamed again. 'One more of Cromwell's bastards, she says,' and stared at the soldier who stood, frozen to the spot. 'Perhaps it's yours? Recognise the mother?' Another scream and Susan turned around and placed herself between the legs of the now hyperventilating Diana. 'Push! And again.' Her words were directed at the corpse of the chicken which sat, headless, blood still dripping from the exposed neck, between Diana's thighs. By Diana's right hand, half-hidden beneath a piece of linen, lay her stiletto. Susan looked up at the soldier, who remained standing by the door, surveying the bloody mess of a room that was set before him. 'How are you on delivering children? Not the kind of bloody mess you appreciate? Then get your pustulant face out of my delivery room.' Susan was virtually shouting now, partly as part of the play, partly through fear that he would call her bluff. But her fears were unfounded, as the soldier turned and left the dining room, pulling the door to behind him. A single feather followed him into the main part of the inn.

Diana carried on moaning and screaming until the innkeeper knocked to say all was clear. Susan let him in.

'What in the name...' he said, plainly shocked.

'Do not fret, man. A simple play.' She threw the headless bird at him. 'My sister here has given birth to your dinner,' she said, laughing. 'Have it cooked and shared about the customers, and add an ale for each man.'

'Great,' said Diana, sitting up on the table. 'I can stop screaming now. Goodness. What a mess.'

The two women set about cleaning up both the room and themselves, and Susan reapplied Diana's outer garments, transforming her back into the lady she purported to be. Susan put on her cloak and they returned to the main room of the inn where they were greeted with raised tankards and thanks by the men who remained. All except one. He was a surly man, thickset and swarthy, his face set in what looked like a permanent frown.

'It's all well and good, but when they realise that you ain't just two common cozening cunts they'll be back,' he said, snarling as he crossed the room towards them. 'Except you whores'll be long gone, and us poor saps'll be your whipping boys. I pity your husbands.' He advanced closer. 'Though I'm doubting you'd either of you catch such a thing as had eyes to see or legs to run with.'

'That'll do, Seth,' said the innkeeper. 'We don't want no trouble. After all, you're happy enough to drink their ale.'

At this, Seth threw his tankard away, spraying ale over the two women in the process. Suddenly, he was face to face with Diana, his breath hot and reeking of drink as he looked down at her, his right hand clutching her crotch tightly. 'Gave birth to our chicken dinner, did it?' he growled. 'Let's see if it can give us all a treat for pudding. I need some of this more than I need ale.'

'Seth!' the innkeeper shouted, and Seth fell silent. The room breathed a sigh of relief. Diana leant forward and Seth dropped his head towards her.

'Now then, Seth my old chap,' whispered Diana. 'How, exactly, will they realise anything unless you tell them?' She paused, smiled and carried on. 'You may have me in what passes as a quite vice-like grip in these parts, but allow me to tell you what will happen next unless you do exactly as I say. You can feel something hard between your legs, can't you? It's a very sharp, pointed Italian dagger called a stiletto. It is pressed against what I imagine is your rapidly shrinking' - at this she coughed - 'manhood. Now, if you want your puny little pizzle to remain able to feel the ever-so-manly attentions of your right hand ever again, I strongly advise that you release me.' His grip relaxed and he made to retreat.

'Uh uh,' said Diana, shaking her head. 'I haven't yet finished. Now, if you even think about informing on us I will hunt you down and when I catch you - and I will - I will make you fit only for guarding the Pasha's harem. I will slice your cock down the middle and rip off your balls. If you're lucky, I'll use a knife, but I'll like as not tear them off with my bare hands. Understand? Good. Now, you break off, laugh and joke as if we're old friends. We buy you ale and you stay for supper.' She smiled once more. Seth retreated, laughed as heartily as he could manage and sat down. 'Another ale for all, and two for Seth,' shouted Diana. Susan was never quite sure who she thought was scared the most when she saw Diana shift into her implacable anger phase, her victim or Susan herself. Such behaviour was beyond her, had always been beyond her. But she was glad that Diana was on her side. The men became ever rowdier, and Susan decided that it was time to retire for the evening and contemplate the most pressing issue. The two women shut the door behind them and left the men behind, gossiping and laughing. They sat down in the quiet of their dining room. 'What are we to do, sister?' said Susan to Diana, a jug of wine set on the table between them.

'I will engineer something,' said Diana. 'But no matter what you think, it is I who am charged with the infiltration of Thurloe to the detriment of all future plans. And unlike you, I have little reputation to lose.'

'It is not your choice,' said Susan. 'You cannot succeed in this mission. I may do so, and while my reputation will not survive, whatever is said of me we two know the truth: I cannot be bought. But this is the price we pay. We do not give our very lives.'

'But perhaps our immortal souls,' said Diana. 'It is my task.'

'Perhaps,' said Susan. 'Perhaps.' It seemed typical to Susan that she was now arguing with Diana over who would be least damaged by this scheme. Doubtless, Lucy, Countess of Carlisle would find such an endeavour as natural as she found having her husband sent abroad that she might play with Buckingham. But then, Lucy was not only one of the first of the Sisters, but, in the words of one correspondent, 'the killing beauty of the world'. Neither Diana nor Susan possessed such attributes, but then, their task was somewhat different. Diana could probably seduce most men by force of will, but what Susan knew of Thurloe was that he was far from being most men. He was a man of principle. He could not be pursued. He must be made to pursue. Like the crow, he would be scared away by the Dianas of this world. He must be lured by glimpses of something. 'Diana,' she said, determined now to assert herself over her companion. 'I must remind you that while we may be sisters we are not equals, and so long as we labour within the aegis of the Knot I am your mistress. You are duty bound to obey my will. And so you shall. I will be Thurloe's morsel. And that is my final word.'

'Yes, sister,' said Diana.

'We cannot catch a crow without subterfuge. We must make him beholden to me, so that I can feign indifference to his thanks. Display no deference, only disdain. Treat him like a lapdog, or better still, a mouser. Then, perhaps, we will prick his curiosity, and the more I remain aloof...'

'The more he will want to understand why,' said Diana, finishing Susan's thoughts. 'He is a spymaster, after all. We must use his nature against him.'

'We still must somehow arrange to meet Thurloe in circumstances in which he suspects everyone but me. And your being arrested will not suffice.'

'I believe you are wrong, sister.'

'You do?' asked Susan.

'Yes,' replied Diana. 'You remember Medea?'

'Yes,' said Susan. 'But I fail to see the relevance.'

'She fooled Creon by pretending to revitalise a goat.'

'Thank you. Am I said goat?' asked Susan.

'No, sister, I am. We spread rumours about me as before. When they come to arrest me, I shall suffer some sort of fit, and you can save me.'

'Thurloe will not fall for your play-acting, Diana,' said Susan, laughing. 'But I know the apothecary Hinton is abroad, as he delivers letters on behalf of the Knot. I can meet him at Greenwich, and ask him for some fast-acting and demonstrative poison, and its antidote.'

'Tomorrow we travel to London,' said Diana. 'But we shall do so independently. I will let slip my destination to Seth, and something of my mission, as I have already suggested. He's too angry not to turn the parliament shilling. You, meanwhile, will travel to Dover and enter London by way of the river. I will lodge at the Mermaid, near to Butcher's Row. You will lodge at your usual address.'

'The Mermaid belongs to the Sisterhood, indeed,' said Susan. 'When the time comes, you shall play the goat, and I the witch.'

'Introduction will have been made, and we can both work on the spymaster,' said Diana. 'Perhaps a wager on who will prevail?'

Susan laughed. 'No, sister. Once your part has been played, you must take the convent.'

'The convent?' said Diana.

'Diana. You know as well as I that a Sister who is compromised in any way must take the convent until such a time as her being once more abroad is deemed safe for all.' Susan suspected that Diana ought already be safe within the society's walls in Antwerp, but she was glad to have such an experienced and committed Sister by her side for a task such as this. And yet still she felt the entire idea was at best ill conceived, at worst... 'I fear that I shall fail, and that my failure will leave us worse off than had we done nothing.'

'Do not fear failure. It is for him to fail, not you. You must merely place yourself somewhere he cannot but fail to resist. And that is just out of his reach.'

'I can see how that might work,' said Susan. 'Be how they treat us: invisible.'

'Yes,' said Diana. 'Nous sommes les Filles d'Ophélie. Nous sommes les agentes invisibles. Nous sommes le premier, le dernier.'

'Et nous sommes la différence,' said Susan.

'And we are the difference,' said Diana. 'As you told Edward, to catch a spy you must bait your hook well.'

'To catch a spymaster you bait your hook with nothingness.'

'You are both bait and hook,' said Diana. 'And be he never so cunning, he will be unable to resist biting. Because he cannot conceive of a hook strong enough, or subtle enough, to entrap him.'

'Now let us sleep, for tomorrow we begin,' said Susan. And snuffed out the candles one by one.

5

Susan awakes

It was the sound of the grate being swept and a new fire set that first penetrated the thick fog enveloping Susan's consciousness. She opened a cautious eye and saw the innkeeper's girl on her knees, coaxing the kindling into life and then sliding the small bunch of flaming twigs into the gap she had left at the fire's base. She watched as the flames teased and caressed the bigger sticks until they, too, began to crackle with energy. The girl arranged some larger pieces of wood so they might benefit from the fireplace's new-found enthusiasm and stood up, dusted off her apron and turned around, only to see Susan staring directly at her. 'Milady,' she said, curtseying brusquely. Susan wasn't convinced that the girl was being entirely genuine, but the thickness in her head was starting to make itself felt in her stomach, so she decided to act according to her nature.

'Fetch some fresh peppermint, and make an infusion of the leaves in boiling water, if you please,' said Susan, but the girl left the room without so much as a nod of the head in acknowledgement. 'Thank you, you've been no help whatsoever,' Susan remarked to herself, before falling back into semi-sleep.

The door opened again, this time swinging with enough vigour to recoil on its hinges until it was almost closed again. The noise drove itself through Susan's ears and directly into her brain, reawakening her with a jolt.

'Wake up, sister,' said an almost aggressively cheerful voice. 'Time to get yourself together. I brought you a mint infusion.' She slapped a great cup onto the table that loitered near Susan's head. 'There's good, cold water coming, too, just the thing you need to wake yourself up. We've a lot to do today, sister.' Diana's entrance was followed closely by the girl's, who appeared to have developed a little humility since she had set the fire. This time her curtsey had some feeling behind it. After she'd set the jugs on the table, Diana addressed her directly. 'Fetch me the boy.'

'Yes, milady,' said the girl, who scuttled off at such a pace that Susan suspected she may have had the slowness of wit to have crossed Diana that morning.

'Whatever did you say to her, Diana?' said Susan. 'You seem to have put the fear of God into the poor girl. I shudder to think what she might have done or said to deserve such a flaying.'

'It wasn't what she did or said so much as her manner,' replied Diana. 'I suggested that if she found she could keep the tongue in her mouth civil then perhaps I would avoid acting the tyrant by removing it.'

'And what did she reply?' asked Susan.

'Well, I may have had my hand in her mouth at the time, so any reply was likely to manifest in deed rather than word,' said Diana, with a look in her eye that was both cruel and mischievous at the same time. Susan had seen this look before, and it engendered in her breast a feeling of admiration shot through with fear.

'Milady?'

'Ah, young man,' said Diana to the innkeeper's son, who'd just walked into the room, face beaming at the prospect of another healthy tip. 'Now then,' she said, kneeling down to place herself at his level. 'I know you can keep a secret, but I have a mission for you, and a secret for you. A secret to sell.' Diana smiled at the lad, who was remarkably clean considering his complete immersion in all of the filthier jobs at the inn, though she put that down to the girl, whom she understood was his sister. 'Now firstly, I want you to take this packet to Sittingbourne, and wait outside wherever passes for a gaol in that town until the two Swordsmen are set free. Ask the tall one if he's Talbot. If he says yes, run. If no, give him the packet, and tell him you are to await his answer. Bring it straight back here. Agreed?' She held out a coin. He took it from her hand. She gave him the packet. 'If you or anyone else opens it,' said Diana, 'I'll cut off your hand.' She paused. 'And believe me, I'll know.'

'Yes, milady,' said the boy.

'And as for the other matter,' said Diana, and she leant forwards until her lips were almost touching his ear, and began to whisper. The boy nodded vigorously at intervals, and when she had finished, she stood and held out another coin. 'You are sure you understand?'

'Yes, milady,' said the boy, snatching the second coin and running out of the room as if the devil himself was on his tail.

'Excellent,' said Diana. 'That's that, then.'

'That's what?' said Susan, sipping her mint infusion. 'What have you done?'

But Diana wasn't listening. She was too busy pulling off her shift. After throwing the garment aside she poured some water into the bowl that the maidservant had set on the table, dipped her hands into it and flung the cold liquid onto her face, gasping as she did so. She followed this up with more little gasps as she splashed the cold water over her breasts and into her armpits and crotch. 'Come on Susan, get yer lazy arse out of bed and woken. It's almost time to breakfast.'

After a bowl of porridge and more mint infusion, Susan began to feel rather more like herself, and she and Diana set about their day with something approaching gusto. A few minor repairs to their clothing, the splitting of their financial resources into manageable and easily concealable portions and the preparation of their horses took the best part of the morning.

'Well,' said Susan. 'I haven't done all this for a few years. I must admit I'm a little nervous.'

'It's like riding a horse,' said Diana. 'You'll be fine. Just trust your instincts. They've always worked before.'

They took their lunch, and they waited. They waited in their room as the inn began to fill with customers. As it approached mid-afternoon, the two women were taking refreshment when the boy came bounding, red faced and breathless, into their room.

'Goodness, child,' said Susan. 'Why the rush? Is there some alarm?'

The boy stood, catching his breath, then spoke. 'Milady, it's a fair few miles to Sittingbourne. But the tall one, Duggan, the Irish, said to tell you that the Bluebells of Scotland was the tune he heard when he awoke this morning.' He looked at her with rapt attention, trying to decide whether he'd done right or not. Diana looked at him gravely for a second before the corners of her mouth began to turn and her frown was replaced by a wide, beaming smile.

'Well done, well done,' she said. 'And here's the second half as promised. Now remember to let us have a good five or six hours before you let Seth in on the secret. And try not to laugh when he tells everyone how marvellous clever he is. Now go get us our mounts.' She ruffled his hair, gave him another coin and sent him on his way. Pulling her scabbard out of her satchel she turned to Susan and spoke in a low, serious voice, strapping the formed leather to her left forearm as she did so. 'Are we ready to go, sister?' Susan nodded. 'Good. We must meet our escorts. And one of them will without doubt be less than happy to see me.'

The women buttoned themselves up, shouldered their bags, offered up a small prayer and left their room. All eyes were on them as they walked through the inn, tracing their journey towards the front door. Seth, who had been sat in his usual spot for nigh-on two hours, spat on the floor in front of Diana as the two ladies passed him. They stopped and Susan looked at him with the indulgence accorded to a not-quite-house-trained puppy on its choosing the most obviously valuable and visible part of the house in which to supply ample evidence of its continued incontinence. He didn't say a word, just smiled. Once the eyes of the inn's customers could no longer feast on the figures of the sisters and had gone back to staring into their cups of ale, the innkeeper, too, went outside.

He found them waiting on his appearance. 'My apologies for the unpleasantness last night, ladies, but...' Susan waved him quiet, and pulled a small purse from her bag.

'There is no need to be obsequious, my good man. You were promised reward and reward you shall have.' She placed the purse into his hands and clasped his fingers around it. 'There. Reward.'

At this they turned from the innkeeper, strapped their bags to their horses and mounted. Diana winked at the innkeeper's boy as they dug heels into flanks and walked off, leaving the King's Arms behind.

'Where are we going, sister, and who are we meeting?' said Susan.

'Ah,' said Diana. 'Two very simple questions. We will meet our escorts at Bluebell Wood, about a mile hence. They are the Swordsmen arrested in Queenborough, the men who crossed the channel with your brother and me yesterday. They are loyal - they bear the sign - and they completed their mission well, namely to prove Manning's betrayal and to destroy whatever trust had been placed in him. They think me a traitoress. So it could be an interesting meeting. So far as they're aware I'm Lady Stanley and you, you shall be Sarah.'

'So why them?' said Susan. 'Why do we need them?'

'As I said before, we must move to London independently. Travelling alone is far too dangerous, and will attract too much attention. We use them because they are close by. I will travel with the Irish. We will go from Bluebell Wood to Charlton House, where we stay as the guest of the Filmers. Sir Robert was a loyal servant. We will be used well there. You will travel with the colonel, via the Thames, and meet Hinton in Greenwich, where you will ask him to provide you with the accoutrements of a wise woman.'

'And when we are safely installed in London?' said Susan.

'We wait,' said Diana.

Susan had been acting as postmistress for the Sealed Knot for some months and, over that time, she had constructed a net of communications that relied not on complex procedures but simple strategies that worked together, making it resilient and resistant to the loss of any individual within it. Were Susan herself to be taken, the network would soon adjust itself, cover up the gap and carry on, if not as before, then at least as efficiently. There were some weak spots, however. The apothecary Hinton was one such. His knowledge of both Susan and her various code names made his work more dangerous than she was happy with. But the great boon of the apothecaries was that they could travel without suspicion. If they were not visiting a client, they were visiting the towns and villages that fell within their range. Susan had recently recruited another apothecary, one called Chase, that she might reduce the burden on Hinton. This meticulous planning and slow adaptation was her forte. Diana, she knew, was a very different type of operator, and had been chosen well for this mission. Diana was at her very best in a crisis. When Susan's back was against the wall, she froze - Diana blossomed. But this meant that Susan was uncomfortable. She needed to know exactly what it was she had to do to complete this mission, even given that she felt it was impossible.

'Sister,' said Susan. 'I need more. I cannot just walk into the lion's den without even an idea of a plan. This is not me. What are we to do?'

'We get the city used to our presence,' said Diana. 'Beyond that, and ensuring that you are close by when needed, there is little we can do. I must be like the fly in Thurloe's web, my every movement designed to attract his attention.'

'I still say it is too dangerous, sister,' said Susan. 'Like the fly, it's passing likely you will lose your life in this venture.'

'I see no other choice. All we can do is what we can do. But we have one great advantage in this game.'

'Which is what, exactly?'

'Our natures,' replied Diana. 'My absolute transparency is what will save me, just as your absolute horror at the part you must play will save you.'

'From what?' asked Susan, but no answer was forthcoming. At this Susan felt some relief: even as she spoke she had realised that this was not a question she much wanted to contemplate, let alone discover an answer to.

The two women continued in a silence broken only by the occasional snort, sneeze or whinny from their mounts. The next half hour passed without incident until Diana spoke.

'You see behind the tree just at the top of that hill?'

'What, sister?'

'Who is perhaps the question,' said Diana. 'I'll lay money on the Irish. We'll find out presently.' They continued their leisurely progress towards the brow of the hill, and when they reached it, stopped for a moment. They could see two horses tied up beneath a large oak that stood at the entrance to a wooded area a hundred yards distant. At the foot of the oak sat a man, back propped up against the trunk, a plumed hat balanced on his face.

'There's the colonel,' said Diana, pointing towards the sleeping figure.

'How can you tell from here?' asked Susan.

'Because you'll never see an Irishman wearing such a hat,' came a voice as if from nowhere. 'At least, not by choice.' The two women turned to see Captain Duggan walking between their mounts, and allowed him to take both horses by the halter. 'I never thought we'd have the pleasure of your company again,' he said. 'The colonel's going to be overjoyed.'

'I'm sure the pleasure will be all mine,' said Diana. 'And I think in future you ought to conceal yourself better. We spotted you "lying in wait" about half a mile back.'

'And what, may I ask, is such a fine and wealthy widow as yourself doing on this road unaccompanied,' he said, casting a disdainful glance at Diana's companion, 'by anyone other than an itinerant?'

'You may well ask,' said Diana, 'but then you wouldn't expect a lady such as myself to grace you with an answer, now would you, Captain Duggan?'

'I see no lady, Lady Stanley,' said Duggan, enunciating her title with as much sarcasm as he could muster, and he slowly led the horses towards his companion. As he walked, he put the thumb and first finger of his free hand to his lips and let off a whistle loud enough to make Susan's horse start slightly. The man under the tree stirred, sat forward and slid his hat from his face onto his head. He stood, dusted off his britches and yawned. He then stooped, picked up his sword and scabbard and draped the leather strap over his shoulder.

'We have woken the colonel, it appears,' said Duggan. 'He's always in a bate when he awakes.' The Irishman smiled as his companion began to walk towards them. 'Colonel!' he shouted, 'I've chanced upon an old friend on the road. Says she and her serving woman here will be more than happy to entertain us this evening.'

'Under normal circumstances I would welcome such generosity,' said the Scotsman, 'but we have business to attend to, as well you know.'

Diana laughed, making Duggan turn around and stare at her. 'I don't see the joke, Lady Stanley, truly I don't.'

'Oh, you will,' said Diana, 'you surely will.'

'Sister, must you antagonise the man so?' said Susan.

'Yes, sister,' said Duggan. 'Must you? Pay heed to your itinerant.' The two parties closed to within twenty yards of each other, close enough for the colonel to make out the faces of the women whose horses were led by his companion-at-arms.

'Well,' said the Scotsman, 'what have we here? Can it be the little roundhead mistress from the boat? It truly is my lucky day.'

'Luckier than you imagine,' said Diana. 'You have captured two highly dangerous women. Women whose chief delight of a morning is to sing of the floral delights of our northernmost territories.' A smile crept across Diana's face as both of the men stopped walking and stared. First at the two women, then at each other.

'You mean to tell...' started Colonel Talbot, but Diana waved him quiet. He tipped his hat, and spoke again. 'I beg your pardon, milady. I wonder, do you have something that might suffice as a gift?'

'For your mistress in Paris?' asked Diana.

'The very same,' replied Talbot. Diana threw him a small token and his countenance changed in an instant. The token and the code were enough for him to identify the women as those the two were charged with escorting. 'Milady, I am at your service,' he said, bowing and doffing his hat. 'And my apologies for my behaviour on and after the boat.'

'But colonel...' said Duggan, confused.

'But nothing, Captain Duggan,' said Talbot. 'This is no parliamentarian. This, these,' he corrected himself, 'these are the women for whom we lay down our lives if needs be.' He slapped Diana's horse on the shoulder and took the reins from Duggan.

'Good colonel,' said Diana. 'You will forgive my toying with you, but you surely understand?'

'Yes, indeed,' said the colonel. 'No better way to cover your tracks and help our disguise than by fomenting conflict in earnest between us.'

'Colonel,' said Duggan. 'After all you said?'

'A mere case of mistaken identity, I assure you,' said Talbot. 'What is your need of us, milady?'

Susan watched their escorts carefully as Diana explained the barest details of the plan to them, and reflected on the fact that these barest details encompassed practically everything but the final objective. It appeared that everything was ultimately being left to chance. Susan could deduce no plan other than their letting their destiny unfold exactly as it would. Not for the first time, Susan wondered whether there was anything to be gained by making plans. Ought we not merely operate as God saw fit to allow us? The freedom of will granted us must, of course, take its place within God's plans for mankind, and to consider any other way was surely to tempt His providence. But what if you were to know His plan? What if you were to know your fate? Was one not bound by the highest of duties to act accordingly, to change direction so as to allow it to unfold, or was that arrogance of the highest order? How could she, Susan Hyde, hope to know how best to proceed? Perhaps Diana's way was for the best, after all. Set out on the journey by all means, but never take the destination for granted.

A peal of laughter brought Susan back into the conversation.

'Sister,' said Diana. 'Are you with us?'

'I am hungry,' she replied. 'Let us eat.'

'Then it's agreed. Duggan and I are for East Sutton, while you and Talbot are for Greenwich, and will travel by water,' said Diana.

'Whatever you say, sister,' said Susan, suddenly feeling tired as well as hungry. 'Whatever you say.'

'Very well, milady,' said the colonel. 'But we must not tarry. It is no small distance to our destinations this evening and we both have need of retaining the goodwill of our hosts.'

The four were soon sitting beneath a great oak, and there they set about their repast with no little enthusiasm, and even less ceremony. The sun began its slow descent, filling the woodland floor with great stripes of shadow that danced as a gentle breeze began to stroke the branches above them. Susan looked at her companion, now laughing and joking with these two men who only the day before had counted Diana as a sworn enemy, and marvelled.

6

Diana steps back

Diana's journey to fille-complète, to being a fully inculcated member of the Sisterhood, had not been without its difficulties, and one of these was to be found at Charlton House. It was at Charlton House that she had been recruited, and at Charlton that her mother, as the Sisters termed those who had introduced them to the order, had cause to regret her decision almost as soon as she had made it. Lady Filmer had seen something in the wild and tempestuous Diana that not only needed directing to a greater purpose, but needed saving from itself. She had, perhaps, also foreseen the impossibility of her paying heed to any warnings regarding her behaviour, and the ensuing inevitability of a disaster befalling her. Lady Filmer, no doubt, also foresaw the nature of the disaster that awaited Diana, as it came in the shape of her son, Samuel Filmer.

Diana had been saved by the Sisterhood, by their refusal to allow anyone to control them through ignorance. The Sisterhood may have been out of step with much of society, but they valued the freedom of the three traditional aspects of mankind, freedom of spirit, of mind, and, most importantly, freedom of body. Diana had often wondered whether Lady Filmer's actions had been rather more pragmatic than charitable - that by making Diana her Sister, she reduced the possibility of her becoming daughter-in-law, or of Diana merely bearing Samuel's bastard. And so Diana approached the house with no little trepidation. It wasn't that she was unsure of her reception; far from it. The problem was she knew all too well what it was likely to be. She hoped the incident with the candles had been forgotten, too. Diana hated to dwell on past events, but she knew that it would be wise to tell her escort everything. Then again, when was Diana ever wise?

'Captain Duggan,' said Diana. 'We will arrive at Charlton House, home to the Filmers, within the hour. Sir Robert was a great supporter of the late king, so much so that he was sorely tested by the army, his lands taken, and himself imprisoned.'

'As have many loyal subjects, Lady Stanley,' replied Duggan. 'Sir Robert is not alone in his troubles.'

'Sadly, we shall not meet Sir Robert,' said Diana, 'on account of his being dead these past two years.' As she spoke, the road along which their horses bore them started to sweep to the left. Diana knew what awaited them at the house, and the dangers that it presented to their journey.

'And his sons?' asked Duggan.

'Samuel I have met,' said Diana, 'though not for several years. He's a hothead, so beware.' Calling Samuel a hothead was the best way she could think of to prepare Duggan for the reception that awaited her without creating enmity between these two men before they had even met.

'I ought fear him?' said Duggan. 'He must be some man.'

'No, Captain,' replied Diana. 'You must fear his temper and his poor judgement leading him to make promises he cannot keep or threats he can neither back up nor back out of. We will do better with him on our side.'

'I will be the model of decorum,' said Duggan, smiling and bowing as he sat astride his mount.

'Just make sure you are, Captain.' The words of explanation caught in her throat, and she knew that a little knowledge, at least on Duggan's part, was a very dangerous thing. Just as she resolved to explain the situation more fully, tell him on what terms she and Samuel had parted, and that no matter what the apparent provocation, he should not look to settle any scores, Duggan spoke once more.

'Lady Stanley,' he said, nodding at the road ahead. 'It appears we are to have company.' As he spoke, Diana caught sight of his meaning. A patrol of three parliamentary horse was making its way towards them. 'You will temper your natural instincts and allow me to deal with them.' He laughed. 'You had best give me your pass and act as demurely as you are able.'

'Yes, Captain,' said Diana, casting her eyes downwards with a smile. The patrol hallooed them and the lead horse broke into a trot. Within seconds the horseman was level with Duggan and had taken the Irishman's reins.

'And what might you good people be doing on the road at this time?' said the horseman, looking at the two travellers carefully while his companions stood off some twenty yards distant. 'I trust you near your destination as this is no road for strangers.'

'We are for Sutton,' said Duggan. 'We should be there within the hour, no?'

'Indeed,' said the horseman. 'And you are?'

'Marchant, Patrick,' said Duggan. 'I travel with Lady Stanley here to Charlton House.'

The horseman doffed his cap to Diana, and turned his horse. 'We will escort you to your destination, milady. There have been some unsavoury characters on this road of late.'

Diana looked at Duggan and raised her eyes to the heavens. 'We are most grateful for your company, sir,' she said. 'And will feel all the safer for your swords.'

'Have you perchance passed any other travellers on your way?' asked the horseman.

'Not for three hours or so,' said Duggan. 'Man and wife. At

least, they argued like they were. She would nag and he shout and she nag some more. They half their time stood just staring and spitting bile at one another.'

'Not newlyweds, then?' said the horseman. 'They are more wont to settle their differences lying than standing, eh?' At this he and his companions roared with laughter.

'Please,' said Duggan. 'Milady...'

'Beg pardon, milady,' said the horseman. 'We are but soldiers, not accustomed to fine company.'

Diana kept her gaze set on her horse's mane to prevent herself from laughing, and gave her mount a little kick. 'Granted,' she said as she rode on ahead a little. They rode like this for another forty minutes, Diana some thirty yards ahead of the four horsemen who were plainly bonding as men were like to do, through enumeration of their conquests, both in battle and in bed.

The evening was still light when they came to an expanse of meadow that sat before a manor house. 'Charlton House,' said Diana to herself as they approached closer, and she wheeled her horse around so that her escort lay between her and her destination. Samuel did not know that she travelled under the name Stanley, so she needed Duggan to introduce her as such, before he ruined her disguise. And Samuel stood in front of the house, accompanied by a girl of no more than seventeen who was throwing a ball at him without much enthusiasm. When the ball reached Samuel he flicked it into the air with a stick and hit it as hard as he could.

'What are they doing?' said Duggan. 'It looks like hurling but not.'

'Cricket,' said the lead horseman.

'Cricket?' replied Duggan.

'It's popular hereabouts,' said the horseman, as he cupped his hands around his mouth and shouted. 'Hoi! Samuel! I hope there's been no wager on this game.'

The man with the ball stopped mid-throw, turned and shouted back at the horseman, who he plainly knew well. 'You know I'd never put money on a game, Jethro. Anyway, I'm just practising.'

'What does he mean?' said Duggan.

'Oh,' said Jethro. 'When Sam was younger, he and a friend played a match, 'gainst four other gentlemen. And he's very good, is our Samuel.' Jethro paused to dismount. 'Two other gentlemen entered into a wager, involving,' he paused, turning to Samuel, 'what was the wager again, Samuel?'

'Candles, Jethro, candles,' replied Samuel.

'Aye, that was it. Candles,' replied Jethro. 'It led to much in the way of trouble.'

'Why the fuss over a few candles?' said Duggan, as the party dismounted.

'It was neither the cricket nor the candles that caused the trouble, eh, Samuel?' said Jethro.

'The act of the wager, perchance?' suggested Duggan.

'No,' replied Samuel. 'We are not so particular here on such matters, and certainly were not back then. It was Bill's refusing to pay up that was the problem. That and Nicholas's taking him to court for said refusal.' Samuel shook hands with Duggan. 'Travelling far?'

'We, myself and Lady Stanley, that is, are in need of a good meal and suitable quarters,' said Duggan. 'Lady Stanley was a friend to Sir Robert, and he a friend to her.'

Samuel looked Duggan up and down. 'You are welcome at Charlton,' said Samuel. He then looked at Diana, whose horse had by now caught up with the men. 'Lady Stanley and I need no introduction, indeed.' He bowed gently. 'Milady.' He took the reins of her horse while she dismounted. And winked.

Duggan took the bat from Samuel's right hand. 'If you don't mind,' he said, and weighed it carefully, before taking a practice swing. 'Would you throw a ball or two at me, Samuel?'

'Of course,' said Samuel, and the two men took their places while the others watched. Samuel threw, Duggan swiped and missed. Samuel threw again with the same result. 'Perhaps you would care for a game while Molly here escorts Lady Stanley into the house and prepares your quarters.'

Duggan smiled. 'I have no candles about me.'

'Seeing as you're a beginner, how about Jethro and me against the three of you?' said Samuel.

Diana left the men to their game and walked up to the young girl, who was standing a few yards apart from the group. 'Pleased to meet you Molly,' said Diana. 'I am Lady Stanley.'

'Milady,' said the girl, curtseying.

Diana took her by the arm and led her towards the house. 'I'm a friend of your late master. Sir Robert was a good man.' She stopped walking all of a sudden and turned towards Molly. 'Now, let me take a look at you.' She smiled broadly. 'Now I remember. You are the housekeeper's girl. We have met before.'

'Indeed, milady?' said Molly.

'Indeed. Though it was several years ago. And you may call me Diana when it's just we two, like you used to.' Diana smiled and the pair continued walking.

'Lady... Diana - when did you marry Lord Stanley?'

Diana leant her head towards the young girl and whispered. 'I didn't. I am merely borrowing his name. After all, he has no need of it now.'

'But what of his family? His heirs?'

'They will not miss it. And my need is certainly the greater.'

'I would love to be a lady,' said Molly with a sigh.

'Oh I doubt it, Molly,' said Diana. 'Certainly, there are some advantages, but all in all, it's terribly limiting. For one thing, one tends to be allowed only to exist in the company of a gentleman, like Master Samuel. Though he is very handsome, don't you think, Molly?'

'He certainly thinks so, but he is no gentleman, he does as he pleases. A gentleman would not...'

'Would not what, Molly?' This was all the confirmation that Diana needed. Nothing had changed at the house, and nothing had changed about Samuel. Excepting that he was now older and presumably rather more experienced. And, of course, he no longer had parents to guide him, or protect the objects of his affections.

'A gentleman just would not,' said Molly, as they entered the house. Behind them they heard shouts and laughter as the game got under way. 'Samuel will win. He always does.'

'Not always,' said Diana.

An hour later the night drew in, and Duggan and Samuel burst into the house, laughing and joking, their shirts wet with sweat. 'Well, Lady Stanley, your chaperone is a liar and a cheat,' said Samuel, tearing off his shirt. 'He fairly thrashed Jethro and me. It appears his practice swings were not entirely indicative of his ability!' He threw the shirt onto the floor. 'Leave your shirt for Molly to wash, Robert, and your bag is upstairs in your room, first on the left. You'll see.'

'Thank you, Samuel,' said Duggan. 'You may wish to be a little less trusting next time - your sport is much like our native hurling.' He left the room still bearing his shirt.

'Molly!' Samuel shouted. 'Where is the lazy slattern?'

'Doing your bidding, naturally,' said Diana.

'Yes, Master Samuel?' said Molly as she appeared from upstairs.

'Pick up Captain Duggan's shirt and see that it is washed, and quickly. Mine can wait,' said Samuel. 'And bring me fresh.' As she turned he grabbed at her buttocks with his hand, and she squirmed out of his grasp.

'You might treat your servant with a little more respect, Samuel,' said Diana, as she left the room.

'Why?' said Samuel. 'She's a servant.'

'What do you want from her? Is it not enough that she serves, that you must humiliate her too?'

Samuel turned to Diana, laughing. 'What would any man want from such a juicy piece?'

'Your father would not be impressed, Samuel, nor your brother,' said Diana.

'It's a good thing neither of them are here, then. Let us eat. You have a long journey tomorrow.'

'Before we eat, Samuel, you recall how you have sworn to help me in any way that you can, in any way I see fit, yes?'

'That is correct. We all want the same thing. To restore the monarchy.'

'Good,' said Diana. 'You will release Molly into my care. I need a servant, and I choose her.'

'I will what?' said Samuel, spluttering in disbelief. 'Release Molly into your care? I do not think so, Diana, no matter what.'

'Now you listen to me, and you listen well,' said Diana, moving close enough that Samuel could feel the heat of her breath on his face. 'You have taken an oath, and by all that's holy you will honour it. I tell you that you will release Molly, and you will do so willingly.'

'Or what, Lady Stanley? What exactly are you going to do?' With this he took her by the throat and pushed her against the wall. 'Don't think I've forgotten how you acted upon your last visit. You're a slut, and you'll always be a slut.' He shook his head, smiling. 'Lady Stanley indeed...'

'Act in haste...' said Diana, squeezing her words out through his grip.

'I have already repented,' said Samuel. 'And anyway, I have plans for young Molly. Truth is I want to keep her more than I want to keep you happy. So the answer's...'

'Yes.' The voice was Duggan's. Samuel's fingers relaxed, his hands dropping down by his side as he moved slowly away from Diana, the point of the Irishman's blade nestling gently between two of the vertebrae of his neck. 'If only to maintain decorum, eh, Lady Stanley?' Duggan gave Diana a look almost as sharp as the point that had persuaded Samuel of the error of his ways.

'She's no more...' began Samuel but his voice faded as he felt the skin on the back of his neck begin to give way to the sharp steel as Duggan increased the pressure he was exerting by the slightest amount.

'We'll have no more of that nonsense,' said Duggan. 'We will eat and sleep and in the morning we'll be gone. Lady Stanley, go and help pack Molly's things. I must have a little chat with young Master Samuel here.'

'Thank you, Captain,' said Diana, and turned to leave.

'And milady,' said Duggan. 'Before you go may I remind you that while Samuel here places himself at your service, as do I, my greater responsibility is to the king? I trust we will not see another occasion such as this, one where the mission appears to take second place to your personal wishes or, dare I say it, vendettas.'

Diana left the two men alone without another word. She and Molly packed everything they considered essential, including several gold pieces that Diana assured Molly were her rightful bounty. As Molly had been released by Samuel, Diana insisted that the four of them eat together. They did so in uncomfortable silence. Following dinner, Samuel took to his closet with a bottle of wine and they heard no more of him.

The next morning, Diana and Duggan left the house for London early, with Molly beside them. Samuel had yet to rise.

7

Susan changes station

By the time Susan and Talbot arrived at Greenwich, the market was packing up for the day. The square was covered in all manner of detritus, from the flyblown corpses of rats to perfectly serviceable vegetables. Susan watched as several dogs and a pig nuzzled their way through the rubbish in search of edible treasures, occasionally receiving a sharp kick from one of the beggars who competed for the same bounty. The squalor, the poverty. It made Susan ashamed to be English. Those like herself had a duty to aid these poor creatures, but the order of the country had been disturbed by the wars, and for all parliament's talk of freedom, it seemed to Susan that the rich had the freedom now to be as covetous as they desired so long as they kept their desires hidden behind a wall of piety, and the poor the freedom to starve on any street corner they chose. Then she caught sight of him. He carried a collection of glass vials in two wicker baskets which hung from the yoke that lay across his shoulders. It was the apothecary, Hinton. She dismounted, handed her horse's reins to Talbot, and walked towards him.

'Anthony,' said Susan. 'It is good to see a friendly face. I trust your journey here was uneventful? Allow me to introduce my escort, Colonel Talbot of the Scottish Regiment of the Dutch Army.'

The apothecary nodded his greeting and took Susan by the arm, leading her away from the Scotsman. 'You trust this man?' he asked, looking back over his shoulder as he spoke. 'I do not know of him.'

'He was selected by those who can be trusted, Anthony,' said Susan, quietly. 'And he knows neither my true identity nor my activities - to him I am Sarah. He is to ensure my safe passage and obey my orders.' Susan gripped the apothecary's arm tightly. 'Thus far, he has acquitted himself well.'

'If you trust him, Miss Susan - Sarah - then I, too, shall do so. But there's no need for him to know any more than is necessary.'

'Indeed not,' said Susan. 'I have need of more than letters from you today. Though this one must be delivered by the Brentwood estate.' With this she handed him a small packet.

'But that route...'

'Has been compromised, yes,' said Susan, smiling.

'Oh, I see,' said the apothecary. 'And as for your other requirements?'

'I need a travelling bag such as wise women and midwives carry.'

'But Miss Susan, there are powerful drugs there.'

'Naturally, Anthony. I know my responsibility to my sisters, and I am not without experience in matters such as these.'

'Of course, your great aunt was a cunning woman, yes,' said the apothecary. 'A street corner is not the best of places to perform such a transaction, but tell me, did you learn much from her?'

'A little,' said Susan as she picked a vial out from the right-hand basket. 'China root. Primarily for use in cases of the French pox. When it's not available, sassafras proves a useful substitute.' She smiled at the apothecary and picked out a root from a jumble of spindly limbs, some feathery and soft, others hard and smooth, that languished in an open basket. 'Helvetius discovered that this is good for intestinal flux,' she said, and placed it back into the bag that contained its companions. 'Nassau root.'

'Well, yes, you have some useful knowledge. I will furnish you with a selection of mostly harmless but efficacious remedies, all of which will be useful for a variety of women's complaints. These will serve as proof that you are who you say you are. The symbols I will copy out into this chapbook, along with a series of receits that you may find useful.'

'Will you give me nothing for the treatment of men?' said Susan, frowning.

'You are but a woman. No man will place themselves in your hands, they will trust only one who has been trained in the art of healing, which, as you know, is not permissible for a woman.'

'Dear Anthony,' began Susan. 'You know as well as I that this is untruth. Women not only may, but do, learn the art as do men. They also have the added advantage of being brought up with remedies at their mother's knee. It is only that women may not be granted licence to practise other than in midwifery.'

'Indeed. That is why no man will trust you. And you well know that the Church has been stripped of the right to issue such licences.'

'Well, I shall travel unlicensed, Anthony,' said Susan, not even trying to hide her exasperation. Parliament not only seemed intent on preventing women from acting as they had done for centuries, but was doing so in such a way as could only serve to punish them simply for being women. She knew she had escaped being challenged by the soldiers at the King's Arms simply because she was loud and covered in blood. But it could so easily have proven the end of their mission.

'You know as well as I do that you must do no such thing, the risk is too great.' With this the apothecary drew closer to

Susan. 'But I will include a licence with your bag. You may sign it with any name you wish; just ensure you dilute the ink overly to make it appear aged. It will be signed by the Bishop of London himself, albeit several years ago.'

'Your forgers are good. Will it suffice?'

'An extant licence is sufficient as it's too much trouble to challenge it, and a midwife on the move is invariably in need of haste. Check the date,' said the apothecary with a wink. 'And there is no forgery involved. I am not without influence.' He smiled to himself. 'I invested in a small quantity of pre-signed papers for use at my convenience several years ago. It is hard to overestimate the gratitude of a man when you have cured his gout.'

'Now that, that is a cure I could make use of.'

'If you were anyone other than yourself, and if it were not already published by Sir Francis Bacon,' said the apothecary, as he reached for pen and ink, 'I would refuse. But it shall be included in your book. You'll struggle to find plaster of diacalcitis anywhere other than in my shop but, if it is the season, you might ply your patient with cherries. I am told that King James used to spend days in some courtier's orchard when the fruit ripened, and no one asked why.'

'Indeed?' replied Susan, glad that at least one man wasn't incapable of doing his job, even when it went against his instincts. 'And now the doughty Talbot and I will make our way to London.'

'In that case, I will take me to Saffron Walden. Then we shall not be seen close,' said the apothecary. 'For how long does your sentinel intend on being your shadow?'

'On our arrival in London he shall attend to me from a distance to ensure no insurmountable problems arise, and on my deciding he is superfluous, he shall return whence he came,' said Susan. 'And in a day or two I shall visit your shop to take possession of my licence to walk alone unmolested.' With this, she turned to Talbot and nodded. He kicked his heels lightly into his horse's flank and began to walk towards the pair. Susan turned again, this time walking close to Hinton and leaning in to whisper. 'I have need of a poison that will produce violent effects almost instantaneously, effects that will cease upon the dispensing of an antidote.'

'A highly unusual request. Do you wish for it now? It is a request I can meet.'

'No time like the present,' said Susan, and the apothecary began searching through his supplies.

He held up two small vials, one with a green wax seal, the other sealed with black. 'The poison's name is not for your ears, while the antidote is from the *Carduus benedictus*, the blessed thistle. It can also be used to induce a fit of casting and thus draw out the humours.'

'Excellent,' said Susan. 'I shall take the thistle, and if you can have the darker vial sent to the Mermaid.'

'The usual place, I presume?' said the apothecary, before nodding his head towards Susan's escort. 'Good luck,' he added, before turning and walking off.

'Colonel,' said Susan.

'Milady,' replied Talbot, who had dismounted and now walked the two horses they had hired the final steps towards her. After assisting Susan's mount, he climbed onto his own horse.

'We ride as far as Southwark, and cross the river on foot,' said Susan, as she spurred her horse onwards. 'And from there you may observe me as suits you best. If I am in need of you, I shall send word. You will need to make contact with the innkeeper of the Mermaid. Hand her this token. She will give you full instructions.' Susan gave him a locket containing a miniature portrait of the king. 'Now let us ride.'

8

Diana gets to work

Diana Gennings, Jennings, Jennens, Stewart or Lady Stanley, depending on who was asking, woke early, as the noise beneath her window began to change from the occasional wagon trundling by with its driver cracking the whip to a cacophony of city sounds. The relative peace of the night was shattered by braying donkeys, barking dogs, neighing horses, arguments and costermongers of every sort competing against each other to see who could shout the loudest. Men, it seemed to Diana, did not even need to drop their hats to square up to one another: it appeared that mere ownership of a hat contrary to another's taste was quite provocation enough. She made a mental note to ask Duggan his views on the belligerent nature of men if she were ever to see him again: she had discharged him on reaching the Mermaid.

Diana sighed, kissed the locket that hung around her neck and uttered a quick prayer. In the days since the dumbshow at the Kentish inn both she and Susan had been busy. Their respective journeys to London had been rendered somewhat more uncomfortable than expected by the advent of unseasonably stormy weather, and Diana, for one, had needed to swap the silks of a lady for a slightly more common thread as a result, but this suited her scheme. A woman on her uppers, in possession of little more than a wastrel husband and delusions of grandeur, was exactly what Thurloe would want to find. Such a woman would betray her principles, assuming she had any left to betray, for mere trinkets. Such a woman was never to be trusted with anything of import, but she was always listening, always watching, always on the lookout for something portable and saleable, whether a gemstone or a piece of information.

Diana had come to understand Molly's troubles with Samuel rather better during their journey, and with each furlong the girl's demeanour had become lighter and sunnier. She slowly revealed an ability to play the innocent born of her constant need to parry Samuel's advances without appearing to know that this was what she did, a skill Diana knew would serve her well. By the time that they had separated, so as not to arrive at the Mermaid together, Diana had come to view her charge as the younger sister she never had. When Molly arrived at the tavern, some time after Diana had settled herself in, a convenient vacancy for a serving girl had opened.

No stomach for strong liquor, that's what they said. But they knew nothing of the strength of a woman, of the strength of sisterhood, of the Sisterhood. Today would be the day. She felt it. She had been in residence for over a week, waiting patiently for Seth's news to reach Thurloe, and for the spymaster to respond in the only way he could, by striking. She had ensured that Susan was close by every morning, and that Molly was primed. They were ready.

The room at the Mermaid was like all the other rooms she had used while on active duty, even though it was a different shape and size. It was floored with rough timber, sported wattle-and-daub walls that had once, albeit some time previously, been freshly limewashed, a single truckle bed with a chamber pot beneath, a mahogany blanket chest, a small table with bowl and water and, set into the wall beneath the window, a two-person bench. On arrival, Diana had dumped her bag on the bed, pulled the pot out from under the bed and squatted over it, surveying the walls and floor as she did so. She counted nailheads to herself as she pissed. 'One, two, three, four, five... then fifteen, sixteen, seventeen. Skip the next... there!' she said as she shook herself a little and slid the pot back underneath the bed. She then advanced to the spot she had identified, unsheathed her stiletto and inserted the point into one of the nail holes. A flap of floorboard loosened, and Diana pulled it clear with her fingers. She had revealed a small box, nine inches by four, that was fitted into the laths that formed the ceiling below and was itself covered in lime plaster. If you did not know it was there, you could stare at it all day and still not see it. She slid it from its hiding place, opened it and inspected the contents. 'Just like all the others. Money, two vials and a letter.' The letter's seal bore the imprint of a nightingale and the letters E A E C I. The sign of the Sisterhood. She opened the letter. As usual, the letter was in code. Diana was meant to remember the key to the cipher but, though she had many qualities, a good memory and a head for figures did not count amongst them. If she met someone who knew her, she assumed that she had borrowed rather more money than they had intended to lend her, and substantially more than she had gotten around to giving back. It was generally a safe bet. What she could make of the letter detailed her escape route and contacts should the mission go badly, though she was struggling to work out what the difference was between this scenario and success seeing as in both cases it appeared that she ended up a prisoner. Loyal as she was, Diana had no intention of taking the traditional Sister's exit in such an eventuality: one of the glass vials was sealed with a blob of wax impressed with the likeness of a fish covered in spines, the other with a rat.

That had been seven days ago, however, and today Diana was

making a deposit, not a withdrawal. She had written her testament the previous day: three pages of neat italic detailing her activities and asking for God's forgiveness. She had signed it with the letters DJ and pressed her left thumb into the molten wax in the approved fashion. She bowed her head, unhooked the silver chain from around her neck and lowered her locket onto the letter which sat on the floor in front of her, and then she wrapped the silver chain around them both. She looked at the packet she had made and held it to her heart for a few moments before placing it carefully into the safe, locket uppermost. She then unbuckled the strip of leather that was wrapped around her forearm and slid out the stiletto that it harboured, holding it up to the murky yellow light that had pushed itself through the room's one window. The thin steel blade tried to glint in the sun but all it could manage was a malevolent glare. 'How I wish you were coming with me, old friend, for you might have found your final sheath,' she said, before kissing it and sliding it back into its resting place. She then placed the scabbard into the box. Finally, she packed in two purses of coin, a promissory note and a silk handkerchief, in which she had wrapped one of the vials. The hook had been baited. She slid the board shut, locked it and set about preparing herself for the day to come.

9

Susan waits

That same morning, Susan Hyde woke in Covent Garden, her customary lodgings, where she was simply known as Miss Susan. She, too, had been disturbed by the market traders and she, like Diana, had adjusted both her clothing and her habits over the past three days. Her dress was now somewhere between that of a gentlewoman and a lady, allowing for her to plough a more commercial, if charitable, furrow than she hitherto had need of. On her return from her sojourn in the countryside, where she had ostensibly been ministering to an ancient aunt on her deathbed, Susan had acted as if her vocation was now clear. Her aunt, so the story went, left her rather more than the chest of medicines that had been delivered to her a few days after her return to the city, as it came with chapbooks detailing the wisdom of its previous owner. These Hinton had sent as a substantive backup to her travelling bag. Susan had also been bequeathed something of a reputation by her silent sponsor, namely that she was a woman who knew things, a woman to whom other women might turn when their bodies rebelled against them, and this reputation now travelled before her.

Susan's testament, like Diana's, was also sealed with a waxen thumbprint and wrapped in a silver chain on which hung a small locket. It was, however, a somewhat shorter document. Her locket bore the same image as Diana's, that of a nightingale. And like Diana, Susan held it to her heart before placing it in a secret compartment in her clothes chest. She dressed herself, sat down on the chair by the window, and waited. It was almost ten o'clock. She didn't expect to have to wait for much longer.

Barely five minutes passed before there was a knock at her door. 'Miss Susan?' said the voice from behind the door. 'There's a boy come with a message for you. Some poor woman at the Mermaid craves your services.'

'Send him on his way with word that I will follow apace,' said Susan. With that, Susan checked that the vial with the green waxen seal was in place, slung her bag around her shoulder and set off.

Walking through the filthy streets of London was always a hazardous proposition for a lone woman, and it was only Susan's medicine bag that gave her licence to do so without a companion. The hazards were not simply due to the prevalence of unsavoury characters set on relieving such a vulnerable citizen of her purse, her innocence, her dignity or, if at all possible, the three as one, though Susan knew full well these characters abounded. It was more the simple motions of the city that sprayed danger all about the alleyways and thoroughfares. If she wasn't slipping in piles of animal dung or sliding in puddles of their stale, she was avoiding the buckets of human waste that appeared from every angle, along with the wasted humans in any combination of drunk, mad or ill who seemed to wish for nothing other than to career into any pedestrian whose course in any way came close to theirs. And once all this was negotiated, there was the matter of the animal life. The kicking, braying, pissing, shitting, trotting, running, flying and fleeing animal life that abounded. It often struck Susan that negotiating one's way through the city was an act that figured somewhere between sheer desperation and heroism, and she suspected that had Odysseus himself begun his great journey in Covent Garden, he would have been lucky to have made Islington, let alone Ithaca.

Susan was more than a little nervous. This was not who she was, the siren, the seductress. But then, this was not who she was to be, either. She was to be nobody. She was to treat him as if he, too, were nobody, invisible, even. It would be his single-mindedness, his dogmatic vision of how things were and how they ought to be, that would allow her access to this unlocker of the hearts of others. And then she would steal from the thief. She saw the signs of Butcher's Row. These were not words but visions. Blood ran down the gutters, and flies were audible before they were visible, the sound reminding Susan of the verses from St John the Divine. 'And there came out of the smoke locusts upon the earth,' she mumbled to herself. 'And their faces were as the faces of men.' It was how the loyal had been represented by some of the more partisan news-sheets, how they had whipped up the fervour of the exact, as those of a more puritan standpoint were known. Taking shallow breaths to minimise the depths to which the smell and taste of the atmosphere polluted her, Susan skirted by the worst of the filth and walked until she saw the sign of the Mermaid. She stepped inside.

One of the tables was already girt with customers, all arranged around a middle-aged woman, handsome in her own way, who looked as though she had not only seen better days, but that they had seen her too. She was, however, drunk and loud.

'Ha!' cried the woman, in response to a question or comment from those who sat drinking with her. 'His wife was an insufferable prig. She took me in, I thought out of pure friendship, but what did I know?' She drew hard on her tankard. 'But it wasn't me so much as my soul she wanted to know.' A filthy laugh followed. 'But him! Colonel Philips...' she looked straight through Susan as she spoke. 'Though he was no military man, I can tell you. They all have discipline and a most erect bearing,' she said, winking as she enunciated the word 'erect' with fastidious care, 'which is more than I can say for the good Colonel.' Another laugh as she held up her right hand, fist clenched apart from her little finger, which started off pointing at the ceiling but gradually curled downwards until it joined its brethren. 'But the Colonel coveted my lilywhite arse,' she said, fluffing her skirts behind her and farting loudly.

'Oh Diana,' said Susan under her breath. 'You are a terrible bitch and a slattern, but my goodness, you do it well.'

The innkeeper was a tall but delicately featured woman with dark, straight hair, and she walked over to where Susan stood admiring Diana's new role. 'Miss Susan?' she said, her English lightly accented, and held out her hand. 'I am Margarita. My friends call me Rita. It's rather less troublesome in this city than so Spanish a name.'

Susan took her hand and looked into Margarita's eyes. They were honest and forthright. She was to be trusted. 'Yes, indeed. Who has need of me?'

'It is one of the girls. Molly. Young, pretty. Pretty naive, to boot,' she said, pointing to the stairs in the corner. 'Up the stairs, third door on the left. I think she's late. Or she has pustules, or she can't piss properly,' she laughed. 'Whatever it is, she won't let me look.'

'Clients?' asked Susan.

'Well, that's the thing,' said Rita. 'She's not that sort of staff. So far as I know, she's a maid. Only been here a week. Wine to water there's nothing there, she's just believing herself ill.'

'Probably feels left out, now she's living amongst the poxy whores of this area,' said Susan, smiling. 'I'll be sure to make it look comprehensive, very dangerous but curable, if only because of her constitution, or piety, or complexion.' She smiled. 'I'll think of something.'

As Susan walked towards the stairs, passing by the table of early morning drinkers as she did so, Diana laughed out loud again. 'Does Cromwell's face scare children? Does the nightingale sing at night? Gentlemen, I cozened the Philips out of £200, and my only regret is that I didn't stay long enough to squeeze more out of them, just as the Colonel wishes he had my arse in front of him at breakfast instead of his priggish wife's face. I know which he thinks the prettier,' she laughed again and coughed. 'Oh God I pissed myself.' Susan walked up the steps one by one as the table erupted in laughter again.

Susan knocked on the door. 'Molly? It's Miss Susan. I've come to help. Molly?' She heard footsteps and the rattle of a bolt. The door creaked open and a small, oval face peered out of the gloom.

'Miss Susan?' she said, her voice trembling.

'Yes, Molly,' said Susan. 'I've come to help.'

'Are you from the nunnery?' said Molly.

'No, I'm not from the nunnery.' The door opened fully and Susan walked into the room. Molly shut and bolted the door behind her. 'Sit down, Molly, and tell me what troubles you,' said Susan.

Molly looked at Susan with a face full of confusion. 'But,' she began, but Susan waved her silent.

'Molly,' she whispered, having leant over so her mouth almost touched the younger girl's ear. 'I know nothing ails you but they don't. Play your part, that of the silly girl who knows nothing, and do as you're told.' Molly nodded, but looked mildly confused. 'What is troubling you, Molly?' said Susan, out loud now.

'But I am troubled, Miss Susan. It burns, Miss Susan.'

'What does, Molly?' She was becoming a little confused

herself. It was traditional that the ailment for which a Sister was summoned in order that they might enter an establishment without arousing suspicion was *hysterico passio*, but Molly was young, and seemed prone to confusion. She may have been a chaffinch, the term given to a Sister's informal assistants, but she was a liability. She would have words with Diana over her choices, if they made it through the next few days.

'My pee, it burns,' said Molly. Then she whispered, 'I heard one of the other girls say it, too. Is it bad?'

'And have you been with a man, Molly?' said Susan. Molly coloured and coughed. Susan began to think that she had a real patient on her hands. This was not a particularly convenient time for such a thing. Susan had work to do, but not with a serving wench.

'I kissed young Billy, the drover's boy.'

'Oh good Lord,' said Susan to herself, not entirely sure that Molly wasn't being totally honest with her here. The innkeeper had said she was naive, but Susan was beginning to think that she didn't know the half of it. The poor girl was going to be swallowed whole by this town. 'Where did you kiss him, Molly?'

'In the cellar.'

'No, Molly. Where on his body? Did you kiss his old man?'

'His father?' said Molly, confused.

'No, Molly, his nether regions. His cock, girl.' Susan was getting frustrated now. She wished Thurloe would bloody well hurry up and come today. If she spent much more time with this idiotic girl she would probably throttle her. As an act of mercy for all concerned.

'Miss Susan, no!' cried Molly. 'Why would I do such a thing?' Molly looked truly disgusted. Susan wondered how long that would last.

'How long have you been here, Molly?' asked Susan.

'Just a sennight,' replied Molly.

'And do you like the taste of ale?'

Molly turned up her nose at the word. 'I detest it, Miss Susan.'

Susan smiled. 'So what do you drink, Molly?' She already knew the answer.

'Nothing much, Miss Susan,' came the answer.

'Show me your chamber pot,' said Susan. Molly handed her the pot. Susan inspected the contents. A small quantity of dark, cloudy and stinking piss lay at the bottom. 'Molly, dear Molly. You have an imbalance in your bladder, nothing more. You'll have to get over the taste, but you simply must drink your small beer. Drink a lot. You need to piss it out.'

'Yes, Miss Susan, thank you, Miss Susan,' said Molly, as there was a knock on the door. Molly unbolted it. The innkeeper stood on the other side.

'Miss Susan, is everything quite alright? I need Molly to work now,' said the innkeeper. 'And one of the other girls says she has a touch of the mother.'

'Ah, the mother,' said Susan, finally understanding that Molly wasn't the chaffinch in the Mermaid after all. She had been an actual patient. 'Yes, everything is fine,' she continued, actually glad that there was now an excuse to stay out of sight for longer. Timing was everything. Serendipity was not something that could be rushed.

'Get yourself tidied up and come downstairs directly,' said Margarita before waving Molly away. 'Well?' she said, looking at Susan directly. 'Anything actually wrong with the girl or is she swinging the lead? I didn't believe her from the very beginning. Something seemed wrong to me, she was nervous.'

'I'm not surprised,' said Susan. 'She'd heard one of the other girls complain of the same problem. She thought she had the pox.'

'But she hasn't so much as touched a man. Did she say which girl?'

'No, but she has kissed the drover's boy.'

'Where?'

'In the cellar,' replied Susan and they both laughed.

'Poor girl,' said Margarita. 'She hasn't got a hope, has she?'

'Not a chance. But if she drinks enough small beer over the next week it will at least stop hurting when she takes a piss. Make her drink so much she spends half her day on the pot. Don't stop until it's clear and doesn't stink.'

'Understood. I'm surprised at her kissing Jack, though. He's not all there, if you know what I mean.' She sighed. 'An ale before you deal with this other girl? It didn't seem urgent.'

'It rarely is, and thank you, yes,' replied Susan, and they both began to walk down the stairs. 'But she said Billy... oh, never mind.'

'This heat's making all manner of people crawl out of the woodwork,' said Margarita. 'And it's not helping their mood. Tell the truth I'm half-expecting the government to shut us down soon.'

'There have been reports of plague?'

'No, well, not as yet, but it won't be long, surely?' she said as she led Susan into the cellars. 'And they're getting far less accommodating these days, if you know what I mean. That's better.' She drew the door closed and unhooked a lantern from the wall as they walked into the earthy gloom. 'It's cooler here and we'll not be disturbed.' The air was moist and yeasty, and Margarita drew off two flagons of ale from a small barrel.

'Have you news?' asked Susan as she took a long draught of ale. 'How fares the Sisterhood here?'

'We still sing unseen,' said Margarita. 'But in truth I am not taken with my latest guest. She may be une belle-fille or even une fille-complète but I do feel she has an agenda separate from that of the Sisterhood.'

'And you a mere petite-fille?' Margarita occupied the lowest rank of the Sisterhood. Les Filles d'Ophélie began as petites-filles, graduated to belles-filles and were elected to the position of filles-complètes. And yet all were sworn to serve. 'How came you to serve here, of all places?'

'I was first recruited when Charles was negotiating with the Spanish,' said Margarita. 'They used me to translate various letters. I like the place. When the letters ceased to arrive, I failed to go home.'

'As has Diana. Come here to serve.'

'I understand your loyalty, and she has mine, too,' said Margarita. 'But we both owe our loyalty to a greater power.'

'Indeed we do. And it is that greater power that has chosen Diana. And we must trust in her judgement.' Susan felt uneasy as she spoke, however. She knew Diana was always one step to the left of where she ought to be. 'We must also trust in my judgement, when I tell you that whosoever seeks me, no matter how distasteful, must be directed to my address in Covent Garden. You understand?'

Margarita opened her mouth to speak but was interrupted by muffled shouts and what sounded like stools being knocked over upstairs. The women rushed up the uneven cellar steps, but no sooner had they opened the door and entered the saloon than their haste left them and they stood, transfixed.

'Thurloe,' said Margarita, the fear in her voice palpable, as she surveyed the scene in what had, but a few short seconds before, been a peaceful establishment.

'Who?' asked Susan, knowing full well which of the men in view was her ultimate target.

'Him,' came the reply, accompanied by an index finger pointing at a thickly waisted man dressed in black and accompanied by three henchmen. 'The spymaster. He is not a man to trifle with, and, if the stories are true, one who enjoys the practical aspect of his job rather too much.'

John Thurloe shot the two women a filthy look but no more before surveying the bar. The table at which Diana had been sitting when Susan had gone upstairs to minister to Molly was overturned. One of her fellow drunks was unconscious on the floor, bleeding from a head wound. Susan saw a small patch of crushed glass on the floor. 'Gennings,' shouted Thurloe. 'Which of you is Gennings?'

Two men pointed to Diana and she slowly rose to her feet. 'I am Diana Gennings,' she said, dress ripped and beer soaked. 'Which one of you ugly sons of camels wants to know?' And then she vomited and fell to the floor, clutching her throat and shaking as she was taken by a fit. Within seconds she was unconscious, even as her body continued its dance. Susan watched and waited. If she went to Diana's aid too quickly, suspicions would be raised... too slowly and the entire plan would die alongside Diana.

'You! Innkeeper!' shouted Thurloe, walking towards the two women. 'How much of your wares has this precious slut consumed this morning?'

'I don't generally keep count, sir,' she replied, 'we just supply the tables. But I'll warrant too little to cause such a purgation.' As Thurloe advanced, Susan made her decision, and set off in the direction of the stricken woman. Inevitably, she met the oncoming spymaster on the way. This was their first meeting, the meeting from which everything else would spring, and it was practically a collision. Thurloe fairly pushed Susan out of his path as if he simply did not see her.

'Watch your place, woman,' he growled as he grabbed the innkeeper and began to interrogate her. Though knocked off balance and winded, Susan made it to Diana's side, knelt down and put her hand to her unconscious sister's forehead. Hinton's drugs were very good. She hoped his antidote would prove as effective.

'This is not the work of ale,' said Susan, addressing the closest of Thurloe's henchmen. 'Get her onto a table, fetch me water and cloth.'

Thurloe turned from the innkeeper and stared directly at Susan. 'And who, pray, are you?' he said.

Susan did not respond, she was too intent on clearing Diana's nose and mouth of vomit, an action that she followed with the raising of her head and torso. 'Are you deaf?' she said to the assembled throng, once more pointedly ignoring Thurloe. 'Get her onto a table. Now. Or we lose her.'

Margarita indicated to the men that they ought to obey, before turning back to Thurloe. His men held their ground. 'She is a healer, an apothecary in all but name, sir,' she said. 'If you wish your prey to live, then you are best advised to follow her instructions.'

At this, Thurloe grunted and nodded to his men, who quickly hauled the still-shaking body onto the next table. When the water arrived Susan bathed Diana's face, rinsed her hair and mouth and made a great show of inspecting her. 'My bag,' she said, pointing in the direction of the stairs, where she had been talking with Margarita. Thurloe himself collected it and handed it to her. She took it without so much as a word, opened the bag, selected the vial, broke it and poured the contents into Diana's mouth and held her close until the shaking subsided. After Diana had been still for a few minutes, Susan wiped her hands and spoke, addressing the most capable looking of the henchmen. 'She must rest for an hour or two, but the worst is over. She will wake with a fierce thirst. It may be assuaged with milk and some broth. No more.' Susan stood back from the table. 'She's all yours. Good luck.'

Thurloe bent over Diana's now calmly sleeping body. 'Thank you. The republic is in your debt Mrs...'

'Susan. Miss Susan,' replied Margarita.

'I didn't ask you, woman,' said Thurloe, turning from Diana.

'It matters not,' she said, 'but if I did not answer you would be none the wiser.'

10

Thurloe takes control

Thurloe looked around the inn, but the innkeeper spoke true: Susan had vanished. He pointed to one of his men. 'Find her and bring her to me,' he said. The man turned to leave. 'But Nathaniel,' he continued, 'use her well. She is to come, but as my guest. I trust you understand. We are to reward her, not punish her.'

'Master Secretary Thurloe,' said Margarita.

'Do I know you?' replied Thurloe.

'No, but everybody knows you, Master Secretary, sir,' she replied. 'Forgive me, but wouldn't your man find his task simpler if he were to have her address?'

'You know this?' asked Thurloe.

'Of course,' replied Margarita. 'How else would I have known where to send for her?'

'You did not send for her,' said Thurloe. 'She was here already.'

'She was here because I sent for her to attend to one of my girls who has been sickly,' said Margarita. 'Now do you wish for Miss Susan's address or will you rely on your powers of deduction?'

'You'd do well to use me kindly, madam,' said Thurloe.

'Do I not do so?' she asked, with a look that suggested that she was beginning to regret having offered. 'She lodges in Covent Garden, no. 17, by the sign of the Raven.'

Thurloe nodded to Nathaniel, who left the tavern in haste. 'I am in your debt,' he said. 'And I shall increase it now. Transfer this creature into a private room where my men may watch over her. One of your girls may attend to her needs.' He paused. 'This is not a request, so that we're clear.'

'Yes, good sir,' said Margarita. 'I understand.' She pointed at a girl who had the misfortune to have walked down the stairs at that moment. 'You. Show these gentlemen up to the third floor and lodge them in the withdrawing room. See that you attend to their needs.' With this she turned to the two henchmen. 'Good sirs, my girl is young and will attend to whatever needs you might have. If, however, you choose to abuse my hospitality, I will see to it that you pay, in both coin and in pain. Do you understand?'

'Do you threaten my men, madam?' asked Thurloe.

'I do, Master Thurloe. I threaten them with your good name and your honour as a servant of the commonweal,' she replied.

'Well said, innkeeper,' replied Thurloe. He looked at his men. 'As the woman says, abuse her hospitality and you answer to me. I will be back in a few hours. I have other business to attend to. When your charge wakes, take a statement from her. Be polite. There is no need to coerce her. Not yet.' With this, Thurloe took his leave of the Mermaid and walked back to Whitehall.

Three hours later, Thurloe was in the Mermaid again. He was not in a good mood. Cromwell was in the process of making some decisions that really ought to have made themselves, and he had received two notes. The first was from Nathaniel, who explained that he had communicated Thurloe's wish to repay the favour done him but had received short shrift, and the second was from one of the men he'd left at the Mermaid, who informed him that the prisoner had woken. On top of that, he did not feel well.

'Innkeeper. Wine,' he bellowed. 'And fetch one of my men.' His orders were obeyed, wine and man arriving simultaneously. 'Well?'

'She will speak only with you,' said his man. 'She is hale. We fed her and gave her milk. She insisted on ale, and we relented. She goes well on it. She seems to think that she has information you will be happy to pay for.'

'She plainly does not know me - Alfred, is it? - or she would be well aware that I am not happy to pay for anything, let alone a woman's prattlings,' said Thurloe.

'Yes, Master Secretary,' said Alfred.

'Now,' said Thurloe. 'Seeing as she's made an almighty mess of my day, let us return the favour.' With this, Thurloe ordered more wine, ale, bread and cheese, and sent one of the innkeeper's boys to his baker's with instructions for his supper. When Alfred had eaten his fill, Thurloe had him relieve the man guarding Diana, who came down to join his employer at the table. Once the second guard had eaten, Thurloe stood up and left for his chambers at Lincoln's Inn. There he remained throughout the next day, and until midday the day after, when, suitably rested, and feeling much improved at having made Diana wait a suitable length of time, he walked back through the city to the upstairs room at the Mermaid, in which she sat, waiting.

11

Diana meets the spymaster

'You took your time, Master Secretary,' she said, as he dismissed her guards.

'You would be wise to take advantage of my current good humour, Miss...?' said Thurloe, before opening the door and calling for more wine, paper and ink.

'Mrs,' replied Diana. 'I am Mrs Gennings. My husband is William Gennings of Essex.'

'The son of the Member for St Albans? But he is barely twenty summers old!' said Thurloe, laughing. 'With all due respect, and let's be honest here, a woman such as you is due precious little, I'm more than a little surprised his father allowed the match.'

'We eloped. What's it to you?'

'Everything interests me, Mrs Gennings, if indeed you are such,' said Thurloe in a low, slow voice that had been known to make such an impression on a prisoner that no further persuasion had been necessary. 'And you will find it much to your advantage to tell me what I'd like to know, and sooner rather than later.'

'And so much is my intent,' said Diana. 'Just so long as we understand one another.'

'You are hardly in a position to be making demands, Mrs Gennings.' He shook his head in disbelief.

'Oh but I am. You see, I have nothing to lose and everything to gain.'

'You'll perhaps forgive me if I reserve judgement until I have heard what you have to offer,' said Thurloe. 'If, indeed, you have anything at all. I believe you had eloped. Do continue.'

Diana remained silent for a minute, then another. Thurloe, it appeared, was more patient than she.

'We travelled to Antwerp, where we lived comfortably enough,' she continued, 'even though we were forced to avoid his friends and relatives, who did not approve, until we became short of money. I occasioned upon a group of royalists in a tavern, and they appeared to be discussing a conspiracy.'

The door opened and the wine appeared. Thurloe took one cup and handed the other to his prisoner. She nodded her thanks. He set the paper and ink on a stool, removed a black quill from within his cloak and began to write.

'Do go on,' said Thurloe, as they supped on their wine. 'You mentioned a conspiracy?'

'Yes, I'll come to that,' said Diana, 'if the terms be agreeable to me.' She paused, but there was nothing to be read into the silence. 'I introduced myself as the wife of Sir Thomas Stanley.'

'Who is in no position to contradict you,' said Thurloe. 'And which terms?'

'Indeed not. And William became my cousin,' Diana laughed. 'The terms under which I will tell you what I know. These royalists were so excited when they discovered that I was a rich widow that they neglected to check my credentials.'

'Indeed?' said Thurloe. 'You'll be most gratified to note that I make no such errors in my work. Everything that can be checked, is checked. Twice. So I'll counsel you to tell the truth, for if you do not I will discover it, and it will not go well for you.'

'Such is your reputation, Master Thurloe, such is your

reputation, and I may be a thief, a liar and a cradle-snatcher, but I am no fool, so if you'd allow me to continue,' said Diana.

'My apologies, Mrs Gennings,' said Thurloe. 'In your own time. Though indulge me, what are you doing here, and why the boasts about your behaviour?'

Diana took a long draught of her wine, smacked her lips and continued. 'I came in part to visit friends, and in part because my hand was forced. Having skinned the Philips for £200, they somehow grew wise to our scheme and clapped my William in irons. I made good my escape, though was almost caught before I crossed the channel, my pursuer arriving too late to do anything but loose off one round at our small boat. I know not where I landed nor whose vessel it was, though its captain and crew, being one and the same man, used me with great courtesy. My companions were an Irishman named Duggan, tall, terribly sick on the journey, and one Talbot. Scots. Very quiet. I know no more about them than their names, sadly.'

'That is of no import,' said Thurloe, 'and neither are they. We have already met them. Gentlemen adventurers led astray by ale and adversity. Somewhat like yourself, is that not so?'

'Sadly my two worst enemies and yet my constant companions,' said Diana. 'Where was I?'

'Your journey. And your terms.'

'Yes, my journey,' said Diana. 'My journey was in part impelled by what I overheard, and the fact that my pursuers do not know that I have intelligence of their plans. They were simply incensed at losing their money to a common coney-catcher.'

'If I might ask you to come to the point, Mrs Gennings, with regard to this information?'

'By all means, but first let us discuss what I might hope for in return, for this is information you will be most glad of, as it is information regarding the fate of the commonweal,' said Diana.

'If it is of such great and paramount importance, then you are duty bound to report your knowledge for the sake of God and your country, are you not?' said Thurloe.

'Neither of us are naive enough to believe that either comes before coin, Master Thurloe,' she said, smiling gently as she spun her tales. She merely needed to be careful how quickly she gave up the names and intentions of her persecutors, for fear that too blithe a story would not be believed. She had fulfilled her part in allowing Susan access to the man, however, and she had her own grudges to settle. She was unsure which of the Philips deserved her scorn more, the priggish, holier-than-thou wife or the lecherous, treacherous husband. It was fitting, perhaps, that they be betrayed together. The very thought of how viciously they would argue once exposed, and the lengths to which each would go that they might save their own skin at their spouse's expense, brought a smile to her face.

'And to set things straight, for I am a man of my word, would you be so kind as to tempt me further?'

'As a gift? Why of course,' said Diana. 'Those of whom I speak direct their words to an apothecary who resides in Covent Garden, a man called Chase. Those letters that arrive to him marked with a dash above the endorsement are sent on, though I know not to where, or to whom.'

'Thank you,' said Thurloe. 'Now, who is it?'

'I beg your pardon?'

'Who is it you wish me to inconvenience in a suitably permanent manner?'

'I think we understand each other,' said Diana. 'And before I bequeath unto you my little bit of vengeance, at the centre of which we find a story of a husband and wife who conspired to assassinate the Lord Protector himself-'

'-a story I most definitely wish to hear,' said Thurloe.

'My terms are as follows,' Diana said, smiling. 'You will

engineer the release of my William from his cell in Antwerp, appoint him to some sinecure worth £100 per annum and you will henceforth leave us be.'

Thurloe hesitated for a second, and his thoughts were interrupted by a knock on the door. The spymaster stood. 'If you'll excuse me.'

Diana strained to hear what he was being told but could not make it out. He re-entered the room. 'It appears I have a rather pressing engagement, but my man here is lettered. You may direct your confession to him,' said Thurloe.

'Confession?' Diana was suddenly wondering if she had misread him. 'I have nothing to confess but the sins of others.'

'Well, indeed, it is their confession. You are merely their proxy. I shall return on the morrow.'

'And my terms?'

'Agreed,' said Thurloe. And with that, he was gone.

Her second interrogator, no more than a notary, entered the room, sat down and immediately stamped on the floor twice. 'Ale, food!' he shouted. 'It's all right for some,' he said to Diana. 'I tramp around all day after him for sixpence and ale, while that pretty little apothecary will make a pound if it's a penny.' He spat into the fireplace. 'And all because she saved your poxy, drunken arse.' He sharpened a quill and dipped it in ink, scratching out some words on the top of the page. 'Go on, then. Tell us everything. He always wants everything.'

Diana smiled to herself. She had achieved three missions at once. The king's, the Sisterhood's, and her own. It sounded as though Susan was in play. It was a pity that Diana had lost the attention of the spymaster, but no matter. With this minion she was in control of the situation. She merely needed to tell a good story, and she could fade into the background with her William. It was a stroke of fortune that her story was not only good, but also largely true. And if the odd detail had been changed to protect the innocent and damn the guilty, well so be it.

'Once upon a time,' she began, 'there were two nasty, spiteful people, and they were called Mr and Mrs Philips...'

12

Thurloe reflects

He had no further business. Not of the State. Of course, there was always business of the State waiting for his attention. Always new rebellions to thwart, new traitors to capture, new intelligencers to unmask, new codes to master, new beating chests containing hearts whose locks needed picking. But John Thurloe was tired. Tired of the relentless bleakness. Tired of chasing the conspirators who hid behind assumed names and false addresses, the S.H.s and Simburbes of this country. Tired of having to do one thing and tell his master another. Sometimes he just wanted to sit down and allow life to wash over him. Even when it was a life as stinking and fetid as Covent Garden during an overly hot summer. And now this woman. For three days she had rejected his repeated offers of reward for the services she had performed. Thurloe was not a man used to rejection, let alone one who took it kindly. He would visit her himself, and be done with it.

When he arrived at Susan's lodgings she was not home, nor was there anyone to take a message, so he sat by the door of the house and waited. He waited for one hour. Then he waited for another. He fell asleep in the warmth of the afternoon, and dreamt of his bed.

'Excuse me, sir,' the words filtered into his dream world and at first he failed to understand what this female voice was doing in his bedchamber. It was certainly not his wife's voice. She, anyway, was back home in the Fens. 'Excuse me, sir.' The voice came again, this time accompanied by a gentle shaking of the shoulder. Thurloe woke, and looked up.

'Oh,' said the woman who stood above him. 'It's you. If you would kindly unblock my doorway that I might enter my home.'

Thurloe shook off his sleep and stood. Susan simply pushed past him.

'I came that I might thank you for your efforts the other morning,' said Thurloe.

'And so you have,' said Susan, walking into the house. 'I bid you good day, sir.' Thurloe pushed the door open once more and followed Susan as she climbed the steep and narrow stairs that penetrated directly into the bowels of the house. When she was halfway up the first flight, Susan stopped. 'I bid you good day, sir,' she said, without even turning to look at the man who was now but a few steps behind her.

'Do you know who I am?' said Thurloe, caught between confusion and anger. 'I am-' he began.

'John Thurloe,' said Susan. 'I know who you are and I know what kind of man you are,' she continued, 'and I bid you good day.' She began her climb once more in earnest.

'You may know my name but not even my wife knows what kind of a man I am,' said Thurloe, following her lead once more. 'I am a man of passion, of passions,' he continued, gaining on his prey every second as she stopped in the hallway in front of her room. With three steps, he was standing behind her. 'I discharge my responsibilities to God and my country, and I discharge them well because I am passionate about them.' As he climbed his voice became more strident.

'A pity you are not so passionate about your marriage vows,' said Susan, opening the door to her room.

'Take supper with me tonight, at my chambers. I'll send a man to pick you up.'

'I bid you good day, sir,' said Susan, shutting the door in his face.

'Eight o'clock. Be ready. He will be instructed not to take no for an answer.' With this, Thurloe stomped down the stairs, not quite believing that this healing woman could have treated him with such disdain.

13

Susan reflects

Susan was uneasy. She sensed a smile forming but it seemed wrong, wicked. She felt polluted, both by her proximity to such an evil man and by her behaviour. Yes, the hook was now baited, and yes, her prey had invited her to attach it to his cheek, so sure was he that there could only be one predator at work here.

Four hours later, Susan found herself sitting in the main room of Thurloe's chambers, hands held demurely in her lap, staring at a point on the wooden panelling directly in front of her. It was a fault in the wood, a knot, the scar that showed where a limb had once projected out into the world from the safety of the tree's trunk. It swirled amidst the dark striations of the tree's rings, like a sudden vortex in the calmest of seas. It was Odysseus' Charybdis, and Susan wondered where her personal Scylla might lie. It had been an eventful few days, and in some ways she was glad to be where she was, effectively detained for dinner at the pleasure of Cromwell's spymaster John Thurloe. The fact that so many of her fellow subjects had sat in front of this man in very different circumstances from those in which she found herself was something that set her teeth on edge. Susan was worried that she would find it impossible to look at his hands without thinking of the blood that they had shed, the pain they had inflicted and the misery they had caused. Thurloe had been leading parliament's war against the royalist resistance for the past three years. It may have been a largely invisible war, but it was war nonetheless, and a brutally oppressive one. Susan feared that he would read her intent as if it were written across her forehead. She feared that she would fail in every way possible. Thurloe was not a man one would choose as an enemy, and certainly he was not a man to challenge. And here was Susan, waiting in the lion's den intent on tweaking his tail when he arrived. He may have commanded through courtesy, but command he did, though he knew not to what degree their fates were entwined. And so she sat, unable to do anything other than sit, and in the quiet she sought to reflect on the situation in which she found herself.

Her joy at seeing her brother Edward had been more than a little tempered by the discomfort afforded her by his singular lack of any meaningful resistance to the king's orders. What he commanded was nothing less than a death sentence. It struck her that while it was one thing to risk one's life in the pursuance of a just cause, having one's life and reputation risked without so much as a by-your-leave was quite something else. Susan would be utterly ruined should she succeed, ignominious should she fail. Disobedient in any case, when he discovered the decision she had made. But no man would then consider her in any way marriageable material. And that, mark you, without the directly convertible status of her having been the king's mistress, or, indeed, mother to the king's bastard. There was no small part of her that suspected this to be Edward's scheme, not that of the king. He had, after all, failed to show Diana and her the actual orders contained in the letter on whose enfolded complexity and cunning he had waxed so lyrical. He had simply tossed it on the fire and, unbeknownst to him, Susan's prospects and reputation had turned to ashes and flown up the chimney with it, followed soon after by her respect for her brother. She resolved to write that she might enlighten him of her feelings of disappointment, if not the subtle change in plan.

It wasn't the act that frightened Susan, should, indeed, it become necessary. After all, it was a natural, beautiful act; that the ordinances of the Sisterhood made clear. It wasn't the danger she was in. No, it was none of these. Susan was a loyal subject, and a fully inculcated Daughter of Ophelia, a fille-complète. As with any other member of the Sisterhood, she would gladly lay down her life if it led to the restoration of the king. It was her duty and her honour to do so. But she wasn't like Diana. The irony of the letter they had sent to 'mother' that described Diana as, how did she put it, an 'untrustworthy, greedy and unprincipled whore who is apt to grab fortune by the forelock'? struck her more keenly now. Did mother know that as a description of Diana it was almost perfect? This was why she was utterly inappropriate. After all, it was far easier to be almost yourself than to try to wear another's life as a cloak. But that was Diana, not Susan. And this was why the original plan, regardless of whose it was, just happened to be fatally flawed. Had Diana been allowed to attempt the infiltration of Thurloe's bed, the plan would have been over before it could have begun. Thurloe, for all his zeal and artistry in the dungeons and cells, for all his patience and largesse retained for the legion of informers he controlled, was a man of great principle. He was not a man to fall for the wiles of a common coney-catcher, even an uncommon one, which was what, in truth, Diana was.

It made perfect sense that Susan should be the one to tempt Thurloe. And it made sense that she ought to treat him with contempt. How better to seduce a man fundamentally unseducible other than to make it plain you could think of nothing more vile than to do so. For it was true that, for all his principles, Thurloe was still a man. It is not merely the devil who can find a way into a man's heart; sometimes it was the devil's heart that was in need of unpicking. What was it her father had said? If you must dance with the devil, be sure to first call the tune. Susan was most definitely calling the tune.

'Beg pardon, Miss Susan,' said her guard and guide, who stood sentinel by the door, but five feet distant.

'I'm sorry?' said Susan, confused.

'You said something, miss,' replied the man.

'I did?' replied Susan, realising as she spoke that she had recited her father's words out loud, as she so often did.

'Yes. It sounded like something about a devil.'

Susan laughed. 'I must have fallen asleep and dreamt of my childhood,' she said, thinking rapidly as her actual words returned to her consciousness. 'We used to play my-espial, did you?'

'Yes, miss.'

'And I always got it backwards,' said Susan, allowing a nervous laugh to escape despite herself. 'I always said what I saw rather than the first letter of the thing. As I fell asleep, all I could see was the panelling there, in front of me, and it's a mess of bevelled edges. It must have been that.'

The man simply nodded and went back to his own daydreaming.

But Susan was beginning to see the logic of her mission, the necessity of it. For the price of one reputation ruined, one innocence sullied, so many lives might be saved, and the soul of England might return, along with God's favour. Both Talbot and Duggan had risked much in their unquestioning behaviour at Queenborough, allowing Diana and Edward to meet Susan without their presence being noticed and their eventually being run to ground.

She could not now decide whether the mission was an honour

or an indication of the disposability of the two women. Were they the only candidates considered or two of many? Her position as the postmistress to the Knot was unofficial. She would never hold such a position in peacetime, unless she were to hold it for her eldest son until he reached majority. But that would necessitate both a husband and fecundity. Her husband had been dead for many years, and their marriage had failed in any case: Susan had never fallen pregnant. She was barren. If there was one thing that could be said for war, it was the fact that one's position became less important than one's ability. Up to a point, of course. Perhaps, she mused, she ought prepare a new postmistress, just in case such a creature became necessary. But whom? Anna was too greedy for position, too ambitious to replace her sister. And ought Susan put her at risk?

But it was she who risked the most. She, Susan Hyde, sister to Sir Edward Hyde, who stood to lose everything. The king stood merely to lose a subject, Edward a sister: Susan stood to lose both her soul and her chances of a future, that is if she did not lose her life. Was it not still adultery if you were unmarried but the other party was not free in any sense of the word? The Sisterhood, of course, was clear that such details sprang from the laws of man, not of woman. Their Bible was clear regarding the creation. Adam and Eve were equal, and had been created simultaneously: Adam and Eve he created them. The story of the rib was merely a late addition designed to confer authority on man through simple primacy. The Sisterhood was clear in its teaching that women were not naturally subservient to men. Aemilia Lanyer had dedicated a poem to the grand mother on the subject. But this was not something they could yet promulgate abroad.

It was she, Susan, who risked all, and for no reward other than the knowledge that she served her king. Not for the first time Susan wondered how different life might have been had the old king's daughter Elizabeth taken the crown those years before when the chance had presented itself, instead of waiting for James to die and allowing Charles to succeed. Yes, she had ruled Bohemia, though for not much longer than a year. And yet her intelligence and skill as politician and leader put her sickly brother to shame. His most regal moment had come in death. In les Filles d'Ophélie, a society had been born that taught its initiates how to live. A society dedicated to restoring Elizabeth's line to the throne. Her countenance hardened as she delved ever deeper into the murky depths of her innermost thoughts and wishes.

She was kicked out of her reverie by the sound of the door slamming. She turned to look, breaking away from the knot that had served her thoughts so well, and saw that it had begun. The spymaster had returned.

'Ah,' said Thurloe, 'it is a delight to return home and find you waiting for me so patiently, Miss Susan.'

'If I am waiting, it is because I have no choice, Master Secretary,' she said, but she was interrupted.

'John, call me John,' he said, pouring them each a cup of wine. 'Recently intercepted contraband,' he added, bringing the cup to his nose, inhaling and then drinking. 'It's very good.' He pulled the chair opposite his guest out from under the table and sat down with a grunt. It had been a long day, and he was very tired. It was only the promise of the evening with Susan that had kept him going.

'I thank you for that, but as I was saying, Master Secretary, I came because I had no choice, just as I waited because I had no choice. And I must remind you that it was your man for whom I waited, not for you, for he is the one who gave me no choice. If, therefore, you consider that either I wait for you or that I do so patiently, or, heavens forfend, both, then you are very much mistaken,' said Susan. 'And, what's more, I would suggest that if this were the case, then your reputation as a man of subtle wit is very much misplaced.' She drank from the cup. 'Though I must admit, your assessment of this wine's quality is not too wide of the mark.'

'Tell me about yourself, Susan,' said Thurloe, drawing his chair underneath the table and signalling with a nod that supper was to be served. Susan was silent while Thurloe's man brought a series of wooden platters to the table. There were great hunks of bread, lumps of cheese, thick slices of cold beef and a terrine. 'You'll find that my fare is much like myself.'

'Lumpen, unsubtle and cold?' suggested Susan.

'Honest, uncomplicated and very English,' countered Thurloe.

Susan took a knife from the table and sliced through the terrine in one single motion, revealing the thick layers of meat inside. She inserted the tip at the point of the first layer, extracted a sample and tasted. 'Duck, cinnamon and venison. And these?' she held up a small, white lump that looked a little like an overgrown seed. 'Like the terrine it came in, these are not exactly English.'

'Pine nuts, I am told.'

The next layer revealed rabbit and boar separated by a layer of sliced apples and nutmeg. 'I wonder if this is more telling of your person than the other plates,' said Susan. 'Wild animal and sophisticated spices, each cushioned from one another by something unexpected, and all in their turn hidden from view by a rough, fire-burnt exterior such that when the true nature is revealed, it is too late to change one's mind. It is all one can do to cope with such complexity.' She cut herself some bread, tore off a corner and began to chew upon it.

'We are not here to wax contemplative about my qualities, Miss Susan,' said Thurloe, filling his own plate with food as he spoke. 'We are here that I might express my gratitude for your assistance this morning at the Mermaid.'

'We are here for no such thing, Master Secretary...'

'John...'

'Master Secretary Thurloe,' said Susan without missing so much as a beat. 'Your gratitude has already been expressed. We are here because,' at this she faltered, the words that were on her mind staying firmly put on the tip of her tongue.

'Because?' asked Thurloe, a smile breaking out on his lips for the first time since he had arrived at his chambers.

'How is Miss...' Susan hesitated. She felt that she was suddenly being interrogated rather than indulging in conversation, no matter how guarded.

'Miss?' continued Thurloe.

Susan was increasingly aware that she was in danger of overplaying her hand. She cast her mind back to when Thurloe had first entered the Mermaid. Had he called Diana by name? Or had he used one of her pseudonyms? 'Your prey that morning. The woman I so usefully restored for you that she might be put to question. What did you say her name was?'

'Gennings. Diana Gennings. What of her?'

'How does she fare?' asked Susan, slicing off a thick piece of the terrine. After all, it may have come from the spymaster's store, but that was no fault of its own, and it was very, very good. 'Has she fully recovered? Did she furnish you with the intelligence you desired?' Susan's eyes flashed suddenly, and her voice quietened. She leant forward towards Thurloe and became a conspirator. 'Is she one of those I have read of in the *Mercurius Politicus*? Did I minister to a real, live she-intelligencer?'

14

Thurloe wonders

Thurloe cut a piece of cheese, speared it with his knife and placed it into his mouth, following it with a good gulp from his cup. He chewed slowly, all the while watching this woman who sat across from him at his own table, her eyes now full of wonder, full of questions. Now, he thought, now she could not deny that she waited for him, though it was still plain that she did not do so patiently. But impatience had different symptoms, different causes. When he had arrived at his chambers, her impatience may have been for that moment, but only in order that she would all the sooner be away from him, and in her lodgings alone. But her impatience was now for him, for that special knowledge that he possessed. The invitation for a heart to be unlocked had been delivered, albeit unwittingly. He swallowed hard. There was, without doubt, something singular about this woman, even if he could not quite put his finger on it. She had an aura of some kind. Thurloe was a pragmatic, intelligent man not given to flights of fancy. For some reason, this woman confused him. Vulnerably independent. It was as if he could not see the cards he held.

'This wine is marvellous strong,' he said. 'It heats my blood excellent well.' He took another, smaller draught and looked into Susan's eyes. They were a light but intense hazel in colour, clear as a summer's day, and behind them burnt a fire the like of which he had not seen for many a year, not since before his first wife left this earth. His eyes dropped a little as he was unexpectedly cast back in time, to another teasing, tempting conversation with a beautiful young woman. 'Miss Susan,' he began. 'Allow me to tell you about she-intelligencers.'

15

Susan waits once more

Susan sat on the cot in her lodgings, waiting for word from Diana. Her head was a little tight as a result of the wine that Thurloe had plied her with. It appeared that its quality was matched only by the quantity of it he possessed and the thirst it engendered in her. Susan had not left his chambers until past midnight, and at such a time she was glad of the escort his man had provided, her shadow Talbot notwithstanding. It was not merely the presence of what was plainly an individual with military experience, both in his size and in the way that he bore himself, but the fact that he was obviously acting as her guard and guide. It was a foolhardy or stupid man who would make an attempt on Susan that night. And it wasn't as if she presented much of a prize; a nurse or midwife out late at night was no uncommon sight, and all she carried of worth besides a few pennies was shut up in her bag, mysterious and marked with symbols such that the uninitiated would not be able to separate poison from panacea. Susan was surprised, perhaps, to see that having delivered her safely, he had not been set as guard. She was certainly gratified, as it indicated that the great spymaster harboured no suspicion of her. Either that or he desired that she think that. The truth would come out easily enough. It was certainly the case that now was not the time to make a collection or delivery. For one thing Thurloe may well have set a close but unseen watch on her, and for another she did not know what Diana had disclosed in order to win her freedom, if, indeed, she had done so. She would wait until the afternoon, when her head had cleared, and pay Molly a visit.

As she waited, Susan took from her bag the same packet she had drawn comfort from at the inn. It seemed like the fateful meeting in Kent was in another age but, in truth, it was barely twelve days previous. This time, however, she unfolded the page and smoothed it out as best she could on the lid of her apothecary's chest. She may have known every crease and stain upon it but sometimes she could barely believe her own memory of the story this ragged piece of paper held.

It had been a sunny day in May 1647 when Jane Whorwood introduced her to William Lilly, the celebrated astrologer and author of popular almanacs such as the *Merlini Anglici Ephemeris.* Many considered him a latter-day Merlin, a wizard and soothsayer, a modern John Dee. But Dee's fate had been exile, following the burning of his library at Mortlake by an angry mob, and he had spent the last years of his life more court jester than magus. Lilly, of course, had his detractors. One such was her friend Dorothy Osborne, with whom she had visited Lilly in the last year. Osborne, of course, wrote to Susan claiming she had always believed him an imposter, dismissing his reading. She found him simple, scoffing that no old woman that passes for a witch could have given her so ridiculous a discourse as a consultation. Susan never admitted to Dorothy that not only had she visited Lilly before, but that his reading of her fate did not seem so ridiculous. A seven-year gap between readings had seen little change in Susan's fate other than its proximity. Lilly had not changed his mind. Neither, it appeared, had fate.

And as Susan traced the lines and symbols of the table with her index finger, she saw how perhaps, just perhaps, she could read his predictions in some way other than the most literal, most final manner: as an opportunity. For seven years, Susan had struggled with Lilly's chart, with its implications, with its sudden silence regarding her future. Her second visit had merely compounded things. Where once the silent curtain fell full eight years away, her visit with Dorothy produced the same result as before, but now less than two years hence. As Susan read and reread both Lilly's chart and his explication, she found it hard to equate his insistence that he could 'read no further' with anything other than a prediction of her death, a death which, surely, was now barely a year away.

Her protestations to Diana had been mere protestations. To call her mission a death sentence was misappropriation: sentence had already been pronounced, albeit in secret. Susan, rather than being terrified at the prospect, now drew comfort from it. While her work as the Hermes of the Sealed Knot was an honour unacknowledged, her new work as a she-intelligencer, her work to undermine the powerhouse of the parliamentary secret service that was John Thurloe, was not only of immense potential importance but also necessarily finite. She would not have to suffer the insults of those who discovered part but not all of the story. She would not even have to answer to her brother for her relative success or failure. Susan was tracing her own trajectory now. Her fate was her own to fashion, and fashion it she would. And she would ensure that the fate of others was so entwined with hers that, when she fell, those she chose to include in her silken web could not help but follow.

Susan would not merely seduce Thurloe, not merely tease out his secrets: she would prove his nemesis. The knowledge that she would to all intents and purposes cease to exist barely a year from now was no longer an indicator that she would fail, but gave her the power and the courage to be his ruin, if not his death. Her new clarity of purpose was soon matched by a clarity of thought, and at around five o'clock she felt that a trip to enquire after her recent patient was not only propitious but properly charitable. And so, bag slung over her shoulder, she set off for the Mermaid.

As she walked through the streets, a feeling of power overtook her, a feeling of calm belonging. She was vigilant without fear, watchful without secrecy, aware without paranoia. She saw no signs of being followed, and she trusted not only that this was the case, but that it mattered not. She had every right to walk where she walked, visit whom she visited. She arrived at the Mermaid and passed the time of day with Margarita, who told her that having been held as a close if informal prisoner since the incident, Diana had been suffered to leave the tavern at two o'clock the previous afternoon, and showed neither signs of being ill-used, nor of being further incarcerated. Molly was upstairs, all but recovered, and would appreciate a visitor.

'Hello?' said Molly when Susan knocked on her door.

'It's Susan, Molly. Open the door,' said Susan, and entered the room. Molly was strangely tongue tied. 'Did anything strange happen after I left?'

Molly hesitated. 'Well, the men did make an awful mess in her room.'

'Whose room?' replied Susan.

'Diana's,' said Molly. 'The woman who stayed here and was ill.'

'You were introduced?'

'Yes,' said Molly. She slid her hand under the pillow and pulled out a blue feather. 'I was set to wait on her while she recovered. We talked at length. She said to give you this, and to tell you how I came to be here.'

Susan smiled, and took the feather. 'Thank you, Molly, and how was that?'

'She took me from Charlton House. As a servant, my master

there was apt to use me ill. But we did not arrive at the Mermaid together.'

'So you knew her better than you made out? Well, Molly, at least you've been honest about something,' said Susan. 'I suppose I'd better check the room.'

'I can show you where, if you like.'

'I know the room. You may stand sentinel if you wish.' Molly smiled. 'How're the waters?'

At this question Molly's smile turned into a look of guilt, which Susan chose to ignore as the two women climbed the stairs to where Diana had slept. 'How are you going to get in? It's locked, you know,' said Molly, following with an 'oh' as Susan, having stood between her and the door, simply pushed it open.

'Now, Molly, pay attention. If anyone comes you must do something that looks like you ought to be doing it, and whistle like this,' at which she warbled a pair of descending lines, not very tunefully, as if they were two crows plummeting from the sky following a collision rather than a pair of songbirds twisting, turning and writhing their songs together as they swept down towards the earth. Molly repeated them precisely. 'Yes, like that,' said Susan, rather confused as to how, or why, she might choose to be so precise. She entered the room and left the door ajar.

The room had been treated rather poorly. Several floorboards and wall panels had been torn out, the mattress ripped open and the chamber pot emptied. 'That was unnecessary,' thought Susan as she searched amongst the remaining boards for the sign. She spotted it within minutes, made the necessary calculations before taking a bodkin from her bag and opening the hidden drawer. Inside was a small letter wrapped in a silver chain bearing a locket. The locket was open. Susan took them both, shut the drawer, re-locked the door and she and Molly went back to her room. When they returned, Susan sat down. 'Now, Molly,' she said, 'fetch me some ale and knock on your return. Do not enter until I say so.'

'Yes, Miss Susan,' said Molly, and left on her errand.

Susan took the packet from her bag, unravelled it and inspected the locket. It was empty. The packet was endorsed FO. Susan broke the seal and unfolded the paper. She read the letter written on the inside.

Deare Sister

I haue been caused to take myself to the Convente, for I find that I may no longer trade securely in this town. I intreate you to honor my choyse of aprentice as I thinke shee is worthy of the position, and hath done me grate favor. I also confesse I did steal her from Charlton House, where master Samuel was using her ill, and was, I'll warrant, apt to ruin her. She reminds me of the girl you described in yourself when you met Jane. She is not as greene as she appeareth - her patienthood was juste a little play betweene us to render you more natural with him.

I comend you to mother and also pray you vse with all necessary kindnesse little John, and that he may finally sleep in peace. Wth regards my dearest sister with whom my latest busines was caried oute, I merely hope that shee remembers mee very affectionatly, and knowe that I tak this action out of neede, not desier. The profitt of my last venture will soone be plaine, and god be thanked all your freinds heare and at home continew very well. I pray god grant the same blessing to you, and all wth you

Your most affectionat

Sister

Susan folded the letter and placed it in her waistband. Diana had played her for something like a fool in setting up Molly as a fake patient. Doubtless the contents of the chamber pot belonged to another. Typical of her to risk everything for a joke. And now she had taken the convent, the traditional sanctuary open to all Sisters, no matter what rank. Diana was now neither responsible nor contactable. She had removed herself from active service, but without the need for such a removal to be permanent. There was a knock on the door. 'Come,' said Susan, and Molly walked in with ale. 'Thank you, Molly. Now lock the door.' Molly did as she was bade. 'Now sit.'

Molly sat as instructed and Susan looked at her carefully. What did Diana see of her in this child? Was this truly why Diana had chosen Molly as her daughter? She did not appear to be, well, anything much. But then, when Susan cast her mind back to the long summer spent at Oxford with Jane, the Susan she was now found it hard to accept that the Susan she was then deserved the opportunity Jane had given her. What had Susan been other than well born? Diana's choice of Molly now made as little sense to her as Jane's choice of Susan in Oxford did. It mattered little, however, as tradition dictated that a Sister who chose the convent, however briefly, was to nominate her daughter, and this nomination must be honoured, so long as they met certain conditions, passed the tests set for them and were not obviously compromised.

'Molly,' said Susan. 'The words that I say to you now must be taken with the utmost seriousness. If at any time you feel that they are being said to you in error, then you must admit as such. Your life, and mine, may, do, depend upon it.'

'Yes, Miss Susan,' said Molly. 'I understand.'

'Diana has left you a legacy, Molly. Not of coin, but of something far more precious. She has bequeathed you a new family. She has identified you as a worthy member of Les Filles d'Ophélie.' Susan paused to gauge Molly's response. 'Have you heard of the Sisterhood, Molly?'

'No,' said Molly.

'Good,' said Susan, 'because we are a close organisation.'

'And you are one of them?' asked Molly.

'Yes,' said Susan. 'As is Diana, though she has taken the convent, of necessity.' Susan looked at the confusion on Molly's face and smiled. 'All this will become clear in time. Now, Molly. You have been chosen to become a member of the Sisterhood. And make no mistake, the Sisterhood is everywhere. And we are powerful. Your nunnery question when first I arrived? The Sisterhood. It was for that reason that Diana made you ask that question of me. She is a saucy wench with little respect for authority, but she is, nevertheless, very dear to me. Even her sickness and recovery was down to the Sisterhood.'

'My illness and recovery?'

'Feigned, as you well know. But it is one I have seen before in girls less canny than you,' said Susan, laughing. 'But we have real power and influence. We help our Sisters and are helped by them. But you must pass your first test.'

'Which is what, Miss Susan?'

'Over the next few days, you will hear all sorts of people mention daughters, sisters, families, secret societies and so forth. They are testing you,' said Susan. 'They wish to loosen your lips. Should they succeed, you will never again hear the name of the Sisterhood.'

'And how will I know when I have passed my test?'

'You will know. Just be assured that there is a *luistervink* in every tree, on every corner of every street.'

'A *luistervink*?'

'An eavesdropper. Literally a listening bird,' said Susan. 'You'll understand soon enough.' Susan saw Molly formulate another question, and knew that each one would give birth to yet more questions, and she was tired. She put her finger to Molly's lips. 'I bid you good night, sister, I must return to my lodgings.'

'Sister?' replied Molly. 'I am an only child. I thank you for your concern, and I am grateful for your advice. I am much improved.'

Susan was impressed that Molly had chosen to refuse to react to the word 'sister' with such speed. There was, of course, no such test. No one would be following her trying to catch her out. It was all a play, just a little something to get Molly in the mood. The thing with secret societies is that they aren't so much secret as it is simply that no one knows they exist. Apart from the people who belong to them. When the Sisterhood sought to welcome a new daughter into its warm embrace, it seemed that a little show of secrecy went a long way. It wasn't long before they understood that true invisibility came not from remaining hidden, but from being in plain sight.

Susan walked from the Mermaid to her lodgings in Covent Garden, where a message awaited her.

II

1

Thurloe rises

Master Secretary John Thurloe sat behind his desk at Whitehall, swung his heavy boots onto it, leant back and smiled to himself. It had been a most fruitful few weeks. He had dined with Miss Susan twice since they had first broken bread together, and he had found her a most interesting and intelligent conversationalist. She had diligently refused to stray into the dangerous territories of either religion or politics, though in truth these days Thurloe saw the gap between the two grow increasingly narrow such that to comment upon one was automatically to begin discussion of the other. Furthermore, he fully suspected this unwillingness to be drawn had prevented several arguments from breaking out between them. Thurloe sensed that the prickly woman who had practically barged straight through him when they first met had mellowed somewhat, though she still evidenced flashes of the woman who had rejected his offers of reward with something less than short shrift, if such a thing were possible. But there was more to Thurloe's mood than the blossoming of a new friendship, though that in itself was a most welcome development - his job tended to get in the way of normal conversation. The ordinance had come through. While he'd been Secretary of the Council of

State for the past two years, effectively the man in charge of knowing things, and during this time had tightened the systems put in place by his predecessor, there had always been something missing from his purview, something without which his job was that much more difficult than it needed to be. The post. Now Cromwell had declared him Postmaster-General, and he could truly get to work. As a result of this, he had been able to send Nathaniel to collect a new assistant for him. And now he could see him over the toes of his boots, sitting nervously in front of his desk.

'Charge of the postage and carriage of all letters and packets, both foreign and inland,' he said. 'Do you know what that means, Isaac?' He looked at the young man Nathaniel had just brought in. Isaac Dorislaus was the kind of man who had most likely spent his youth being picked on for his studiousness, and was now working his way through a list of his tormentors. Alphabetically.

'That you are Postmaster-General, Secretary Thurloe?' replied Isaac.

'Yes, obviously, Isaac. Why do you think I have asked you to attend me this morning, Isaac?'

'The Dutch have finally found who was responsible for my father's death and you wish me to be the first to know?'

'No, Isaac,' said Thurloe, 'and seeing as your case was put to them four years hence with no response, I think we can be quite clear that we are unlikely ever to discover who was responsible.'

'Though we know they were enemies of the commonweal.'

'That we do know, Isaac, that we do.' He swung his boots onto the floor and leant forward, placing his elbows on the desk and his chin on his hands. His office had light. Natural light. Thurloe was enjoying himself already. 'Isaac,' he said. 'I've long been impressed by you. Ever since that deputation. To put your name to an affidavit accusing a sovereign nation of harbouring murderers when barely at the age of majority...'

'But they do harbour them,' said Isaac, passion reddening his cheeks. 'They know who murdered my father, and they protect them.'

'Of course they do,' said Thurloe. 'All nations harbour murderers, cut-throats, intelligencers.' Thurloe paused to watch his new, unknowing employee. 'And you chose a method you could control to try to apprehend them. After all, Isaac, you're hardly a man of action.'

'No, Secretary,' replied Isaac, downcast.

'But I admire your dedication to your chosen sphere, and your abilities as a translator, a secretary, a reader are of great use to me. I wish for you to play the intelligencer.'

'I? Intelligencer?' said Isaac, confused. 'But I am not a man for the open road, the inn, the marketplace.'

'No, you are not. But there is a place where you and your talents will be of great use to both me and my country.'

'There is?'

'There is. It's ironic, really, that for such an intelligent creature, master of languages, master of hands, able to sniff out a single misplaced character in the most mundane letter.' He paused. Isaac simply waited. 'It's ironic that for such a subtle creature you are sometimes unable to see the nose upon your face.'

'Yes, Secretary,' said Isaac, once more casting his eyes at the floor. Thurloe saw his mistake. When Nathaniel had appeared to summon Isaac to Whitehall, his thoughts would have flown to his father's murderers, and his heart must have almost burst with joy. Naturally he thought that his summons was to announce that the guilty parties, harboured by his father's own country even though foreigners themselves, were finally to be handed over. But no. Thurloe could see he now thought he had been summoned simply so that Thurloe might berate him. 'I need no reminding of my many faults, Master Secretary.'

'Soft, Isaac,' said Thurloe. 'You belong in the Black Chamber is all I mean.'

'With Alexandrine?' asked Isaac, looking more confused than ever. 'What interest do we have in the letters that slip through the hands of the Countess of Thurn and Taxis? Though I suppose I can read most all of the languages that are used in the Holy Roman Empire, so in that sense... but I could not countenance affecting Papistry, no, you must not ask this of me...'

'Isaac, Isaac,' said Thurloe, interrupting his flow. 'If I were to infiltrate the organisation of Alexandrine, I do not suppose I would choose you for the task. No, Isaac. I wish for you to create a Black Chamber for us, here in Whitehall.' For the first time, Thurloe saw Isaac smile. He wasn't entirely sure that he liked it. 'And Master Dorislaus,' he continued, 'know that this chamber is not the place for you to pursue your own vendetta.'

'No, Secretary,' said Isaac, his face falling once more.

'But should you happen upon likely individuals, I will gladly assist in any way that I, that is, the State, can.' Secretary Thurloe, Postmaster-General, leant back on his chair and folded his arms. 'Now, Nathaniel will show you your new home. There is coin for whatever supplies you need, including an apprentice. And remember, you are now a representative of the Lord Protector. You do not have to request that people assist you. Unless you wish to. Go create your own commonweal, Isaac, and let us begin our great work.' With this, Thurloe took a black feather from the selection in front of him. He held it to the light, and took up his penknife. 'Still here, Isaac? Have I not explained your task suitably?'

'Yes, Master Secretary.'

As his newest recruit stood, bowed and followed Nathaniel into the corridors of government, Thurloe knew that this was a man who, meek as he was, would be as tenacious in the seeking of revenge for his father as a hungry terrier chasing a rat. In fact, he was relying on it.

2

Nathaniel gets to work

Nathaniel led Isaac through dark corridors hung with lanterns and populated with great oaken doors, some of which lay ajar, allowing glimpses of great desks covered in ledgers, tapestries, food, drink and people. They walked across great cobbled courtyards in which nondescript courtiers skulked in corners speaking behind open palms and then down stone staircases which led them into new corridors, now closer, stone walled and lit by torches, the air thickening as they descended for what seemed like an age, with every new door proving a disappointment, until, at last, they stopped.

'Here,' said Nathaniel, pointing at what was less a door than a dark oak obstacle. 'Here is your new home-from-home.' With that he took a large key from his bag and inserted it into the door.

'Who else holds a copy, Nathaniel?' asked Isaac as the key rattled, took, and the lock suddenly gave.

'Just Master Secretary,' he replied. 'And, of course, there are the keys held in the guardhouse.' The door swung open, and Nathaniel took a taper to the candles that sat on an oak table, their light revealing a small, airless room panelled in dark oak.

Isaac pulled a chair from underneath the table and sat. 'Do you read, Nathaniel?'

'Yes, I do,' he replied. 'Write, too.'

'And you are attached to me now?'

'No, I take my orders from Master Secretary Thurloe, but I am also at your service,' he said. 'My orders beyond obeying him are to assist you in any way you see fit.'

'Excellent. We'd better start with some stores. Fetch ink, paper and sand. I must make out a list for you, Nathaniel.'

'You'll see such things by the fireplace there,' said Nathaniel, watching Isaac survey his rather dark and dingy domain.

Nathaniel brought the supplies to the table, and Isaac sharpened his quill before beginning to make his list. He spoke out loud as he wrote: 'By order of I. Dorislaus, on behalf of...'

Nathaniel interrupted him. 'No need for that,' he said, laughing gently. 'I am your authorisation. What cannot be obtained through ready cash I will simply acquire on your behalf.' He watched as the list took shape. 'Item: Jonny, the printer's apprentice,' he read out. 'In this case, however, it would be of no little use were you to furnish me with a little more information. Preferably the name of the printer he's apprenticed to.'

'Field, Nathaniel, Field. I'll write him a note so he knows that it's truly me who requests him.'

'Ah, Mr Field,' said Nathaniel, a warm smile curling up the corners of his eyes and lighting up his face. 'Consider it done, and with pleasure. Though I wonder what use an apprentice might be.' He took the hastily scrawled note from Isaac's hand.

'The boy has a gift with languages that astounds me. He is sharp and loyal. We will get great use out of him.'

'Shall I return him here?'

'Yes,' said Isaac. 'No. Bring him to the Three Suns in Fleet Street. We must celebrate and lunch there. The rest of the items you may have sent here.' Isaac paused. 'It took an inordinate amount of time to get to our little chamber. I fear I may not find it again, Nathaniel.'

Nathaniel laughed. 'On the contrary, it is easy to find. Follow me.' Isaac locked the door to his new home and followed Nathaniel up two flights of stairs and across a courtyard. 'Your key will work here, too.' They were suddenly on the embankment of the great river, the Thames.

'Well, how convenient,' said Isaac, and walked off in the direction of Fleet Street while Nathaniel made directly for Field's print shop.

The back of the printing house was a confusion of papers being pulled from the press, inspected and draped on lines to dry, then piled atop one another. He had arrived on a print day. The place was not only a mess, but a chaotic buzz of energy. Nathaniel motioned to a journeyman printer, who was flattening a great pile of paper with a hammer.

'My good man, kindly send Mr Field to see me, I have business with him, urgent business.'

'Are you blind?' replied the journeyman. 'It is a print day. He'll have none of your business today. Try tomorrow. Better yet try getting along and never coming back.' He went back to his task.

'Every day is a print day,' said Nathaniel, 'other than for you, who is merely called when extra help is needed. Tell him Secretary Thurloe craves a word.'

'You are not the Secretary,' said the journeyman.

'I am so much as it concerns you,' said Nathaniel, tossing him a coin. 'Now fetch Master Field or I shall stop the press and do so myself.'

The journeyman stopped, put his hammer down and walked into the chaos. Within a minute a small but exceptionally loud man, his face, hands and clothes blackened with printer's ink, walked out of the shop and straight at Nathaniel.

'I'm Field,' he said, a ball of aggressive intent. 'Who bloody well wants to know?' Nathaniel looked at him for a second, allowing him enough time to add a vocal 'Well?' to his thoughts before replying.

'I represent Master Secretary John Thurloe, and by his word, I request that you give to me your apprentice boy, goes by the name of Jonny,' said Nathaniel.

'Impossible,' said Field. 'For one thing he's an indentured apprentice, and for another he's extremely busy. Tell that to the Master Secretary.'

'I'll be happy to take you to him should you wish to deliver your answer in those words, but I would counsel against it.' With this he gave Field a little smile. 'But we can undo the indentures, as you know, and we can also take him by force if we so choose.'

'I will have words with the Lord Protector!' shouted Field. 'I am his appointed printer, you know.'

'I do indeed, and I also know the power such an appointment fails to give you,' said Nathaniel. 'And gaining audience with the Protector on demand is definitely one of them.' He paused for effect, looking Field straight in the eye. 'The boy.'

'And what if I simply refuse? What then, eh? Are you going to walk in and take...' Field's sentence was interrupted by Nathaniel's fist crashing into his jaw.

As Field fell to the ground, Nathaniel walked into the now silent shop. Men stood with ink-soaked beaters resting on the type, bleeding sticky ink into the crevices between the letterforms. They absent-mindedly filled composing sticks with the wrong letters. They held great broadsheets up ready to be dried on the lines that criss-crossed the printing-shop like so many spiders' webs. They stood by the furnace, crucible in hand. They could not decide whether to look at the prostrate form of their master as he lay, crumpled like a forgotten index on the floor, or at this man who had simply walked in off the street and knocked him out. 'Jonny?' said Nathaniel. 'Where's Jonny?'

Nathaniel's request was met with silence.

'No need to be afeared, Jonny,' said Nathaniel. 'I bring word from a friend.' With this he handed the note that Isaac had written to one of the journeymen, who took it into the knot of workers. After a few minutes a slight boy of about seventeen years of age walked out from the melee of the print shop towards Nathaniel.

'Here I am,' said Jonny.

'We're going to go on a little trip,' said Nathaniel, 'and don't worry, you're much better off now.' Jonny stopped by the moaning figure of Field, whose first thoughts as the mists began to clear were that any overly hasty attempt at getting to his feet was not merely superfluous but might perhaps prove positively dangerous. 'Go on, Jonny. If you want to,' said Nathaniel.

'Stupid old pisspot,' said Jonny, and he kicked Field hard, in the rump. A small cheer went up.

'Felt good, eh?' said Nathaniel. 'Savour it. Now let's go.' Nathaniel and Jonny walked off leaving the cursing Field behind. 'He's a nasty piece of work, that one,' said Nathaniel, as they were well on their way. 'I got on the wrong side of him several times when I was your age. It felt good to repay the compliment.' They laughed.

'Where are we going, mister?'

'Call me Nathaniel. First, we're going to the Three Suns where the writer of that note is waiting for you. A friend of yours, I believe.'

'Isaac,' said Jonny. He paused. 'What does he want me for?'

'He'll explain,' said Nathaniel. 'Something about a chamber.'

The two carried on through the chaotic streets chatting

amiably about nothing in particular and were approaching Butcher's Row when they heard a scream in a side alley.

'Best see what's up, eh Jonny?' said Nathaniel, putting his right hand on the hilt of his sword. As they turned into the alley they began to laugh, as they saw a young girl finish what had presumably been an argument with a well-placed kick. 'I don't know about you, Jonny, but I felt that from here!' The man she had kicked at first fell to the ground, but after a few moments he stood up, albeit a little gingerly, and made to draw a dagger but Nathaniel had stuck his fingers in his mouth and whistled loudly. The man looked over at Nathaniel and Jonny and ran. 'Yes, best you run now, fella. At least, as much as you're able,' said Nathaniel as they watched him disappear and the girl give chase for a few steps, then turn and devote her attention to an old woman with some birdcages. 'Right, Jonny. Our work here is done. And I'm hungry.' With this the two men turned and carried on to Fleet Street, where Isaac waited in the Three Suns.

3

Susan questions Molly

Susan was waiting for Molly when she returned to her room at the Mermaid, and waved her quiet as she launched into some story about an old woman with birds who had been attacked by a man intent on stealing her purse. Molly's innocent enthusiasm for the story raised a smile to Susan's lips, and she began to think that perhaps Diana had been right after all, and Molly truly was a younger version of herself.

'Did anyone ask you about the Sisterhood?' said Susan.

'The what?' replied Molly.

'That's better,' said Susan. 'Now you may tell me of this strange incident.'

'Well,' said Molly. 'I was walking up near Butcher's Row when I saw an old lady with some birds in cages turn into an alley, and a very rough-looking cove follow her. He looked as though he was up to no good so I went in after him.'

'That was very brave,' said Susan, thinking that it sounded rather more stupid than brave, and then contemplating where one ended and another began.

'It's just what you do.'

'For a Sister?' asked Susan.

'For anyone. Anyway. I was right. He made a grab for her

purse and she resisted, at which he pushed her to the ground. The birdcages followed and I screamed at him. He turned and I kicked him full between the legs.'

Now Susan began to think that Diana rather saw herself in this young woman. Her spirit and her total self-belief were similar. She rather hoped Molly's moral compass was better aligned, but she herself might help ensure that. Certainly, Molly seemed to revel in the reliving of the tale.

'He hit the ground but soon got up again,' said Molly, her voice getting higher, the pace of her words quickening. 'And I saw him reach for a dagger. I felt scared for the first time but my fear was misplaced. I heard a whistle, and both me and the man looked to its source. It was a big man, accompanied by a younger one, and the big one put his hand to his sword. At this my attacker turned and ran.'

'And what did your saviours do?'

'Laughed and walked off,' said Molly. 'I looked to the old lady but her cages were broken. She lost a nightingale and two robins.'

'The robin redbreast and the nightingale never live long in cages,' said Susan. 'But here, and partly in honour of your bravery, allow me to present you with a gift.' With this, Susan held out her hand, fist closed. She smiled and slowly opened it, revealing a locket on a silver chain. On the front it bore the image of a nightingale.

Molly's eyes widened. 'For me?' she stuttered.

'For you,' said Susan. 'The nightingale is the symbol of Les Filles d'Ophélie.'

'Imagine that,' said Molly, giggling. 'Me, a fully-fledged Fille d'Ophélie!'

Susan laughed. 'Good heavens, no. Not yet you aren't. You are but on the right road to becoming une belle-fille.'

'Oh,' said Molly, a little crestfallen. 'What next?'

'Well, first you must be sworn in,' said Susan. With this she took out a small pair of scissors and leant forwards, cutting a tress of Molly's hair. She then cut one from her own head, entwined the two, trimmed the ends and sealed them with blue wax. She opened the locket that hung from Molly's neck and placed the twist of hair into it. 'By rights it ought be your mother's and yours but I am acting as surrogate.' She closed the locket. 'Now,' she said, trying to give Molly a serious look, but Molly's smile was so wide that Susan could not help but join her. 'Hold the locket in your right hand, and hold the hand over your heart. Let the chain hang loose. Repeat this after me, and with each line, wrap the chain around your hand. Understand?' Molly nodded, and Susan began, reciting the daughters' creed.

'Nous sommes les Filles d'Ophélie,' said Susan. She nodded at Molly, who started to speak, quietly, nervously.

'Noo somm lay fee dofeely.'

'You have no French?' asked Susan.

'Why would I?'

'Whyever did I think otherwise? It's not usual but for you... we are the invisible agents,' said Susan, wrapping her chain around her hand once more.

'We are the invisible agents,' said Molly, following Susan in word and deed.

'We are the first, the last.'

'We are the first, the last.'

'And we are the difference,' said Susan.

'Et nous sommes la différence,' said Molly, her accent impeccable.

'I thought you said you had no French?'

'I lied. Lady Filmer insisted we girls all learnt the language.'

The two women sat in silence for a moment, and Susan kissed Molly on the forehead. 'Congratulations,' she said. 'You are now an initiate. A petite-fille.'

'Not a Sister?' said Molly, disappointed.

'We're all sisters, Molly, but you're not yet a Sister,' said Susan. 'Wear your locket with pride, but keep it out of sight.'

'Like where?'

'Between your breasts. Any man who looks there will be looking for anything but a locket.' Molly turned around and lifted the hair from her neck while Susan dropped the locket over her head and drew the chain around her neck before fastening it.

'Thank you, Miss Susan,' said Molly, throwing her arms around her new mother.

'Anyway, enough of all that. It's time to pack your bags, as you're about to have a very interesting few weeks. I believe your poor aunt is unwell.' Susan wondered whether Molly had really believed that there was a test. But then again, when Jane had initiated her, she saw Sisters in every crowd, willing her to fail. The truth, when she learnt it, made perfect sense. Once she had recovered from the embarrassment.

'Aunt?' said Molly. 'What are you talking about?'

'You must tend to her needs,' said Susan.

'Whose needs?'

'Good God, girl, wake up!'

'Oh,' said Molly. 'I see.'

There was a knock on the door. 'Molly?'

'Yes?' replied Molly.

'Time for you to start your shift,' said the innkeeper.

'Oh, it's not my aunt?' said Molly.

'Your aunt?' replied the innkeeper.

'Patience, girl,' said Susan. 'Enjoy your time. I'll see you soon. Go to work.'

4

Jonny meets his saviour

After the incident on birdcage walk, as he would later refer to it, Jonny and Nathaniel walked through the city at a sedate pace. While Jonny had been Field's apprentice for almost nine years now, he could count the times he had been allowed out of the print shop on the fingers of, well, if not one hand, most definitely five or six hands. Jonny still retained a little of the wide-eyed country boy he had been at the age of eight when he had not only been orphaned but given to Field within a matter of weeks. He hardly knew his father other than that he had died serving the cause of freedom, while his mother was never talked of. Jonny really had no idea whether she was alive or not. Before his father's death, however, Jonny had at least been well educated, and already possessed a decent grasp of the classical languages, a grasp he had transformed into a very solid understanding by reading everything that passed through Field's presses. Jonny had been to Venice with Coryat, Newfoundland with Hakluyt, and even sailed to Atlantis with Bacon. His knowledge of the city in which he lived was minimal, however, and as for his home town, he knew it not. And so as they walked, Jonny stared.

'Right,' said Nathaniel. 'The Three Suns. You'll find Isaac in there somewhere. I'm off to play dice for a lady.'

'Dice?' said Jonny, stung into a confused response.

'Don't worry, Jonny,' he said. 'I speak in jest. Dice are a challenge to God's providence, and have been banned, as well you know.' And with that, Nathaniel was gone.

Jonny was not used to taverns, though his old friend Jim, a journeyman for Field, was known to spend much of his leisure time at one called the Mermaid, just off Butcher's Row. In less guarded moments Jim had let slip that he was sweet on the innkeeper, who was part Spanish, or something. Jonny summoned up the courage and strode inside. He saw Isaac immediately, asleep on a table. He shook him by the shoulders to wake him.

'Isaac, Isaac?' said Jonny. 'Wake up. Isaac?'

'What? Oh, Jonny, sorry. I'm really no drinker. It sends me right off. We should get back to the chamber. But first, if you'll excuse me.' Isaac stood and ambled in the direction of the privy.

'Ah, Jonny,' said Isaac, as he returned to the table. 'That's better. Let's go and see the chamber, eh?' And with that he led Jonny out of the tavern.

They walked through the narrow streets, blinking in the brightness of the late afternoon sun, their eyes having grown accustomed to the tavern's dingy interior. The Three Suns was one of London's dingiest taverns, and this in a field in which competition was fierce. They had gone a few streets before Jonny realised that he had no idea where he was going, or what he was going to do when he got there. Where he was going to live. How to get food. The more he contemplated his situation the more he felt that Field wasn't so bad.

'I bet you're glad to get out of Field's clutches,' said Isaac. 'I'm glad that Nathaniel persuaded him to release you, Jonny. I think we're going to have a lot of fun, you and I.'

'He certainly was extremely persuasive,' said Jonny. 'I didn't know indentures could be revoked.'

'Neither did I. It's a strange new world in which we live, Jonny.'

'He mentioned a chamber. What is it? It sounds awfully macabre.'

'Ah, the chamber is where we unravel the secrets of men's hearts, where we dip our pens into men's lives, where we enfold ourselves and thus may overhear their most private conversations,' said Isaac, drifting off into his thoughts to such an extent that Jonny was forced to take his arm in order that he might prevent him from walking under a horse and cart that were trotting along gently in the opposite direction.

'It sounds awfully like a torture chamber,' said Jonny, 'and I'm pretty certain that's no place for me. Or for you, Isaac. You belong in the republic of letters, lording it over Latin and Greek, harrying hands and capturing cipher.'

'Well, you'll see soon enough.' With this, he removed a key from some inner part of his garments and walked towards a small door set in the wall they'd been walking alongside for the past few hundred yards. The door yielded to his touch and they entered the courtyard. Having locked away the outside world they walked a few, short steps to a stairway, and thence to another door, though this one needed no key, it just swung open. Isaac held out his arm. 'Behold, the Black Chamber.'

Jonny looked into the room and smiled. 'Well, Isaac, I have to hand it to you. I couldn't have come up with a better name myself.'

Isaac pushed him aside. 'Imagination, Jonny. Use your imagination.'

5

Thurloe in two minds

Thurloe had been waiting in the chamber, his lantern blacked out, for the past hour. He found it relaxing, and he had much to ponder. He spoke before they realised he was there. 'Imagination is all very well, Isaac, but I want facts,' he said. 'I want you to make this room the biggest spy-catching web the world will never see.' He removed the shutters from his lantern. 'Have you sent Nathaniel on an errand?'

'Yes, Master Secretary,' said Isaac, lying just a little. 'And may I introduce my apprentice, Jonny, er... do you have a surname, Jonny?'

'No, Isaac, unless you count "getcha arse overear", or any of the many choice epithets Master Field would attach to my given name.'

'Well, Master Secretary,' continued Isaac, 'Field had no idea what he had in this boy.'

'I'll take your word for it, Isaac,' said Thurloe, ignoring Jonny completely. 'I am for my supper, and I shall visit you in a day or two, and perhaps bring you some real letters to work on.'

'Letters?' said Jonny, his voice now touched with wonder.

'Yes, boy, letters,' said Thurloe. 'What did you think you'd be working with?'

With this Thurloe left the Black Chamber-in-waiting, and tramped his way back to Lincoln's Inn Fields. The evenings were slowly drawing in as the summer lounged its way towards autumn, so it was still light when he reached his chambers, and it was not yet so chill that a fire was necessary for anything other than domestic purposes. He pushed open the door, and was greeted with a sight more warming than a blazing fire. Miss Susan sitting at his table.

'You see, Master Secretary? I not only await your presence but do so patiently,' said Susan.

'Master Secretary Postmaster-General,' said Thurloe, as he picked up a jug of wine.

'I beg your pardon?' said Susan, though she heard full well. It was simply that she was caught unawares by his announcement, and this was a revelation that needed some thought, and such thought needed time, and composure. It was this time she hoped to buy in asking a question to which she knew the answer, if not the outcome.

'Master Secretary Postmaster-General,' he repeated. 'Wine?'

Susan nodded. She was in more need than usual. She could not decide whether this news bade good or ill. Ill, she supposed, in that Thurloe would now have access unfettered to every letter in the kingdom, unless purposely hidden from his view, an act which in itself had drawbacks. And on the other hand, it was good that such power was concentrated so near to her grasp. But Postmaster-General? This news alone justified her actions, as a delay of but two or three days in her discovering it might have been sufficient for a damning letter to have passed through his hands. She would have to make her excuses and leave early, try to prevent any letters going into the system. She would have to speak with the apothecary, Hinton, perhaps with Chase, her alternative delivery man, and organise a new path with a more permanent basis than had been used hitherto. She was still frantically looking through her own last letters in her imagination, to whom they were addressed and when they went out and what they said when Thurloe's voice broke through the images of endorsements and seals.

'Susan?' he said. 'Are you quite all right? You look sudden pale and distracted.' His face was mere inches from hers and Susan felt as though he was peering into her skull, gently unfolding each letter as it presented itself to her and nodding as he noted every plot, every plotter and every detail.

Susan didn't feel everything go black. She went straight from feeling rather strange to trying but failing to focus on a face above her while her hand became warm and she felt cool air on her breast.

'Susan, Susan, thank the Lord,' said Thurloe. 'I thought you had left us for a minute.' Susan was about to scream when he spoke again. 'I cut your lace, dear Susan.'

'Thank you, Master Secretary,' she said, as she recovered consciousness, focus and poise. And humour. 'I hope you have some spare twine I might use, or my exit from here may appear particularly suspicious.' With Thurloe's help she regained her place at the table, all possibility of an early exit lost. 'It's been a long, tiring day, and I have lacked sustenance.'

'Well, you have come to the right place,' said Thurloe, uncovering yet another handsome supper. 'Do eat your fill. I have a matter or two which demand my immediate attention. I will not be upwards of twenty minutes.' He stopped as he reached the door. Susan looked at the man who was to be her prey, felt the breeze on her neck and instinctively reached for her locket. 'Patience is indeed a virtue, and virtue does not go unrewarded, Susan.' And with that, he was gone.

'Except in the cases of adulterers and dissemblers, naturally,' she said, but more to herself than to anyone, the room's emptiness notwithstanding. 'And I wonder, will you quiz me over what lies beneath my lace?' As she ate, she surveyed the room carefully. Not for clues to hidden stashes of information, though she expected one day that these would occupy her thoughts greatly, but simply for clues to the man. It was when her eyes alighted on the board from which her supper had been harvested that she both saw and comprehended simultaneously. On the board were several sprigs of parsley. Uncut, just sprigs.

'Oh my goodness,' said Susan, this time most definitely to herself. 'He means this night to kiss me.' A mixture of apprehension and revulsion were set beside an unexpectedly youthful thrill. 'Dear God,' she said. 'You are actually excited!'

6

Susan sends a letter

Susan awoke late. The events of the previous day, and perhaps, more unexpectedly, the evening that followed it, had taken their toll. She had not been able to leave Thurloe's chambers early on account of her indisposition, but equally it had allowed her to avoid staying late, as well as ensuring that he postpone his parsley-sweetened plans. Until the following evening, when she was to attend his pleasure once more. On arriving back at her lodgings Susan had taken a sleeping draught of her own concoction. It was both swift and long acting. The sun was well past its zenith when she finally stirred. The fog in her head took a little longer to dissipate but, as it did so, it presaged a day of revelation.

'I must visit the apothecary, today,' she said. Not for the first time did she bemoan the fact that her current circumstances did not allow for a lady's maid. There appeared to be little that she was not having to sacrifice in order that the Knot might survive. Or, she thought to herself, perhaps it was more accurate to say that there was little that Edward was unwilling to have her sacrifice.

Susan washed, dressed and sat at her makeshift desk in her room. She sharpened her quill and opened her pot of ink. It was dried up. A splash of urine failed to revive it suitably so she placed paper, ink pot, wax and seal into her medicine bag, slung it over her shoulder and set off to the Bailey. It was an area which made a chill run down the spine of anyone who tended to live at odds with the law of the land, for it was here that the capital's criminal courts resided, and the resultant flow of miscreants along its streets made the Covent Garden regulars appear to be positively shining examples of urban health and moral rectitude. Her journey was without incident, in itself rarely to be remarked upon other than she was not in a state of mind that would have allowed her to react in the manner she would usually choose. Her fatigue and general confusion regarding recent events made it more likely that she would respond to, say, an attempt to relieve her of her purse with instinctive force rather than considered subtlety.

She arrived at Hinton's shop only to find him out, the decks manned by his wife, a pleasant enough if perhaps rather uncomplicated soul. Susan bade her good day and she bade Susan wait while she finish mixing a receit. Susan sat, and when the woman was done with her measurements she requested oak gall and iron sulphate but was given a freshly mixed pot of ink instead. It stank and Susan wondered who had mixed it, as whoever was responsible was unwell. She laid out her paper and began to write:

Sir,

It has beene some time since I had any from you, but I haue not had cause yet to visit the apoteke's, so there is little tidings regards my health at present. It will be news met with great pleasure, I am sure, that young John do wax well, and that his new favorite game is blind man's bluff. The aim of this game is to guess the person the others describe while you are blindfold. He becomes so expert we suspect him of reading the game cards in secret. Certainly he cheate us all somehow. He dotes also on his new pet. My sister is in the cuntry, and all attend her needs. I think that the trade that you began on your last visit proceedeth well, and the profit from it will soon be visible, though your merchant is not as you intended. You may wish to send new stock within the year. I heare also that your shop is well-liked by its customers, but that there will soon be a new tax introduced which may harm your business. I am euer hopeful that your next voyage might prefigure a longer stay in the place where your stock is held, and I wish you all happiness in your affayers, be they of the hart or of businesse. With prayers that God protect you and bring ioy of your soule and hers that really is

Euer your most humble seruant,

S.H.

Susan poured a handful of fine sand onto the paper, poured it off, and began the process of folding the letter into a complex booby trap with a long triangle of paper threaded through the packet's centre, several pieces of floss that looked as if they merely wrapped around the package but actually penetrated the whole packet, and a wafer in between. On top of this she applied wax and the seal of the Knot. If anyone interfered with this letter, Edward would know.

Finally, she endorsed the packet with the words *Mr D'Esmond, Paris.*

Her letter finished, she sat, and waited. Her fatigue was such that she took to making a mental tally of Hinton's wares to prevent sleep from claiming her once again. Hinton's shop had two rooms, the front dedicated to display, including the theatre that accompanied the mixing of the many ingredients that sat in their jars, barrels and boxes into the concoction that best suited the individual. Susan, along with many less dependent on the performative aspects of the medical arts, preferred to use specificks such as Peruvian bark that attended to the ailment in question rather than mix a combination of ingredients designed to act on the humours or an organ. Such treatments, which in themselves were designed around the age, constitution and humoral disposition of a patient, often resulted in visible evacuation of the malady via purging or sweating. Susan was of a mind that a treatment's efficacy was its best recommendation, but Hinton was very much of the old school, and the front of his shop was thus arranged in order that it might best display this obsession with outward appearance. The unexpected advantage was that, to Susan, the shop itself was worth considering, if only as an exercise in taxonomy. This display did, however, make for a far more interesting object of study, even if it did rather contradict Bacon's thoughts on the presentation of information.

She began by enumerating the inhabitants of shelves behind the counter, shelves which held fifty-seven glass jars, ninety-four pots and twenty-five small boxes, while twelve small barrels languished at their feet. The jars held the more exciting of the wares available, or at least pretended to, as many of them were simply filled with coloured water. They also boasted the more ostentatious of the simples, and the purely exotic such as lizards and snakes, both dried and pickled. The pots took care of those things recognisable by name, such as gum arabic, scurvy grass seed, witch hazel, henbane and the like. The boxes were unlabelled, the barrels of spirits of varying kinds, with rose oil as a base for perfumes and so on. On the counter in front of the shelves were those exotic stuffs that had been transformed from medicine to luxury items such as chocolate, tobacco and coffee.

There were also items of manufacturing expertise such as mortars, pestles, weights, beams, alembics and kettles and pans. Above the whole show hung a dried fish, bloated and covered in spines like a bleached amphibious hedgepig. Hinton had once had a dried alligator hanging there too but it had perished in the face of a sustained assault carried out by a monkey. The monkey had been sitting on a customer's head as he walked in, and had thus come face to face with the alligator's jaws. Prompted by shock into a violent panic, it had jumped onto its back and torn it to pieces. Such was the danger of surprising people, she supposed.

'The real value is in the back room,' said a voice. It was the apothecary himself, Hinton, returned from his travels. 'I presume you were counting and assessing my stock?'

'You know me too well,' said Susan, standing to follow him through into the back room, where he kept the substances of value, the gold leaf, the ambigris, the bezoar stones. 'Though I see no plaister of diacalcitis.' From here they could enter the courtyard which, when its copper stills were stoked up and roaring, allowed them to talk without danger of being overheard.

'We may speak freely, Susan,' said Hinton.

'Thank you, Anthony. Our first order of business is for you to make out a bill of exchange to Dr Morley for the sum of fifty pounds, payable by John Shaw.' She opened her medicine bag and drew out five small leather bags of coin. 'You may count them now, Anthony,' she said, and the apothecary walked back into the shop's back room to count, weigh and assess the money given him. He returned within minutes.

'Your coin is a little over, but I'll top up your bag with a specifick or two, just to balance things out, and perhaps a small bag of diacalcitis for your use. Which reminds me. Did our little concoction prove itself effective?'

'Yes, indeed it did,' said Susan. 'If anything she was too sudden sick and well. But there were no suspicions raised.'

'Most gratifying, but you said the first order of business. What, pray, might the second comprise, Susan?'

'There is the matter of a letter to Paris,' she said, handing over the packet to the apothecary. 'And I know not if you have heard, but Secretary Thurloe has a new position,' said Susan.

'Well, he can't be much worse than he is already, surely?' said the apothecary, placing the packet in his bag. 'Can he?'

'I rather fear that he can. Secretary Thurloe is now Postmaster-General.'

'So, he finally controls both ends of the pony.'

'And then we must find another courier.'

'And, naturally, your thoughts flew to Asclepius,' said the apothecary. 'And such a move makes perfect sense. Though it is one thing to look to one humour and quite another to begin to work with all four. One artery cannot hold all the blood of a body, Susan. And if it should block?'

'I would appreciate your advice in this matter, Anthony, but the fact is that the channels must be kept open, or the rebellion will founder, deprived of its lifeblood, information.'

'And so the court will shrivel and die, bereft of *its* lifeblood, money,' said the apothecary. 'You must have a second route. Might I suggest John Chase? We tended the princes together in '48. He is loyal, trustworthy and able.'

'His shop is near my lodgings, so perhaps I ought to approach him through you,' said Susan. 'Naturally, a suitable consideration will be forthcoming for His Majesty's most loyal subjects.' The apothecary smiled and held out his hand. 'And one more thing, Anthony.'

'A third indeed, Susan?'

'You have a sure and deadly poison, I recall.'

'I couldn't possibly say, but I hear that the lesser regions of the puffer fish render up a toxin most efficacious,' said the apothecary. 'But what need have you of such a thing? You cannot mean to poison Thurloe? Such an act would be almost doomed to fail, and if not, it would lead to the demise of many a loyal man.'

'It is not your place to question my actions nor speculate on my motives, Anthony,' said Susan. 'Your place is but to supply me with what I request.'

'But Miss Susan-' said Hinton, his voice betraying his fear.

'But me no buts! Do you have such a toxin or no?'

Hinton's face fell, as Susan's authority was real. 'Yes, Miss Susan, I have such a toxin. Death comes quickly through paralysis. But beware, Miss Susan, I am told that if you give an insufficient dose the victim may appear dead but subsequently revive.' He opened a drawer in one of the cabinets and pressed on a panel inside. The panel gave way, yielding its secret in the shape of a wooden board in which eight vials of a clear liquid nestled innocently. Hinton took one and handed it to her. 'You know not whence it came. Such poisons are understandably proscribed. Seal it and keep it safe.'

'I understand,' said Susan, took his hand in hers and the deal was made.

7

Thurloe waxes ill

Secretary Thurloe smiled to himself as he read the confession, taken by proxy, of Diana Gennings. It mattered little that he had lost track of her almost as soon as she had been released. The sinecure that Thurloe had procured for her husband had been sold within moments, on a five-year lease, for ready cash, so there was no way of tracing her there. It was almost as if Diana didn't trust him not to pursue them, and in this he had to admit she showed impeccable judgement. It worried him a little that her behaviour also indicated a belief that he would not be interested in either her or her husband five years from now. In this he feared she might also be rather prescient, for two reasons, the first being the beginnings of the pain in his groin that presaged the attempted evacuation of a kidney stone.

'Nathaniel,' said Thurloe.

'Yes, Master Secretary?' replied Nathaniel.

'Tell me, how has Isaac's young protégé settled into his new role?'

'He and Isaac are thick as thieves, Master Secretary. They appear to have formulated a sort of method for this eavesdropping. There are too many letters to give them all their full attention, so Isaac selects and cuts the seal, while Jonny scans the first and last lines for words of interest, and one or other of them transcribes those that qualify.'

'It has thrown up a few interesting letters already,' said Thurloe. 'Which reminds me, I must commend Alfred on his work with Diana. A most thorough and illuminating document.'

'Indeed, Master Secretary, it was almost as if she enjoyed betraying the conspiracy. Alfred isn't a man you'd put to a complex situation, but with her I think she lorded it over him, giving him things he wouldn't understand.'

'Yes, indeed Nathaniel,' said Thurloe, 'and she mentions the two Swordsmen.'

'The ones you told me to arrest? Yes, indeed she does. If you remember there was nothing special about them, though I'd swear I'd seen one of them before. But there was nothing to hold them with, or even to question them on. They really seemed to know nothing. But they're on our watch list now, for what it's worth.'

'Good work on both counts,' said Thurloe, wincing as he spoke. 'Hell hath no fury, or so they say. I'd certainly think twice before imprisoning her husband. But when it comes to pain,' - Thurloe's own pain was increasing steadily, now fluctuating between a direct stabbing and an intense wave - 'I fear I may be passing a stone,' he said, his voice now quieter, more measured, as if any overly loud speech would be translated directly into fire by the small, irregular piece of calcium that was currently attempting to travel from his bladder to the outside world through a tube considerably smaller than itself. And the pressure behind it would soon build, as it had before. Several days of agony awaited him. And if the stone could not make its way, an excruciatingly painful and extremely dangerous operation would be his only chance of survival. 'Never mind a woman scorned, for sheer furious pain nothing bar gout comes close to the stone.'

He retched. 'Fetch me an apothecary,' he said. 'Fetch me John Chase.'

'The apothecary named by Gennings?' asked Nathaniel, as he stood and pulled on his jerkin.

'The very same,' said Thurloe, slowly lifting himself out of his chair. 'He's a new name to us so we may as well kill two birds with one... oh, an unfortunate turn of phrase. But we already have our eye on Hinton.' He paused to catch his breath. 'Get my cot and a pot, Nathaniel, I'll not be making chambers this evening. And send a note for Miss Susan, also. If she's not home, take yourself to Lincoln's Inn. Tell her I am detained by business and will not return for supper, and so she ought not attend me. In fact,' he said, the pain now becoming more intense, 'tell her I have had to leave town for a few days, and to await my word.' At this he doubled up. 'But first, the apothecary. And be quick about it.' Thurloe vomited into the pot Nathaniel had provided while he received instructions, and fell into the cot, pale and shaking.

8

Susan receives a letter

Deare Sister,

I receved your letter of the 25th instant and felt compelled to write straightways to inform you of an illness that has beset yr cosin. She has been in Pariss this sennight, accompanied by an Irish of your acquaintance. They have taken supper with Inchiquin on more than one occasion, and all seemely. Yet I must tell you this...

Susan sat in her lodgings and clutched the letter to her breast, the enclosure it had contained remaining where it had fallen, at her feet. It was always a bittersweet experience to read her brother Edward's hand on a letter - what she read inside was always furtive, complex and difficult where she longed for a letter in which her brother Edward could be simply that: her brother Edward. But at least she now knew where Diana had scuttled off to. She plainly hadn't taken the convent for long, if at all, but then times were difficult, and Diana was nothing if not unpredictable. She was in Paris, the city in which Charles Stuart's court was to be found, and where her brother was effectively secretary to a state of confusion and chaos.

Hinton had supplied the letter with another interesting piece of information, however, namely that Lady Stanley, too, was in Paris. It was unlike Diana to reuse an alias in such a way, as it exposed her to discovery, but she had plainly found that rich widowhood suited her. There was no news of her husband William. Hinton suggested that Lady Stanley had been exchanging correspondence through the network with a man who could only have been Robert Honywood, steward to Elizabeth, grand mother of the Sisterhood and Queen of Bohemia.

Paris made perfect sense for Diana, as it not only housed the court of Charles Stuart, but also of his mother, Henrietta Maria, and her court comprised a divisive, factional collection of hangers-on and ne'er-do-wells. Diana would certainly feel at home there, and it was ripe with fools intent on frittering away what little money they had as ostentatiously as possible, as if it were some sort of game. And that was a game that Diana was exceptionally good at. But it wasn't simply money that was spent with profligate abandon, as it seemed as if these players were possessed of an almost reflex indiscretion, pouring what paltry secrets they were party to into any ear that cocked itself in their direction. One such, she knew, was Inchiquin, an Irishman of notorious incompetence and looseness of tongue, even within the circles he frequented. His notoriety had a more serious side, as well. Here was a man responsible for the death of thousands of Catholic Irish but a few years previously. It was from him that Diana, or so she had claimed, acquired her new formulation of invisible ink - she had apparently stolen the recipe and then convinced him he'd burnt it by mistake. Susan found his association with Diana more than troubling. But there was little she could accomplish from Covent Garden, so she turned her attention to the letter's enclosure. It was unsigned and anonymous:

I ame confident you haue heard alreadie of a riche ladie Stanlie that did cheat poore Collonel Philips and wife of 200 pound, and had cheated more if M^{ris} Mohun had not discouered her, when she was at Antwerp, she knew her, her name is Skinner, and a take away the K. out of her name and you will finde her trade.

This information was not, of course, entirely news to Susan, though Diana had put the transaction in a more flattering light. But the link to Philly Moon, a well-respected Sister, was more troubling, and as for the riddle at the end, it wasn't entirely clear what Diana was being accused of. Anyone who knew Diana for more than an hour or two would find it hard to believe she was a lady of unimpeachable virtue, and as for theft, it was her modus operandi. But the opprobrium of Mistress Moon worried Susan.

While she contemplated this letter's import, Edward's letter had continued to muddy the waters in which Susan currently swam.

I can onlye assume that, now that the prime merchandise has been exported, the shop in London is closed, and needs no more support.

This mission, that was not Diana's to carry out, was now assumed by Edward to have been abandoned - a perfectly reasonable assumption given the circumstances. Whatever Diana was up to in Paris, it could only help Susan by drawing attention away from her. But Diana was no longer a pressing concern. Susan had work to do.

She was due at John's for supper within the hour. Instinctively, she slid the letter and its enclosure into a fold in her dress before pausing and smiling. 'Hardly the safest place, Susan,' she muttered to herself, hid it carefully amongst the clothing in her trunk and quickly readied herself. She had been observing her prey closely and her diligence had, she suspected, finally borne fruit. Susan had noticed something in Thurloe's chambers during her last visit. It was just the slightest smattering of dust on the wooden floor, hard by the wall. It was such a small, insignificant thing that Susan assumed that it was more a paranoia brought on by her time working for the Knot than any real evidence of anything of importance. But then again, she often found that it was not searching for the thing itself that bore fruit, but observing changes, however small, and considering possible causes for them. From there discovery often proved simple. There were a number of possible causes for this delicate dusty smattering, so far as Susan could tell, but only one proved interesting enough to warrant further investigation. If this were plaster dust, as she suspected it was, it might suggest an uncaring removal and subsequently hasty replacement of one of the oak panels immediately above. Such haste might indicate the existence of a hollow in the wall, and one may well speculate as to its contents. What might Thurloe wish to keep secure from casual discovery? It was perhaps designed to contain papers of a sensitive nature. And it was time that Susan lived up to the title of she-intelligencer. This evening she would investigate further, given the opportunity. And if not this evening, the next evening she attended Thurloe at his chambers. Patience was perhaps Susan's greatest ally. It was a quality conspicuous in its absence with Diana. She slipped out of her lodgings and into the bustle of Covent Garden. Within a few steps she saw one of her apothecaries with Thurloe's man, heading directly towards her.

It struck Susan as a wonder that she so often appeared to see without being seen, her training notwithstanding, and certainly it amazed her that Chase and Nathaniel could pass so close by and not notice her, but there did seem to be some urgency at hand. It was apparent that they had a goal in mind that did not include her presence. It was also apparent that her initial fear at seeing the two men together was unfounded, as Chase had plainly not been arrested. That left two possibilities. Either Chase was working for Thurloe, or Thurloe was ill. The fact that the two men hurried away from his chambers meant that like as not he was not at home. Susan increased her pace. It was a rare thing for such an opportunity to present itself, and she meant to take full advantage.

Over the weeks that Susan had been dining with Thurloe she had made herself just as inconspicuous at his chambers as she was on the streets. Most days she would enter them without passing another soul other than the porter with whom Thurloe had an understanding, and on those rare days when traffic was heavy around his door, she would simply melt into insignificance. Today was much like every other, and it was a matter of seconds between her walking into the relative calm of Lincoln's Inn Fields and shutting Thurloe's door behind herself. The rooms were empty. She was early. It was time.

Susan set about her work quickly, first arranging a chair so that it would be struck by the door upon opening, spilling a jug of old wine to justify the movement, and placing a cloth by the spill. She then took out her bodkin and, following a careful inspection of each of the panels that might have caused the plaster dust, isolated the most likely candidate. It was the third panel from the floor, and it bore light scratch marks on one of its edges. She inserted the bodkin into the gap between the frame and the scratches on the thin oaken panel and gently prised it open. Behind it lay, as she hoped, a small hollow, in which two solid, masculine ledgers well bound in black morocco leather nestled intimately, a gathering of loose papers beneath them. She slid the top ledger carefully from the embrace of its partner, and turned the pages until she found the most recent entry. Susan drew a short breath, stopping at the moment she saw the initials R.H. and 'his mistress, Parris' written in Thurloe's neat secretary hand. Robert Honeywood, she presumed. The steward to Elizabeth

Stewart. If it was no surprise that Thurloe had a mole in The Hague, it came as a shock that it was one so well placed. All the more reason to place her faith solely in the hands of the Sisterhood, as even the men who worked for them did so unwittingly. There was no other identification, simply the sum of ten pounds in the right-hand column. A few lines up from these words she read another familiar name, that of Chase. There was no sum of money beside his name. Honeywood could be dealt with presently. That he was in communication with Diana was altogether more problematic. And then there was Chase. What was he doing here? Did the lack of a sum next to his name indicate that he was yet to turn but that he was a target?

Susan looked at the name above the apothecary's. This name had a short passage attached to it. Susan read it out loud: 'whose *Rhetorick* is *Ribaldry*, whose Element is *Drinke*, whose wit is in *Baudery*, and whose Beauty is blasted with her own Breath, it being a damp that will kill a *Spider*.' The name attached was 'Mrs. Phil. Mohun.' This, at least, indicated pretty clearly that Philly Moon was not to be turned.

Susan held the ledger loosely in her hands, suddenly unsure what to do. It wasn't clear why these names were here, in Thurloe's black book, but the fact that they were had surprised her greatly. It made her heart thump loudly within her breast, as if it were trying to counsel her to make her escape while she could, and her hands turned from their usual soft warmth to a cold clamminess that reminded her of the brown trout that her father Henry used to snatch from the river Nadder near their home in Dinton, Wiltshire. Her father would bash the fish over the head with a mallet, and the recollection of this image was enough to bring Susan back into the present. Her equilibrium recovered, she quickly copied out the relevant parts onto a scrap of paper using Thurloe's own pen and carefully slid the ledger back into its resting place. She then slid out the sheaf of papers.

The hand was different, a little rougher than Thurloe's, but legible enough for her to read the first few words:

> *The Lady Genninges wife to Sr William Genninges of Essex saith that her Husband and selfe haueing liued a yeare...*

It was the account of Diana's interrogation. Susan read on, her face draining of colour as she did so. But it did not simply detail the interrogation itself, but was annotated in Thurloe's own script. Here it all lay, in the margins. Diana's handing of Chase to the parliamentarians, her betrayal of the assassination plot being concocted by the Philips. The deal she had cut with the devil. Susan felt hollow. Diana had left the Mermaid unharmed, she had been told. This was betrayal, pure and simple.

There was a voice in the corridor that she recognised. Susan rapidly slid the papers back into their hiding place and followed this rehousing with that of the panel, albeit rather more roughly than she would have liked. She then fell to her hands and knees as the door opened and immediately collided with the waiting chair.

'Who's there?' came the voice. 'What is the meaning of this?' The door swung again with greater vehemence, this time less colliding than crashing into the oak that barred its path.

'Soft, Nathaniel, soft,' cried Susan. 'It is but I. Some wine spilled and I had to move the chair to reach it.' She stood and pulled the chair away from its defensive position. Nathaniel entered.

'Miss Susan. I come bearing news from Master Secretary Thurloe. He is inconvenienced on account of matters of State and will be in the countryside for the next few days. He sends his apologies but supper must await his pleasure.' Nathaniel looked at Susan, the remains of the wine on the floor, the table. 'You have been writing, Miss Susan, or perhaps are intent on doing so?'

Susan pinned up her hair, concealing the scrap she had just written on as she did so, then rubbed her hands together. 'Yes, indeed. I was going to write a short note to the Master Secretary, which was the reason for my spilling the wine.'

Nathaniel looked at her, his eyes narrowing slightly. 'On what subject, Miss Susan?'

'Never you mind, Nathaniel, never you mind,' said Susan, laughing as rudely as she could. In fact, she was trying to channel Diana. Every part except for the betrayal part. That part was still sinking in. She simply couldn't believe that she'd given Thurloe the Philips' plot and, more importantly, Chase. Chase had been an important part of her plan to protect her network, a plan that now appeared flawed. But she could not simply abandon him as this would show that Diana's betrayal had been revealed, and through that she would surely be revealed herself.

'Miss Susan!' The words forced themselves through the clouds of Diana that surrounded her consciousness. She looked up and saw Nathaniel's face staring at her. 'I can take a message to the Master Secretary if you wish.'

All Susan could see was the third panel from the floor. Its grain ran horizontally, unlike the rest of the panels. Nathaniel might not notice, but John surely would. 'I'll write one after I've cleaned up the last of this wine...' But Nathaniel had opened the door wide, and began to usher Susan out of the room. She knew that to resist the man would immediately awake his suspicion. She looked back as she walked through the opening, willing the panel to turn. Susan turned her back on Thurloe's chambers and heard both the door shut and the rattle of a key in the lock. There was going to be no turning of the panel, not tonight. But this was not the most important turning that Susan was concerned with, however. With her double-dealing with Thurloe, it was looking very much as if Diana was less the cozener and more the counter-intelligencer. Susan knew that

Diana was a highly volatile character; this was what made her so effective and, she grudgingly admitted, such fun to be around. Diana made Susan feel alive, but with this action, her vitality had endangered the coherence of the Knot itself. Diana may not have given Thurloe the information that would allow him to unravel the Knot, but her actions may well have reminded him of Alexander's own technique for solving such problems.

'Her name was Skinner... take away the k and you have her trade' said Susan to herself. Now she understood what the anonymous writer of the enclosure had meant. Diana had been testified against by a Sister, and the accusation was that her first thoughts were not to kinship: there was no more damaging accusation to lay at a Sister's feet. The laws of the Sisterhood were clear. Diana was now persona non grata until such time as her guilt or otherwise could be ascertained by the Sisterhood's court of session. What was plain, however, was that the woman had no loyalty except to herself. In her statement Diana had deviated from her mission, taking the opportunity to revenge herself on those she felt had wronged her, while simply selling her information to the most persuasive bidder. This was not behaviour that befitted one of the Sisterhood. Outside chambers Susan took her leave of Nathaniel and deliberately set off in the direction opposite to his.

The London streets appeared more frenetic and febrile than ever. Perhaps this was simply the result of Susan's realisation that she was now truly alone in her endeavour. Molly was too young to be of much use, quite beside the fact that she was not party to Susan's task. Yes, Susan was alone, and the realisation had settled onto her like the first snows of a hard winter, smoothing out the sharp edges of her fear and wrapping itself around her core, keeping the warmth of her self-belief and sense of duty both hidden and preserved. In many ways it was something of a relief. Susan need no longer rely on any others to achieve her goal. Success, or indeed failure, was now hers and hers alone. The streets appeared to know this, and obligingly placed a whole series of obstacles in her path. As if she did not have enough to consider. Drunken, lecherous men grabbed at her rear through her skirts as they staggered past her. Skittish horses reared up at runaway dogs and threatened to trample her with panicked hooves while the carts they drew lost their wheels and barrels of soap fell, cracking open to leach their cargo, rendered glutinous by the summer heat. But there was to be no Jane hiding gold within these gallons to smuggle them through parliamentary lines. All they did was drip yet more treachery into her path. But though the city conspired against her she moved between its conspiracies with ease, less walking than gliding, impervious to outside influence. There was now no outside for Susan, just Thurloe's chambers, and the secrets that lay within.

Susan was afraid.

9

Thurloe toys with Isaac

As the long summer of 1655 slipped into autumn, John Thurloe found himself beset with several questions, and holding few answers. During his last fit of the stone, which had been longer and more debilitating than ever, the Black Chamber had continued its work efficiently, albeit with rather less success than was customary. Isaac, Thurloe knew, was of the opinion that it was best to allow the chamber simply to uncover what it would rather than seek specific goals. Light, not fruit, was how he put it. But Thurloe craved results, and to him, the relative silence of the various lines of communication they had uncovered was not indicative of success, but of failure. There were other approaches open to them, however, one of which he had just presented to the Lord Protector himself. It had been Isaac's idea, and he and Jonny had worked together on it for several weeks. When Thurloe pushed open the door to the Black Chamber, Isaac looked at him as if he were a bridegroom awaiting the unveiling of his bride.

'Well?' asked Isaac, 'Are you going to tell us in what manner the Lord Protector spoke of my work?'

'Oh, Isaac, Isaac,' said Thurloe. 'You are so impatient sometimes. What do you say, Jonny?'

'Well, Master Secretary,' he began. 'I do say that we are prey to the rushing onset of winter...'

'Is it winter already?' cried Thurloe. 'What have we been doing for the past six weeks?'

'There is the little matter of the...' said Jonny, but was prevented from finishing by Isaac's attempt to reassert his hold on the conversation.

'Impatient, Master Secretary?' said Isaac, his expectation curdling and the irritation floating to the top. 'You consider me impatient because I wish to know what the Lord Protector thought of my work's value?'

'You know full well the Lord Protector finds your work here in the Black Chamber of very great import,' said Thurloe. 'It is impossible to gauge it fully, of course, until we actually thwart a major royalist plot, but we will, Isaac, we will.' Thurloe smiled at Jonny who tried, but failed, to hide his amusement as Isaac was given a lesson in obfuscation. 'And what's more, he proposes to increase our purse that we may range more completely. Furthermore, he notes that we, sirs, are the first official secret service, and as such it is time we made our methods plain. The Protector wishes that we produce a text such that the service might continue without us. As you know, Isaac, every spymaster until now has kept their own records, used their own methods, and bought information with their own purse. We, or rather you, Isaac, are to document our activities to this end, and formulate a coherent method to ensure that the service shall no longer rely on the continuing good health of its head.' Thurloe paused. 'That is how much your work is valued, Isaac.'

'Master Secretary!' cried Isaac, his face beginning to change colour. 'You are being purposely obtuse. You know full well I refer to the tract.'

Thurloe's face fell. 'Obtuse?' he said, kicking Jonny, who was starting to laugh. 'Did you just call me obtuse?'

'Yes, no, sorry Master Secretary,' said Isaac, his voice revealing a slight edge of panic. 'You know I didn't mean anything by it...'

'And anyway, Isaac,' said Thurloe, his face lighting up again. 'I seem to recall that young Jonny here also wrote a not unsubstantial proportion of said tract, am I right, Jonny?'

'Yes, Master Secretary,' said Jonny, 'a not unsubstantial proportion indeed.' Thurloe turned his gaze to Isaac and raised his right eyebrow.

'Yes, yes,' said Isaac. 'Our tract. What did the Lord Protector make of *our* tract?'

'Well, it's interesting that you should ask,' said Thurloe, but he was interrupted by the entrance of another into the room. 'Ah, Nathaniel,' he continued, as if all thoughts of tracts and Lord Protectors had been banished by this sudden appearance.

'Give me strength,' said Isaac.

'Good sir,' said Thurloe, continuing unabated. 'What news from the enlightened world that might give succour to these poor, shadow-dwelling souls?'

'Oh,' said Nathaniel. 'Wasn't there some pamphlet that was being written?' He smiled at Jonny who by now had his hand clamped firmly over his mouth.

'I must visit the privy,' said Jonny, plainly unable to contain more than just his laughter.

'Fret not, Isaac,' said Thurloe, clapping him on the back, and picking up the letter he was working on. 'The Lord Protector approves of your handicraft.' He read a few lines and tossed it back onto the pile. 'In fact, he was so taken with your tract that he wishes you to take it to Field himself in order that it might be published by the end of the month.'

'Thank you, Master Secretary,' said Isaac, all the tension leaving his face. 'Is that why your mood is so playful today?'

'Playful?' said Thurloe. 'Do I seem in a playful frame of mind to you, Nathaniel?'

'Well, Master Secretary,' said Nathaniel. 'I must admit you do seem somewhat lighter in aspect than usual. And while you have enjoyed better health since your last inconvenience, today does seem to find you marvellous merry.'

'Well, my good fellows,' said Thurloe. 'Best we all make the most of it, no? Let us take the remainder of the day for our own amusement.' He flicked each of them a coin. 'And allow me to make purchase of your suppers for you, too.'

'Why thank you, Master Secretary,' they said, and prepared to leave.

'One more thing, Isaac,' he said, sitting down and flipping his boots onto the desk in front of him. 'With regard to the tract and Mr Field.'

'Yes, Master Secretary?' replied Isaac.

'I think we ought entrust the task to young Jonny,' he said. 'It strikes me that it would be nicely poetic. I imagine he's capable of supervising the work and ensuring it is carried out most excellently well?'

'Of that I have no doubt,' said Isaac. 'He is a more than capable amanuensis and overseer. He is quick, diligent and precise. Let's hope for Field's sake that he doesn't attempt to fob him off with inferior paper or compositor.'

'Indeed not,' said Thurloe. 'Enjoy the afternoon, and - Isaac? - best you send Jonny off tomorrow morning to annoy good Mr Field. Tell him he must stop the presses for the Lord Protector.'

'Did I hear the name of Field?' said Jonny, as he re-entered the chamber.

'Yes, Jonny,' said Thurloe. 'Isaac will explain.' He handed him a coin. 'Now, begone the lot of you. I shall attend to the chamber.'

'Yes, Master Secretary,' said Isaac, and the three disappeared into the warren of corridors, leaving Thurloe alone in his Black Chamber.

Thurloe leant back into the large chair that was his allotted place. Lord of all he surveyed, that's what he was. There was no other logical way to describe it. He had, through hard work, humility and the grace of God, placed himself at the head of the intelligence table. From here he could finally take the fight directly to the Knot. He knew almost everyone involved now, as his chamber was finally beginning to work as he knew it ought. The relative silence was but temporary, and in any case, winter was always a quiet period. But he would eventually lure the ludicrously named Mrs Simburbe, Mrs Edwards and S.H., the three figures around whom the conspiracy revolved, into an indiscretion. Thurloe was not to be fooled by the ringleaders using the rather unbecoming conceit of giving themselves women's names, but he was content to play the spider, hidden under the leaf, with one leg resting on the silken thread that would tell him when his prey was near. These men would stumble into his web eventually.

As for matters closer to home, there again his plans were proceeding apace. There was no guard at his door now, it was simply not necessary. Susan was no longer wont to slip out if unattended, nor was coercion necessary to have her take supper with him. It merely warranted some measure of subtlety on her part, in order that she might enter his chambers without being seen by anyone other than the porter who effected her ingress.

He stood and almost immediately stumbled, the pain in his left foot as sudden as it was sharp. Ah, the fall. He could not pretend he had not invited God's displeasure, or perhaps this was merely a memento mori, a reminder that behind his self-satisfaction lay a mere man. He looked to the heavens. 'Thank you, Lord,' he said, before resting on the desk and scribbling a short note. Then he hobbled out of the Black Chamber, gave the note to a servant to be delivered and made his way slowly to Lincoln's Inn. His gout would serve him as a reminder that humility was perhaps the most desirable of qualities to find in a man.

Back at his chambers, Thurloe sat, his left leg resting on a pillow on another chair, and tried to drink himself to sleep with a bottle of port wine that had recently come into his possession, a gift from a royalist conspirator he had recently dissuaded from further activities. It had been mildly successful, and he dozed fitfully, but the throbbing in his foot was not only increasing in intensity, but it was changing in its consistency, too. Where once were thick gobs of pain, intense but only capable of gradual motion, there were now wide sheets of excruciating agony that took up formation in motile layers as if his skin were now on fire and his blood molten rock.

'Master Secretary Thurloe,' came a voice that offered him temporary respite from his torments. 'Master Secretary. Did you truly think that I would abandon you in this hour of need?'

'Susan,' said Thurloe. 'My dear Susan. How your voice is like balm to my soul.'

'That's all well and good, Master Secretary,' replied Susan. 'But the balm you need is not for your soul, I fear, but for your poor foot.' With this she leant over the chair and inspected the offending appendage. 'It's very red,' she said, and poked at his big toe.

The invective that spewed from Thurloe's mouth quite took Susan by surprise. 'Master Secretary!' she said, her face betraying her astonishment. 'And you purport to be a godly man.'

'You have no clue,' said Thurloe, his voice weak and tremulous. 'You have no clue of how, how total, how complete this pain is. The pain of being deprived of our Lord's love cannot be much worse.'

Susan looked at this man, this scourge of the royalists, this tormentor of men, his face now pale and covered with beads of sweat. Was this the man whose name mothers used to quieten unruly children at bedtime? Was this the man she herself had called a very devil? So weak, so vulnerable. She stood and reached for her bag.

'I will cure you,' said Susan.

'You cannot...' said Thurloe, but she silenced him with a look of pure devotion.

'I can and will,' said Susan. 'I have the receit of Sir Francis Bacon himself. It is a goodly cure. Stay still and I will fetch some necessities.'

'No,' said Thurloe. 'Call down for an attendant. Get one of them to do so.'

'I must do so myself,' said Susan. 'Be patient.'

Within the hour, Susan was applying the poultice, stage one of the process. After another three, she was bathing the affected foot, and by nightfall, Thurloe's foot was wrapped in a plaister, and he was asleep.

At 7am Nathaniel entered the chamber. Susan was asleep on the floor by Thurloe's chair. 'Beg pardon, Miss Susan,' he said. 'This letter came urgent for Master Secretary.'

Both Susan and Thurloe woke.

'Good heavens,' said Thurloe. 'I do believe it worked.'

'Master Secretary,' said Nathaniel, handing him the letter. Thurloe took it and waved the carrier away. He opened the letter and read.

'John?' said Susan. 'Are you quite well? You look sudden melancholy.'

Even Susan's first use of his given name, though it relit a fire he thought long since burnt out, could not compensate for the lines he read. If anything, they merely accentuated his torment.

10

Jonny makes plans

Having been granted the afternoon as a boon, Jonny had left Nathaniel and Isaac to their own devices, as he reckoned that if he was to show Field up good and proper as he wanted to, then it were best he had an inside man to keep him wise of any tricks his old owner - for apprentices were fundamentally owned by their masters - might get up to. He walked past the carnage of Butcher's Row, turned the corner, and in front of him stood the Mermaid. It had been Jim's tavern of choice for some time, so if he wasn't yet there, he would show up eventually. Jonny was practically walking on air after Thurloe had told him that he could take charge of producing such an important tract. And one, mark you, written by the Lord Protector himself. Albeit with a fair amount of help from Jonny and Isaac. The tavern was virtually empty, and there was no sign of Jim, so he picked a table and sat. He caught the eye of one of the serving girls and she walked up to him.

'What'll it be?' she said.

Jonny looked at her, but didn't say anything.

'Hey mister,' she said, rather abruptly. 'I'm not here for the good of my health, you know. What'll it be?'

'Sorry,' said Jonny. 'You look familiar somehow...'

'If I had a penny for every time I've heard that line, mister... what'll it be?'

'Hang on,' said Jonny. 'I've got it. Did you go to help an old lady with birdcages after some scoundrel tried to steal her purse... you kicked him in the, well, you know...'

'Oh my!' said the girl. 'It was you that scared him off? My very own Redcrosse knight!'

'Hardly,' said Jonny. 'That was Nathaniel, not me.' He smiled as winning a smile as he could muster. 'But I'm happy to take responsibility.' He held out his hand. 'Jonny.'

'Molly,' said the girl, pointedly ignoring it. 'First ale on the house... Redcrosse.' And she leant over the table to pour.

'I like your locket,' said Jonny. 'May I?'

'It, it was my aunt's,' said Molly, a little unsurely. She stayed leant over so Jonny could look at it more closely. He took the locket softly in his hand and examined it.

'It's beautiful,' he said. He looked a little closer. On one side it bore the image of a bird. On the reverse, there was writing. Jonny half-expected a love-token, but the words were not English. '"Ego avis enim cantans inaspecta." Interesting. I am the bird that sings unseen,' he said. 'Or *a* bird.'

'Oh,' said Molly. 'You are well lettered! Is that what it means?'

'Yes. I have more Latin and Greek than Shakespeare, and Hebrew into the bargain.' He inspected the locket once more. 'Looking at the front, it must be the nightingale. It refers to the legend of Philomela, surely,' he continued.

'Tell it to me, Jonny.'

'It's quite violent. I'm not sure it's suitable for your ears.'

'I'll be the judge of that,' said Molly as she gave Jonny a look he couldn't quite place. Or compete with. 'Tell it to me, Jonny. I don't bite,' she added, with another look that seemed to suggest she had better weapons than her teeth. 'And in any case, we're not exactly busy.' And with that, she sat.

Jonny took the cup that Molly had filled. He drank. 'Philomela,' he began, 'had a sister named Procne, who was married to Tereus, king of Thrace, and Procne wanted to visit her sister in Athens, but instead Tereus agreed to travel to Athens and escort Philomela back to his kingdom, where the two sisters might do whatever sisters do when they get together.'

'What do you mean, Jonny?' asked Molly, but Jonny just looked at her blankly and carried on with his story.

'King Pandion, Philomela's father, was worried about his last remaining daughter - well, his last daughter remaining at home, anyway - travelling so he had Tereus promise to protect her as if he were her father. Tereus agreed, but Philomela was so beautiful, and Tereus such a rogue, that on arrival in Thrace he could no longer control himself, and forced himself upon her in a cabin in the woods.'

'Vile man. Much like all,' - she checked herself - 'most men.'

'Indeed,' said Jonny. And on he continued. 'Tereus told Philomela that she was not to tell a soul. After all, he was king, no one would believe her, he'd say it was witchcraft, and so on. But Philomela refused to bend to his will and said she would tell the whole world. At this, Tereus cut out her tongue and left her for dead in the cabin.'

'Typical king.'

'True enough,' said Jonny, and carried on. 'Philomela did not die, however, but instead wove a tapestry depicting her rape by Tereus and took it to her sister.'

'And what did her sister do?'

'Procne was incensed, and killed the son given her by Tereus, feeding him to the king in a pie,' said Jonny, taking a good swig of ale to aid his voice. 'After he had eaten his fill, the sisters presented him with his son's head on a platter. The king was mightily displeased at the turn of events,' he continued.

'Mightily displeased at the turn of events?' repeated Molly, looking Jonny in the eye once more. 'Jonny,' she said, in a threatening tone.

'Did I say mightily displeased? He flew into a murderous rage, chasing after the sisters with an axe, intent on butchering them. But the sisters-'

'The sisters turned on him, disarmed him and slowly cut him to pieces with his own axe, only pausing to enjoy his suffering?' suggested Molly.

'No, you vile creature. What made you think that? They prayed that the gods might save them and just as Tereus was about to catch them they were both transformed into birds, Procne into a swallow and Philomela into a nightingale.' He drank a little more ale, satisfied at a job well done.

'I preferred my ending,' said Molly. 'Where did you learn that?'

'Oh,' said Jonny, wondering whether he ought talk of the books that he found dotted around Whitehall, but thought better of it. 'I'm a printer...' he started, adding 'apprentice' when he saw the look that Molly was giving him.

'Oh, I just love books,' said Molly, excitedly. 'I can't afford them and you don't find many left behind on tables here.' She smiled as Jonny's face obviously betrayed his confusion. 'No, indeed, Master Jonny. You don't find any.'

'So that's the story behind the nightingale, anyway,' said Jonny. 'I suppose Philomela was a woman who sang unheard, and was transformed into a bird that sings unseen.'

'It's a beautiful story. I'm not sure that I'd allow myself to be turned into a bird, though.'

'I'm glad. I think you are quite lovely just as you are.'

'Thank you. And you may call me Molly.'

There was a shout from across the room. 'Jonny!' It was Jim. He'd finally finished for the day. 'Great to see you, Jonny!' he said, as he sat down at the table with a thump. 'A jug of ale, my lovely,' said Jim, aiming a slap at Molly's backside. She evaded it deftly, and Jim almost fell off his stool. Molly laughed, looked directly at Jonny and winked. Jim looked at Molly, then at Jonny. 'You sly old dog, you!' He slapped him on the back and finished his cup of ale for him. 'Now then, Jonny m'lad. What can I do for you?'

11

Jonny goes to work

Isaac Dorislaus was already at the desk when Jonny arrived, grinning from ear to ear. Isaac, however, was hunched over a letter, his index finger poised on the first line. It remained stationary while he addressed his young charge.

'Before you start, I wax ill, and I don't want to hear about your evening, your night or your morning,' said Isaac, without raising his head. 'In fact, I don't wish to hear your voice, or, indeed, anything whatsoever.'

'What ails you this fine morning, good Master Dorislaus?' asked Jonny.

'Allow me to pass down some of the wisdom that is gained with age,' said Isaac. 'Never, ever go drinking with Nathaniel. Don't be tempted, persuaded or otherwise led astray.' At this, his face fell directly onto his letter. He groaned. 'I cannot see, let alone read. As for thinking...' his voice drifted away as he spoke. 'Just let me die alone, Jonny.'

'I fear Master Secretary Thurloe would take umbrage, Isaac.'

'For my being dead or for your being elsewhere at the time? In any case, you have an assignment today.'

'I do?' said Jonny. 'Is it exciting?'

'You know full well it is. You are to take the final text of our

Lord Protector's tract to Field's for printing. And you are to instruct him to stop the presses in its favour, also. Obviously, if there is any problem you might find Nathaniel is the man for you. Just don't go to the tavern with him, Jonny.'

'Oh, as if I'd forgotten,' he said, with a wry smile. 'Where is the approved version?'

Isaac pointed to a tied bundle of papers sat on the table. 'Don't hurry back,' he said.

Jonny picked up the bundle and strode out into the courtyard. It was October and London was beginning to get cold, though it was still dry, a fact that made Jonny a happy man as he had yet to save the money for a good winter coat. He had, however, finally been accorded the honour of having his own key, which saved him from an awful lot of talking to guards and an awful lot of wasted time. This also meant that he could spend more time inside the Black Chamber, where it was at least warm. He was beginning to worry about the state of his lodgings, however. Primary amongst the ways in which his lodging was unfit was through the inability of the room's roof to prevent the ingress of water when the rain came. It was because of this that he was developing a habit of working late and accidentally falling asleep inside Whitehall. The previous evening, however, he had neither worked late nor returned to his leaky room. But the Black Chamber wasn't the most comfortable of bedrooms, being effectively a windowless and airless box, and in the weeks that it had been functioning Jonny had formulated three separate explanations of its name. Depending on the audience for whom he performed, it was so named on account of the deeds both uncovered and instigated within it, from the colour of its walls or of those who worked within.

Jonny had begun to notice how certain trades seeped into the very pores of a man. Printers suffered from stained everything and were often poisoned by the tools of their trade. Tanners smelt like the piss they used to create the lye so vital to the process. The denizens of the Black Chamber, however, suffered primarily as a result of the dozens of tallow candles necessary to produce suitable levels of light for the transcription and deciphering of letters. By the end of a shift illuminated by these dull yellow tubes, whose light came at the price of prodigious amounts of greasy smoke, the forensic amanuenses within found themselves set loose on London, their clothes damp and sticky, as if they had been sweating grease. What's more, their faces were often darkened enough by the smoke for them to be mistaken for Spaniards, an irony which failed to escape them, though thankfully they had only once had to escape the wrath of the common man. It was a filthy life, though there were worse places to work, and one of them was his old workplace and current destination, John Field's printing-house in Blackfriars, where Jonny had been virtually incarcerated until Nathaniel had rescued him. His current lodgings, with all their faults, were rather better than the room he had at Field's, which made him feel like a sparrow, tucked up under the eaves as he was.

As the cold nipped at his ears, Jonny began to think that it was likely to be a long, unpleasant winter unless he could secure a pay rise, or perhaps a bonus. Perhaps he ought to spend more than the occasional night with Isaac, whose annuity, granted following his father's murder by royalists, allowed him to wallow with his as yet uneffected vengeance in relative luxury. Or perhaps, just perhaps, there was another way to acquire a small lump sum to wrap around himself and cheat Jack Frost.

But now, as he walked by the river to pay a visit on his old master, John Field, his mind was drawn to other matters. Field was a pompous, self-important ass at the best of times, and seeing as his official title of printer to Parliament had been very recently changed to printer to His Highness the Lord Protector, Jonny could only dream of the levels his excitement with himself had reached. Furthermore, Jonny was beginning to notice just how quickly Cromwell, the so-called 'Lord Protector', was drawing around himself the things he needed to make himself king in all but name, including the institution of the King's Printers. It might be a somewhat tricky job to persuade Field to obey his one-time apprentice in this matter without some type of extra inducement, such as Nathaniel was wont to supply, but Jonny was going to enjoy trying.

It was too late to consider his strategy now, however, as he had reached his destination, the print-shop adjacent to St Andrew-by-the-Wardrobe. It was, as ever, a hub of activity.

'Shop!' shouted Jonny, and within minutes out Field scurried, for all the world like some kind of demented spider. His hands and face were black enough, a colour that changed little as he smiled.

'Oh,' said Field. 'If it's not little Jonny know-it-all.' He spat into the ground. 'Piss off, there's a good Jonny,' he said with a sneer. 'We are appointed to the Lord Protector now, so stick that up your arse and call it a feather. We're not doing it.'

'I presume your work is as shoddy as ever,' said Jonny. 'I bet the Lord Protector doesn't know about that, now does he?'

'Sod off you little shit. Which part of *we're not doing it* don't you understand?' said Field, his words staccato and aggressive. 'And don't think your heavy can scare me, either. Firstly I have my own now, and secondly I have the protection of the *Lord Protector*, so really, why don't you piss off and tell your oh-so-important author what I think of him.'

'Right-ho!' said Jonny, getting the manuscript out from his leather bag. 'I'll just go and tell him now, let me see,' - he flicked through the sheets of paper ostentatiously - 'oh yes, here we are, just a second.' Jonny was stretching it out for as long as he could. 'Here it is. The author being... His Highness, the Lord Protector...' Jonny smiled. 'Right then, I'm off.' But he hadn't walked two paces when he turned and said. 'Oh, no, sorry. What I really have to say is stop the presses and load this up.' With this, Jonny handed Field the bundle. 'And we'll have neat work - no cheap paper and clear print. I know this inside out and I will stamp on you.' He smiled a smile of victory. 'It's forty pages, in quarto, so five quires.' He paused. For effect. 'Tonight.'

'But Jonny, for heaven's sake, you know how this shop works,' said Field. 'I can't possibly get it done that fast.'

'I'm for my breakfast,' said Jonny, 'and when I get back, in say, an hour or so, you'll have the type for the first sheet on the stone, and the paper wet and ready, or I'll take over your shop for the day and do it myself.' At this, Jonny turned and walked away, heading for Covent Garden. He had a plan.

12

Susan frets

Susan sat in her room in Covent Garden, going over and over the night before last in her head, trying to attach some sort of meaning to it that wasn't the meaning it appeared to have. If only Diana hadn't turned out to be... it was just so frustrating, not knowing what to do. And she had to do something, that was for certain. The brutal truth of the matter was that John, Thurloe, was a target, nothing else. Susan shared his supper on account of his being full of secrets, specifically the secrets that the Knot were trying to keep to themselves. The Knot needed to know which of them he had uncovered and Susan was set the task of attaining this knowledge. This was her job, this was her mission, though she still needed to find time to keep the post running, a task made more difficult now that Thurloe controlled both ends of the chain. Hinton and Chase were doing an excellent job in the circumstances, but only in the circumstances - having to assume Chase's route was compromised made life that little bit more complicated. The real problem, however, was simple. Susan was beginning to have feelings for the man she had been spying on from the start, and from the start intended, at the last, to assassinate. Where were her thirty pieces of silver? These feelings weren't so much beginning as they were beginning to overwhelm her. It was beginning to feel like a betrayal, but of both king and John. Susan was in trouble. And the only soul she could talk about it with was Diana, who had first taken the convent and then apparently taken up with the enemy. And then there was Molly.

Molly. There was a suitable distraction for her. She would head to the Mermaid. After all, she was practically a Sister now. There just remained the tiny matter of the final test. Susan picked up her medicine bag, hid a couple of letters in a secret compartment and walked into the carnival that was Covent Garden on market day. As she walked out onto the riverside, she bought herself an apple, and as she bit into it she saw a young, good-looking youth exiting a chop shop clutching a sheaf of paper and smiling to himself. It was the smile of a plan coming together, of closing a good deal, of sealing another with a kiss. It became Susan's smile too as she was transported back to that moment in Thurloe's chambers. It was the moment that everything changed. It was the moment that Susan began her own civil war. It was that moment.

It was also the moment that a cutpurse chose to walk directly into Susan and relieve her of the burden of a purse of coin. Susan had tied it carefully to the bag itself but the cutpurse was skilful and quick enough to lift it and jag into the crowd before Susan realised what had happened. It took a second to steal and Susan knew it had gone within three. 'Stupid woman!' she said, chastising herself as she searched the crowd in vain. 'That's what happens when you start some silly, girlish daydreaming.' Her anger increased when she realised that it wasn't a loose change purse that had gone missing but a golden one. 'Idiot!' She was furious.

Susan swung around quickly when she felt the hand on her shoulder, nails ready and fist swinging. She checked herself just in time as she saw that the man was no assailant. He was of above average height, well dressed with fine bone structure and wore a small moustache. His wig was wavy and fair, and only his eyes betrayed a certain world-weariness that belied the rakish exterior. He did not flinch, however, merely stating his name and intentions. 'Sir Samuel Morland, at your service, ma'am.'

'Mrs Diana Jennens,' replied Susan. Instinctively. She truly was a she-intelligencer now. She lied without thinking.

'My pleasure, Mrs Jennens,' replied Morland, before raising a small purse in his right hand. 'I believe you have just misplaced this?' he said, smiling.

'Thank heavens,' said Susan, smiling back at the man, who leant forward, conspiratorially.

'Are you placed within the government of this Emerald Isle?' he said, and Susan shook her head. 'Good,' said Morland. 'They'll not know I'm home yet, and I'd like to keep it that way.' He looked around him. 'I spent rather more of our dear Lord Protector's money giving succour to the Piedmont poor than he might have liked. And a fair amount of it relieving myself.'

'How did...' began Susan. She not only had no idea who this man was but why he was talking to her about his work for parliament. Unless he was simply lying, of course. 'Intelligencer!' she said to herself, triumphantly.

'Well, it's all a matter of the right equipment allied with vigilance,' said Morland. 'I saw this miscreant steal a few times, then predicted she would come to you next. I then cut off her escape route and hooked her.' With this, Morland stepped to his side to reveal a young girl of about twelve years of age on the floor, unconscious, a ring of violet cuts around her left leg. 'A new invention,' he said, holding up a metal cane with what looked like a set of teeth on a chain at the end. 'Ho hum, must get on with getting on,' he said, and was gone.

Susan picked the now waking girl up by the arm and practically dragged her to the Mermaid, with her kicking and screaming all the way. Just by the door, Susan got down to the girl's eye level and, holding her by the shoulders, shook her and spoke. 'Now look here,' she said. 'I'm trying to help you. I can help you.' The girl spat in Susan's face and kicked out with enough force to allow her to wriggle free. Susan put her hand to her mouth. There was blood. The child, however, was nowhere to be seen. A drunk man staggered from the inn, followed by Molly, who had just escorted him from the premises.

'And don't,' started Molly as her one-time customer fell into the street, but stopped when she saw Susan. 'We'd better clean that up. There's no helping some people.' And the two of them went inside.

'Why, haven't we blossomed, sister?' said Susan, as they sat down to eat.

'I was told it can make a great difference,' said Molly. She leant closer to Susan. 'Diana had a scabbard like hers made for me!'

'Ah, that's good. A proper coming-out gift for a mother to give her daughter. I'm very pleased, and I'm willing to bet Diana's very proud. Congratulations.' Susan touched her lip and flinched. Now was perhaps not the time to approach the subject of Diana's change of status. 'I think we need to talk about men.'

'We do?' replied Molly, a little confused.

'Well,' said Susan, smiling at her charge. 'Perhaps I need to talk about men.'

'I see,' said Molly, playing with as straight a face as she could manage. 'Have you recently kissed a man?'

'Yes, I confess I have done so.'

'Where did you kiss him?' asked Molly, suppressing a giggle as she did so.

'In his chambers.'

'And are you displaying any symptoms?'

'Yes. Breathlessness, absent-mindedness, obsession with minutiae, a feeling of helplessness in the face of it all.'

'Oh dear,' said Molly, 'I don't think this sounds good at all. We may well need to drink some wine.'

'It is the cure for many ailments, indeed. And I need a cure. Because I fear.'

13

Jonny takes pleasure in small revenge

Jonny felt that all was at one with the world as he snaked his way back to Blackfriars, half willing Field to have disobeyed so that he might have Nathaniel teach him a lesson. The other half of him, however, wanted Field fully distracted so that he might put his little money-making scheme into practice. And then there was the serving girl from the Mermaid. He had a plan for her too. He straightened himself, tucked the paper he carried into his jerkin and strode back into Field's as if he owned the place. Maybe he could make enough to start his own, some day? The sight of Field himself, face like thunder, punctured the sunny daydream and brought Jonny back into the cold of a Blackfriars morning.

'I trust you enjoyed your breakfast, Master,' - Field hesitated, as he had no idea what Jonny's surname was - 'Master Come-lately.' The improvisation pleased him and he smiled grimly as he welcomed his temporary master back into the printing-house. 'And be under no illusion, know-it-all,' he spat in a whisper, 'this humiliation will be remembered and returned in Biblical fashion.'

'Vengeance is mine, sayeth the Lord,' said Jonny.

'And I say I shall be avenged sevenfold,' said Field. The two men walked to the press. They resumed their normal speaking volume. 'One stone, ready and waiting for your approval,' said Field.

'Ink it and press it. Bring me the proof, and bring me Jim, too. I will speak with the compositor.' Jonny walked into the corner of the room in which there was a booth that sufficed as an office. He took a quill from the rack, sharpened it and awaited the arrival of the first proof. He put his boots on the table for good measure. Jim walked in.

'Jonny, lad,' said Jim with a wink. 'Funny to see you sat there. Strange enough to see you back. Field is like to explode his fury is so great.' Jim smiled. He, too, had been apprenticed, but to Field's father, Richard. And what they said about fathers and sons was true. Jim had recognised Jonny's potential early, and schooled him in the printer's art when Field was absent, drunk or both.

'It's good to be back,' said Jonny. 'But only because I'm in charge.'

'Be careful, Jonny,' said Jim. 'Field has a long memory, and bears a grudge well.'

'I am beyond his reach now.'

'So long as Master Secretary Thurloe remains in favour, yes. But look to these lines.' He handed Jonny a small scrap of paper covered in letters and numbers. 'Here are the mistakes Field made me insert.'

'Thank you, Jim,' said Jonny, handing him his own paper. 'I need to put this through, as well,' he said.

Jim took the page and scanned it. 'A bill for a chop shop? This is a strange business for the Master Secretary to be involved in.' He looked at Jonny. 'Does governmental service not pay well, Master Jonny?'

'Let's just say I have some extraordinary expenses coming

up, and my change of employ has come with certain added obligations.'

'It'll be a woman, then,' said Jim. 'Hold on, Jonny. Sounds like the proof's dry. I'll get on composing this and keep Field away. When we're up and running he'll to the tavern, and we can press it then.'

Field entered bearing the barely dry broadsheet and laid it on the table. It looked good enough at first sight, but Jonny was not only forewarned but more experienced at the process than Field knew, his education having been largely carried out under cover. Jonny looked at Field, then transferred his attentions to the text. He smiled to himself as he scanned the four pages of the first gathering. There was something wrong. 'This signature is out of sequence,' said Jonny, as he scanned the text itself. 'Eyeskip. Repetition.' He circled a sentence. 'This should read "And the reason why States may proceed in this maner" rather than "And the reason why States may *not* proceed in this maner", as it states here.'

'Are you quite sure, Master Secretary's instrument, or would you like me to fetch your text?' said Field.

'Quite sure, Master Field,' said Jonny. 'After all, I wrote it.' He smiled. 'If I didn't know you better, I'd suspect you of trying to sabotage my position by having me sign off a text incorrect in vital areas.' Jonny looked back at the broadsheet in front of him. 'You are dismissed. I'll bring the corrected proof to the stone when I'm finished.' He signed his name at the top of the broadsheet. 'And I'll be hanging onto this,' he added. 'For old time's sake.'

Field muttered something under his breath, grabbed his coat and stomped off. Jonny was trying not to laugh when Jim walked into the booth once more.

'That was quick,' said the compositor. 'I'll set up your page while you finish the proofs, then?'

'Thank you, Jim. I can adjust the type, though I'd appreciate your casting your eye over it before we go to press,' said Jonny.

'It will be my pleasure,' said Jim, and left Jonny to finish his task.

After half an hour, Jonny was easing the quoins that held the type tightly in its frame, and methodically correcting the errors on the stone, both Field's interventions and the usual typographical hitches. Having finished his work, he called Jim over. Another half hour of tinkering and adjusting, making sure that no errant letter sat proudly, waiting to rip into the sheets of paper that lay in piles, moist and ready to take the kiss of the press to their hearts, and it was time.

'Let 'er rip!' he bellowed. It was hardly the most traditional of beginnings to a print run, but it seemed appropriate that Jonny should use Jim's favourite phrase to start things off.

The run began. The type inked, the broadsheets attached to the frisket, then the moment of impress, when paper and ink became one, before the sheet, now groggy after its ordeal, was hung up to dry. Jonny had always loved this moment, the first pressing. It was a fitting act of creation following on from the painstaking work of writing, editing and setting the text. Jonny was publishing his first book. And it was a delicious feeling. But there were other matters to attend to while he was here. Jim had set Jonny's other text such that he would get sixteen bills per broadsheet. It wouldn't take long to produce what he'd promised, and then to convert them into a winter coat and a more comfortable resting-place for the winter. What he was doing might have appeared to be simple theft, but when Jonny considered the man from whom he stole, and the way he had been treated when apprenticed to him, it seemed far more like the final repayment of a debt accrued over a period of years. In many ways, Jonny felt that Field was getting off lightly.

Even when running Field's two presses at full capacity, and

with two quires printed in an adjacent print shop under Jim's supervision, it was late in the afternoon before the constituent parts of the tract were all drying on the lines in the printing house. As soon as was possible, Jonny took the sheets for one copy down from the lines and folded them into the book he had just printed. He stitched the quires together, trimmed them and wrapped the uncut book in another sheet of paper and wrote a name and address on it. He then took the wrap of silk he had bought with his last coin that very morning, and tied it around the package. He called the latest apprentice, gave him the address and sent him on his way. He then took the bills to the chop shop, exchanged them for ready money, accepted the offer of dinner and returned to Field's press.

His work was almost done.

14

Molly receives a gift

There was a knock on Molly's door. 'Package for you, Molly,' came the voice of one of the other girls. 'Boy downstairs has it. Says he's to see it placed in your hand before he can leave.'

'Did you tell him you were me?' said Molly, looking at Susan as she did so.

'Yes, but he took one look at me, shook his head and said "Molly" at me, like he knew you,' said the voice.

'Alright, Kate,' said Molly. 'I'll be down presently.' She stood and tucked her locket into the collar of her dress so that it hid rather inefficiently in the fold of material. She trotted down the stairs, where a young boy she didn't recognise was waiting. He was clutching a paper package wrapped in a piece of silk. 'I'm Molly. Who sends this to me?' The boy simply looked at Molly, his eyes disbelieving. Molly leant down so that her head was nearer to his. 'I'm Molly,' she repeated. 'Who sent this?'

The boy smiled all of a sudden. 'Molly,' he said, handing her the package. 'For you.'

Molly took the package, but before she could say thank you, the boy was gone. She shrugged her shoulders and went back to her room, where Susan waited, all expectation.

'Well, what was all that about?' asked Susan.

'I have no idea,' said Molly. 'I said I was me, he didn't believe me, so I bent down to tell him again, and he did. He gave me this and ran off.'

'Who was he?'

'I've no idea, but judging by the state of his hands I'd say a printer's boy.'

'Well,' said Susan. 'Don't keep us in suspense. Let's see what all the fuss is about.'

Molly untied the silk, looked at the endorsement and smiled.

'What does it say?' asked Susan.

'To the girl who makes the nightingale sing,' said Molly. She smiled. 'It's from Jonny,' she added.

'Who?' asked Susan.

'Jonny,' said Molly. 'He's apprentice to a printer, and he was in the Mermaid yesterday. He's nice. We chatted.'

'But the nightingale?' asked Susan.

'He saw my locket. I told him it was an heirloom passed down by my late aunt.'

'Good thinking. And this gift comes from his printing-house, presumably?' said Susan.

'Yes. The note says it's nothing as exciting as the story of Philomela but it is the first copy of the first book he has ever been charged with printing.' She smiled, handing the book over to Susan. Susan took it from her and read. Her face fell. 'Oh, come on, Miss Susan,' said Molly, rather confused by her reaction. 'It's such a sweet comment!'

Susan merely shook her head, and read out loud. '*A declaration of His Highnes, by the advice of his council, shewing the reasons of their proceedings for securing peace of the Commonwealth, upon occasion of the late insurrection and rebellion*,' she said. 'It's uncut. Give me a knife, Molly.'

'What?' said Molly, confused. 'It's a gift from an admirer. You can't cut it. It's mine.'

'Oh for heaven's sake, girl,' said Susan. 'Are you blind? The title page has "Hall and Field, printers to His Highness the Lord Protector" emblazoned upon it. Is Cromwell not content with being regicide that he has to declare himself king in all but name? It is but adding to his long list of crimes.' With that, Susan reached across Molly and grabbed her knife. She inserted the blade between the uncut foldings of the first quire and ripped upwards as if disembowelling a deer hung head down after the hunt. She opened the pages and rubbed them flat with the bottom of her hand.

'Susan, please, you're scaring me.'

Susan simply held out her right hand. 'Your Jonny is complicit in the crimes of this man,' she said, and began to read.

'No. He's just an apprentice. He merely works to live.'

'Maybe,' said Susan as she looked up at the young woman in front of her, and kissed her on the forehead.

'Jonny is a good man.'

'You've met him once!' said Susan, in disbelief. She then looked back at the text in front of her and continued to read, slitting each uncut page as it turned into her path, her face darkening as page followed page. 'My God,' she said suddenly. 'They knew it all. They knew everything and were simply waiting for us to move.'

'Susan? What do you mean?'

'Listen to this, Molly,' said Susan, skipping back a few pages. 'The Lord Protector writes that "the Walks of Conspirators, who are a sly and secret Generation of men, are ever in the Dark, and the measure of all their Feet cannot be exactly taken and compared, yet many of their Steps, having been discovered through the goodness of the all-seeing God, We shall set down such part thereof as may be of use to make publicque", meaning that we are watching your every move. But that's not the worst of it, not by any measure.' She skipped forward. 'Ah yes, here we are. The delightful author writes that "the reason why States may proceed in this maner, is, because that which is intended to be Exemplary, for the terrifying men from such Attempts for the future, will not other ways be proportionable to the danger of the past Offence", that is, we will capture you, torture you and kill you. Not for what you have done, but to dissuade you from doing what you may otherwise do in the future.' Susan threw the tract onto the floor.

'Miss Susan!' said Molly, the tears beginning to fall as the man she had imagined Jonny to be fell victim to her sister's ire.

Susan looked at her with something approaching contempt. 'Pull yourself together, girl,' she said, a hard edge in her voice that Molly had not heard before. 'You are a member of the Sisterhood. You do not simper and cry at the first signs of difficulty. You stand up. You are counted. You are not found wanting. Nous sommes la différence.'

'We are the difference,' said Molly.

'That's better. There is much work to be done, Molly, and it is down to us to carry it out.' She paused, trying to reconcile herself with the Susan who had not only kissed Master Secretary Thurloe, but had enjoyed it. 'There is a way,' she said, out loud.

'There is?'

'There is what?'

'You said, "there is a way", what did you mean?'

'Oh, I was talking to myself,' said Susan. 'Shall we take supper here tonight, together?'

'Yes, that would be nice.'

'Remember the hidden drawer in the Mermaid, Molly,' said Susan. 'In extremis, remember the drawer.'

'Yes, I shall,' replied Molly.

'And reply to young Jonny,' said Susan. 'This is plainly a love token. Accept it and get close to him. We may be able to make use of his position with Field. In every setback there is opportunity. Remember that, Molly.'

'Yes, sister.'

Susan stood and readied herself for the outside world. She had feelings for Thurloe, yes, and he was her enemy, yes, and this troubled her, yes. But she realised that she, too, had been presented with a great opportunity. Her feelings were how she would get her job done. They were the reason she would succeed. Ils sont la différence. And, what's more, her loyal service to the cause and the Sisterhood despite her personal attachment merely accentuated her fitness to serve. And serve she would. She would visit him that night, and give him more than a kiss.

'Now, what would Edward think of that?' she said, absent-mindedly. And of the tract, she wondered. Still, winter was here and with the cold and the storms came a lull in active duty, though not for Susan. She would move her lodgings to near Baynard's Castle to prevent her remaining too close to those of her circle. The proximity of Blackfriars also conferred certain other advantages, as the area's population was becoming increasingly fluid, especially now that the theatres were being pulled down and replaced by tenements. And she would prepare Master Secretary John Thurloe for his new role as her intelligencer. She sat down with pen and paper.

15

Thurloe bemoans his fate

Master Secretary Thurloe, Postmaster-General and spymaster for the protectorate, answered to but one person below God, and that was the Lord Protector himself, Oliver Cromwell. Now, it seemed, he was beholden to a woman, also. That this woman was not his wife was a complication he preferred not to consider, but with God, Cromwell and now Susan his position was one of choice - his wife was merely obligation. He did not love her. Their marriage was, like many others, one of convenience. He had loved her predecessor, and now Susan. Susan was like to his first wife, and she both brought back memories and represented the promise of new ones. And now his obligation would separate them, just as Susan and he had moved into a new realm. It seemed most odd to him but it appeared that the turning point in her feelings for him had not been seeing his power, but his vulnerability.

Master Secretary Thurloe, Postmaster-General and spymaster for the protectorate, who, it was said, could pick the lock to the heart of the darkest of men, was increasingly clear about one thing: he did not understand women and likely never would.

'So, Master Secretary Postmaster-General,' said Thurloe, savouring his titles as he sat back in his carriage, and speaking only to himself. 'So, John Thurloe,' he continued. 'Here you sit, leaving the woman you...' - he checked himself - 'Leaving the life that is truly yours in order that you might fulfil your obligation to society.' He looked out of the window at the chaos that was the Thames. 'And to God. And yet he sees fit to present you with a taste of happiness. Just before he reminds you of your proper place.' There was a rapping on the carriage door.

'Master Secretary,' said a breathless Nathaniel. 'I went to your chambers as instructed, with the intent of sending your baggage after you, when I came across this.' He handed a small letter through the open window. 'It was tucked into the gap between the door and its frame. I felt that you would wish to see it immediately.'

Thurloe took the letter from Nathaniel's hand and inspected it. It was sealed with a single blob of wax, which bore the imprint of the letter S. The endorsement read 'John Thurloe, Lincoln's Inn Fields'. He felt for his pocket knife but found nothing. 'Nathaniel, the seal, if you would,' he said, handing it back through the window. 'And be aware that I will like as not be gone for more than a month. Tell Isaac that the chamber is to continue its work, and that he is to send me a compendium of intelligence, by courier, each sennight. I have made provision for Miss Susan to be rewarded for her nursing of me during my attack of the gout. See that the money reaches her.'

'Yes, Master Secretary,' said Nathaniel, handing back the letter, its seal now sliced neatly from its home. 'Our best wishes for the health of your family.'

'Thank you,' said Thurloe, and he rapped on the ceiling of the carriage. 'Let's go.' As the carriage began to move, he unfolded the paper and read out loud.

My deare Iohn,

Words cannot expresse my feelings as my eyes opened this morning. I haue long thought my selfe incapable, since the death of my dear husband. But you, deare Iohn, have awakened this part of me.

I have been struggling with my dutie, too, though I cannot but feel that God has willed us to meet, and as the guardian of my hart it is onlye he that can re-ignite it so.

Since your illnesse the thought has troubled mee greately, whether I commit adultery or no.

Satisfy my consyence, I pray, and I shal lay my seruice at yr feete.

Evr yr deuoted seruant,

Susan

The previous evening had differed markedly from their usual pattern. Typically, they would first eat their fill of his store, drink his wine and sit in front of his fire talking. At no time would the distance between them be forgotten. Not of class nor of position nor of sex. That he, Thurloe, was natural lord and master was unquestioned. He could not easily explain the sudden onset of good humour that had seized him the previous day though he was often left unaccountably cheerful following a successful interrogation. Certainly his men might have found a strange sort of amusement in the way that his fingers had entwined with Susan's in front of the dying embers of his fire that previous evening, and they would likely have commented on his morning's work: he had been busy confirming the confession of a royalist conspirator through the tried and tested method of inserting lighted matches under the man's fingernails. Thurloe could not put his own finger on what had changed between them, but change it most certainly had.

There had been something else that evening, something very different indeed. It wasn't that he remembered the conversation as if they were still deep within it, though he did. It wasn't that he remembered the look in her eyes as if it were burnt onto his, though he did. It wasn't even that he felt her hands in his as if their fingers still entwined, though he did. It was the taste of her lips. Thurloe held the letter to his breast. He could almost feel her heartbeat.

But this was the second letter he had received that day. The first had torn the contentment with which he had awoken from him. Like Icarus, his waxen wings had failed, melted by the heat of the reality that inhered in his wife's illness, which had worsened since he had first been advised of it, that morning when he had awoken pain-free, with Miss Susan asleep at the foot of his chair. Now his responsibility as husband and father drew him back to the Fens. It drew him back to the life that he had been pretending was not still his. It drew him back to his family outside of the Black Chamber.

He watched the streets of London stream past his carriage and wondered how long it would be before he could return to where he truly belonged.

16

Jonny's work pays dividends

'I take it you received your present?' said Jonny, as he waited for Molly to pour his ale.

'Yes, Jonny, and thank you,' said Molly. 'I was going to write a thank you note this evening but, well…'

'You'd rather thank me in person?'

'Yes, well, now that you're here,' said Molly, letting a smile slip out that Jonny felt down to his toes. She leant across the table, so that Jonny could almost touch her lips and, as she filled his cup, whispered to him. 'I'm going to spill your ale. Swear, throw your cup over me and leave.' Jonny looked at her, too distracted by her lips to quite understand what she was saying. 'I'll see you down the alleyway in a few minutes.' And then she poured ale all over the table. Jonny sat there, still a little confused, until Molly shot him a pained smile.

'Stupid woman!' shouted Jonny out of nowhere as he stood up, knocking his stool over. He picked up his cup and threw the contents directly at Molly's face, but didn't quite hit his target, hitting her neck instead. He turned and left, aware of some commotion behind him but ignoring it. He turned out of the tavern and ducked down the alley and waited. And waited.

It was the softest, most welcoming of kisses, and she tasted of strawberries. 'I suppose that answers that question, then,' he said as they finally drew apart, lips still wet, tongues still poised and ready to begin again.

'Which question is that?' she said, drawing away slightly so she could see his eyes properly. Their hands still touched.

Jonny looked at Molly as she looked at him. 'Whether you liked your gift or not. That question.'

'I think so.' Her dress was soaking and Jonny was doing his best not to stare. 'Look. I need to change and they'll notice if I take too long, so look lively and follow me.' With this she took off. Jonny hesitated for a second but then followed. He followed as she ducked through a small window opening and into the Mermaid's rather higgledy-piggledy insides.

'Where are you taking me?' asked Jonny as they scampered up a set of stairs.

Molly stopped, turned and looked at him as if he were simple. 'My room. Where else?' she said. And she opened the door. Jonny hopped inside. Molly followed, shut it and leant against it. She looked at Jonny and beamed once again. 'Tell me again what you were saying about my lips, Jonny,' she said, grabbing his shirt and pulling him towards her.

'I didn't say anything about them,' said Jonny, confused. 'I...' But Molly was one step ahead of him.

'Shhh,' said Molly, placing her finger to his mouth. 'Perhaps you'd better kiss me again before I change my mind.' She leant towards him and turned her head just a little. Their lips met, parted, and met again. Jonny felt as though his heart would burst. Then Molly pushed him away and started to take off her dress. She stopped and looked at him, her smile turning into a frown. 'Jonny, avert your eyes! You are my Redcrosse knight, not the john of some speckled minx.' And they both burst into laughter.

Jonny took the opportunity to inspect Molly's room as she dealt with her ale-soaked dress. It was as sparse as could be imagined; the only items that stood out were the unbound quires he had sent her, which had been cut, and a leather tube that had buckles on one side. He picked up the tube. 'Whatever is this?' he said, but Molly took it from him, putting it straight back in the chest. 'Oi, I was looking at that!' he said, somewhat put out.

'It's just a leather armlet; it helps to steady my hand when I'm working. It's a sort of brace, a support, yes, a support,' said Molly. 'Nothing exciting.' She turned him round again. 'It's rude to stare.'

Jonny waited patiently. As patiently as a man who'd just kissed - no, been kissed - by a beautiful woman who was now semi-naked and but a yard from him could wait. Then her hands were over his eyes and he could feel the damp of her dress pressing into his back and her hot breath on his neck.

'Don't turn around, just listen, Redcrosse, as I must go back to work,' she said, in a voice that dripped into his ears like honey. 'And tomorrow I must tend to my uncle's affairs. I will be away for a few weeks. If you'd like to write to me while I'm away I'd be happy to return the favour,' she said. 'In English, if you please. Leave your letters with the innkeeper, she'll get them to me. Wait here for a few minutes and then leave.' And with that, Molly was gone.

Jonny stood, confused, elated and overflowing with every other emotion he could think of as he waited to leave.

In the chest, poking out of its leather harness, Molly's stiletto winked at him in the candlelight.

17

Thurloe reads

Miss Susan, Covent Garden, by the sign of the Raven

My deare Susan,

I received your last of November 14th instant as I was leaving the cittie, there being urgent matters that demanded my time of me, though I was wont to remaine close to you. It was not in my power to informe you of my travels. But you can only guess at how your words warmed my very soul. It may seeme as if I run from you just as youre hart is open to mine but I assure you this is far from the case.

I almost wish another attack of the gout that I may employe you as nurse once more. I still marvel at how you and Sir Francis together did render a ready cure for me. Would that he might tell how to release those hostages to fortune that keep me from your side.

I knowe that I, too, sinne in thought and deede but cannot but think that God would not render such purity and beauty as I finde in you and yet warrant it evil.

My consyence is yet clear, and I hope and pray that yours does not see fit to trouble you on these winter evenings.

If you wouldst write to me direct your mail to my chambers at Lincoln's Inn. Endorse your packet J.T., nothing more.

I am ever at your mercie,

John

Enclosed in a letter addressed to Anthony Hinton, Apothecary

Sister,

We both are prey to distance and absence, my being away from both you and RC who are, besides D, my dearest frends on this earth, and you from your own J. Needs must wee beleve in that old saying about its strengthening of harts and forging of bonds.

My second training proceedeth right well, and I am granted muche in the way of prayse for my dedication. My instructors asserte me as a credit to both my earthly mothers, and that I have in me the best qualities of you both. I pray that I might make you both proude in all that I may accomplishe in service when I doe take orders.

Evr yr deuoted sister,

M

Mr D'Esmond, Paris

Sir,

I pray this findes you in good healthe and hale, and that the travails you spake on in yours of October 20 haue left you and your house undimmed. I haue myself been troubled with misfortunate days, and sleepless nights, and must tell you that for all I have attended the market most euery euening, still there is no new merchandise either on display or under the tablecloth. I haue made euery entreatie to the shopkeeper but to no avail. I thinke that where once he did cheat vs, he now prefers to do business with others. He also has gone abroad, and while I thinke not that he taketh our custom in vaine, it seeme he prefereth to keep his stock until the market is highe.

You are euer in my prayers and may God keepe you safe in the knowledge of his loue and of mine, who is euer your most humble seruant,

S.H.

Molly, by way of the Mermaid

My darling Molly,

I wrote you a sonnett. The most nice and beauteous of the poetic forms, it seem'd thusly the most auspicious maner in wh^{ch} *to blazon my feelings. Poesy is the highest of the artes - it is name stems from the Greeke poein, to make. But your beauty is beyond my meager skil to expres, if not beyond the forme itself.*

Know only that each night I spende without you is torment, and myne onlye solace is that the bird that sings unseen is heartie yet, just as my hart can do nothing but stare into the depths of my loneliness.

Sing, muse, of the girl that the nightingale takes as its tune.

I have no more than this: but more you have no need of.

With all expectation of holding you in my arms again this twelfth night.

Ever your servant,

Jonny

18

Thurloe is caught in a trap

'John,' came the voice from the other end of the house. 'There is a man to see you.'

John Thurloe sat at his desk, his account books spread out in front of him, the rest of its surface covered with transcripts of letters sent to him by Isaac. In the weeks since his return to his family he had busied himself with local minutiae. His family's affairs, and, indeed, those of every family of note near Wisbech, were in the most scrupulous order as he sought to bury his sin with hard work. December had proved a most unpleasant month and the seasonal flooding had returned, washing away lines of communication and all but cutting him off from his other home that was in Whitehall. He stood and walked to the kitchen where his wife, as hale and hearty as she had been when he arrived three short weeks previously, was fussing over the mud-caked courier who stood, dripping with rain, in the middle of the room. It was the first delivery he had received for over a sennight.

'My wife appears to have things in hand, Alfred, is it?' said Thurloe.

'Yes, Master Secretary,' said Alfred. 'Good of you to remember. The roads are uncommon difficult, and the journey has taken several days.'

'Well. You must rest here for a day at the very least while I prepare answers to those missives you bring.' Thurloe took the bag Alfred had brought and sifted through its contents, muttering to himself as he did so and cuffing one of his children gently on the back of his head as he grabbed at the strap. 'Joshua, no!' he said, and as his fingers landed on one of the packets they paused. This package bore within it some child of its own. He turned to his wife. 'Furnish Alfred with anything he needs, and find him a clean bed. I must work through these papers ere I can allow him to leave.'

'Yes, John,' said his wife. 'I will call when supper is ready.'

'Have it brought up to me,' said Thurloe. 'I will dine with my duty this evening.'

'And which duty will that be, husband?' replied his wife. Thurloe simply stared at her for a few seconds before disappearing up the stairs, his footfall uncharacteristically heavy. There had been a time when his wife would have felt the full force of his anger at her open challenge, but with distance from Susan came the recognition of his guilt. It was, however, a guilt he appeared, if not to relish, then at the very least one he refused to address.

Thurloe sat back into his chair with a thump. His left foot was beginning to ache once more. He tore at the letter. It was from Isaac, and it detailed the various interceptions made, the transcripts sent and carried by the courier and the minor plots uncovered therein, the double agents installed. None of this registered as Thurloe grasped at the enclosure that it contained. It bore the letters J.T., nothing else.

'Susan,' he said to himself and he held the packet tightly, offering up a prayer as he did so. There was a knock at his door. He palmed the packet and shifted his weight on his chair. 'Come,' he said. The door opened and his wife walked in bearing a tray.

'Your supper, husband,' she said, setting the tray down on an oaken chest as she spoke. 'Will you be working late tonight?'

'In truth, I believe I must.'

'What is truth?' she said, turned, and left.

Thurloe sat in silence for a moment, then opened the letter.

My dearest John,

While it pains me to write with such secrecie I also finde it strangely exciting. I feel like a she-spie, on a secrete mission of the greatest danger and importance: to discover and capture the hart of the feared John Thurloe.

In truthe I am much vexed by this winter cold, and long to sit and warm myself by your fire.

I thanke you for the consideration, and while I do nothing with you for anie reward but your respect and love, the monies Nathaniel passed to me have been put to greate use.

In haste, as your mercury awaits.

Ever yrs,

Susan

John Thurloe refolded the letter and walked to the fire, hobbling very slightly. He took a draught of his wine. Too late to ask for Bacon's receit, he thought to himself. But then again, was it the treatment or was it the nurse? Which had effected his recovery? He sat down once more and tucked the letter into a small drawer in his desk. He picked up the letter within which Isaac had conveyed Susan's words.

Master Secretary,

In truth there is little to report. S.H. writes once more to mr D'Esmond of Paris, though merely to complain of some recalcitrant merchant. There are whispers of a new conspiracy abroad but as yet no matter. One of the Swordsmen, the Irish, has returned to the continent while the other remains we know not where. Chase delivers little, though we beleeve we have identified another of their postmen. Manning, who served us well, is uncovered and forfeited his life. Field makes more noise than action and we have employed nurse Alkin to sniff out a newe presse that vexes us.

All other information is included in the transcripts.

Your servant,

I. Dorislaus

Thurloe began to eat. It was going to be a dark and unpleasant winter.

III

I

March 1656
Thurloe's mood darkens

'It is perhaps time you made an honest woman out of young Molly,' said Thurloe, as he paced about the chamber. 'It's been three months at least, has it not?'

'Yes, Master Secretary, almost. But she will not take a husband, she says.'

'Then she will remain a common slut, Jonny,' said Thurloe. Jonny stood up, bristling.

'Peace, Jonny, peace,' said Isaac. 'For one thing you play outside of your court, and for another Master Secretary means merely in terms of the law.' He redirected his attention. 'Does he not, Master Secretary?'

'It is the law as it stands,' said Thurloe. 'If she will not marry, then perhaps she might find value in a short sojourn to the country, to visit an aunt, where she could find herself married and sadly widowed in quick succession. Thus she might hold property in her "own" name, so to speak.'

'And where, Master Secretary, might she find a spouse who has the good grace to pass away within weeks of their wedding?' asked Jonny.

'These things are not my affair, but I'm sure you might

discover a parish where neither Church nor State stand in the way of business, if you looked hard enough.'

'Master Secretary,' said Jonny. 'Are you recommending that I needs must pay two bribes, to the man of God and his parson, though they are one and the same?'

'How dare you suggest such a thing of me?' said Thurloe. 'I say merely that it is not unknown in certain places.' The chamber quietened as the two seated men continued about their business, and the third paced behind them. 'I find it hard to believe that there are no plots being hatched, Isaac. Why is it that we uncover so little these days?'

'I truly cannot say, Master Secretary,' said Isaac, prising the seal off a letter so roughly that it cracked. Thurloe stopped pacing and leant over Isaac's chair.

'Isaac?' said Thurloe.

'Yes, Master Secretary?'

'You do understand the work that we do here, Isaac?' replied Thurloe, as he picked up the letter that had just received such loving attention.

'Yes, Master Secretary. We open, inspect and copy letters as they pass through our hands.'

'And then we reseal them and send them on their way such that the addressee has no inkling that we are hanging on their every word, so that their words might hang them.' At this he threw down the mangled paper onto the table and clipped the seated man around the ear. 'Isaac, dear Isaac, one of the Winter Queen's monkeys could do a neater job. You'd make a better butcher.'

'Yes, Master Thurloe,' said Isaac. 'I'll look into it right away.'

'Don't be an idiot, Isaac. I wonder perhaps our prey has realised that we are watching them. We shall seek assistance. I know a certain Samuel Morland who boasts the skills you lack.'

'Yes, Master Secretary,' said Isaac. 'Shall I make enquiries?'

'It's almost as if you read my mind on occasion, Isaac. Bring him to me. We need to play our game harder.'

'I shall acquire another chair also, Master Secretary,' said Isaac. The door swung open. The wet chill of winter was yet to dispel, and it became a swirling oppressive chill as Nathaniel entered the room. 'Kindly shut the door smartly, Nathaniel. The chamber was almost warm until you arrived.'

'Yes, Isaac, and I will refresh the fire,' said Nathaniel. 'I trust you have not yet seen this, Isaac?'

'And what might "this" be, my good man?' said Isaac.

'Merely a response to your tract, I mean, our Lord Protector's tract, of last year, and by none other than Sir Edward Hyde,' said Nathaniel. 'Sent direct to Master Secretary Thurloe. We can only assume that he means to publish. I suspect the Protector will not be best pleased.'

On this, Nathaniel handed the letter to Isaac, who inspected it.

'Isaac,' said Thurloe, 'read it out, man.'

'Very well. It goes by this title, to whit, *A Letter from a true and lawfull member of Parliament, and One faithfully engaged with it, from the beginning of the War to the End. To one of the Lords of his Highness Councell, upon occasion of the last Declaration, shewing the Reasons of their proceedings for securing the Peace of the Commonwealth, published on the 31st of October 1655*, as wordy a title as the work to which it makes its reply. It witters on about the executions of traitors, and...'

'Give it here, man,' said Thurloe, snatching it from Isaac's grasp. He mumbled through the text, then paused, and spoke. '"Trust me," says Hyde, "you have gotten nothing by those Spectacles, and men return from them more confirmed in detestation of you, then terrified from any of their purposes towards you," he continues, suggesting that "if they shall perish in or upon their Attempt, what a Glorious Fame will they leave behind them? what a sweet Odour will their Memories have with the present and succeeding Ages," because obviously, the traitors are concerned with immortal fame. Immortal infamy, perhaps. But he continues thus, "Statues will be erected to them, and their Names recorded in those Roles, which have preserved the *Bruti*, the *Horatii*, the *Fabii*, and all those who have dyed out of debt to their Country, by having paid the utmost that they owed to it." Now isn't that sweet?' he said. 'I think Hyde wants us to martyr these traitors. Well, we ought not be so churlish as to disobey a "true and lawfull member of Parliament", now ought we?' He threw the letter down on the table. 'Find me some new traitors to martyr,' he said, 'preferably boasting the name "Hyde". Then Sir Edward can list their names when he publishes.' And he left, leaving his words resounding around the chamber.

2

The Black Chamber confers

'I feel Master Secretary's mood is not as we would wish it,' said Isaac. 'I will summon this Morland fellow. We shall see if he can improve matters.'

'Or he may bear the worst of it on our behalf,' said Jonny. 'He ought not have said that about Molly. Think it he is serious?'

'Perhaps not, but you are practically living as man and wife, Jonny,' said Nathaniel.

'If a husband's lot is to crawl into his bed through a window only accessible by climbing over the roof of the adjacent whorehouse, then yes,' said Jonny. 'Practically man and wife, as you say.'

'Is the roof not icy?' asked Nathaniel. 'Or does the heat of your lust melt all before it?'

'I do wish you two were less interested in my evening entertainments,' said Jonny. 'A man has to keep some things private, you know.'

'It is merely because we have none to call our own, Jonny,' said Isaac. 'Jealousy, pure, unadulterated jealousy.'

'Speak for yourself, Isaac,' said Nathaniel, laughing.

'Indeed, Nathaniel?' said Isaac with a snort. 'And the name of the poor unfortunate?'

'Well,' said Nathaniel, 'there's Anna, Bethany, Charlotte, Erica...'

'No one for the letter "D", good Nathaniel?' said Jonny. 'For shame, you are a disgrace to the menfolk of the Black Chamber, with your inability to provide suitable material for an Abecedarium d'Amour.'

'In truth you are both never so witty, but none of this will help us in our current predicament,' said Isaac.

'Though they may prove succour if Master Secretary's mood should blacken further,' said Nathaniel. 'May we not simply arrest a Hyde and trouble them for an explanation?'

'We cannot simply walk about the city arresting anyone with the name Hyde,' said Isaac.

'Whyever not?' said Jonny. 'In fact, it's a most excellent plan.'

'It is?' said Isaac. 'Why so? Convince me and we shall do so without pause.'

'Well,' said Jonny. 'We know, or at least, we suspect, that those we seek are aware, or at least suspicious, of their post being less private than perhaps they might have hoped.'

'That is correct,' said Isaac.

'It follows that they are using other methods to allow their letters free access to their circles. So they must be using individual couriers.'

'But we know that. Chase is one such.'

'But he is quiet, again as if he suspects,' said Jonny. 'Let us widen the net, and simultaneously make some arrests, but almost at random. That will make them think we have information.'

'Or that we are clutching at straws,' said Isaac.

'No,' said Nathaniel. 'Jonny's right. They'll think we have new information, and their habits will change, which will inconvenience them and perhaps make them visible.'

'Or they'll be emboldened, thinking we know nothing,' said Jonny.

'Either way, a change in habit may expose their secret ways,' said Nathaniel.

'We hold the candle under the letter,' said Isaac.

'And the invisible is made visible,' said Jonny.

3

Susan takes stock

'Anthony,' said Susan. 'Are we stocked with cordial?'

'Alas, stores run somewhat low,' said the apothecary. 'As does our store of communications.'

'Indeed, since the rumours of the Spanish coming to the aid of Charles Stuart there has been little traffic. Think you that it is intercepted?'

'Perhaps, but I do have one for Mr Gotherintone, and one for Mrs Simburbe, if you would care to peruse them.' As the apothecary handed over the letters, Susan grimaced. 'Are you quite well, Miss Susan?' he asked, as she slit the first letter open. 'There is also the small matter of a hat box.'

'Cousin Lowes, yes,' said Susan. 'I will deal with that situation presently. But this cold is too much for me.' She unfolded the letter and read it out.

Mr Gotherintone

I want 5 yrds of ye finest Gray cloth cane bee had to send my sonne into France if you will deliuer so much to the bearer of this one yr word, and make choise of the best mixt Gray you haue you shall not faill of yr mony at Michaelmase next, this I beleiue you will doe when I remember you trusted mee in a greater concerne, and I faild you not, nor will I now that ame

yr freind

K. Ayliffe

'Is it merely the cold, Miss Susan?' asked the apothecary.

'I believe so,' said Susan. 'I wonder is it not time to consider visiting my aunt for some respite?' Susan's aunt, however, would ask more questions of her than even the good apothecary. If the weeks when John was away had been difficult, she found that since he had returned, his excess of choler was proving most unpleasant. Or perhaps it was she, Susan, who acted out of turn. She had been ill these past three days, however, and so had not visited Lincoln's Inn. Was she failing in her duty? If so, to whom?

'Respite from the cold?' said Molly. 'Or does your charge become sudden demanding?'

'Demanding of what, Molly?' said Susan.

'Your favour, Miss Susan, your favour,' said Molly. 'It seems to have stirred Jonny's blood, that is for certain. He climbs through my casement most every night.'

'Molly, that I do not need to know,' said Susan.

'I mean it as it is said,' replied Molly, laughing. 'He climbs through my casement in a very literal sense.' She leant closer to Susan, and whispered in her ear. 'And then...'

'I do not want to hear,' said Susan, standing. 'I must get Kate's "gray cloth" ready for delivery.'

'The usual arrangement with Mr Shaw?' asked the apothecary.

'Yes,' said Susan, 'but I must speak first with our supporters. The gold is not so easily acquired in winter - the cold makes people tighten up - and the dates on these letters suggest no little interference. This was sent some time ago. There is something in the air. I will write to cousin James, inform him of my imminent progress. But I will obfuscate in case my letters are intercepted. We can be clear that only Anthony here has safe passage.'

'Miss Susan?' said Molly, her concern clear in her voice as her sister sat down heavily, looking pale.

'I am not myself, no,' said Susan. 'I shall visit Kate and take the air. March can be a trying month.' At this she took the second letter in hand. 'Ah, dear brother,' she said, her tone betraying her distaste for what she believed was inside. 'Are you to berate your common strumpet of a sister for not performing her squalid duties efficiently enough?'

'You must not talk of yourself in those terms,' said Molly.

'You may leave us, Anthony,' said Susan, 'but pray you supply some more mint, for my stomach ails me.'

'Yes, Miss Susan,' he said, and left the room. Susan recommenced reading.

'Molly,' she said. 'My brother is a pretty piece of work. Good God he's a pretty piece of work.' She held the letter by her side. 'Have you any spirits, Molly?'

'Some brandy wine, if you're of a mind.'

'I most definitely am. And you will comprehend my reasons right presently.' Susan waited while Molly reached into her bag and took out a small bottle, took a swig, shrugged at Susan and passed it to her. Susan took two big swigs and handed the bottle back.

'Well? I trust this will be worth it.'

'Indeed it will,' said Susan. 'Firstly I was correct. He does not explicitly berate me for being an adultress so much as for forcing him to carry the knowledge that his sister is fundamentally incompetent when it comes to her job as intelligencer. After all, it's one thing having a common adultress in the family if she is extracting vital secrets from the enemy, quite another if she appears simply to be a common adultress.' Susan took back Molly's bottle and drank off some more of the brandy wine. 'This is typical Edward. Never one to attend to the beam when there's a mote on offer. How does my darling brother think his precious court can get its daily bread if not through me? Through Shaw? How does he think I keep our post flowing, what post there is, if not through working each and every day?'

'Is there a secondly?'

'Oh my. Is there ever?'

It was Molly's turn to drink.

'You remember that tract of Cromwell's your Jonny was so kind as to give you, gift wrapped, last winter?' asked Susan.

'Yes,' said Molly. 'I still have it safely stored in my chest.'

'Well,' said Susan. 'Darling brother in his most infinite wisdom has taken it upon himself to pen a response, thus both dignifying and justifying Cromwell's argument.' She sighed. 'Worse than that, young Molly, is that in it he positively invites Cromwell to create more martyrs. It's almost as if he wants us to be caught, seeing as we're achieving little other than turning Sir Edward Hyde's sister into a common whore. He intends to publish it presently, and I doubt that he will listen to my opinion. After all, I am merely a woman.'

'This may not end well.'

'It rarely does,' said Susan. 'It rarely does. I will to the country. Bring me paper and ink.'

4

The Black Chamber expands

'Whom do we have on our list we could arrest, just a little, as a shot across the bows, so to speak?' said Isaac, as he, Jonny and Nathaniel sat in the Three Suns, contemplating lunch on a day that was so cold that time appeared to have slowed down, much like the horses that felt the full weight of their burden as their hooves cracked through the sheets on icy puddles to the freezing mud below.

'There's Chase,' suggested Nathaniel, 'the one given up by that drunken, poxy whore we caught last year.'

'Who we've been following successfully for weeks,' said Jonny, 'and we're not about to kill that goose quite yet. Not till he's laid us at least one egg.'

'He is but one of a great number of subtle and sly fellows in and about the City, who are paid by a common purse of that respective faction by whom they are employed, whose daily business is it to go laden with intelligence, and instructions,' said Isaac. 'We cannot take them piecemeal. We must swoop on them altogether.'

'Especially that other apothecary, what's his name again?' asked Jonny.

'Hinton, yes,' said Isaac. 'He's particularly slippery.'

'Do we know their schedules, Isaac?' asked Nathaniel.

'They seem to change on an irregular basis,' said Isaac. 'So allow me to propose that we set a man on each, and give the man on Hinton a runner. When Hinton leaves town next, the runner informs us, then Chase's man, and we take Chase here knowing Hinton will be apprehended with all his packets. We just have to pray that they're interesting.'

'I will take Hinton,' said Nathaniel. 'Who will take Chase?'

'I shall,' said a bewigged figure who stood behind Nathaniel's chair. Nathaniel stood and stared at the man, who appeared not to be as perturbed as he ought to have been.

'You are amongst company that neither suits nor desires yours, sir,' said Nathaniel. 'I recommend that you take your leave immediately.'

'And should I refuse?' replied the man, leaning nonchalantly on a metal cane.

'I will give it to you, sir,' said Nathaniel. The menace in both his voice and his stance cleared the adjacent table, though none reckoned the stranger with a prayer, even if his cane contained a blade of some sort.

'I'm sure you would,' said the man. 'Master Secretary told me to be wary of you, Nathaniel.'

'He is a wise man,' replied Nathaniel, the menace falling from him as quickly as it had risen. 'I imagine, then, that you are Samuel Morland.'

'You imagine correctly,' said Morland. 'At your service.' He looked around the table. 'Might I squeeze in?'

Morland sat between Jonny and Isaac, across from Nathaniel. The innkeeper, who had seen the potential for trouble and had gone to the table to defuse it, now merely stood by, a sitting target for a thirsty man. 'Ah, innkeeper, might I trouble you for some sack?'

'Sack?' replied the innkeeper. 'Where do you think you are, sir?'

'I heard tell this was a tavern, dedicated to the distribution of beverages of an alcoholic nature in return for donations of coins of the realm. Sack is such a beverage, so kindly source some and bring it to me.' With this he threw a coin in his direction.

'Jenny,' said the innkeeper, addressing one of the more buxom of his staff. 'Get yourself to the Mitre and ask Jim for a jug or two of sack. He knows I'm good for it.'

'You see, gentlemen,' said Morland. 'Authority and gold will get you anything.' He smiled and took out a pipe, stuffed some tobacco in the bowl and lit it with a taper. 'We are charged, I believe, with expediting matters, no?'

'Indeed, Master Morland,' said Jonny.

'Sir Samuel, if you please,' replied Morland. 'And, as you will discover presently from the mouth of Master Secretary Thurloe, I am, from this moment, chief of operations for our little office.' He smiled once more, and drew a key from his pocket. 'Which will, I believe, be relocating in the very near future.' He returned the key to its resting place, placed his hands on the table and looked at the three men in turn. 'I believe we lack material evidence on which we may act. I also believe I have a solution.'

'Do go on, Sir Samuel,' said Isaac, his words crawling with contempt.

'Dr James Hyde,' said Morland. 'Sir Edward's cousin.' He paused while from behind him a jug and a pewter mug appeared. 'Why thank you, Penny.'

'Jenny,' said the girl, but her frown dissolved in the sustained assault of Morland's attentions and an actual penny besides.

Morland drank deeply. 'Now, where was I? Oh yes,' he continued before his question could be answered, 'Dr James Hyde.' He took another deep draught. 'His arrest would send a suitably personal message to Sir Edward, even if we release him after a few days. And if we're lucky we'll catch him in possession of a letter or two.'

'Are we to presume you know his tailor?' said Isaac.

'As a matter of fact I do,' said Morland. 'John Honyatt of Boar's Head Alley, Fleet Street. Though I fail to see how that fact is pertinent in any way.'

Nathaniel stood up, wearily. 'Well, I suppose I'll go and knock on Dr Hyde's door,' he said. 'I don't suppose you have anything useful such as his address, by any chance?' Morland shook his head. 'That's why we must know his tailor, Sir Samuel.' He surveyed the men sitting at the table. 'Come on Jonny, Isaac, we haven't got all day. I don't know about you, but I've always wanted my own tailor.'

Morland made to stand up and join them but Jonny placed his hand on his shoulder, arresting his movement. 'Why keep a pack of dogs and course the hare yourself, Sir Samuel? Stay and enjoy the conviviality of the Three Suns. We shall return with information.' With that he joined his two companions and they left the inn, Nathaniel turning to the innkeeper as they did so.

'Sir Samuel will clear up our slate,' he said. 'Privilege of rank.' He smiled at Morland with a look that made it clear that he knew Morland was yet to receive his title.

Boar's Head Alley was only a short walk away and while Honyatt was at first angry to be drawn away from his meal and then perturbed on realising in whose name he had been so drawn, he was relieved to discover that all that was necessary for him to return to his dinner was the small matter of a client's address. That and the promise of an extra discount for Nathaniel and his two friends should they require new clothing, which they most assuredly did.

James Hyde, however, went from perturbed to scared to unconscious in double-quick time, and from there to a rather poorly appointed prison cell. While Nathaniel booked him into his new lodgings, Isaac and Jonny returned to the inn. There they found Morland, drunk as the lord he would some day become. They escorted him back to the chamber, where they were soon employed in reading a series of very interesting letters while Morland snored in the corner.

5

Thurloe's mood worsens

Master Secretary John Thurloe sat in his chambers and waited. The winter had been cold, and appeared in no hurry to change its mind. It was too cold to open a window or door unless egress was necessary, so while the usual stench of an overpopulated London was kept at bay, it was reproduced in microcosm in every building as woodsmoke, tallow, sweat and the noxious emissions caused by unfortunate eating habits simply picked up fresh pollutions with every circuit of the rooms within. With the only wind for days being that generated by the city's inhabitants, it was a small mercy that the chill made Thurloe's nose run, as it insulated him from the worst of the unpleasantness. Still, he mused, it wasn't all bad. It was not as though such weather led him to expect the sounding of the bells that announced the arrival of the scourge of Europe's cities, the plague.

He hadn't seen Susan for almost a week. It seemed that every time he had invited her to supper he had ended up sending her a last-minute cancellation. His mood was blackening in almost direct proportion to his desire, the former not being helped by a series of letters from his wife that detailed the glorious existence his family were enjoying in the Fens, inclemency notwithstanding, while simultaneously indicating her increasing displeasure at the length of his absence. He had tried explaining to her that his position necessitated his residing in the capital, even in the cold of winter, when it was likely that those who plotted against the Lord Protector would make an error of judgement, their desire to take action heating their blood as much as the season frustrated their intentions. He had seen the opposite effect the previous year when he had taken the turncoat Gennings, even if her whereabouts had remained a mystery to him since, as her testimony had allowed him to dismantle one conspiracy and infiltrate another. It was ever an irony Thurloe enjoyed, the fact that in the heat of high summer the spirit is inspired to bold if not foolhardy action while the body wishes simply to lie down and let the heat wash over it, while in winter the desire to act was partially impelled by the impossibility of doing so. His wife, however, was unmoved by such arguments. And so tonight, while Thurloe's spirit wished to shake the tree and harvest the conspirators he knew were gathering in its branches, he knew that the fruit still ripened, that their time was not yet. While his spirit wished him to act to smooth away the guilt that washed over him, his body craved Miss Susan.

Tonight there was no need to cancel; tonight Thurloe sat and waited for his lover, a platter of food on his table, a jug of wine besides. Tonight she had not arrived by the six o'clock watch, nor the seven. Thurloe was beginning to lose patience. And he was beginning to run out of wine. There was a knock at his door. His impatience vanished and he stood to allow Miss Susan in. At the door stood Nathaniel.

'Good God, man,' said Thurloe. 'I am busy. Begone with you. Whatever it is can wait until the morrow.'

Nathaniel opened his mouth to respond, but Thurloe simply slammed the door in his face. Nathaniel knew better than to protest further. Instead he traipsed back to the chamber, where the letter-reading was in full flow, wrote out a quick note and then, thinking better of it, threw it into the bucket that held all waste paper.

Thurloe, meanwhile, his mood back to blackening again, poured himself a cup of wine and drained it. Followed by another. And another. And a twinge in his groin. There was something untoward, too, something that sat in the back of his mind like a toad; squat, ugly, venomous. It might have been weeks ago, but it still rankled. Thurloe was by nature a close man. Exact. Tidy. Consistent. He looked about the room, and it was suddenly as plain as yesterday. The panel. It was wrong. It hadn't quite fitted since... surely, he thought to himself, Susan would never... And it was then that she appeared.

'Your door was open, John,' said Susan. 'I felt it not presumptuous to enter unannounced.' She crouched by his side.

'You're late,' said Thurloe, slurring his words just a little.

'The world waxes ill and I am busy,' said Susan. 'But I am here now, am I not?'

'I have waited on you these past two hours, woman.'

'Soft, John. This is not the John Thurloe I know and...' she hesitated.

'Yes, Miss Susan? Know and cozen?'

'I beg your pardon?' said Susan, standing once more. 'You are in your cups, Master Secretary. Shame on you to speak to me thus.'

'I will speak to you howsoever I please, woman!' his voice rose in volume as he spoke. 'I will speak to you howsoever I please.'

'Well, Master Secretary. You do have that right, indeed. But you shall find in that case that I exercise my right not to listen.'

Thurloe grabbed Susan by the wrist and pulled her towards him. 'I commit adultery for you,' he said, almost snarling. 'I do not expect to be gainsaid.'

'You wish for meek and mild? Get thee to Wisbech,' said

Susan. 'You will find you one there.' She ripped her wrist free of his grip. 'Your adultery is not my concern. It is for you and your conscience alone to consider.' She knocked the jug of wine from the table. 'Sober up, Master Secretary. You commit adultery for yourself. I have a higher purpose.'

6

Susan fears

With her last words stinging her lips, Susan turned and walked directly to the Mermaid. She had worked so hard and for so long with John that she had quite forgotten herself. She was Susan Hyde. She was une fille d'Ophélie. And yet she reacted to Thurloe's mood as if she were a man. She had a charge, and she had carried out that charge well. Too well. She had spoken to Thurloe as if they were equal, not he the spymaster, she the spy. He was too sharp, even when in his cups and with the dark clouds gathering about his soul, to fail to notice Susan's final rebuke. He would investigate. And that investigation could reach but one conclusion.

She entered the Mermaid, where she found Molly, not yet retired to her lodgings.

'Does Jonny visit you tonight?' said Susan.

'It is most likely, Miss Susan, why?'

'I have made an error and must leave immediately, I cannot wait a night, let alone a sennight,' said Susan. 'Send word that you wax ill. Go to my lodgings at Baynard's Castle and pack everything into my chest. I shall attend you at your lodgings. Take no risks. If there appear to be strangers acting strangely in the vicinity, then leave straightways. If I have uncovered myself, it shall only be myself I have uncovered. I will give them means to find me such that they may not therefore seek my accomplices.' Susan sat down heavily. 'I feel unwell. Did Anthony bring more peppermint? Remember the drawer. Ask him for his extract of exotic fish.'

'I will discover some on my travels,' said Molly as she pulled up the left sleeve of her dress and buckled up her leather scabbard. 'Have no fear, sister,' she added, kissing her locket. 'I will see you safe or die in the attempt.'

Molly kissed Susan on the forehead and disappeared into the night. Susan sat waiting for the wave of nausea to finish with her. She was beginning to think that she had perhaps been overconfident with regard to the security of their post. It was beginning to seem impossible that it was not compromised. She was even beginning to wonder whether John wasn't using her. Perhaps he had known from the very start. If that were the case, she was in a great deal of trouble.

7

The Black Chamber awakes

'Dr Hyde has certainly been a busy man,' said Isaac, as he filed the last of the letters. 'But he would have done well to have filed these elsewhere, if he meant not to destroy them. Sadly they tell us little we do not already know. Other than perhaps his mother is over-fond of the bottle.'

'It struck me at first that it might have been code but at the last it did seem rather too rambling to be battered into any sense at all,' said Jonny.

'There is still the one delivered at the last, the one as yet unopened,' said Isaac.

'Ah yes,' said Jonny. As he spoke the snoring behind them, the snoring to which they had become accustomed if not fond over the two hours since their return from the Three Suns with Morland around their necks, the snoring behind them stopped. The door opened and in walked Nathaniel.

'Ah, Nathaniel,' said Morland, shaking his head in an attempt to wake it up. 'Do we have small beer?'

'In the usual place, Samuel,' replied Nathaniel.

'Fetch me a quart,' said Morland, his voice lacking the penetrative power that it usually possessed. 'If you'd be so very kind.'

'No,' said Nathaniel. 'You plainly mistake me for one of your other lackeys.' He walked to Jonny and put his hands on the back of his chair. 'And anyway,' he continued. 'I am most definitely not kind.' He pulled a small packet from his jerkin and handed it to Jonny. 'For you.'

'Oh, thanks,' said Jonny. 'Ah, it's from Molly. It looks like it's going to be a long night, chaps!' At this the three laughed while Morland vomited into a pot.

'Sir Samuel, really!' said Nathaniel. Morland took the pot and left the room.

'Why must we suffer this buffoon,' said Isaac, 'when everything was going so nicely?'

'Because, Isaac,' said Jonny, 'because you are a butcher, remember? And Sir Samuel has golden fingers.'

'It's a pity he hasn't an iron stomach,' said Nathaniel. 'Because he'll need one if he continues to drink like that.'

'Says the last of the fish of London Town,' added Isaac.

'Just because two ales are a surfeit for you, Dorislaus!' said Nathaniel. 'Anyway, what does the delectable Molly promise you tonight, Jonny?'

Jonny broke the seal and opened the letter. His face grew longer as he read. 'Well?' said Isaac, 'I, at least, must live vicariously through your exploits, so I must know them.'

'She waxes ill and cannot see me tonight,' said Jonny, downcast.

'It must be in the air,' said Nathaniel. 'The Master Secretary was in a filthy mood when I visited him. I felt it wise to wait until the morrow before informing him of our actions.'

'No doubt he was tarrying with that piece he keeps, whoever she is,' said Isaac.

'Miss Susan, I believe is her name,' said Nathaniel. 'Commoner, apothecary, healer.'

'She cannot be apothecary,' said Isaac. 'The "she" being the obvious fly in that one of her ointments.'

'I hear tell her husband's was the name on the books, but hers were the brains,' said Nathaniel.

'I heard the gift was her grandmother's, and was handed down to her on the old woman's deathbed, along with her simples,' said Jonny.

'It matters not, as she was not there,' said Nathaniel. 'Which goes a long way to explaining his mood. Unless he is about to suffer a fit of the stone.'

'A fit of the stone?' came the voice of Morland. 'Heavens forfend. If Master Secretary Thurloe is suffering from a fit of the stone then I am de facto head of operations,' he said, not a little triumphantly.

'Well,' said Nathaniel, 'firstly Master Secretary Thurloe is not ill, and secondly, you know where you can stick your head of operations.'

'Let us look at this unopened missive,' said Isaac, placing the packet on the table. Morland reached over and took it.

'Allow me,' said Morland, waving away Isaac's protests. 'It's time I gave you a masterclass in our way.'

'We have been doing this for no little time, Sir Samuel,' said Isaac, the indignation set fair on his face.

'Well,' said Morland, as he turned the packet around in his hand. 'It's a wonder that you're not in possession of rather more sophisticated skills, isn't it, Master Dorislaus?' Morland ushered Isaac from his chair and sat down. 'Watch, and learn,' he said, and set about the packet.

Isaac stood to his right, face like thunder, his arms folded.

'Firstly, it has a rather strange address,' said Morland, as he read it out.

To Dr Hyde thse present

at Sa.s Greetname

'Sa.s Greetname, anybody?' he said. 'No? Well, onwards.' He turned the packet in his hand and inspected it more closely. 'It has been locked, but it is a simple lock. Whoever sent it is either unskilled, though it doesn't look that way, or was lacking time. I suspect the latter. Now, to open it without damage.'

'Not possible,' said Isaac, handing Morland the thinnest of the chamber's knives.

'You're right, Isaac,' said Morland. 'It's certainly impossible if that's as sophisticated as you get.' Morland chuckled to himself. 'Nathaniel, my good man, would you perhaps be able to acquire us some quicksilver?'

'Of course, Sir Samuel, seeing as you ask so kindly,' replied Nathaniel, and walked out of the room.

'Well, while Nathaniel is gone we might take some supper,' said Morland. 'Will the kitchens be open?'

Isaac and Jonny looked at each other and ushered their hungry colleague out of the chamber and down to the kitchens, where there was always somebody loitering. They acquired bread, cheese, cold beef and ale and returned to the chamber. When they returned Nathaniel was waiting for them.

'My, that was quick,' said Morland.

'Well,' said Nathaniel, 'acquisition is one of my many talents.'

'And I had you down as a meathead,' said Morland. 'My humble apologies.'

'Accepted,' said Nathaniel, 'unless you've failed to bring enough for me, in which case I may return to more expected behaviour.'

'There is plenty,' said Jonny. 'We shall eat before we witness what will be quite a feat, if Sir Samuel here can deliver on his promises.'

'Believe me,' said Morland, 'he can and will. But you are right. First things first: food and ale.' Morland was keen to make some great revelation, or at least to impress his new comrades with his skills so that he might justify the promises he had made to Master Secretary Thurloe. Thurloe had come to Morland on account of his reputation as a master of the dark arts of the Black Chamber. This reputation, however, had been created by Morland himself. It wasn't that he wasn't a master at opening, reading and resealing all but the most complicated foldings undetectably, it was simply that Morland was the only person who knew that this was the case, and his talents went somewhat further than messing around with letters. His greatest gift, or so some argued, was the gift of self-promotion. Morland had promised much, and John Thurloe, Cromwell's spymaster and right-hand man, was well known for many things, but a sense of humour and patience in the face of failure did not number amongst them. Samuel had to deliver. And now, he sensed, was his time.

The four men ate their fill, the shared repast serving to soften much of the rancour between them. At the last, Morland sat in front of the letter, and took it in his hands. He inspected it once more before he spoke. 'Quicksilver and knife, gentlemen,' he said. On receiving these he shook his head. 'Try in my bag. There's a roll of silk.' Nathaniel handed it to him. It was fine, padded silk finely embroidered with highly detailed but very strange designs. 'Oriental. They make exquisite blades.' At this he unrolled the silk and took out a blade so thin it was impossible to see how it might be sharpened. The three men watched in awe as Morland first softened the waxen blob with the quicksilver and then gently persuaded the seal to leave both letter and lock using his knife.

'Well,' said Isaac. 'I must say I'm impressed. I do hope what's inside justifies the effort.

'Et voilà,' said Morland, opening the letter with its lock still intact. He then unfolded it and laid it on the table. 'Obviously, reconstructing a letter is another matter, but you'll get used to it soon enough.' He placed the knife back in the silk sheath and rolled it up, tying it shut with a bow. 'Now, for the meat of our meal. Isaac, would you care to do the honours, as I believe this is an area in which your skills *are* actually unsurpassed?'

'Neat. Either female or, perhaps more likely, affecting a female hand to dress himself in women's weeds to throw us off his scent. But it is a familiar hand: I think S.H. but under duress. Stress, perhaps, time pressing or illness,' said Isaac. 'Write down these passages, Jonny, if you would.' Isaac read the letter through quickly. 'Interesting. I should say time pressure. This first passage has much matter,' he said, and read it out loud while Jonny transcribed.

Sr

These are to present my most humble serues to you desiring you to doe mee the like fauoure to my Cosen Lowes.

I ame thanke God very well as Dr Hydes and haue an oppertuniti of a coach to Sirencester, wher I shall meets by Ms Ayliffes seruants, so that I shall be at her house on tusday, wher I shall stay a fortnight at least, And whilst I am at greet name, our convoy must be by Londone, And if you please to diricte yours for mee to Ms Lane widdow ouer against Sant Pullkers Church, she will convay them with hers to mee, I presume you receiued myne by our carrer together with your hat case, since that I suppose you haue on from your gouerner, in acknowlegment of yours.

'So,' continued Isaac, 'we know where S.H. is off to, and how to intercept any messages that travel in any direction. What follows concerns placement of a nephew and is either coded or actually concerns the placement of a nephew. The ending perhaps will be made clear by another letter. And it is fresh. Sent just yesterday.'

'Excellent work, my good fellows,' said Morland. 'Might I humbly suggest we call it a night and reconvene tomorrow?'

'Certainly,' said Nathaniel. He looked at Jonny. 'Well, seeing as you're out of luck tonight, would you care to accompany me to the tavern?'

'I'd be delighted,' Jonny replied, and they left the chamber.

Isaac looked at Morland. 'It's not going to end prettily,' he said, and they snuffed out the candles one by one, drew their coats tight and walked together into the cold of night.

8

Susan breathes again

Susan stepped out of the coach at Cirencester after a journey she would have gladly forgotten had her body allowed her such a luxury. It had begun well enough, as Susan had dressed like the lady she was for the first time in months. While her attire did serve to remind her that at least half of the affectations adopted by the upper classes were a direct consequence of the sheer discomfort caused by their clothing, she felt herself once more. Susan Hyde. Sister to Sir Edward Hyde. No healing woman she. Her baggage loaded, she clasped her locket tightly and the coach began its journey as the misty tendrils of dawn wrapped themselves like a cutpurse's fingers around the trees that lined their route.

It was at this point that things began to go wrong. The first problem occurred when one of her fellow passengers lit a pipe, the odour of which made Susan vomit. In fact, it turned out that even the slightest hint of a strong odour made her vomit. They drove past a farm's compost heaps; Susan vomited. A new passenger brought out their lunch; Susan vomited. She made herself monumentally unpopular with her fellow passengers even though she had managed to avoid vomiting over any of them, or indeed, spilling the pot, but no one seemed to much appreciate these niceties. Then there was the passenger who insisted on praying constantly as if they were in the bowels of a ship in the teeth of a gale. The man who insisted on making crude references to Susan's decolletage every ten minutes as if they were the first pair of breasts he had ever almost seen. And the dog. Good God, the dog. It didn't realise how lucky it was to make it to the first major stop alive.

By the time the coach arrived in Cirencester and Susan finally alighted, where at least one of those who remained inside was heard to take the Lord's name in vain as they gave thanks for the safe completion of her journey, she hurt. Her back hurt from being bounced along on the hard wooden seats. Her legs hurt from being in the same position for so long. Her stomach hurt from vomiting. Her stomach actually just hurt. When she alighted, she was met by her maid of three-and-twenty years, Mary, and by Mrs Chaffin, wife of some court official in exile who Susan had forgotten. The pair of them stared at the pale, unsteady creature who stood in front of them.

'Good heavens, Mistress Susan!' cried Mary, only just resisting the urge to fling her arms around her mistress. 'What has that city done to you?'

'Mary,' said Susan, quietly. 'You truly have no idea quite how wonderful it is to see you. Just how wonderful it is to be back in civilisation again.' The men in attendance dealt with Susan's luggage and the three women climbed into the carriage ready for the trip to Greetenham, the village in which the Ayliffes resided. As they rolled through the countryside, the questions came thick and fast. Susan simply held up the palms of her hands. 'Peace, peace,' she said. 'I am tired, dirty and wax ill. I want nothing more than a hot bath, a change of clothes and a good meal. I have had none of these for I cannot say how long.'

'Mistress Susan,' said Mary. 'Your bath will be ready on our return, or I'll want to know the reason why!'

Susan smiled at this, remembering just how fearsome Mary could be when the need arose. Or the opportunity, yes, perhaps that was more to the point. Mary took the opportunity wherever and whenever she could. Susan heard Mary continue but her mind was suddenly concerned only with where to vomit. The window was the obvious choice. She apologised to the man who rode on the footplate.

'Oh mistress,' said Mary. 'I'll take that as a no, then, shall I?' With that she put away the slice of pie she had brought to assuage any immediate signs of hunger.

'I'm sorry, Mary,' said Susan. 'I fear I ought ride atop the carriage.'

'As you wish,' said Mrs Chaffin, who rapped her stick on the ceiling, bringing the carriage to a halt. Susan climbed onto the bench next to the driver with the aid of the slightly soiled footman, and they recommenced their journey.

The driver was a long-term family servant, who had known Susan since her brother Edward had married Anne Ayliffe some twenty-four years previously. It was still something of a mystery that the family connection endured long after the marriage had ended, though the manner in which it did was surely much of the reason. Anne had died in childbirth just months after the marriage, uniting the two families in grief, and this bond was one that endured. Joseph had been in his thirties then, and he was something of a fixture in the Ayliffe household now he approached his sixties, both on account of his longevity and the laconic manner with which he dispensed the wisdom he had accrued over this time. He was also a man who tended to get straight to the point.

'Married?' said Joseph.

'I beg your pardon, Joseph,' said Susan, as they bounced over a stone. 'Ouch.'

'Pardon me, mistress,' said Joseph. 'I meant, is he married, mistress?'

'Is who married, Joseph?' said Susan. 'I must admit, I truly have no idea what you speak of.'

'The gentleman who has caused you to leave the city with such haste,' said Joseph.

'And what makes you think that I left London on account of a gentleman, Joseph?' replied Susan.

'Beg pardon, mistress,' said Joseph, as he swerved gently to avoid a pothole, 'but I know of no other way for a lady to be with child.' He paused. 'Other than Our Lady, of course, mistress.'

'No, indeed not, Joseph,' said Susan, and not one more word passed between them for the rest of the journey.

9

The Black Chamber at play

'No Jonny this morning?' said Morland, as he wandered into the Black Chamber just before lunch.

'Remember in whose hands you last saw him, Samuel?' said Isaac, arching his eyebrow as he spoke.

'Ah, yes,' said Morland. 'I do recall the scene. Two young men walking into the depths of a winter's evening, with nothing but companionship, camaraderie and maybe even brotherhood on their minds, only to discover later that Beth or Diana is rather a distraction and before they know what has happened, they're beneath London Bridge with two wenches bent over in front of them with their skirts about their ears, though all the while their grubby hands are emptying their pockets and their minds are on their next customer.'

'You don't know Jonny, do you, Samuel?' said Isaac, laughing gently to himself.

'Then perhaps they toasted their brotherhood long into the night, only to find themselves asleep in the corner of some tavern come cock crow, their heads pounding like the broadside of a man-o-war, their stomachs churning like the alchemist's alembic and their tongues taking up twice the room in their mouths than they ought and fit for nothing but smoothing wood,' suggested Morland.

'You don't know Nathaniel, do you, Samuel?' said Isaac.

'Apparently not, good Isaac,' said Morland. 'Perhaps you'd care to enlighten me? Make complete my inculcation into the brotherhood of the Black Chamber?'

'It would be my pleasure, Samuel,' said Isaac. 'We might profitably discuss such matters over dinner? We stole a march on today's letters yestere'en, we are short staffed and the good Master Secretary has yet to make his pleasure clear following our pre-emptive action concerning the royalist postal channels.'

'Indeed. Do you think that Nathaniel will have informed him of our escapades, Isaac?'

'If he has not done so, it will not be on account of any overindulgence on his part, but merely the result of some black mood of the Master Secretary's making the delivery of any such intelligence a somewhat delicate operation,' said Isaac. He set down the letter on which he had been pretending to work and slid a piece of paper out from under a pile of other letters. 'Come. I hear tell this chop shop in Covent Garden is worth visiting.' He handed the paper to Morland.

'Interesting. How does a chop shop afford such a bill?'

'It appears they must know someone with access to a printing-house but who doesn't feel the need to pay for ink, paper or manpower,' said Isaac, standing up and accompanying Morland out of the Black Chamber and into the courtyard. 'And said person must run off a few dozen broadsheets without anyone noticing, or being able to act should they notice, dry them, cut them and deliver them.'

'And do we know such an individual?' asked Morland, as they locked the gate behind them and strode along the river.

'Well, it was noted that following his mission to take the Lord Protector's tract to John Fields to be printed, and within said mission his being given carte blanche, so to speak, with regard to how he carry out his duties, so long as they be carried out that day…'

'I am all ears,' said Morland, as they approached their destination.

'It was noted that following his mission many of these bills did suddenly find themselves public, and a young gentleman of our acquaintance, one with no stomach for strong liquor, did present himself in possession of a new winter's coat and did also change his lodging not long afterwards,' said Isaac. They entered the shop, its atmosphere thick with the rich aroma of mutton fat, and sat at one of the benches. A simple signal and two portions of hot mutton stew were placed in front of them. 'Furthermore, this very bill found its way into our chamber, by means unknown.'

'I imagine this to be an ale-only establishment, Isaac?'

Isaac nodded, both at his companion and their server, who brought two tankards to the table. The two men ate, spearing lumps of fatty mutton with their knives and mopping up the gravy with hunks of bread torn from the loaf that had also appeared in front of them.

'Who knew that young Jonny was so sharp, Isaac?' said Morland, in between mouthfuls.

'I did. I knew that he was so sharp. I used to work with Field as a translator when Jonny was apprenticed to the irascible old bugger, and while he had no clue as to Jonny's talents, I sought to nurture them. When Master Secretary brought me into his Black Chamber, I brought Jonny.'

'And now you accuse him of theft?'

'No, no,' said Isaac, 'though technically he is guilty of it, from Field at least. The old man deserved to be robbed just for the manner in which he treated Jonny.' Isaac paused to wash down a particularly fatty bit of meat. 'I merely seek to demonstrate his ability, ambition and loyalty.'

'Loyalty?' said Morland, confused by Isaac's choice of illustration. 'How does his theft from Field indicate loyalty?'

'It's quite simple. Loyalty is reciprocity. You treat Jonny as a brother, and he will treat you in the same manner. He will be Cain to your Abel or, or...'

'I'm not sure the book will come to your aid on this subject, Isaac,' said Morland, laughing gently.

'You're right,' said Isaac. 'Brothers tend not to end well. My point was that Jonny doesn't forget a slight.'

'And what about sisters?'

'I have no idea about sisters,' said Isaac. 'Their whys and wherefores are not my strong suit. But Jonny is a man who will forget neither kindness nor malice. And he will repay both sevenfold.'

'It strikes me as good that I like the boy. But you never quite explained his absence today.'

'No, indeed I did not,' said Isaac. 'Though I did predict it, in part, at least. Perhaps you will understand when you accompany Nathaniel to the tavern on an evening that holds no more fragrant calls upon your time.'

'I beg your pardon?' said Morland.

'Last night Jonny's girl, Molly, sent word that she waxed ill and that she could not receive him that evening,' said Isaac. 'In her stead, he went with Nathaniel on a drinking spree. Having made the same error I can attest to its dangers. Jonny is no doubt still unconscious in an alley somewhere or at his lodgings receiving an excellent purgation for free.'

'Hardly for free,' said Morland. 'Someone has to pay for the ale. So merely the result of an evening's entertainment. And what of Nathaniel? In what state will he find himself this morning?'

'You may ask him, if you wish,' said Isaac.

'I may?' replied Morland.

'Well, he's walking towards us with intent,' said Isaac, 'and by the look on his face he has recently had audience with Master Secretary Thurloe, and it was a not entirely pleasant experience.'

'Good Nathaniel,' said Morland, as Nathaniel walked within hailing range. 'To what do we owe the pleasure?'

'Samuel, Isaac.' He paused. 'No Jonny?'

'Unsurprisingly,' said Isaac.

'Ah,' said Nathaniel, 'I fear I may have had a hand in that. He's a game one, is Jonny. Not one to allow himself to be outdone,' he laughed as he saw that his two companions were smiling, 'I take it you have deduced the outcome of last night's revels, then?'

'It had crossed our minds that he might struggle to keep up,' said Morland. 'But is there news that we ought to have shared with us?'

'Yes, Sir Samuel,' said Nathaniel. 'Firstly, Master Secretary Thurloe is most pleased with our actions last night, and especially with the initiative thus taken. He agrees that the tree must be shaken every so often that we may dislodge the riper of the hanging fruits. He is most perturbed, angry, even, that his mistress not only insulted and left him to his supper alone yesterday, but appears either to be ignoring his messages or is not in a position to read them.'

'Perturbing indeed, Nathaniel,' said Isaac.

'And as his mood worsens, I hesitate to inform him that I have no word of her. She has, for all the world, vanished.'

'This bodes ill,' said Morland. 'I suggest we at the very least look busy. Fetch Jonny, Nathaniel, and we'll come up with a plan.'

10

Susan's worries are washed away

Susan stood in the best room in the house, and allowed herself to be slowly undressed. As Mary removed each layer, unhooking buttons, unlacing stays and otherwise unravelling, unwrapping and unbinding her mistress, she placed it in a basket next to her. The only exception was the silk dress Susan wore, which Mary hung up that it might receive her personal attention later that day. Susan drew breath audibly as her corset was unlaced, but she could not see the look of concern that crossed Mary's face. As she slowly approached nakedness, a series of servant girls came into the room bearing bucket upon bucket of hot water, each one poured into the large bath that dominated the room. The water had been scented with rose petals but all Susan longed for was to be clean and asleep in this bed, which she knew to be the most comfortable in the house.

'There, Mistress Susan,' said Mary as the very last item fell into the basket by her side. Mary signalled for the basket to be removed and the final bucket-wielding maid, whose bucket was to be left by the fire for later use, took the various items to be washed. Mary smoothed down her mistress's hair. 'Would you care to step into your bath, mistress?' Susan placed a toe in the water, recoiled slightly then slowly, gradually, she slid her right leg into the bath. She followed with her left leg and, hands gripping tight on the bath's rim, she gradually lowered her body in, feeling the caress of warm fluidity along the backs of her legs, up between her thighs, over her buttocks and then, as if gripped in the fist of some water sprite, simultaneously on both back and stomach. Susan shuddered in sensual delight as she slid further and further into the bath's comforting embrace, once again drawing in her breath sharply as her breasts sank beneath the water.

'Oh Mary, Mary,' said Susan, 'you simply cannot imagine how the thought of this moment has sustained me over the past few days.' And she leant back and sighed.

'It is wonderful to be able to attend to you once more, mistress,' said Mary as she began to rub a cake of soap vigorously on a flannel that she might attend to Susan more comprehensively. She took Susan's left arm and began to soap her down, starting with each of her fingers individually and then slowly moving up to her shoulder. As she soaped Susan's armpit Mary noticed her wince slightly. 'Anything wrong, Mistress Susan?' she asked, as she pushed her forwards and began to scrub her back.

'No, just a little tender, that's all,' said Susan, luxuriating in the attention her back was getting. 'It's the weather,' she added, mumbling almost directly into the bath water. Mary took the right arm and repeated the process. Once more, Susan winced, though more obviously as Mary was purposefully rougher with her. 'Be gentle, good Mary,' said Susan.

'There's no clean comes with gentle, mistress, just as there's no smoke without fire. Stand up, mistress,' she said, and began to work on her right leg, moving up towards Susan's crotch. 'Scuse my asking, Mistress Susan, but when did you last have the flowers?'

'Mary, Mary. How can you ask such a thing?'

'Are you saying, hand on heart, that you have taken no lover, Mistress Susan? I ask because you are sore in the breast and seem to be unable to stomach strong smells. When did you last bleed?'

Susan was quiet for a second, and then sat down in the bath with a splash. 'It was twelfth night, Mary.'

'And the father?'

'Will not and cannot ever know. Nor can he be known.'

'It will grow up a bastard, then, Mistress Susan.'

'Yes, it must. If it be suffered to grow at all, Mary.'

'But Mistress Susan, what you talk of is mortal sin.'

'Better mortal sin than give birth to the bastard son of the devil,' said Susan, biting her tongue as she spoke such words of hatred about the man she loved. 'Leave me, but send my dear sister to me, and Mary,' she added, 'you are not to breathe a word of this, not to a soul, living or dead.'

'Yes, mistress.' Mary left the room in tears, crossing herself as she did so.

Susan sat in the bath, head on her knees and her arms wrapped around them, just a single tear forming in her right eye. This was not going to plan. She had successfully infiltrated the bed of Secretary Thurloe, though he had hardly let one unguarded comment slip from his mouth, and those few that had escaped appeared, in retrospect, to have been pyrrhic pillow talk, costing the royalist cause far more than they earnt by them. All else they had achieved was her effective removal from active service. She clutched at her throat but her locket had been removed along with her clothing. It languished out of reach on the dresser. Now more than ever she needed the comfort of the Sisterhood. Just the knowledge that she was not alone would make the difference. Nous sommes la différence.

The door creaked and shut. Her hostess was now with her. 'Good day, sister,' said Susan.

'Sister,' replied Kate Ayliffe and walked across the room,

pausing only to pick up Susan's locket, which she placed around her neck, fastening the chain and allowing it to hang freely. 'Mary tells me you asked for me,' she said, sitting by the bath on a stool. 'I presume you are with child, Susan?'

'How did you...' began Susan, but she was cut off by the wave of her hand.

'I am old and have seen much, Susan. And I certainly know a pregnant woman when I see one.'

'I cannot yet be certain, not unless we can see the clouds in my urine. But I last bled on twelfth night.'

'So we have a week to prepare for the worst. Have you considered your options? I presume that the father is known to you, as surety.'

'Yes. If there is a father, then his identity is sure enough.'

'And am I to take it that he is neither aware of this possibility nor is he a suitable match?'

'No. A most unsuitable match. An impossible match. He is never to know.'

'Married, then, I presume?'

'Yes, but that is the least of the reasons for his unsuitability,' said Susan. 'It would perhaps be best if you enquire no further and we concentrate on the things we can control.'

'Yes, you are right,' said Kate. 'Is your intention to keep the child, should such a child exist?'

'I would rather cut off my breasts than give succour to the child of the devil.' Diana had cast her as Medea at the start of this ill-starred venture. She cannot have known just how truthful that would turn out to be, that the witch who brought a goat back to life would end up killing her own child.

'Soft, child,' said Kate. 'The father cannot be so loathsome to you.'

'He can and he is,' replied Susan. 'He is the very antithesis of what we, the Sisterhood, love, cherish and nourish. He is an evil man.'

'Then surely he needs must have taken you by force, Susan.'

'He did not. He did not.'

'Then why, child, why?' asked Kate.

'I cannot say. When will it next be possible to be rid of it?'

'You mean to murder it?'

'Yes,' said Susan. 'Just as I ought murder its father, and will yet, if the chance presents itself. If it is in my belly, it is not yet quick. And if it is not quick, it is no sin to remove it, as there is no life to extinguish.' As she spoke she avoided her companion's eyes, willing her own to remain dry and her true feelings to thus remain hidden.

Kate stood silent for a few seconds. Then she spoke. 'If I'm not mistaken, the woman you seek will next pass this way at the beginning of next month. It is but a fortnight. I will make the arrangements.' She paused. 'Is there no chance you might change your mind, child?'

'None,' said Susan. 'See to it, and send Mary to me. This bath grows cold.'

As the door shut behind Kate, Susan kissed her locket, and held it tight. 'Diana,' she said. 'Why? Your sister needs you.'

IV

1

Friday 4th April 1656

The Black Chamber meets with success

'We have the apothecary!' said Morland, his words reverberating along the corridors and into the small, oak-panelled room into which he ran. Inside, Isaac and Jonny sat hunched over the solid oak table that dominated it, dealing with the day's post.

'The apothecary?' said Isaac. 'Hinton? It's taken long enough.'

'It took him this long to take to the road, but we have him now, and he was carrying letters,' said Morland.

Isaac flinched as a small leather bag flew over his shoulder and landed on the table's hard oak, the air it displaced in doing so making the candles that were the room's only source of light flicker and sputter.

'These are they,' said Morland. 'They take priority over everything, including our sleep. Master Secretary Thurloe wants to see the transcripts by morning. And if his fit of the stone allows, he may even be able to read them.'

'Perfect,' said Isaac. 'I was looking forward to my Friday night.'

'Me too,' said Jonny. 'I was for the tavern.' He chuckled to himself, a laugh almost as dark as his ink-blackened fingers. 'Young Molly has promised me a bath tonight.'

At this Isaac laughed loudly. 'We'd best get on with the job, then,' he said. 'Good Sir Samuel, did our kindly superior say anything about sending these letters on their way, or will he be content to allow me to butcher them?'

'Indeed he did not, good Master Isaac,' replied Morland. 'You may butcher them to your heart's content. Tonight we are drawn against time, not technique.'

'A butcher indeed,' said Isaac. 'Pass me the cleaver of letters,' he added, holding out the palm of his right hand for Jonny to slap the handle of his penknife into. 'I thank you, kind sir.' He paused, then held the letter up in front of his face. 'So this is addressed to our old friend Honyatt the tailor, in Boar's Head Alley.'

'That's near Molly's tavern,' said Jonny. 'Pray you find some errand within to send me upon post haste, Isaac.'

'Well Mr Honyatt, tailor. I'll act the butcher,' and he slid the knife into the letter's gullet and slit it from top to tail. 'That's how we beat the letter-folders,' he said, as a smaller packet fell out of the gutted missive. 'What do we have here?' He tossed the packet to Jonny. 'A child born unto our letter?'

'Ah, and this one is interesting,' said Jonny. 'No fewer than two seals, and black at that.'

'Bless them, they must think we were born simple,' said Isaac, 'to think we'd take it for a letter of condolence. Inscription?'

'To a Mr Edwardes at Antwerp, to be left with a Mr John Shawe Merchant in the same town. 'Shall I open it?' he added.

'Slit its gizzard,' said Isaac, as he unfolded the first letter in front of him and read out its contents. '*These are only to desire you to cast these inclosed into the post house.* Blah blah, *your friend, S.H.*' He set the letter down. 'Another old friend. What of the enclosed?'

There was the sound of paper tearing and Jonny displayed a long slither of the enclosure, inspected it for ink and, upon finding none, held it in the flame of the nearest candle and watched as the paper caught light. 'A nice lock, but sadly wasted.'

'And what does the letter say, that you have so artfully destroyed, Jonny?' came Morland's voice from behind them. 'Well?'

'I thought he'd gone, Isaac,' said Jonny. 'Did you think so, too?'

'I most certainly did, Jonny, but it appears I was mistook,' said Isaac.

'*Sir*,' said Jonny. '*This is the third since I had any from you, yet possible you have been as kinde, and my journying or the apothecary's, may hinder me from the good tidings of your happy health which you, or my gossupe haue derived to mee, and if mine went right you both know I am as present in my one...*'

'For the love of God, man. So much is nonsense,' said Morland. 'You'll be reading out laundry requests next. Get to the meat of the matter.' With this he snatched the letter from Jonny's hands and scanned the paper rapidly, his right-hand index finger drawing itself across the page as if sucking up the letter's import. '*I must warn you not to trust My country man Mr. R.H. who hath a Mrs in Paris that he furnishes with the rarest commodities of your shopes.*' At this he stopped. 'Do we have an R.H.?' he said.

'Not to my knowledge,' said Isaac. 'The Master Secretary does not share all with his minions.'

'Not to worry, though it sounds pertinent,' said Morland. He proceeded to mumble through the rest of the letter until he came to a stop. '*Which when you have determined let me know your minde by the old way the hartichockes as soone as you can, and I shall decree it accordingly.* Interesting. I don't know what this artichoke thing is. Some form of unseen ink, perhaps?

Or an enclosure within an enclosure, perhaps? And "by the old way?" - isn't this what the wise women call their methods? It just shows that we shouldn't butcher these letters, Isaac. Who knows what secrets young Jonny set fire to when he disposed of this letter's tongue?' He inspected the letter carefully, folding it and unfolding it several times as he reconstructed its original form. 'A nice piece of folding. And good quality wax.' He held the letter up to a candle, then shone the light onto the inky surface. 'Fine sand for blotting, and good paper. French, if I'm not mistaken. I don't think this is your everyday traitor.' He looked at the endorsement at the bottom of the script. 'S.H. again. Do we know much of this one, Isaac?'

'Royalist of some hue, and is either female or affects a female hand, though Master Secretary will have none of it,' said Isaac. 'No witchcraft, so far as I'm aware. Do you not recall? We opened a similar letter but a week hence.'

'We have other letters bearing this mark?'

'Yes,' said Isaac.

'Bring them to me,' said Morland.

Isaac started to rummage around in one of the chests that filled the otherwise unemployed areas of the chamber, and within minutes dumped a thick sheaf of paper onto the table. 'What are we looking for?' he asked.

'Anything,' came the reply, and they began poring over the letters both to and from S.H. 'This one's from '53,' said Morland. He handed it to Isaac.

'Before my time,' said Isaac. 'I started last year when Master Secretary Thurloe was appointed Postmaster-General.'

'So,' said Morland. 'Look at those before your time. See if they tell you anything.' Isaac shuffled through the papers and then began again, inspecting each letter carefully. He let out a small noise. 'What?'

'This letter,' Isaac began.

'Yes?' said Morland, urging him to make some great revelation.

'This letter,' continued Isaac, 'is in the king's hand.' He corrected himself quickly. 'In the hand of the traitor Charles Stuart.'

Morland was stunned into silence, albeit momentarily. 'My goodness. That is rare. You are sure, Master Dorislaus?'

'Oh yes. It's his hand without doubt.'

'So. S.H. must be of great import. If only...'

'We knew his whereabouts,' interrupted Isaac.

'Or hers,' repeated Morland.

'But we do,' said Jonny, passing another letter to Morland. 'We know exactly where he or she is, or at least their destination but a week ago.'

Morland scanned the letter and smiled. He was about to make good on his promises. 'Mrs Ayliffe's. Greet Name, near Cirencester,' he said out loud. 'Jonny, take this letter to Master Secretary Thurloe's chambers,' he said, as he rapidly scratched out a few lines, folded the letter in two, dripped sealing wax over the join and stamped it with his ring. 'Then get us two swift horses. We must have S.H. in our hands before anyone misses the apothecary.'

2

Saturday 5th April
Molly has an unexpected visitor

From the very moment that Molly opened her eyes she knew that something was amiss. She could feel the presence. Working under the assumption that whoever or whatever it was that was currently in her room had yet to ascertain that she was awake - her head was turned towards the wall - she decided that she would lie awhile and assess the situation before acting.

'I trust it fits well,' said a female voice, a voice that Molly not only recognised but that filled her with excitement.

'Diana!' she fairly shouted, as she sprang out of bed and threw herself around the intruder's neck.

'Steady on, Molly,' said Diana, as both she and the chair she occupied reeled backwards under the sheer momentum of Molly's embrace.

'What on earth are you doing here?' said Molly. 'You took the convent.'

'Well, yes... but such a season is now gone, and I return to be by your side, where I belong,' said Diana.

The two women remained silent for a minute.

'Why are you here, sister?'

'You will not yet have heard, but the apothecary Hinton is taken by Thurloe's men.'

'Taken?' Molly's voice betrayed both her shock and confusion. 'How, where?'

'On the road to Cambridge. It appears they have been monitoring him for some time. Chase, too.' She paused. 'I am mighty hungry. It has been a long walk. Might we acquire some breakfast, Molly?'

'Of course. Help me dress.' Within minutes the two sisters were seated, bread and small beer in front of them. 'I loved the present, by the way. And indeed, it fits perfectly.'

'I'm glad. Pray you never have to use its resident, but at, well, extremely close quarters it has no equal.' Diana took a swig from her mug and continued her explanation. 'Hinton was caught before he could pass his burden on to the next man. I know not what he may have had on him but it's easy to imagine that one or more of the letters had Susan at their heart. We cannot but assume that Susan is compromised.'

'But Diana. Miss Susan has already left London.'

'She has? That is good news indeed. So she already knew of Hinton's arrest?'

'No, she knew not about Hinton,' said Molly. 'She left nigh on two weeks ago saying she had made an error, but did not say of what sort.'

'So she is not safe?'

'I cannot say.'

'Cannot or will not, Molly? While I may have taken the convent I have returned. There is no time for us to observe the niceties of the Sisterhood. Where is she?'

Molly looked at her companion and said nothing.

'Molly,' said Diana, 'Molly! Susan is both sister and friend. I do not violate the Sisterhood by caring for her in either capacity.

I apologise for my forthrightness but I am a woman desperately in fear for her sister's safety.'

'I quite understand, Diana. You, however, do not. I will not comment on Susan's safety as I do not know where she is.' Molly looked around them at the streets of Covent Garden as they began to fill with the day's travellers. 'I do know one thing, however,' said Molly.

'Yes?' said Diana.

3

Sunday 6th April
Susan awakes

It was a Sunday morning and Susan lay in her bed, half-asleep, running through the events of the past year. It seemed a lifetime ago that she, Diana and Edward had sat in the back room of the inn in Boxley, and her king had pronounced what was, in the end, to be a sentence of death upon her by means of a letter. Though Susan could not have known the manner in which she, Susan Hyde, sister to Sir Edward Hyde, was to meet her end, she was fully aware then, as now, that this letter proclaimed her fate every bit as much as had Lilly's symbols. But for it to culminate in her endangering her mortal soul by destroying the bastard child of Master Secretary John Thurloe, spymaster to Cromwell and scourge of the royalist cause, that had never so much as crossed her mind. Susan had failed. She had failed her king; she had failed the Sisterhood. All she had succeeded in doing was ruining herself. And for what? At this point, it almost felt like she was being rewarded for her incompetence. It was she, after all, who luxuriated in her bed this April morning, woken not by the shouts and curses of the market traders of Covent Garden, but by a cockerel lording itself over its harem, and she woke not to the stench of London, all sewage, sweat, smoke and suffering, but to the cool, clear air of the Wiltshire countryside. It may only have been the calm before the storm, but she was determined to spend in peace these few days that remained before she would join the foolish parlourmaids, professionals and papists in having her sins taken from her. For all the lofty aims that her mission had sought to accomplish, Susan was well aware that in its flawed execution she was, all things considered, no better than a common adultress. Worse, in fact, as she had convinced herself that she served greater powers than herself and also, and here she felt perhaps more guilty than in any other aspect of her behaviour, she had developed feelings for this brute of a man. More than feelings. She had developed them, she was sure, as a simple ruse, to allow her to carry out her allotted task. She had developed them the better to fool the great and subtle wit of the man. Most of all, however, she feared that she had not developed them at all: they had simply developed.

As she lay in bed what she really felt was that she missed John.

Susan began to drift back into sleep when unusual noises began downstairs, and entered into her dream world. She was suddenly back in the Mermaid, speaking with the innkeeper about Molly's chances in the city, at the moment when the kerfuffle had started up and she knew that Diana's plan had begun, that she would soon meet with Thurloe and her fate would be sealed.

Susan sat up in bed with a start as the realisation hit her that these noises were not a dream but were actually downstairs, in Mrs Ayliffe's house. She grabbed the locket around her neck and kissed it. At that moment the door flew open and in burst three men, two of whom she recognised, though she could not place them. She ripped the locket from her neck and flung it into the corner of the room.

'What is the meaning of this? Who dares enter my chamber

uninvited?' said Susan, mustering up as much indignation as she could.

'Peace, S.H., peace,' said the man who was obviously in charge. 'While I regret the manner in which I am forced to make your acquaintance and must apologise profusely for it, it is, sadly, necessary to prevent your destroying any evidence you might have about your person.'

At this the gentleman waved his pistol and the third man, the man she did not recognise, walked towards her.

'Escort the lady downstairs and lock her in the pantry,' said the gentleman. 'And there stand guard. Only Master Jonny here or myself may order her release. Do you understand?'

'Yes, Sir Samuel,' said the man, and walked towards the bed.

There was a sudden shout as Joseph entered the room, a sword in his hand. 'Don't you dare touch Mistress Susan!' he shouted. 'The first man who does loses his hand.'

'Joseph!' cried Susan.

'Oh, good heavens,' said Morland, 'Joseph, Joseph. Your sense of honour and duty are admirable, and duly noted, but really.' He pointed his pistol at him. 'Don't be silly. Put the sword down.'

'You coward,' shouted Joseph. 'First you enter a lady's bedchamber uninvited and second you won't even fight like a man. Have at you!' Morland simply stood there.

'Oh dear,' said Morland, handing his pistol to Jonny. 'If by any chance he wins, shoot him.' He turned to Joseph and unsheathed his rapier. 'Now, my good fellow, I admire your courage, but you cannot go around hurling the c-word at a gentleman and expect to get away with it.' He tore a cross in the air with his blade. The bystanders pressed themselves into the corners for safety.

'En garde!' said Joseph.

'Oh, please,' said Morland.

Joseph threw himself forward with all the fury of a pack of dogs. He lunged at Morland with a great thrust but his target simply vanished, and his sword was turned away.

'Predictable,' said Morland, who simply moved into the centre of the room and parried or sidestepped each attack without any apparent effort. 'I'll give you ten out of ten for enthusiasm,' and he followed a parried attack with a lightning-fast counter-thrust that removed the top button from Joseph's shirt. 'But I'm afraid you struggle to earn a single point for technique.' And so it continued, as Joseph became redder and redder from the effort and his shirt progressively more open. 'Enough!' cried Morland and lowered the point of his sword to the ground. 'Enough, I say. Your point is made. Bravo.'

At this Joseph made one final, desperate assault. It ended with his sword flying across the room and the point of Morland's rapier at his throat. 'I said enough,' repeated Morland. 'I have no desire to kill you but kill you I shall if you leave me no choice. Accept defeat, and accept my mercy.' He looked at where Joseph's sword lay. 'You could have had someone's eye out with that.' He sheathed his blade. 'I'm sure Mistress Susan will come quietly, will she not?'

'Yes,' said Susan, 'she will.'

'Search her trunk,' said Morland. Susan looked at him askance. 'My apologies, but we must.' She stood dumbfounded as Jonny went through her trunk. 'I'm presuming you have nothing about your person? We do not have a woman to search you so I would appreciate not being forced to do so ourselves.' Susan shook her head, showing that her shift had no obvious secret places. 'Thank you. Now as I said before, into the pantry.' He looked at Joseph. 'You, sir, may prepare a carriage. We leave within the hour.'

4

Sunday 6th April

Jonny makes a discovery

As the third man escorted Susan down the stairs at the point of his pistol, Morland and Jonny stood motionless, Jonny still with a pistol in each hand.

'Where did you learn to fight like that?' asked Jonny, his face still wide open in awe.

'Oh,' said Morland. 'I'm an earl, well, in waiting. It's what we do in our spare time, which is all the time. We learn things. Especially useful things such as how to win a duel, whether with pistol or rapier, and how to escape very fast on a horse when you have done so. And believe me, young Jonny, when you live your life as I do, these are not skills of luxury, but of necessity.'

'What sort of life do you mean, Sir Samuel? You are a denizen of the Black Chamber. That is your life.'

'Not in the least, Jonny,' said Morland. 'My life is one of wine, women and song. Though not necessarily in that order. Every penny of mine not spent on those, my chief delights, I consider a penny wasted.'

'So why the Black Chamber?'

'Ah, because I have great ambition, and my hobbies are great expenses. I seek position and opportunity, Jonny. Position to best place myself where there lies the greatest opportunity. Now we have much work to do, and much opportunity to make. Let us first search the rest of this room, and thoroughly.'

Jonny nodded, and headed straight for the corner where he had seen their prisoner throw something as they had burst in. He quickly saw what he was looking for. It was a small, silver locket on a chain. It bore an engraving of a bird on one side and an inscription in Latin on the other.

'Found something interesting?' said Morland, who was placing several purses of coin into a leather bag he had taken from a hook on the inside of the door and emptied of everything but the two bundles of mint that scented it.

'Just something I think Molly will like,' said Jonny. 'It will make a nice gift.'

'Good thinking, Jonny,' said Morland. He tossed him a bag of coin. 'This ought to come in useful, too.' Jonny caught the bag and stashed it alongside the locket inside his clothing. He wondered what possible reason there might be for this traitor to the commonweal to be in possession of a locket bearing the same design as one sported by his beloved. It made little sense to him, but then, little concerning today did. He did not understand the need for guns, and then he had not understood Joseph's behaviour, especially once bested. He certainly did not understand Morland's greed when he surely could not be short of coin. And finally, he could not understand the need for the woman to be locked in the pantry.

'Ah,' said Morland, who appeared to have finished acquiring all the coin in the room. 'Now we are getting somewhere.' He held up a sheaf of letters. 'Recognise the hand? Impressive that Isaac identified it as a woman's.'

Jonny looked closely. It was S.H., that much seemed certain. It didn't seem to say much, but then, very few of the letters that he'd read in the Black Chamber said very much. Most of them, and especially those written by women, rarely contained anything of greater import than what their nephew had eaten for supper, where they'd gone to escape the weather or how could they get their cousin's nephew's sweetheart a position in court before the inevitable happens and she has a baby on her hip.

He'd once read a letter from a colonel in Ireland, who was generally speaking the single most boring correspondent he'd ever known, and whose letters revolved solely around hunting and the relative merits or otherwise of his latest hawk or hound, in which he'd talked about the women in his vicinity. He wrote that they were so fond of yellow hair that those who did not have it by nature would dye it, and that with lye and a local moss. Now Jonny knew that there were several ways of acquiring lye, and he hoped that none of these poor women were forced to use the chamber variety, as good Lord they must have stunk to high heaven. The colonel also noted that with such women he often saw 'blacke bottoms with yellow topps', but Jonny could not make head nor tail of that, and so had given it no more thought. Letters, he had concluded, were like memories, and flattered to deceive.

'I feel our work is done, Jonny,' said Morland. 'Go downstairs, fetch the maid and allow her to pack.' He looked around the room, and his eyes alighted on an embroidered bag. 'Allow her to pack that, and no more. And a trunk for our evidence. I shall search the rest of these rooms upstairs.'

Jonny went downstairs where he found Susan's maid, crying and keening, and set her to complaining even more before charging their escort with ensuring the carriage was ready. After half an hour Morland returned, his bag now full.

'Thief!' cried Mrs Ayliffe, as he loaded up his pickings onto the carriage.

'No, Madam Ayliffe,' said Morland, as he stood on the carriage's runners, 'I am merely a servant of my country confiscating items of value that have aroused suspicion in me from the house that harbours a notorious she-intelligencer.'

'Thief,' she muttered again. 'Are you not going to allow Miss Susan to eat? A lady in her...' she choked the words down.

'A lady in her, hmm?' replied Morland. 'No. We have a tedious journey. We leave in five minutes. Either be ready to go or wave goodbye by that time.'

Jonny took Susan by the arm, and gently escorted her to the carriage. As he did so, Susan racked her brain trying to place him, but the stress of the morning denied her.

'Jonny,' she said. 'It is Jonny, yes?'

'Yes,' he said. 'Why do you ask?'

'When you were searching my room,' said Susan, 'did you find a locket?'

'*I am the bird that sings unseen*?' replied Jonny.

'Yes,' said Susan. 'You have Latin. I'm impressed. Do you have the locket?'

'I do,' said Jonny. 'What of it?'

'I know I have no right to ask this of you, and I fully expect you to refuse my request and I will not curse you for it,' she said, 'but it is of great sentimental value to me. It holds the hair of my mother and sister, and I would be very grateful if you would return it so that they may accompany me wherever my fate may take me.'

Jonny looked at Susan and saw merely honesty. He took the locket from his inside pocket and placed it in her hand.

'God bless you, Jonny,' said Susan, and kissed the hand that returned her locket to her.

At that the carriage shook. 'On deck, Jonny,' cried Morland, and Jonny climbed up to the front of the carriage while their escort and Mary joined Susan in the carriage.

'Marlborough,' said Morland to Joseph. 'And no hard feelings about the swashbuckling, eh?'

'No sir, very good sir,' said Joseph, somewhat truculently, and off they went.

5

Monday 7th April
Thurloe's work bears fruit

Master Secretary John Thurloe sat in the Black Chamber, his mood darker than his heart. 'Where in the name of all that's holy is Morland?' he said, his voice trembling and on the verge of cracking. 'And Jonny?' he added.

'They left on Friday, Master Secretary,' said Isaac. Isaac was not enjoying his time alone with Thurloe.

'And why, pray?' said Thurloe, his voice quieter now. Isaac feared the quiet Thurloe more than the thundering version. 'Why did they leave on Friday?'

'We discovered something, Master Secretary, and Sir Samuel thought it best to act, what with your indisposition.'

'And why is it that I cannot get word to Chase? I thought we were watching him?' If Thurloe objected to one thing, it was this. He hated not knowing. He hated not knowing what his own men were up to, what his own office had discovered and what it was he was meant to be doing. Thurloe was a man of action, even if that action was merely giving an order, or opening a letter. To sit and be unaware of what was taking place around him, and especially knowing that it was taking place without him, was anathema.

Isaac hesitated, then spoke, the confusion in his voice evident. 'But Master Secretary, we have Chase. We arrested him.'

'You did what?' said Thurloe, his voice now dipping into the dangerously quiet zone.

'We arrested him,' said Nathaniel, at whose sudden entrance Isaac breathed a sigh of relief. 'And Hinton, as planned. They are held close at Lambeth House.'

'And why, pray, did no one think to inform me?' said Thurloe, squeezing the words out through gritted teeth.

'You were indisposed, Master Secretary, and we thought it best for both you and the country that we continue as planned,' said Nathaniel. 'We arrested Hinton because the opportunity presented itself. You said you wished for new martyrs. Chase, naturally, we took at the same time. Chase was clean but Hinton had some interesting letters about his person, including this one, Master Secretary.' At this Nathaniel picked up an unfolded letter and presented it to Thurloe, who read it quickly.

'Addressed "To Mr John Honyatt A Tayler at his house In Bores head ally Next to the 3 sunes in ffleetstreet", yes, we know this man. He sent us to James Hyde.' He read on.

Mr Honiard

These ar of only to desire you to cast these inclosed into the post house, according to my Request to you from Oxforde, so with my Best remembrances to you and your wife And daughter wishing al health I rest

Your frinde

S.H.

September the 3

'Intriguing,' said Thurloe. 'And the enclosure?'

'Well,' said Nathaniel. 'That's where things got really interesting.' With this, Nathaniel handed over another piece of paper, this time with rather more text.

'Thank you, Nathaniel,' said Thurloe, his mood visibly improving. He read through the letter, picking out phrases as he went along. 'So, what do we have here? "To Mr Edwardes these present. To be left with Mr John Shawe Marchant at his house in Antwerpe." And do we know these individuals?'

'We do, Master Secretary,' said Isaac.

'And do they interest us in any way, Isaac?' said Thurloe, as he scanned the letter quickly. 'I see.' He began to read again. '"I must warn you not to trust My country man Mr. R.H. who hath a Mrs in Paris that hee furnishes with the rarest commodityes of your shope, before any of the other Ladies can be adorned therewith, and this he did this last summer to the prejudice of your trade there."' At this, Thurloe paused. 'R.H. is one of ours. He is uncovered.'

'We were not sure, but it appears so, Master Secretary,' said Isaac.

'Set a man to watch and see who takes him,' said Thurloe. 'It may be instructive.'

'Yes, Master Secretary.'

'And this? "I must desire your caution, being so much concerned in your trade, that if you fail, I breake, I hope you have receiued the goods from your corresponds a month since, little John is your seruant", do we know to whom this refers?' asked Thurloe.

'We do not,' said Isaac. 'More's the pity.'

'And we have seen this one before, this S.H., have we not?' said Thurloe. 'And Shaw, do we not. What of Edwardes?'

'John Shaw we do know, indeed. He is the John Shaw who acts as a clearing house and banker for the traitors in exile.'

'And Edwardes? Please tell me he's more interesting than Shaw?'

'Oh yes,' said Isaac. 'He definitely is that. He's the traitor, Charles Stuart.'

Thurloe leant back in his chair and slowly let his hands fall to rest on his legs. 'The traitor?' he said, mildly incredulous. 'S.H. is writing directly to the traitor?'

'Yes, Master Secretary. That is exactly what S.H. is doing.'

'I thought not that this S.H. could be so connected. We must find this individual,' said Thurloe. 'And as soon as possible.' Isaac allowed himself the liberty of a smile. Thurloe noticed immediately and his dark mood returned. 'Do you think we are playing in this chamber, Dorislaus?' he said, his voice rising once more as he stood, wincing with pain as he did so.

'Peace, Master Secretary, peace,' said Nathaniel. 'Isaac smiles simply because he knows that you have no cause other than to be pleased. Samuel and Jonny left London with the express purpose of delivering S.H. into custody.'

'We know where he is?' asked Thurloe.

'We did,' said Nathaniel, 'and we chose to act before the arrest of Hinton was promulgated abroad. Though we do believe it is a she.'

'This is most excellently done,' said Thurloe. 'Though I doubt not that he affects a woman's hand. We shall see soon enough. Now we needs must unpick the lock that guards the heart of the good apothecary, and we will have achieved much.'

'You will have your martyr yet, Master Secretary,' said Nathaniel. 'But think not that the apothecary will prove a challenging heart to penetrate.' With this, Nathaniel waved a piece of paper in front of him. 'I come straight from Lambeth House, where the good apothecary, perhaps having heard tell of your methods by a fellow prisoner with whom he spoke unseen, bade me give you this note.'

'You are a close one, Nathaniel, indeed,' said Thurloe, taking the note from his hand. 'Now, let us see what the apothecary wishes to say.' With this, Thurloe unfolded the note and read to himself, mumbling through the words. 'He wishes there to be "a speedy dispatch to farther examination" and adds that while he had at first refused to talk, he now "hopes to receiue your more fauourable opinion, which may add much towards my release."' Thurloe smiled. It was the widest smile Isaac had seen for some time. But the smile turned into a grimace. 'Is there an apothecary we have not yet arrested, Nathaniel?' he said. 'For I am in great need of one.' He paused. 'If only Miss Susan had not left this town. Nathaniel, you must find Miss Susan,' he said. 'But in the meantime, any apothecary without a grudge will do. Hinton will just have to wait.'

6

Tuesday 8th April, 10am
Susan fears

Since waking that Sunday morning, when she had spread herself out on her bed and had simply drunk in the luxury of calm, the luxury of quiet and the luxury of clean having escaped the city, Susan had not tasted sleep. It was now Tuesday, and her captors awaited the stage - it seemed they had no transport of their own, and that they drew the line at stealing horse and carriage. It was perfectly fine to fleece the women of every penny that could be found, however. This Morland was an odd fellow, and she had finally recalled their previous meeting. It was ironic that he should now be playing the cutpurse rather than deliverer of justice, though, of course, to him she had changed from being the damsel in distress to the traitor she-intelligencer. Perhaps the Catholics were right, and it wasn't who you were at heart so much as who you appeared to be that truly mattered. And to him, to Sir Samuel, as he continually reminded everyone, Susan looked very much like an opportunity. At least, she gathered from his attitude towards her that he did not recognise her true nature or her true name. He didn't even seem to be aware that she, his captive, knew his immediate superior rather better than he did.

Susan didn't imagine it would take long for the truth to come out. But John's feelings for her... how would he manage to abide by them and look to show that he was still in command? She-intelligencers were generally treated more gently than their male counterparts - after all, how could a mere woman hope to plot and scheme without a man's direction? The Sisterhood knew, but men, even men like John, they had yet to understand the things a woman could achieve, much less conceive. John would spirit her away. She would take the convent. She was sure of that. He would not suspect that he had been her prey right from the start. That was his weakness, yes. Diana had been right all along. It was his weakness then, and it would be his weakness now. No stomach for strong liquor indeed. These men had no clue.

They tarried at an inn, which suited Susan as she was tired and hungry, and while sleep eluded her, at least she might eat. It suited Morland, too, who sampled the establishment's fare to the point of obsession. Joseph had twice indicated he might disarm him and free them all but Susan, rightly, had shaken her head. They were in a parliamentary town. There was nowhere to go. And anyway, there was still Jonny to contend with. While Morland was a buffoon, he was a clever one, though his overriding belief in his natural superiority and his understanding that the world was, at its heart, here to serve his every whim was a serious weak point. In not considering the possibility that a Joseph, once bested, might try to gain freedom for himself and those around him, Morland increased the possibility of its occurrence. Jonny, however, was young, sharp and ambitious. He watched, he learned, he remembered. As did Susan, as she finally recalled where she had seen him before, too, in the city. He had been radiating triumph that day, the same day that Molly's... they couldn't be the same Jonny, surely. But he was the printer's boy. Had been the printer's boy. She hoped it wasn't so, for his sake as much as hers.

The door to the inn opened, and the local muscle who had accompanied Morland and Jonny as they arrested Susan walked in. He was unpleasant and uncouth and Susan would be happy to be rid of him. In this, she believed, she reflected the sentiments of the rest of the party.

'Coach's here,' said the man. 'Come to take you back where you belong, close in the Tower with the other traitors.'

'Really,' said Morland. 'Must you be so vile?' He threw him a coin. 'You have done sterling service and your country is proud of you. You may go on your way.'

'Thank you, Sir Samuel,' he said and, having thrown a filthy look at Susan, he was gone.

'My apologies, Miss Susan,' said Morland. 'A necessary evil.'

'But the Tower?' said Susan, feeling rather faint at the prospect.

'Pay him no heed. You will be kept close, but in the manner that befits your status. I trust you are ready?'

'Yes, thank you, Sir Samuel.'

Having loaded the carriage with persons and baggage, Morland opened the door, stepped in and handed Susan a large bunch of fresh mint. 'For the journey, Miss Susan,' he said, before shutting the door and instructing the driver to get going.

'How thoughtful,' said Susan as the carriage rolled along the road to London.

7

Tuesday 8th April, 8pm

Molly makes an unwelcome discovery

'These are dangerous times.'

'But we don't know what's going on,' said Molly.

'Exactly why they're so dangerous, Molly,' said Diana. 'We don't know what, if anything, Hinton was carrying when they arrested him. We don't know where Susan is other than gone. We don't know what Thurloe knows, whether he's discovered Susan's real identity or her mission.'

'Wait a minute, Diana,' said Molly, confused. 'Say that again.'

'Which bit?'

'The bit about Thurloe.'

'You mean, the "we don't know what Thurloe knows, whether he's discovered Susan's real identity or her mission" bit?'

'All of those.'

'You do know the mission?'

'Well, of course I know,' said Molly, rolling her eyes up into her skull. 'Susan is the postmistress of the Sealed Knot. She keeps the channels open.'

'You know her true identity? You know that she is Susan Hyde, sister to Sir Edward?'

'Advisor to the king in exile, Sir Edward Hyde?' Molly said, suddenly less sure of her position in Susan's confidence. 'Jonny's mentioned him.'

'Jonny?'

'My beau,' said Molly.

'Oh, I am behind the times. And have you told Jonny of Susan's identity?'

'Don't be silly.'

'Who is Jonny, anyway?' Diana asked, as she started to get a little agitated.

'He is the printer's apprentice.'

'How is it that he knows of Edward Hyde?'

'Like I said, the printer's apprentice,' said Molly. 'The king's printers, well, the Lord Protector's. So he reads. He often works in Whitehall on pamphlets, official stuff, especially when there's something complex being worked on and it must be done securely. I don't know exactly where. Well, I know exactly where as if I send notes they must be directed to the very room.'

'And where is he now?'

'I know not,' said Molly, 'for I have a visitor.'

'Charmed, I'm sure. Do you know with whom he works?'

'Only by reputation. Nathaniel is nice. Friendly,' said Molly. 'Unless you annoy him or one of his friends then he's a total bastard. Isaac, he's the scholarly one, shy, retiring, razor wit. Recently they've been joined by another. Jonny can't work him out but I think he's a disaster waiting to happen.'

'Oh Molly, Molly,' said Diana. 'You know of Susan's mission?'

'No, it appears that I do not.'

'She is to gain the confidence of John Thurloe,' said Diana.

'John Thurloe? You mean, spymaster, let's put burning matches under your fingers until you talk Master Secretary Thurloe? The Thurloe who arrested you?'

'The very same. And it is for Susan to spy on the spymaster.'

'So Susan's John is... no! She could not, she would not.'

Molly's voice was just a little quieter than usual, her natural effervescence muted.

'She could and she has. And now we know not whether Thurloe knows that he has been cozened. And as for your Jonny, have you met this Nathaniel?'

'No. I have met none of Jonny's colleagues. I know them by repute only.'

'If Nathaniel was a soldier, then I believe we have met,' said Diana. 'I think he may work for Thurloe.'

'If that were so, then Jonny must also work for Thurloe,' said Molly. 'And that's ridiculous. I know Jonny works for parliament by default, but he wouldn't... would he?' She sat down heavily. 'The stories of Thurloe... oh goodness, they make my toes curl. And Susan is on a mission that involves him?'

'No,' said Diana. 'Thurloe is her mission.'

'This scares me. And if Thurloe is our enemy, that makes Jonny our enemy, too.' She paused, and looked directly at Diana. 'Oh, this is not good. This is very not good indeed.'

8

Wednesday 9th April
Susan is made a prisoner

As the coach drew to a standstill Jonny leapt off the rear platform where he had been riding and helped Miss Susan down from inside, much to Joseph's chagrin, as he was left with Mary's hand to hold as she, too, alighted.

'Where are we?' said Susan, as their baggage was unloaded and left in the road. 'What are we to do now?' The mint had helped her stomach somewhat but she was tired, so very tired. Her captor spoke.

'We, Miss Susan, are to attend the grand council,' said Morland, 'and they will doubtless ignore you for an hour or two before committing you to prison,' at which word he paused rather obviously for effect, 'or, most likely, to house arrest. In this latter case I shall lobby to keep you at my house, which is not far.' He signalled at Jonny to attend him. 'Jonny, go,' he said, giving him a card with an address scratched upon it along with Morland's own sign and seal. 'Show this to the man at the door, and beg him attend with the cart in all haste, and transport all to the safety of my domicile.' He looked around. 'We shall attend your return so make haste!'

Jonny rushed into the crowds and Susan sat heavily upon the

trunk that Morland had brought to transport his spoils. As the crowds swirled about them Susan tried to shut out Joseph's moaning about respect, Mary's continuous comments about delicate ladies and Morland's accusations regarding recalcitrant prisoners. She focused on her John, the John she knew bore a love for her that would move him to remove her from Morland's clutches, perhaps spirit her away to a place of safety. Perhaps she would take the convent after all, and Lilly's predictions concerned her name and not her body. She tried to shut out all other thoughts. Jonny returned, breathless.

'He's on his way,' said Jonny. 'May I...'

'You will attend to the luggage and see it safely delivered,' said Morland, 'and then...'

'May I...' enquired Jonny.

'And then you will attend my pleasure,' said Morland. 'Come,' he instructed the others. 'To the grand council.' With this, Morland walked through a large set of doors a few yards from where they had alighted, followed by his prisoner and her attendants.

'And how may I help you?' said the guard on the inner doors.

'Sir Samuel Morland, Clerk to His Highness's Signet, to present a prisoner, a Miss Susan, she-spy, for your disposal, sir,' said Morland.

'Wait here,' said the guard and disappeared through the next set of doors. Morland turned to his charges and smiled. They did not smile back. The guard reappeared. 'You,' he said, pointing at Morland, Joseph and Mary, 'wait over there. You, come with me.'

'But my good man...' began Morland. The guard simply glared at him until he sat down.

'Thank you,' said the guard, and led Susan away. In the chamber was a long table at which sat several men discussing various topics with great seriousness. The guard announced her;

one of the men waved his arm without even casting a glance in her direction and indicated that she stand and await their pleasure. The guard returned to his post.

Susan stood. Tired, hungry, thirsty. She stood while the men discussed the latest news on the Spanish, the problems with the Scots, several different problems with trees, yet another ban on duelling and an interminable list of pleas to the council for this, pleas to the council for that and Susan began to get sore feet and then her legs began to ache, and then her back, and it became harder to stand and suddenly - 'Who is this woman? Hold her close by and bother us no more.' The guard led her out to find Morland, Joseph and Mary still sitting, waiting if not patiently, at least waiting.

'You, Clerk,' said the guard. 'She is to be held at your convenience and expense until further notice. Now stop cluttering up my workplace.'

'Two hours,' said Morland. He scratched his head. 'And not a word?'

'There were plenty of words,' said Susan. 'Just none directed at me.' She smiled, though it was a forced smile. 'Now, Sir Samuel, I am tired and hungry. And your guest. Kindly extend your hospitality.' She smiled again, but this time it was a wry smile. 'After all, we know who's footing the bill.'

With this, Morland led them to his house at Westminster, where Jonny waited, even more impatiently than usual.

'Sir Samuel?' he said, the tone in his voice denying any need for further explanation.

'Go on, Jonny,' said Morland. 'But have a care you're back bright and early.'

'Of course,' he said, and within a minute was flying down the alleyways and through the back ways as fast as he could go. There was so much to tell Molly he could hardly wait.

9

Wednesday 9th April
Molly makes her choice

Molly jumped when she heard the knock on her window. She'd been expecting it for what seemed like weeks but had only been a few days. She'd sent him a couple of notes since the one saying she was ill, but no Jonny. She half missed him and was half worried about him, even though she knew full well that he was more than capable of looking after himself. But this was the longest they'd neither seen nor communicated with each other since she had completed her training. And Molly did not like it one little bit. And that was without considering the information that Diana had brought her. She was as yet unconvinced, however, and would take no action without evidence. But before evidence came interrogation. And before interrogation came reunion.

She opened the casement and in Jonny tumbled. Into her room and into her bed. They made love as though it was the first and last time and then they lay side by side, exhausted but happy, staring at the ceiling of her room as if each other's eyes were too deep, too dangerous.

'Oh Molly,' said Jonny. 'It's been amazing.'

'Wasn't it just, Jonny?'

'The past few days have been amazing,' he said, and it simply burst out of him before he could register the look on Molly's face. 'So we got this tip-off, and we knew we had to act even though nobody knew except for us and we had to make the call and we did and we hired horses, riding hard for hours, swapping our tired mounts for fresh horses twice and finally we were there. We hadn't slept and it was dawn and we took a soldier from a nearby town and then saw the house and we drew our pistols and shouted "Where is she?" and we discovered her room and broke down the door and...'

'Peace, peace my love,' said Molly, interrupting his flow. 'Take some wine and refresh yourself. It certainly appears that the life of a printer's apprentice is far more exciting than I had thought possible. Or have you changed your place of employ?'

'Thank you. Well, maybe we weren't entirely involved in the business of publishing per se.'

'And who's we, anyway, Jonny?'

'Oh, Molly. You know if I told you I'd have to kill you!'

'So,' said Molly. 'You've broken down some poor woman's door on a Sunday morning. Delightful behaviour.'

'You don't understand, Molly. She was...' he hesitated.

'She was what, Jonny? A milkmaid? A dangerous washerwoman? A widow?'

'Well,' said Jonny, wrestling with himself. 'I suppose when we marry we'll not have secrets, eh Molly?'

'No,' said Molly. 'Assuming I take you of course.'

Jonny kissed her on the forehead. 'You're so sweet,' he said, and then looked around the room and put his index finger to his lips and made an exaggerated shhh... 'She-intelligencer!' he whispered, triumphantly.

'Oh my!' said Molly, feigning shock. 'You're so brave, Jonny!'

'Very funny, Molly,' said Jonny, before carrying on. 'As we entered the room I saw her throw something into the corner of the room but then there was this great shout and in ran a servant, he must have been sixty if he was a day, and he threatens us with a sword.'

'Oh no! What did you do then?'

'Well, we have guns, so of course Sir Samuel...'

'Sir Samuel?'

'Well, we call him that even though he has yet to be titled,' said Jonny. 'Sir Samuel points his pistol at the man and invites him to be less foolish and lay down his weapon but he simply calls Sir Samuel a coward!'

'How frightfully rude!' said Molly.

'Exactly. So Sir Samuel gives me his pistol and...'

'Is mortally wounded but you bravely best the servant in single combat?' suggested Molly.

'No, nothing like that, but it was extraordinary. The servant launched attack after attack but Sir Samuel was simply never where the other man's sword was. I've never seen anything like it.'

'And then he ran the servant through!' said Molly, hopefully.

'No, Molly, that would have been ungentlemanly. Sir Samuel simply tore off the servant's shirt buttons one by one with the point of his sword before laying it down and saying "That's enough".'

'Oh, how disappointing.'

'But the servant launched a final, furious assault at which Sir Samuel disarmed him and held him with the tip of his blade at the servant's throat.'

'I don't suppose...' asked Molly but Jonny shook his head. 'Pity.'

'No, but like I said, it was extraordinary. Sir Samuel even gave Joseph...'

'Joseph?'

'The servant,' replied Jonny. 'He even gave him a new shirt as he'd ruined his old one.'

'Sounds the very model citizen, Jonny. Am I to consider my place in your affections under jeopardy?

'As if anyone could replace you, my love. Anyway, for all his gentlemanly ways, he has a very particular attitude to personal possessions.'

'In what sense?'

'In an "I'd very much like to take personal control of your possessions" sort of sense,' said Jonny. 'Especially those possessions of a golden nature.'

'What did you steal, Jonny?' Diana, it appears, was right. Jonny was no printer's boy, just as Molly was more than a serving girl.

'Nothing,' said Jonny, 'but I didn't tell you about the thing I found, the thing that I saw the she-intelligencer throw away.'

'Now that does sound exciting, Jonny.'

'Well, it got all the more interesting when she later asked me whether I had found anything in the room, and I said I had, and she described it, and I said yes, that was it, and she begged me to let her have it, as she said it was very dear to her and it held remembrances of her mother and sister in it.' Jonny stopped talking and looked at Molly.

'What did you do, Jonny?'

'I gave it to her, of course,' said Jonny. 'I wonder that you need to ask me that question. But can you guess what it was, my love?'

'You must enlighten me, my darling.'

'It was a locket. Small, silver, with an engraving of a bird and a Latin motto that translates as "I am the bird that sings unseen".' Molly's arm drew him towards her as he spoke. 'Does that sound familiar, Molly?'

'Yes. It's the same as the locket I have.'

'Yes, it is.' He paused. 'You know what this means, of course?'

'Yes, I do,' said Molly, as a tear fell down her cheek. 'It means you are a good man, my love. A man amongst men.' With this she put her arms around his neck.

'It means that you have been keeping secrets from me, my love. But the locket, Molly, the locket.'

'You're right, of course, we ought have no secrets. And from this day, there will be none.'

'Good,' said Jonny. 'Very good. But what does it mean?'

'I'm sorry, my love,' Molly said, tears filling her eyes. 'But whatever happens, just know that I love you, Jonny, and I'll never love another.'

'Peace, Molly,' said Jonny. 'Why the tears?'

'I love you, Jonny,' she said, 'and I'm so very sorry.' With this Molly grasped the handle of the stiletto that she had hidden by the bed with her right hand and placed the point gently at the base of Jonny's skull.

'That tickles,' said Jonny.

'Forgive me, my Redcrosse, my love,' and with those words she drove the stiletto up through the base of his skull into his brain with all the force she could muster. 'Forgive me.'

Molly sat with Jonny in her arms for what felt like a lifetime, her tears dripping down onto his bare shoulder until she heard a quiet knock on the door. Molly lay Jonny down on the bed, gently, placing a folded piece of linen to the wound to stop the blood from getting everywhere. She looked at him for a second, his face as peaceful as if he were merely asleep, happily in her arms. She placed a kiss on his forehead and stroked his hair. 'Goodbye, Jonny,' she said and opened the door.

'About time,' said Diana. She looked at Molly. 'Oh, you poor girl,' she said, and embraced her. 'But we can't tarry. Do you have the route organised?' Molly nodded but too subtly for Diana to notice. 'The route!' Molly nodded with extra vigour. 'Excellent.'

Diana looked at Jonny's corpse and sighed. 'Molly, dear Molly,' said Diana, disapprovingly. 'Next time, Molly, make sure they dress themselves before you dispense with them. It's a nightmare doing it afterwards.'

Molly simply burst into tears, and began beating Diana's chest with her fists. 'For the love of God,' she said, between deep, wrenching sobs. 'I just murdered the man I...' her words were cut off by a slap to the face.

'Never use that word again, and pull yourself together, sister,' said Diana. 'You had no choice.'

'But if I could have explained, if...' but Molly stopped herself this time, conscious of the look she was receiving.

'Better. Now, check his pockets and Molly, for heaven's sake, girl.' Diana simply stood, transfixed. 'That was a gift to you, it's not to be left in Jonny's brain.'

Molly slowly walked over to the corpse, took a firm grip on the handle of the stiletto with her right hand, pressed her left against the back of his head and... 'Just a second,' said Diana. She pressed the linen firmly around the point of entry. 'Now go ahead.' Molly pulled but nothing happened. 'You have to wiggle it a bit,' said Diana. A slight noise was followed by a smooth slither as the blade exited. Molly wiped it clean. 'Good. Pockets.'

Molly suddenly reached into the corner and grasped her chamber pot, and vomited noisily into it.

Diana waited until the retching ceased. 'Are we quite finished?' Molly looked at Diana and nodded gently, retching again quietly as she did so. 'Pockets.' The two women checked every pocket in the few items of clothing that lay crumpled on a chair.

'There's this,' said Molly, brandishing a small card. She looked at it closely in the dull candlelight. 'An address in Westminster and a sign. Looks like Morland, Sir Samuel Morland.'

'If we follow him he'll perhaps lead us to Susan,' said Diana. 'Now let's dress him.'

It took twenty minutes, a fair bit of swearing and quite a lot of sweat before they finally had Jonny looking as he had done on arrival, albeit now somewhat less animated. Diana took a small hemp and some twine from a bag and handed the twine to Molly. They bound his hands and feet and then attached the hemp around his middle. Molly took the free end and climbed out of the room onto the roof through the casement he had entered by.

'Keeps him from swirling about,' said Molly as she took up the slack. Molly heaved and Jonny's lifeless form was raised a few inches and then he thumped back down onto the floor. Another heave met with the same result. And a third. 'It's no use,' said Molly, panting. 'We both need to be up here.'

Diana joined Molly and the two women dragged Jonny's corpse out of the room, across the roof of the brothel and down into a back alley. As they untied him they looked for suitable places to put him.

'There,' said Diana, pointing at a shadowy corner.

'Too close to home.' Molly shook her head.

'Not at all,' said Diana. 'Close is good because no one hides a body anywhere other than where they killed it or streets away. And here we can tuck him up and he won't be spotted until well into the evening.' They squeezed him into the shadows and slunk back into Molly's room. Diana gave Molly a hug.

'Thank you,' said Molly, getting a small bottle out of her trunk. 'This will help, too.'

'Hang on,' said Diana, standing up almost as soon as she sat down, and rummaged between the horsehair cushions. 'What's this?' She was holding up a key.

'It must be Jonny's,' said Molly. 'It's not the key to his lodgings, though. I already have that.'

10

Thursday 10th April, 2pm
Susan reaches out

If there was one thing that Susan could say for Sir Samuel Morland it was that he kept an extremely comfortable house. Joseph and Mary were also appointed comfortable chambers, though they were situated at the other end of the building. Susan was not entirely pleased to find herself thus isolated, and Sir Samuel was perhaps over-punctilious in assuring himself that he was the perfect host, even though his behaviour did not seem to include his worrying overmuch about his guests. Things might have been much, much worse.

'Mary,' said Susan, as she sat in the withdrawing room. 'Could you fetch me paper and ink, if it pleases you? If you are challenged say that I write my confession.' She paused. 'First I must sleep.' As Mary turned to leave, Susan called after her. 'One more thing, Mary. Soak me an egg in vinegar. Wake me in three or four hours.'

'Of course, Mistress Susan,' she said, and went to do her mistress's bidding. Susan realised that it was time that she took control of the situation. She would contact Talbot, make sure that she had at least one card up her sleeve. She lay her head down and within seconds was dozing. And she dreamt.

Several hours later and Susan awoke, the word 'Mistress?' in her ear as Mary shook her from her dream. 'You were moaning quite awfully.'

'A bad dream,' said Susan. 'I really am awfully tired, and under the circumstances I suppose it's only to be expected.'

'Yes, Mistress Susan,' said Mary. 'And it will only get worse.'

'If only they had come two days later I would not be in this godforsaken estate.'

'God never forsakes us,' said Mary. 'Here is paper and ink, as requested. And your egg.'

'Thank you,' said Susan. With this, she took two of the various pieces of paper that Mary had brought, one of which was barely an inch square, and wrote a short message on each. She folded the larger piece, dripped wax upon it and sealed it with her thumb, wincing a little at the heat of the wax on her flesh. She then took the egg and squeezed it gently, feeling the vinegar-softened shell flex with the pressure from her fingers. She took her penknife and sliced a narrow slit through which she slid the smaller of the two messages. She gave both note and egg to Mary.

'Give the note somehow to the boy who delivers to this address. If there be friends close by, they will find it. Soak the egg in water for an hour, let it dry, then take it to the Mermaid, and give it to the mistress there.' Mary left the room, and Susan, weary again, lay on the day bed.

As she lay down, not quite asleep, not quite awake, Susan contemplated her strange situation. She found this holding cell quite odd. Having been arrested with such violence and bundled away without so much as a bite to eat before the journey, she now languished in a gaol that just happened to be in keeping with the highest of fashion and she was being fed exceeding well. While Sir Samuel was perhaps not the most dependable of men, he was highly cultured and witty with it. If there was one thing of which she was truly grateful, it was his company. She knew she might be incarcerated for days or even weeks, so it was a joy unexpected to be able to pass a fair proportion of them immersed in Sir Samuel's library. She was looking forward to re-translating Chapman's Homer back into the Greek, or comparing the relative merits of Jonson's work with, say, Dryden's. With Chapman running through her head, Susan soon fell back into the clutches of Morpheus.

Susan had been sleeping for perhaps half an hour when a knock at the door woke her.

'Enter,' she said, and Morland walked in.

'I wanted merely to enquire after your stomach. Does it still protest, Miss Susan?' he asked. 'I have changed our order of bread to manchet. I believe it to be easier on the digestion.'

'I thank you, Sir Samuel,' said Susan. 'I shall be sure to report to your superiors, though they may be that in name only, that you have used me with great kindness.'

'Why thank you,' said Morland, his eyes drawn to the paper on the table. 'It is the least one can do in such unpleasant circumstances,' he added. 'After all, we may be on different sides, but you are still a lady, and I still a gentleman.'

'I wonder, might I enquire as to the nature of this engine here?' She pointed at a round, brass instrument with numbers and figures set round a series of concentric dials.

'You are of a natural philosophical bent?' said Morland. 'Most excellent. It is a device of my own devising, designed to allow the user to manipulate money with ease. Through the simple turning of these wheels, amounts of money may be added to one another, subtracted from one another, multiplied by one another and divided into one another. It will revolutionise commerce, taxation and indeed any activity that relies upon quick and accurate calculations. A similar engine might also be applied to navigation, and even cryptography.' He spoke the final three words with a whisper.

'Cryptography? What, pray...'

'Ah,' said Morland. 'Cryptography is the rendering of writing into code such that no one without the key can read it.' He smiled. 'This engine will be the universal key. When I have ironed out some little inconsistencies, at least. I believe it will soon be time to take supper, so I shall take my leave of you until then.' At that, Morland turned and left the room.

11

Thursday 10th April, 4pm
Nathaniel investigates

Nathaniel was en route to Lambeth House, but first he was intent on giving young Jonny a kick up the arse. Surely he had been overly distracted by the charms of young Molly, so he made a diversion by way of the Mermaid. Molly was absent but expected so he sat down for some ale and pie. He ate steadily and, some twenty minutes later, watched as Molly walked into the tavern and gave a letter to the innkeeper. The innkeeper pointed at Nathaniel and Molly hesitated, turned to leave but, obviously conscious that he was watching, changed her mind.

'Young Molly,' said Nathaniel. 'You don't know me, but I've been waiting for you. Come have a drink.' He saw Molly's hesitation. 'That is not a request, Molly. I work with young Jonny. My name is Nathaniel.'

Molly's countenance changed in a second. 'Nathaniel!' she beamed. 'How lovely to meet you at last. Jonny speaks very highly of you.' She sat down at his table, and a sudden thought hit her. 'Is he all right?'

'I was about to ask the same question.'

'Oh?' said Molly. 'Why so?'

'He has yet to come to work, Molly. This is most unlike him. I figured he had woken entwined in your delightful arms and had decided that it was the place to be today.' He smiled at Molly, and winked. 'Can't say I'd blame him.'

'I didn't know he was back. And if he's entwined in anyone's arms they certainly aren't mine.' She frowned. 'Some little slut's got her claws in him, no doubt,' she said, looking every inch the jilted lover.

'Behave, Molly,' said Nathaniel. 'He dotes on you. It's getting a bit annoying, frankly. Can you not do something to rile him so he'll stop going on about how bloody perfect you are?' He watched Molly's face carefully, as a tear broke free from what was plainly a fierce attempt at self-control.

'I fear for him, Nathaniel.'

'Oh, Molly. He'll be fine. It's just that he returned to London yesterday, ran off to see you and has pretty much vanished.'

'Well, he never found me,' said Molly. 'I hope he's not in trouble.'

'Oh, don't you worry. He's a sharp one. It'd take one hell of a girl to pull the wool over his eyes. And as for catching them, there's no one compares with you, Molly. So stop blubbing. He'll turn up. It's just that things are a little testy and we could use his hands on the pump, so to speak.' As Molly looked at Nathaniel, it was obvious that he scared her. His best efforts at making it appear that he was merely worried about Jonny had plainly failed. But any attempt to turn him, one way or the other, would be as difficult as it was dangerous. 'Well,' he said. 'Send him to me the moment he surfaces. And don't scratch his eyes out. We need them.'

The net was closing in on Molly, though it was plain that she had no idea whose boat it was being thrown from.

Nathaniel led Molly down a couple of alleys to confirm that she was following him before turning into a busy thoroughfare where he lost her. He then visited the chamber where none but Isaac sat working through the day's post. No Jonny.

12

Thursday 10th April, 8pm
Diana prefers blondes

'You are not safe, Molly,' said Diana, running her fingers through Molly's hair. 'You are too well known in these parts, dear sister.'

Molly smiled. 'Some might say you are the notorious one.'

'I think that was a compliment.'

'You must take it in sense that feel it.'

'When they find poor Jonny, you will be under suspicion of at least some sort of involvement,' said Diana. 'And we really ought to get you somewhere safe.'

'I'm not running away, dear sister. Not while Miss Susan remains in danger.'

'I should hope not. But luckily, I have a plan.'

'Why does that thought not fill me with joy, Diana?' said Molly.

Diana stood and led Molly back to her lodgings, taking a circuitous route to make sure that anyone following them would give themselves away through excessive boldness or lose track of them through timidity. When they were both sure that they were untracked, they went in through the back way, and Diana left Molly in her room, though not before giving instructions. She then disappeared, returning an hour later carrying a bucket and a large packet. She shut and bolted the door behind her.

'Have you prepared things as I instructed?' asked Diana, setting down her bucket carefully and placing the packet on the bed.

'Yes, but why in God's name do you carry that bucket of foulness with you? It stinks like a tavern privy in summer. What is it?'

'It is what we shall use to change your appearance. Well, that and the contents of that package.'

'And how, prey, do you intend to do that?'

'It's a trick my grandmother taught me,' said Diana, as she unwrapped the packet carefully and placed some of the contents into a bowl. She then took a ladle and mixed in some of the liquid, and in doing so, filled the room with such a stench as made Molly dry heave. 'It's chamber lye.'

'Chamber lye?' said Molly, incredulous. 'Fermented piss?'

'Indeed it is,' said Diana, mixing more of the packet's contents with the lye, making a thick paste. 'The original recipe calls for lye made from the ash of burnt ashwood, but we have neither the time nor the timber. And anyway, this was in the laundry room.' She smiled at her charge. 'But it's fine. These are herbs and lichens, finely chopped to mix with it that will,' she hesitated, 'help.' Molly just stared. 'Now, while we wait for that to cure, we can close-crop you.' With this, Diana reached into her bag and brought out a pair of shears.

'You jest, surely, sister?' said Molly as Diana approached her, shears in hand.

Diana shook her head. 'Just keep still. It's the sheep as struggles loses more than its fleece, or so they say.'

Molly took a deep breath and closed her eyes. 'I trust you're skilled in the art, sister?' Diana shook her head.

'You're my first.' And she began to snip. Molly crossed her

fingers. After ten minutes Diana was starting to sing to herself as she cut Molly's hair closer and closer to her scalp. 'You'll make a very handsome boy.' A further five minutes was all Diana needed. She stepped back and admired her handiwork. 'Not bad, even though I say so myself,' she said, placing the shears back into her bag and surveying the mass of hair that now surrounded her unwilling model. 'Now for stage two.' And with this she picked up the bowl in which she had mixed the paste. 'Put the linen around your neck and dip your hair in the hot water.' She watched Molly obey. 'Good. Now rest the back of your neck on the side of my bowl here.'

'You must be joking, I'm not putting my head anywhere near that, that stuff.'

'Sister!' said Diana, sharply. 'Qu'est-ce que tu me dit? Est-tu une vraie fille d'Ophélie ou une autre?'

'Yes, sister, I apologise.' And she lay her head on the edge of the bowl on Diana's lap.

'Now,' said Diana, 'this will not be pleasant, but these are desperate times, and we are also pitted against desperate men. What we do now may allow us a second longer in which to act. And that second may be our second. It may be la différence.' With this she began to brush the stinking paste she had made onto Molly's newly cropped hair. When she was finished, she wrapped her head in strips of linen. 'There. That will need two or three hours to take.' She looked at Molly. 'I wouldn't sit up, if I were you.' She paused while Molly simply looked quizzical. 'A lump of lye-soaked herbage is not something you wish to have sliding down your face.'

'I'd normally say I've had worse, but I fear in this case it would be a lie,' said Molly. 'Though I feel sure the same cannot be said for you.'

And the two women were silent.

13

Friday 11th April, 2pm
Thurloe in torment

He had woken drenched in cold, clammy sweat as his body sought to turn itself inside out, his viscera evacuate themselves and his skin fold inwards. An overwhelming sense of foreboding had strapped his arms tight onto his cot and clamped its hand over his mouth. The scream, when it came, was from somewhere so animal deep inside him that he had turned his head in terror towards the open door, but kept his eyes closed, unsure what he feared most: to be torn asunder by beast unknown or to stare into the jaws of his destruction. But this was no unknown assailant that had moved him from sleep to the edge of unconsciousness in a matter of moments with a pain like none other. It was a stone bigger than any he had previously seen, let alone evacuated. The walk to Lambeth House had been his first exercise in days, and with each step he was reminded of the unwelcome guest that had seen fit to leave in the middle of Tuesday night. This Sisyphean block of calcium was the eagle that feasted on his kidneys. And still they came, albeit ever smaller, still they came. Thurloe could no less escape the conclusion he was being punished for his adultery than the knowledge that now would be an unfortunate time to be interrogated by him. Revenge may keep his own wounds green, which otherwise would heal, but it helped assuage the pain, if only temporarily. It was more than this, however, as he did not much like important arrests or discoveries happening without him. This was how control was lost. It was how mistakes happened. It was how people escaped. Today, he would be unlikely to escape the feeling that if the object of his attentions did not feel substantially less comfortable than he, someone was not doing their job properly. Today, Thurloe was troubled.

He called the guard, who opened the heavy oak door and unchained the prisoner, who fell to his knees jabbering his thanks and promising to tell everything.

'Save it for Master Secretary Thurloe,' said Nathaniel. 'He suffers from the stone and thus will suffer neither fools nor dissemblers, but make them suffer. He finds it most excellent physic.'

'I will tell all,' said the apothecary. 'Even how to deaden the pain.'

'Just pray that he finds matter in the telling, or you will know it straightways,' said Nathaniel. 'Here we are. Just remember to leave Master Secretary Thurloe satisfied, or it will be the worse for you.' He pushed the door open and ushered Thurloe into the room. 'The apothecary, Master Secretary.'

'Ensure someone remains hard by the door on the outside. I will summon them as becomes necessary,' said Thurloe. 'You may visit Morland and attend me in my chambers tomorrow afternoon.' Nathaniel smiled, nodded, left the room and shut the door behind him.

'Now, Anthony,' said Thurloe. 'It is Anthony Hinton of the Bailey, correct?'

'Yes, Master Secretary,' replied Hinton, his voice quiet.

'Speak up, man!' said Thurloe, raising his voice.

'Yes, Master Secretary.' Hinton tried once more, forcing himself to be more strident.

'Nathaniel has doubtless informed you that I am suffering a fit of the stone,' said Thurloe. 'I no more wish to be here than you. I am impatient at the best of times, but today I will only ask a question once. If I do not receive immediate satisfaction it will hurt. Do you understand, apothecary?'

'Yes, Master Secretary.' Hinton's voice cracked as he spoke.

'Explain to me the system.'

'Yes, Master Secretary. I receive letters addressed to me, which contain letters within. I open them, extract the enclosures and, having decoded the addresses as written, deliver them as appropriate.'

'Good,' said Thurloe. 'Now, a test. Any attempt to lie and I will begin to question you hard.'

'Yes, Master Secretary.'

'Code names first,' said Thurloe. 'Who is John Shaw?'

'That is not a code name, Master Secretary. John Shaw is a merchant of Antwerp. It is through him that money is sent to the court.'

'The court?' said Thurloe, bristling.

'My apologies, Master Secretary,' said Hinton, his voice now tremulous with fear. Hinton had treated several men unfortunate enough to have been subject to one of Thurloe's questionings. His understanding was that his treatment of prisoners was more dependent on his mood than whether his questions were answered. And his mood was darkening. 'The traitor and his followers. Several times these three or four years I have supplied money through him. Sometimes forty pounds. Sometimes fifty or sixty at a time; all which sums were returned by bills of exchange to Dr Morley, payable by Mr John Shaw.'

'Good, good. Who is Mr Edwardes?'

Hinton hesitated. Thurloe stared at him. 'The k... Charles Stuart, Master Secretary.'

'Good. We know as much.' With these words of Thurloe's, Hinton began to relax. It was perhaps a little presumptuous. 'Now, the next questions are vitally important. Your fingers will not appreciate any obfuscation.'

'No, Master Secretary,' said Hinton, as he began to sweat again.

'Code names,' said Thurloe. 'Andrews.'

'John Earle, Bishop of Salisbury,' replied Hinton.

'Westenbergh.'

'Dr Hammond.'

'Mrs Edwards.'

'Susan Hyde.'

'A woman? Who is she?'

'Indeed, sir, she is sister to Sir Edward,' replied Hinton.

'He has a sister?' asked Thurloe.

'Indeed.'

'Interesting,' said Thurloe. 'Mrs Simburbe.'

'Susan Hyde.'

'Really?' said Thurloe. 'No need to ask who goes by the code S.H., then? She is a busy woman,' said Thurloe. 'And where might I find the mistress of spies?'

'Last I heard she had left town to visit relatives in the country.'

Thurloe smiled. 'On this point, it appears I have more information than you,' he said. 'She was in the country, but she now stays in London as my guest.' Susan Hyde? Thurloe had landed a big fish. At least, the sister of a big fish, though it did appear as if this woman was rather more involved in this business than he had thought possible. 'Make yourself comfortable, apothecary. You're still a spy. You will most likely never leave Lambeth. Enjoy your stay.' With that, Thurloe was gone. Hinton spent the journey back to his cell in prayer.

14

Friday 11th April, 10pm

Morland's house guest is vexed

After supper, when Mary and Joseph had retired, and Susan was drifting off to sleep once more, Morland burst into her chamber with two servants.

'Wake up, Miss Susan, and show me the letter you have written!' shouted Morland.

'What?' said Susan. 'Who wakes me?'

'Show me the letter,' shouted Morland again, 'the letter!'

'I wrote no letter, Sir Samuel, if it please you. I was intent on writing my testament, but could not bring myself to begin.'

'Get out of bed, traitor,' shouted Morland. 'You mean to escape and see me hanged! After I have used you so well. We will take you straightways to Lambeth House.' He pointed to his servants, who searched the room and found nothing. 'Fetch muskets, pistols.'

'Why do you vex me so, Sir Samuel?' Susan was beginning to shake with fear. 'Why do you vex me so?'

Morland gesticulated once more and the two servants tore off her night clothes. 'We will take you away in the morning. Until then you will go nowhere.' And as suddenly as they had arrived, he and his servants were gone, the door locked behind them. Susan lay on the bed, naked and shaking from head to toe.

And that was how Mary found her the next morning. She and Joseph calmed her down and made her as comfortable in her bed as they could, trying to ignore her ramblings about her captors trying to kill her. She heard a knocking at the front door. It was a delivery boy. She told Joseph to watch over Susan and went downstairs. When she arrived at the bottom of the stairs Sir Samuel was on the street talking with the boy while his servant took the comestibles from his basket to transfer to the kitchen. Mary ran to the door.

'Sir Samuel,' she said, all a-fluster. 'Did he bring the mint as requested? My mistress has a sore stomach still.'

'Yes, Mary,' he replied, handing her the bunch of green. 'Is Miss Susan otherwise well this morning?' Morland spoke as though nothing had happened the night before. Mary considered it wise to take the same approach.

'Yes, thank you,' she replied, 'though she wishes to take her breakfast in her chamber, an it please you.'

'Of course, as she wishes,' said Morland.

Mary then turned to the boy. 'Thank you, thank you,' she said, palming the boy a penny.

Morland caught his wrist. 'What did she give you, boy?' he said, gravely. 'Let me see.'

'It was a penny, sir, that's all,' said the boy as he opened his fist to demonstrate that he told the truth.

'Well, my apologies to you,' he said to the boy, before turning to Mary. 'And to you, kind Mary.' As he turned to continue, Mary pointed at her waistband, where the note was almost completely hidden. Before the conversation was over, and Mary had left to take Susan her mint, the boy had lifted the note expertly and hidden it under a cuff. He then took the penny Morland offered and went about his business.

15

Saturday 12th April
Diana watches

Molly walked down the alley and into the courtyard, where Diana waited for her. She took great pains to ensure she was not followed.

'Nothing,' said Molly. 'No movement as yet. No one in, no one out.'

'That's no use to us,' said Diana. 'We can't get led to Susan if there's no one to follow. Still, it's early. I've heard nothing of Jonny, either.'

'You won't,' said Molly, whose eyes were red from crying. 'We murdered him, remember?'

'I meant that he's not yet been found. That's all.'

'So?'

'Until they find him, we're pretty safe, as they won't be wanting to speak with anyone who knows him as a matter of urgency. Plus there's the key.'

'The key?'

'The key we found,' said Diana. 'If he's still undiscovered tonight then we should see if it's of any use.'

'You mean, break into his place of work, where the

parliamentarians plot our demise? I must admit, I thought I had some crazy ideas on occasion but you are something else.'

'Not break in, walk in. You said you knew how to find where he worked, so it only seems wise to check every avenue open to us, and that one has got to have enough potential to be worth the risk, no?'

'I suppose so,' said Molly. 'I said I knew how to get a note delivered, which is not quite the same. But two women walking through government corridors alone?'

'Molly, I said you'd make a lovely boy with cropped hair. Now, get back to your lodgings and relieve me in an hour.' With this, Diana kissed her fingers and held them to Molly's locket. 'Be vigilant, sister,' she said, and skipped back down the alley to continue the surveillance of Morland's house.

As the morning wore on there was much movement in the street, but none at Morland's house until a boy wandered up to the front door with a basketful of food. 'Ah, so you have guests, Sir Samuel?' she said under her breath as she watched a maid appear, then a second. There was a short altercation that ended kindly enough, but there was something else. The second maid had allowed the boy to steal something from her waistband. She had seen enough. As the boy left and the front door closed she scuttled after him, catching him up around the corner.

'Boy!' she called, holding up a penny. 'One penny to come speak to me; another if I like what I hear.' The boy hesitated, looked around, and then ran to her and snatched the penny from her fingers.

'Yes,' was all he said.

'What did you deliver and how much?' asked Diana, holding another penny just out of the boy's reach.

'Two manchet loaves, a venison pie, artichokes, a dozen apples, some cheese and a great bunch of mint. And he asked for some more small beer,' said the boy.

'Thank you,' said Diana, giving him the second penny. 'One more question,' she began.

'Another penny?'

'Yes,' said Diana. The boy nodded greedily. 'Did the maid give you a note?'

'Yes,' said the boy, handing the letter to Diana. 'I heard voices within. They seemed to be rehearsing a nativity.'

'I beg your pardon?'

'I couldn't make out much other than Mary and Joseph, though,' said the boy.

'That is excellent work,' said Diana, handing him the third penny. 'If you hear anything else, you come and find me,' she laughed. 'After all, I'm not hard to find! There are more pennies for you.' The boy rushed off before she changed her mind. Today had gone well so far. Diana waited until Molly returned before opening the letter.

Sister,

I am held close by. I fear. May the man with the feather in his cap attend my pleasure.

'Sister,' said Molly. 'What does this mean?'

'We must get word to Talbot to be ready to act,' said Diana.

'Talbot?'

'I'll explain later,' said Diana, 'I shall remain here, while you return to the Mermaid and give this to Margarita.' Molly nodded her head, took the letter and melted into the crowded streets.

16

Saturday 12th April, 2pm

Nathaniel shares his information

Nathaniel left Morland's house rather more confused and a lot more worried than when he had arrived. He could feel the tension that had enveloped the denizens of the Black Chamber since Morland and Jonny had undertaken their madcap ride to capture S.H., who now awaited the Master Secretary's pleasure at Morland's well-appointed residence. There she was kept in a luxury not enjoyed by those who had uncovered her, as were her maidservant and attendant. It appeared that Morland had an indulgent streak matched only, he presumed, by that of the father at whose expense he lived. He certainly could not keep such a house on the wages he received in Thurloe's employ. But still, at least S.H. could be closely watched, a task that would have been more easily achieved had Jonny seen fit to return to work that day instead of luxuriating in young Molly's embrace - the girl was plainly lying about Jonny's whereabouts. Still, Nathaniel could hardly blame her for that. He would fetch Jonny later. In the meantime, he decided not to let Susan's prison warder in on the little secret he was party to, and her state when he visited ensured that she had no idea that her identity, or both her identities, as appeared to be more relevant, had fallen prey to Thurloe's network.

Within half an hour Nathaniel was knocking on the door of Thurloe's chambers. Thurloe bade him enter and inside he found the Master Secretary stretched out on the bed staring at the ceiling. He had a small knife in one hand and was slowly, painstakingly, peeling an apple, the single strip of green coiling like a snake around its prey.

'You are ill again?' asked Nathaniel.

'I am on the mend,' said Thurloe. 'I believe there is but the one stone yet to complete its journey. I will be in my bed for the next day or two.' He paused with his peeling, motioning to Nathaniel to pass him the bottle that sat by him. He took a drink from it. 'Passing tolerable relief,' he said. 'No sign of Jonny?'

'No,' said Nathaniel. 'Molly says she knows nothing but she lies.'

'Interesting.'

'And Samuel's house is being watched by a woman who I swear I've seen before. And I have intelligence.'

'And I too,' said Thurloe.

'The apothecary?' asked Nathaniel.

'Indeed,' said Thurloe. 'So keen to talk, as if like the nightingale the dark encourages the song.'

'And his notes?'

'Most agreeable. It turns out our correspondent S.H. is none other than Susan Hyde, sister to Sir Edward Hyde. She has been running a pretty little postal service. But I will see her suffer for it. I trust your intelligence is less interesting?'

'More, Master Secretary, more,' said Nathaniel. He wasn't exactly looking forward to sharing his news.

'Well, come on, man,' said Thurloe, somewhat exasperated. 'If it's of more interest than that, you must say.'

'It is Miss Susan, Master Secretary.'

'Yes, what of her?' said Thurloe, the excitement in his voice betraying him. 'Have you intelligence of her whereabouts?

'I know her position precisely, Master Secretary.'

'Well, out with it, man,' said Thurloe.

'She is currently with Sir Samuel Morland.'

Thurloe went quiet, his excitement now confusion. 'She throws me over for that excuse of a man? Have them brought to me.'

'No, Master Secretary. You misunderstand. Miss Susan is S.H. She is Susan Hyde.'

Thurloe went pale. His fist closed tight over the knife and apple. 'Are you sure?' He paused, and took more from the bottle. 'Nathaniel!'

'Yes, Master Secretary,' said Nathaniel. 'Quite sure.' He waited for the inevitable reaction. It would be swift, brutal and final.

'This cannot be known, Nathaniel,' said Thurloe, his once pale brow darkening. 'Transfer her to Lambeth House. There keep her close, remove all signs from her. Use her ill. I do not expect her to see the spring. Take my signet but make all obscure.'

'Yes, Master Secretary.' There was a knock on the door. Nathaniel answered and was handed a note. He indicated that it was for Thurloe, who nodded that he ought open it. 'It is from Isaac. It is not good news. They have found Jonny. It appears that he was murdered.'

'This is sad news indeed,' said Thurloe. 'Miss Susan a spy and Jonny murdered. I cannot but believe that these facts are not unconnected. Arrest his girl. She will know something, if not everything. Now be gone.'

17

Saturday 12th April, 3pm
Thurloe has a revelation

It was not until Nathaniel had left that Thurloe released his fist. The blood ran over the apple and its serpentine peel as if to remind Thurloe of his sin once more. Surely this could not be true? Susan, his Susan, the woman with whom he sinned in word, thought and deed, she could not be a royalist, let alone a she-intelligencer. He knew such women. Base, faithless, morally bankrupt. They would sell their unborn child. But Susan was as pure and as kind a soul as he had ever known. She had never tried to seduce him, if anything she'd pushed him away. She... and then it struck him. She had worried about the poxy whore she'd saved. She'd asked about she-intelligencers. And her kiss. It had quite entranced him. Thurloe cast his mind back to one of S.H.'s letters. It had mentioned the 'old ways', and he had thought she wrote 'mystically'. Thurloe knew then that he had fallen victim to a witch.

The blood dripped onto the floor as his arm fell loose, and his hand released both fruit and blade.

18

Saturday 12th April, 4pm

Morland's house guest is moved

'Sir Samuel,' said Mary. 'I fear that Miss Susan is more than passing inconvenienced, and so have taken the liberty of sending for a nurse more capable than I in these matters.'

'I'm not sure I appreciate your presumption, Mary,' said Morland. 'Do you think me incapable of employing a suitable attendant for Miss Susan?'

'As you wish, Sir Samuel,' replied Mary. 'I bow to your superior knowledge of women's matters, and will welcome whomever you think most fit to attend Miss Susan. I'm sure that no one will apportion blame in your direction should your choice be unable to provide suitable care.'

Morland stood for a while, scratching his chin. 'Women's matters, you say?'

'Indeed, Sir Samuel,' replied Mary.

'Why didn't you say so earlier?' said Morland. 'When does your nurse arrive?'

'Mrs Chaffin is expected presently,' said Mary. 'Am I at liberty to acquire what simples are necessary?'

'Of course,' said Morland. 'But you will need an escort.'

'Naturally,' replied Mary, who returned to Susan's chamber to find her sleeping lightly, Joseph by her side. 'Has she shown any sign of recovery?' asked Mary.

'She sleeps better, as you can see,' said Joseph. 'And when last she awoke she had greater control of her senses.'

'Good,' said Mary. 'We will have assistance soon to help tend to her.' There was a knock at the door. 'That will be her now,' said Mary, and she bustled downstairs only to find Morland by the door, speaking with a thickset gentleman. Mary stopped on the stairs to see if she could ascertain what it was the man wanted, but it was already too late.

'My good Mary,' said Morland. 'I am afraid there has been a change of plan, and Miss Susan is to be transferred to a location more fitting for a whore and she-intelligencer.'

'Sir Samuel, for shame,' said Mary. 'How can you use such language of a lady?'

'Like I said, a whore and she-intelligencer,' repeated Morland. 'No lady she.'

'And you no gentleman, despite your title, Sir Samuel,' said Mary. 'Your part in this shall not be forgotten.'

'By whom?' Morland said, laughing. 'By an ageing lady's maid and a country bumpkin servant. Well are you named Joseph and Mary, for 'twould be a miracle indeed if you were to give birth to any manner of intrigue.' At this, Morland whispered something to the man who stood on the threshold. 'I wouldn't bother packing Miss Susan's effects. All she needs where she's going is a clear conscience. And I'm not convinced she will ever have one of those.'

Mary spat at Morland's feet but he simply laughed and directed the visitor to go upstairs. Two more men entered the house and the three of them went directly to Susan's chamber. Within seconds an unsettling sound began to drift down the stairs, a low moaning that grew in both pitch and volume as it transformed itself into a scream and, then, silence.

'You are a sorry, pathetic individual,' said Mary, as she strode toward the stairs, intent on aiding her charge, but Morland held her back.

'You may attend to her when I say you may,' said Morland. 'And at this moment, you may not.'

Morland was smiling as the three men carried a motionless figure wrapped only in a sheet down the stairs and towards the house's still open door.

'Set her down,' said Morland, and the men held her upright in front of him. She began to wake; the moaning starting once more. Morland slapped her across the face, hard. 'Be silent.'

The force of the blow brought Susan back into full consciousness, and she stared back at her captor. 'If I am silent it is because I choose to be,' she said.

'What is this?' said Morland, ripping Susan's locket from her throat and inspecting it. 'How sweet. It even has a motto. *Ego avis enim cantans inaspecta.* The nightingale. And yet Philomela could not sing but instead was seen. Explain this.' He opened the locket, took out the entwined hairlocks and waved them in her face. 'And this.'

Susan smiled. 'You will know when it is time for you to know.'

'Get her out of my sight,' said Morland, and the men carried the now silent and subdued Susan out into the street, where a cart awaited them. They dumped her in the back and one man sat either side of her while the third grabbed the whip and the cart trotted off. 'Good riddance to her,' said Morland as he looked at the locket more closely. 'A nice piece. As ever, I thrive in another's adversity.'

Mary simply stood and glared at the man who was so triumphant with so little cause. Another knock, and this time it was Mrs Chaffin. Mary spoke with her briefly and then looked to Morland.

'Lambeth House, for all the good it will do you,' said

Morland. 'You are welcome to follow, for all the good it will do her. They may allow it, they may not. 'Tis out of my hands.'

Joseph and Mary packed what few of Susan's effects were still undamaged and left the house alongside Mrs Chaffin.

19

Sunday 13th April, 2pm
Susan is put to question

The cart ride was cold and uncomfortable, but most of all it was humiliating. It was insult enough that Susan was being transported in a cart but for her to be wrapped solely in a sheet was simply despicable. Even Charles had been treated with appropriate decorum when led to his murder on the scaffold. This insult could not be borne. And yet, for all that, Susan hoped that her brother might never hear of this. He had already stripped away her chastity by putting her in such a position that she had to become mistress to Thurloe, though following her childless marriage she assumed that he believed, like all others, that she was barren. At least had this proven still to be true Edward would not have had to worry about the proof of her adultery that now slept in her stomach. Edward had forsaken her the moment he had thrown that letter on the fire. She prayed he would not find cause or opportunity to forsake her again. She would at least be due the martyr's memorial in his great book, that was clear.

The cart entered the yard at Lambeth House and as soon as it stopped she was taken roughly by the wrists, manhandled towards the main door and then inside, where she was further pushed and pulled down corridor and stairway, the atmosphere growing colder and damper as she progressed. Her captors were not intent on her longevity. They arrived. She perceived this because they stopped at an open doorway. The chief amongst them took Susan by the arms and pushed her into the damp cell and sat her on a bench.

'Thank you, Nathaniel,' said a voice she recognised. 'You may leave us.'

'John,' she said simply, as the door closed with an achingly final thud.

The cell was as dark as it was dank, and Susan could not make out the features of the man she both loved and despised in equal measure. She could feel his anger, his vitriol, as it filled the empty spaces around her, hemming her in. It imprisoned her as effectively as any stone.

'Master Secretary Thurloe to you, Miss Hyde,' said Thurloe. 'Though you deserve neither title, as you are no better than a nameless nothing.'

'If that makes you feel better about your adultery, John, then so be it,' replied Susan.

'You seduced me, bewitched me,' said Thurloe.

'It was you who pursued me, John.'

'Because of your spells. I should have known. You wrote your guilt. "Let me know your mind by the old way, the hartichokes," was one such admission. Before I knew who you were, when you were just S.H. to me, I annotated one of your letters "by the one who writes mystically", and it appears I was correct, as usual. You are a witch, and you shall die as one.'

'It is ironic that you are akin to a devil. I am barren, and yet your seed lives in me. I will not hang, John, your child here will not allow it.' She stroked her belly and smiled, letting her sheet fall away. She knew the proscription against destroying the unborn, no matter the offence of the mother. 'Behold your whore, your witch, mother of your child.'

'You lie,' said Thurloe. 'You lie as you always lied.'

'And you lust as you always lusted, but I lied for a cause greater than myself, for the return of the rule of God and king over this land. You lusted for your own pleasure. This child does not lie.'

'What makes you think I did not know you from the start?' said Thurloe, but Susan just laughed.

'I will make a deal with you, devil.' Thurloe made to speak but she quietened him with the barest of movement in her index finger. Susan felt the power she wielded as if it were lightning. It surged through her, emboldening her. This was not the power of the Sisterhood, nor even of a mother. This was a power that came because the only things that Susan had to lose, her life and that of her child, their child, were things she actively wished to be rid of. 'I will make a deal with you, devil,' she repeated. 'But it is a one-time offer, and there will be no negotiation. Refuse and I shall go to my doom, yes, but by all that is sacred I will take you down with me. Will you hear the terms?'

'Yes,' said Thurloe.

'Good,' said Susan. 'They are these. You will allow my maid and a nurse of her choosing to attend to me. It will show kindness and intent to preserve life on your part, so is nothing but good for you. You will allow them to treat me with drugs that pacify. I shall sleep else rave like a mad woman. Do you agree so far?'

'So far, all seems agreeable enough.'

'You will allow me a visit from my minister, that I might write my testament.'

'And what good will that do you?'

'I am an adulteress who carries the spawn of the devil inside me. I fear no judgement,' replied Susan, 'but I fear being misrepresented.'

'And why should I allow such a thing?'

'There are two good reasons, John. The first is that you owe your life to me.'

'In what sense, harlot?'

'In the sense that at any time of my choosing, I might have become Judith to your Holophones.'

'And the second?' said Thurloe. 'What you might have done is of no value here. It remains undone.'

'The second is that I have written our testament already. It lies in a letter addressed to the Lord Protector himself, which will be delivered by an innocent hand on the fifth of May if word does not reach them to destroy it.'

'Our testament?'

'Yes,' said Susan. 'Our testament. If you wish for your cupidity, your lust, your adultery and dishonour to remain known only to you, then you will allow me to send word to my minister.'

'And if I do not?'

'Your protector will discover all, which you do not desire.' Susan did not wish to reveal that she had found what were presumably his secret archives, books that he could only be keeping as insurance against any change of his status within the governmental apparatus.

'Do I have any choice?'

'No. There is no way to cheat fate. Allow me my solace and I will tell you the sign that will lead to the destruction of the letter. Then you may do as you will.'

'And why should I not simply extract the information?'

Susan placed her hand on her belly. 'Not even you would dare,' she said. 'I do not ask if you agree. You must and you know it. And be not minded to betray my trust, as such will be your betrayal of yourself. Our story is written. Once I have salved my conscience, it shall be destroyed in all but yours.'

'And so our saga comes to its end.'

'Indeed it does. Kindly allow my maid to attend to me that I may make suitable arrangements. And deliver me of pen, paper and ink.'

'It shall be done,' said Thurloe, and left Susan alone in her cell.

Susan drew her sheet tighter around herself and shivered. Thurloe would not stick to his part of the bargain, this she knew full well. But this knowledge would, she hoped, be enough to allow her to thwart his intentions. He meant for her to hang, of this she was sure. But she would not give him the satisfaction.

The cell door swung open.

'Write,' said Thurloe, and watched as Susan did as she was bidden.

'It needs no seal. I know it will not go unread,' said Susan, handing him the folded paper. 'I hope this is the last we see of each other.' Thurloe took the letter, and turned to leave. 'In another time this may have ended differently, John.'

Thurloe shut the cell door behind him and walked from Susan's cell, limping slightly. He called for Nathaniel.

20

Sunday 13th April, 3pm
Nathaniel makes a choice

Nathaniel had remained hard by the cell door but neither of the occupants had raised their voices sufficiently to allow him to ascertain the meat of their conference. As it ended he had quickly slunk away, as much as he was capable of slinking. On hearing his name called he turned and made as if he were walking back to the cell. He met Thurloe, whose countenance was darker even than when in the grip of the stone.

'I have made a deal with the witch,' said Thurloe. 'But we shall capture a whole nest of them. Arrange for her maid to attend to her and allow a nurse of her choosing access also. Watch them closely. Find me a wise woman who can abort the child she carries that we might hang her.'

'Sir?' said Nathaniel. 'Is that necessary, Master Secretary? An innocent must die?' Nathaniel had seen more than his fair share of death, and been responsible for a large proportion of it, but he had never been unfair. Those who met their end at his hand were either actively engaged in an attempt on Nathaniel's life or working towards such a thing. But an unborn child? Quite apart from its being anathema, it was plain wrong. Nathaniel was a soldier. He obeyed orders. He was not especially religious, but he knew right from wrong.

'It is no innocent, Nathaniel, it is the issue of a malignant and a witch. And she will hang. But first I needs must recover a dangerous document. You will take this letter to Isaac, and once he has transcribed it you must deliver it. But keep a close watch on the recipient.'

'Yes, Master Secretary,' said Nathaniel. And he left Lambeth House, unsure of how to do right by Miss Susan. She may have been a she-intelligencer, but there was the innocent child. Thurloe was, he felt, being led by his heart and not his head. By the time he had reached the Black Chamber that he might deliver this letter, he had purposed a course of action.

'I must visit the apothecary once more,' said Nathaniel, handing Isaac Susan's letter. 'But first you must unpick this that I must deliver post haste.'

'You look perfectly well to me,' said Isaac, taking the letter from Nathaniel's hand and unfolding it. 'A minister? I will transcribe and discover it.'

'And so I am, but I am bid to carry out some distasteful work,' said Nathaniel. He waited calmly for Isaac to finish, then took the letter and walked directly to the Mermaid.

'Innkeeper,' said Nathaniel as he walked through the doors, speaking loudly enough to quieten the clientele. Margarita attended to him almost instantaneously. 'Innkeeper,' he now spoke *sotto voce*, 'I have a letter. It is from Miss Susan to an unknown recipient. Beyond that I cannot say, other than there is coin for your trouble.' With this, Nathaniel turned and walked out into the street. He knew what would happen next, as this part of the distribution of information Hinton had recently revealed to his master. At the side of the tavern was an area that men used to relieve themselves, either on the wall itself or in one of the buckets left there for this very purpose. Here also were a series of hollows cut out of the wall just above waist height, where messages could be secreted and from where they might be recovered. Nathaniel found a suitable vantage point, not too obvious and yet close enough to ensure a relatively simple job of following the man who would surely collect Miss Susan's letter.

Nathaniel stood for over an hour before there was a break in the stream of less-than-gentlemen releasing their own streams of steaming piss wherever their drunken hands happened to direct them. It was a small boy, and Nathaniel watched as he first checked to make sure that the coast was clear and then walked up to the wall, sprayed a cursory quantity of urine about the place and dipped his hand into one of the hollows, fishing out the letter. On turning to leave, the two made eye contact and the boy immediately started to run. Nathaniel gave chase, but his prey was nimble and shook him off with ease, dodging between the carts and horses and people who flowed like a tide of living excrement through the streets.

'Well, I'm not going to win this one,' said Nathaniel to himself, as the boy disappeared from view. 'I may as well visit the apothecary, and then I might attend to the burial of poor Jonny.' He performed one more sweep of the street scene, turned and walked away.

21

Sunday 13th April, 5pm

Talbot glimpses his nemesis

On one corner a man with a feather in his hat bent down to listen to a small boy who pointed at Nathaniel. 'That is good work, Billy,' said the man, in a soft Scots accent. 'You have the letter?' Billy nodded, exchanging it for a handful of coin, and disappeared. 'Well, Nathaniel,' said Colonel Talbot. 'Our paths cross once again.'

22

Monday 14th April

Diana and Molly get into trouble

'I tell you I can still smell it,' said Molly. 'It's as though I fell asleep by the road in the sun and an entire troop of horse, every one of 'em hot and thirsty after hours in the saddle, decided to piss on me, and I didn't wake up until the sun had cured me nicely.' She hawked and spat. 'I'm going to smell like a privy for the rest of my life.'

'Oh, Molly,' said Diana. 'Don't be so melodramatic. It's really not as bad as you think. I can barely smell a thing unless I bury my nose in your hair, and then I grant you it's a little high, but that'll pass with another wash and some rose water.' Diana had her fingers crossed as she spoke. It was something she did a lot, crossing her fingers as she spoke. Sometimes even Diana was unsure when she was lying, and at such times she had long ago decided that it was best to assume that she was. She was quite sure that Molly had yet to come to such a conclusion. Still, there was ample time for such a realisation.

'Rose water? You haven't been drinking, have you, sister?' She hawked and spat again, this time following it with a long draught of wine which she swilled around her mouth, gargled and spat into the chamber pot. She then sucked wine up each nostril and did the same.

'Now that is seductive! Step up and see, fellas,' said Diana, laughing. Molly scowled at her, then stood up.

'Be silent, Diana,' said Molly, her face darkening. 'Jonny barely cold in his corner and you insult me like that. It seems wrong, leaving him there, at the mercy of Lord knows what,' said Molly. 'It's bad enough that we murdered him, without our defiling his corpse.'

There was still no word on his discovery. It would be a long time before Diana forgave Jonny for forcing her to make Molly deal with him. She hadn't been sure whether Molly was ready for such an action but well knew that were Diana to have carried out the assassination the relationship between her and Molly would have turned bitter. 'Molly, sister,' she said, grabbing her companion by the shoulders and looking her in the eye. 'We're not playing here. This is real. He's dead, we're not. I'm sorry, and I feel for you, but that's the way it is.'

'I don't think you understand, I...' but Diana interrupted her.

'I understand better than you know, sister,' said Diana, turning her grip into a hug as Molly's tears began again. 'We are women. We lose all that we love. We give everything, we give life, and all around us it is being taken away. I know. It was ever thus. It will ever be thus.'

The two women stood for a few minutes in each other's arms before Molly gave Diana a little squeeze and broke away.

'I understand, sister,' said Molly. 'Now. How do we get into his workplace without it being obvious?'

'Well. I have an idea but I'm not sure you'll like it.'

'Try me.'

'We let Jonny take us.'

'Jonny's dead, Diana,' said Molly. 'Don't rub it in.'

'We know that, but no one else appears to. Go to his lodgings

- after all, you're his girl - and pick up his remaining clothes, maybe that coat he loves. Loved.'

'And then what?'

'You may become Jonny,' said Diana. 'Then entering the lion's den will become rather less intimidating.'

'I can't believe...' began Molly, but Diana's eyes silenced her.

Diana took a good look at Molly. 'Smart girl,' she said. 'In fact, Molly should run away from the Mermaid, tonight. You can become a man, be my beau. I'll call you Denny.'

'You're serious.'

'Yes, Denny. I'm serious. Get you gone and come back a new man.' Diana kissed Molly and watched as she ran off.

Diana took the opportunity to quench her thirst. It was, as she well knew, unquenchable, however. It was a thirst for more than ale, more than money, more than revenge. It was a thirst for autonomy. All Diana wanted was to be allowed to be without having to justify herself. She could not help but push back against those who wished to place her. Talbot on the boat, insisting that she declare her allegiance. Seth that she existed for his pleasure. Samuel Filmer insisting that he knew her, could possess her. Thurloe, Thurloe... she was lost in her thoughts and supping her third ale when Molly returned, wearing Jonny's spare shirt and britches underneath the winter coat he had bought the previous year - or, as Jonny had put it, the coat generously donated to him as a gift by Mr Field. Diana figured Molly's breasts too small to be noticed under such loose clothing, and with her now blonde hair hidden under Jonny's old cap and a smear of dirt on her face, she looked every inch the well-favoured if scarce-bearded youth. Diana was impressed by the transformation.

'Hello Denny,' said Diana. 'I'm a little drunk. Sorry.'

'Typical. I'll just nip upstairs. Have a piss and get ready.' With that Molly ran up the stairs to her room, fetched the key, strapped her stiletto to her left arm, and returned to find Diana locked in an embrace with some man. 'Oi, you! Put my sister down right now!'

'Yes, mate,' said the man. 'Just as soon as your balls drop.'

Molly walked up behind Diana, shoved her right arm between her sister's legs and grabbed the man's testicles. 'Yours have, now shall I pull them off or are you going to fuck off?' She twisted and the man let go, screaming. 'Come on, sis,' said Molly and they left the tavern amidst peals of uproarious laughter.

They walked down the street, turned the corner and Molly pushed Diana against the wall of the alley. 'What are you playing at?' she hissed, and Diana laughed.

'My, you make a forceful man, Molly.' Diana was no longer slurring. 'I just wanted to see you could still be the man under duress, that's all. And I must say you did a fine job. If push comes to shove the push will be me against the wall and the shove your using me like a common slut.'

'Damn you, pick your moments,' said Molly. 'Shall we do this?'

'Let's.'

The two women walked the embankment route to the door Molly had seen Jonny open on several occasions, namely those occasions when she had followed him. Having checked there was no one watching or even within sight, Molly unlocked the door and they slipped into the courtyard. The night was clear enough and bright, their route across the courtyard and down the steps clearly illuminated. They came to a corridor which contained several doors.

'It must be one of these,' said Molly, and got out the key. She tried it in one while Diana looked at the others.

'Here.' Diana pointed at one of the doors.

'How can you tell?'

'It's the only one that's locked.' Molly struggled with the key as Diana lit a taper from the corridor. The door opened. The two women stood transfixed.

'Go on,' said Molly. 'Go find a candle.'

Diana walked in and picked up a candelabra with four candles stuck to its spindly arms. Molly lit them one by one and with each new flame the room became lighter and yet darker. 'It's funny,' said Diana. 'But the light makes the shadows deeper.'

'There can be no shadow without light, sister. So. What do they do all day in this forsaken room?'

Diana held up the light and as their eyes grew accustomed to the gloom that the candelabra shed into the darkness they took stock of its contents. At the room's heart stood a great oak table pushed up against the wall, with three chairs sitting obediently, tucked in tightly. On its top sat two wicker baskets, one at each end, and in front of each chair was an assortment of implements, pens, thin knives, inks, small pots of indeterminate substances, sticks of wax in various colours, bowls of sand, paper, brass seals, wafers and floss. Everything in front of the middle of the three chairs was arranged perfectly. It was almost as if they were looking at a Holbein. A row of unbound quires sat against the oak-panelled walls, and above them two broadsheets were pinned, covered in names and numbers in neat tables, some with other names written next to them. Small squares of paper were pinned all over the wall panels, each one bearing a name, a number, a place or a date.

'Whatever it is, they're seriously tidy. Well, one of them is, at any rate. They must write a lot of letters here.'

Molly looked into the baskets. 'They do. These baskets are full of letters, sister. Who are they sending them all to?' She picked up a quill, as black as the shadows that danced in the corners of the room. 'Black feathers?'

'Crow,' said Diana. 'I've seen these before.' She brought the light closer and they looked at the letters still on the table. 'Oh my God. They're not writing letters, they're opening them. It's the post. They're opening the post. All of it. They're reading everything.'

'The knot is undone,' said Molly.

'What do we do?'

'Nothing,' said Molly. 'Or they'll know we've been.' Molly's gaze was attracted by an unfolded piece of paper that sat upon the table, with the words 'Miss Susan' emblazoned upon it. It was short. 'Diana,' she said, holding up the paper. 'We must take this and show it to the Sisters. Susan means to act.'

'Let's get out of here before someone comes,' said Diana. They snuffed the candles, locked the door, ran up the stairs and across the courtyard. As they got to the door to the outside world a shout rang out.

'Oi!' it said. 'What do you think you're doing?' This was followed by the clatter of an armed man running over cobbles.

Diana lifted up her dress. 'Fuck me, fuck me now,' she said, and drew Molly's hips in between her open legs. 'Can't an honest working girl get some privacy?' she shouted at the guard.

'Not here,' said the guard, who already had his pistol levelled at the couple. 'How'd you get in, anyhow?'

'Door's open,' said Diana. The guard tried it; it opened.

'Shit,' he said. 'That shouldn't be open.' He turned to the couple. 'Now clear off out of it and find somewhere else to fuck.'

'Come on mister,' said Diana. 'Let me finish him and I'll give you a freebie.'

'Now!' said the guard. 'Before I shoot you both.'

They uncoupled and ran through the open gate, laughing, running until they were back at Molly's lodgings, where the adrenaline ran out, and they allowed sleep to envelop them.

Diana woke fully clothed, in Molly's arms.

23

Tuesday 15th April
Nathaniel takes action

Nathaniel arrived at the chamber in time to see Isaac Dorislaus unlocking the door and walking into the gloomy room ahead of him. His feet were as heavy as he knew Isaac's to be, as not only was there a full day's work to attend to - a new boxful of letters sat by the door awaiting his attention - but he was to prepare to assess the various boys who had been recommended as replacements for poor Jonny. As he walked through the doorway, he saw that Isaac looked confused.

'Something wrong, Isaac?' said Nathaniel, as he picked up the box of letters. The chamber was still somewhat dark. 'Isaac, man. Set a light to guide me.'

'Nathaniel,' said Isaac, turning to face his colleague. 'The candlestick has moved.'

'Truly?' asked Nathaniel, dumping the box on the table with a thump, and walking into a chair as he did so. He understood Isaac's discomposure now. While his need to have everything in the chamber 'just so' was sometimes rather comical, it did mean that items such as the candlestick always remained in their allotted place, even when Isaac was not the last to leave the chamber. It did so simply because no one could bear Isaac's constant questioning as he sought to discover who had moved it. And yet today it was out of place.

Nathaniel knew that one key was as yet unaccounted for since Jonny's disappearance - his had neither been found on his body nor in his lodgings. He walked out into the courtyard where the duty guard was about to be replaced.

'You there,' said Nathaniel. 'Anything to report?'

'The usual nothing,' said the guard. 'Except that one of you lot left the gate unlocked. I caught some slut with a customer in the courtyard.'

'Oh?' said Nathaniel. Isaac had been the last to leave the chamber on the previous day and the idea of his not locking the gate was laughable. 'Remember anything about them?'

'The tart was a mouthy one, and her john wore a thick winter coat, like Master Jonny's, and a cap like to his, too,' said the guard.

'How did you see it was like to Jonny's?' asked Nathaniel.

'Beggin' pardon, sir,' said the guard, 'but it's hardly winter coat weather. Plus it had a tear on the back. My wife was going to mend it for him. She's a seamstress, and...'

'Thank you, my good man,' said Nathaniel, interrupting. It seemed as though the guards always wanted to tell him their life story. But Master Secretary Thurloe would find this an interesting development. Jonny's coat seen skulking about with a prostitute while Jonny himself lay murdered in an alleyway. Obviously his key had been stolen, but how would the thief know which door it opened? More to the point, why on earth would a common thief risk walking into this den of governmental iniquity? Master Secretary Thurloe would definitely find this interesting. He walked back to the chamber where Isaac, candlestick now in hand, still looked worried.

'I am lonely,' said Isaac, without so much as looking up. 'And suspicious. Things are afoot. I fear you ought relay to Master

Secretary that I am troubled. I'm trying to work out who might have killed Jonny, specifically someone who knew where he lived and worked.'

'It must be a short list of suspects,' said Nathaniel.

'Yes, indeed,' said Isaac. 'Very short indeed. In fact, present company excepted, there's only one possibility. Which reminds me, have you found Molly?'

'No. And I doubt I will. Both her lodgings and Jonny's have been emptied. I fear for her.'

'This just lends weight to my fears.'

'Which are?'

'That it's Molly. She must be using his clothing to disguise herself as a young man.'

'But surely she wouldn't - I mean, Molly?' said Nathaniel. 'She's just a girl.'

'It seems strange, indeed.'

'But the way that Jonny died showed us that he died by the actions of someone skilled with a blade,' said Nathaniel.

'Skilled?' said Isaac.

'Most definitely. It was either a very skilful or very lucky strike. An exceptionally neat wound, from behind, at very close quarters.'

'A Swordsman?'

'One such would fit the bill. Perhaps Molly has become embroiled with some malignant or other.' He paused. 'Perhaps they hold her.'

'You think so?' said Isaac.

'I have no idea,' said Nathaniel. 'But it does worry me. I'll borrow an extra couple of men. One to look to you, the other to keep watch over Master Secretary Thurloe. Once they realise that the element of surprise has escaped them they will melt away into the night.'

'And Molly?'

'She is easy to spot so they'll not let her show her face, at least not during the day. And the night will not cover her well.'

'Unless she presents as a youth,' said Isaac. 'And she is a malignant rather than simply being taken by them.'

'Molly? I doubt it. And as for the guard's report,' - Nathaniel laughed - 'if that were so we'd be on the lookout for two women, one dressed as a man. Are we reviving the playhouse on our London's streets, Isaac?'

'I have seen stranger things, Nathaniel. And if I might have the transcript of Miss Susan's letter back that I might unpick it...'

'I do not have it, Isaac. Whatever makes you think I have it?'

'Its absence,' said Isaac. 'Ask Master Secretary, as I find it hard to unpick letters I do not possess.'

'I will,' said Nathaniel, and left the chamber, somewhat perturbed. As he walked along the river on his way to Lambeth House, he saw suspicious pairs everywhere. Any man who walked with a certain swagger and was accompanied by a young woman was a potential assassin. Nathaniel was a soldier, and a good one, but he was the first to admit his skills with the blade were based on strength, both of arm and character. The Swordsmen - young, skilful and dedicated to following Prince Rupert, warrior prince Palatine - were cut from a different cloth, and felt themselves superior to fighters such as he. And they were well known for being impulsive, hot-headed men. In a weaponless altercation Nathaniel had yet to meet the man who could best him, but as for the couple of Swordsmen he had fought, it was a different matter entirely. The first had Nathaniel at his mercy and was intent on telling him so when he quite lost his head. Chivalry has its place, Nathaniel knew that, but the field of battle was not it. Hesitate, like his conqueror had, and you may fall victim to a handy bit of pistol work. His second experience showed how much Nathaniel had learnt from his first. Never fight on someone else's terms. He had retreated and retreated, ignoring the cries of coward, until he found himself at an advantage. The advantage was a halberd, with which he shattered first his opponent's sword and then his leg, before removing any doubt as to the victor from his shoulders. But he knew that in the event of a surprise assault, from behind, he was gone. Whether or not their code allowed for such a thing was unclear. Nathaniel's code had always been win first, play nicely later. If ever.

Once he arrived at Lambeth House, he felt rather more at home. He went straight to the apothecary's cell.

'Good apothecary, you are looking well,' Nathaniel lied. The apothecary looked awful, but he was still alive. 'I bring you hope of some shortening of your stay. Just answer well. We seek a substance that will rid us of someone troublesome.'

'Why?' replied the apothecary.

'Because we do,' said Nathaniel. 'That's all you need to know. You know we can make you tell us.'

'Yes, yes, yes,' said the apothecary, beginning to sweat. 'Of course. Forgive me. I would use extract of puffer fish,' said the apothecary. 'It kills in a very short space of time, and is easy to dispense, as little is needed and its taste is weak.'

'You have tried it?'

'Not to kill, but it numbs the tongue for hours, just the tiniest drop.'

'And there is an antidote?'

'None but mithridatum,' said the apothecary, 'and I have not seen that for years. Unicorn horn may work.'

'Where might I find such poison?'

'I know of just the one place,' said the apothecary.

'Well?'

'My shop in the Bailey. In the back room, third cabinet from the left, third drawer down. There's a secret panel. Inside there are seven vials of it, marked so,' he drew a shape in the soil of the floor. 'But mind you use a whole vial, or you will merely paralyse the victim, and they have been known to recover subsequently. Also it is better if fresher. Whom do you intend to poison?'

'It matters not.'

'It matters to me.'

'All you need know is that I requested a drug to dispense with a child unborn,' said Nathaniel.

'You need an abortifacient?' said the apothecary.

'A what?' replied Nathaniel.

'A drug to abort a child. Is the child quick?'

'I do not know,' said Nathaniel.

'If it is quick, it is murder and a mortal sin, you know that?'

'Of course I know that, fool,' Nathaniel shouted, raising his right hand. 'But the child must die so that the mother may be hanged.'

'I cannot be a party to this.'

'But you already are,' said Nathaniel. 'I have been charged with killing her child. That I cannot in all conscience do. I therefore seek a sure method from you, but you lie, on account of your conscience.'

'But the child still perishes,' said the apothecary.

'Indeed,' said Nathaniel. 'Whether quick or not. But we do not in this slaughter the innocent. Least not straightways.'

'And for my part?'

'You were deceived by me,' said Nathaniel. 'Your conscience is clear.'

'But I will suffer for it.'

'In this world, yes,' said Nathaniel. 'But I will endeavour to be somewhat overenthusiastic as I discover why the remedy you proposed was fatal to the mother, and in doing so end your suffering on this earth. You are already sentenced. Before I do so, however, I shall arrange for some improvement in your victuals. And some wine. I am sorry to have to do this, but I see no other way.'

24

Thursday 17th April

Molly is given a mission

'Sister,' said Molly. 'I crave a word.'

Mrs Chaffin stopped and looked closely at the boy who had spoken to her. Her eyes were drawn to the locket about his neck. 'Hello, sister,' she said. 'You are dressed mighty strange.'

'Needs must,' said Molly. 'And it not only keeps attention off me but it affords me access where a lady might otherwise struggle to go freely. But to business.'

'Indeed, sister,' said Mrs Chaffin. 'And my business is of great import.'

'Concerning Miss Susan, no doubt.'

'How...' asked Mrs Chaffin.

'We, my sister here and I,' said Molly, pointing at Diana, who was still in the shadows. 'My sister and I have been in attendance to Miss Susan.'

'Sister? That is no Sister, young lady.' Her voice was stern and implacable. 'That woman is well known to us, and may not affect kinship with the Sisterhood.'

'What do you mean? Yes, she took the convent, but now she's back.'

'This woman is anathema,' said Mrs Chaffin. 'She has been termed a sinner. We have nothing to say to her.'

Diana bristled, and leant in close to her accuser. 'Yes, sister, I have been anathema, but I am here now as a friend of Miss Susan's, and you block my path at your peril.'

'And I, too, am with Diana,' said Molly. 'And you are either with us or against us.'

At this, Mrs Chaffin fell silent. Molly and Diana were close enough to touch her. She made a decision. 'She languishes in Lambeth House,' she said. 'We cannot hope to aid her escape.'

'We have news of Sister Susan's intentions,' said Molly.

'What news?' replied Mrs Chaffin.

'We found this,' said Molly, handing her the transcript of Susan's letter, which she then read aloud.

Most reverend father,

Please attend your sister at Lambeth House this Tuesday that you might take my testament and allow me to follow my mother's fate with a firm hand and a ready wit. Would that myne owne love were divine, for then I might drink the wrath of God from my uncle's cup with joy in this life, and not the next. 10.9.16.4.18.7.

Your loving sister, etc

Mrs Chaffin cast her eyes downwards and muttered to herself, words that Molly could neither recognise nor understand. She raised her head. 'This is unwelcome news. She means to self-slaughter,' she said. 'We must act, and act fast.'

'This makes sense to you?' said Molly.

'Yes,' said Mrs Chaffin. 'She directs the recipient to take the third of seven vials and then deliver it to her to drink and thenceforth die. Presumably she means from Hinton's shop.'

'How do you read that?' asked Molly.

'She is a daughter of Ophelia - her mother's fate is to die,' said

Mrs Chaffin. 'Would that mine own love were divine - John the Divine, the Book of Revelation. The numbers are chapter and verse. Look them up.'

'So what is it we must do?'

'The only thing we can do, namely turn adversity into advantage. Susan requests that her minister administers poison when he collects her testament. And tells him where to find it.'

'And so what do we do?' asked Molly with an exaggerated firmness.

'We must assume that there will be no persuading her minister, even if we were party to his identity. We must also assume that this is the poison the apothecary has custody over and which is only given to members of the Sisterhood on certain missions, either to allow them to fulfil them or to protect the Sisterhood should they fail.'

'Protect the Sisterhood?' said Molly, confused and becoming increasingly frightened.

'Molly,' said Diana, placing her arm around her shoulder. 'The vial, you remember, at the Mermaid. It is not merely for use against our enemies.'

'We must get to the source of this poison and weaken it,' said Mrs Chaffin. 'Too little merely paralyses temporarily. You and Diana must first break into Hinton's shop.'

'Must we steal?' asked Molly.

'This poison is held only by Hinton, and that in secret. But he, too, is in Lambeth House and his wife is simple, bless her. It is unlawful to hold such a drug, and her husband may feel that such secrets are best kept close. And even if she did know of such stocks, she would not tell anyone she does not know, and she knows none of us, nor is she a Sister.'

'Leave it to us,' said Molly. 'Where is it and what must we do with it when we find it?'

'In the back room, third cabinet from the left, third drawer down. It has a secret opening. There are seven vials of it. You must locate it and place a weakened dose in place of the third one. You can make this from the one in the Mermaid. If you have time, you must replace half of the other ones with water and seal them again with the nightingale. If not we must gamble.'

'What does that achieve?'

'It gives the minister a drug Susan desires him to have, but in the quantity we desire,' said Mrs Chaffin. 'But no, it will not kill, merely give the illusion of death - enough to fool a raging, thwarted man when observed in the bleak oubliette in which she languishes. It is our only hope. And it is a thin one, at best.'

'And then?' asked Diana.

'You must make good your escape. London is not safe for you now,' said Mrs Chaffin. 'This must be done today. We cannot risk being caught in this act - we will see each other again in the convent, whether we be side by side with our fallen Sisters or sat next each other at high table.' As she said these words she stared at Diana, but she and Molly wrapped their hands around the one locket they possessed together, and the three women joined hands in silent prayer. 'Go,' she said. 'Act. Prepare the way. We can but pray for your success. Soyez la différence.'

25

Friday 18th April

Nathaniel takes possession

Nathaniel slipped through the narrow alley and clambered over the tired wall and into the yard. He crouched down and looked about the doors, windows and nooks, dagger drawn. He didn't like this sort of work. He was much more the walk in through the front door and tell people what, exactly, they were about to do for him kind of man. Few were foolish enough to gainsay him. Now, however, he skulked like a common thief. It really was beneath him. He made a decision, shook his head, stood up, sheathed his weapon and dusted himself down. Then he strode towards the apothecary shop's inner yard, with its crucibles and fires. He walked straight past them and through the unlocked back door into the back room. He stood silently still for a few moments while his eyes accustomed themselves to the light, then muttered to himself before walking to a cabinet, forcing the drawer open and looking at the contents.

'I'm sure he said there would be seven of them,' he said, before reaching in and taking one of the six vials that sat side by side in the drawer. He placed it in a leather purse and tied it to his belt. He then walked to the front of the shop and directly out into the street. He stood at the side of the filthy thoroughfare and stared directly at a young lad who leant up against a wall. He was slight, with dirty blond hair, and was accompanied by an older woman who stood to his side and whispered in his ear. Her face was hidden. A horse and dray passed between the watcher and the watched and the pair were gone.

The vial still bobbed up and down on his belt as he turned right and began to walk towards the river. As he did so he saw a man walking towards him, smiling. His hat sported a tall feather and he looked strangely familiar. As they passed by one another they locked eyes, only breaking contact when their shoulders were virtually touching. A moment after they passed each other Nathaniel turned sharply around. He scanned the throng of people until he caught sight of the feather. It had increased its pace and was gaining on the horse and dray. Nathaniel watched as the man stopped, turned and smiled just before he cut in front of the horse. Nathaniel sped up, pushing pedestrians out of his way in an attempt to catch up, but as he rounded the horse someone walked directly into him. The pedestrian remonstrated with him but he raised his fist and was about to strike when he saw that it was the blond boy. Nathaniel looked up to see the feather disappear down a side alley. He looked back to the boy but he was gone. The feathered man, too, had eluded him. Still, he had achieved what he had set out to achieve. He would worry about the sudden reappearance of the man from Queenborough later.

26

Saturday 19th April
Diana jumps ship

The boat was making good headway, the combination of calm seas and steady wind making conditions perfect for what was a somewhat solemn journey. Diana and Molly sat in the boat's prow, arms linked, and stared at the horizon. They were wrapped in the same piece of cambric that Diana had used on her trip the previous year, when the whole sorry enterprise had begun. Behind them Duggan hung over the boat's side, as miserably sick as ever.

'What are we going to do in Antwerp?' said Molly.

'Don't you worry about that, Molly,' said Diana. 'Just remember you're going home. Anyway, I'll not be coming to Antwerp with you. I have unfinished business in Paris.'

'Paris?'

'Yes, Paris.'

'Then I, too, am going to Paris,' said Molly. 'I've always wanted to visit.'

'You must go to Antwerp, sister. Your place is with your sisters.'

'You are my sister, Diana. And my place is with you. I am for Paris.' Molly tightened her grip on her companion's arm. 'I have no home other than with you.' Her eyes moistened. 'Not since Jonny.'

Diana motioned to speak but Molly silenced her. She looked wistfully at the approaching coastline, the spray from the boat mixing with the salt of her tears. 'Strange to leave England behind,' she said. 'Though not as strange as bumping into Nathaniel. I wonder what he was doing hanging around the Bailey.' And she fell silent once more. 'I do have one question, sister.'

'Just the one?' replied Diana.

'For now,' said Molly. 'What did our ferryman mean when he said "I don't believe I've had the pleasure, milady" - what exactly? The way he smiled it was almost as if you knew one another.'

'I couldn't possibly say.' Diana's look, however, gave her away.

27

Monday 21st April, 4pm

Visitors arrive at Lambeth House

Mary and Mrs Chaffin stood in front of the thick, metal-studded door of Lambeth House. The door swung open and the guard looked them up and down. 'Give us them baskets,' he said, pointing at the women's burden. They proffered them gently only to have them snatched from their grasp and rifled through in front of them. He laughed. 'Picking up a relative whose visit ended early, are we?'

'Mother,' said Mrs Chaffin. 'I see you bring yours to work,' she added, nodding in the direction of the mastiff bitch that was tied up next to him. They walked through into the courtyard. They were almost across when the guard began shouting abuse at them. 'Idiot,' said Mrs Chaffin, with a laugh that convinced neither her nor Mary that theirs was anything but an extremely dangerous situation.

When they reached the entrance to the notorious prison they called House, as if it were more a place of luxury than bestiality, they waited once more while their names were taken and written in a large book. There was no laughter as they were ushered into a room where two women searched them rather more thoroughly than had been the case at the main gate. Then they waited while their escort was summoned. They were not waiting for long.

'This way,' said Nathaniel. 'Master Secretary awaits.'

'Has Miss Susan sought release from her torment?' asked Mrs Chaffin.

'She has borne it squarely,' said Nathaniel. 'But we expect a minister presently.' He led them down into the damper, danker regions of the prison. As they walked, they began to hear a strange noise.

'What is that noise, sir?' said Mary. 'It has an infernal sound to it.'

Nathaniel laughed. 'No need to grasp the good book to your breasts, ladies,' he said. 'It is merely a goat.'

'A goat?' replied Mary. 'What possesses you to allow a goat to reside in this godforsaken place? To terrify the inmates further with its diabolical noise?'

'Peace, woman, peace,' said Nathaniel. 'We are arrived. First I shall enquire about the minister, then you may attend to your charge as you see fit.'

'Thank you,' said Mrs Chaffin, and the two women stood as still as they could in the middle of the corridor, as if the stone walls were hungry for their souls, and too close a proximity would lead to the pair of them being absorbed into the very guts of the prison. Then there were voices. Subdued at first, then louder. A roar of laughter was followed by the words "If they think it's within their power to save the immortal soul of that monster then they are welcome to try." The rest they could not make out.

Nathaniel emerged from the room from which the bleating still came. 'I shall return to the gate and take the minister to the prisoner when he arrives. You will attend Master Secretary Thurloe's pleasure,' he said. With that, Nathaniel walked off. A voice thundered out from the room.

28

Monday 21st April, 4pm

Thurloe plays the devil

'Enter!' It was Thurloe, and the goat echoed his command. The look of relief on the faces of the two women as they walked slowly into the room suggested to Thurloe that they feared that the noises they had heard emanated from the spymaster himself rather than the animal that was tethered in the room. He laughed. 'By the looks on your faces you expected to find me in possession of cloven hooves, and perhaps with horns hidden under a voluminous hat. You must be wondering why the goat?' With this he leant towards them and lowered his voice to a whisper. 'I'm not the devil, you know. Sit down.'

'We would rather we were allowed to see Miss Susan as soon as possible, Master Secretary,' said Mrs Chaffin. Mary nodded her agreement. 'The way you treat that poor, innocent girl is an abomination against God.'

'All in good time,' said Thurloe. He stood up, a little slowly, and walked over to the goat. He knelt down and ruffled its head. 'But first you are going to take part in a little demonstration, and this poor chap is about to be sacrificed for the good of his creator and this country he blesses. My apologies are due to him, for he is truly innocent of any crime,' he said, turning to the two women. 'And you, you are like to be his doom.' Thurloe was minded to discover the lengths to which these women would go in order to see his prisoner. He thought it never so poetic that he should take revenge for Creon, and fool the witch with the same gambit Medea had used against the old king. He had prepared the stage, and now it was time to set forth the play. He handed them a flask of wine. 'This flask was brought to me two weeks ago by that girl for whom you feign such care. That soul unsullied by sin. She meant for me to drink it.' He looked down at the goat that was nuzzling his leg. 'What do you think, mister goat? Will they drink it themselves or feed it to you?' He raised his head and looked at the two women. 'For that is your choice. You either drink the wine yourself or make the goat drink.' They stared at him blankly. 'Decide.'

The wine itself was nothing to do with Susan. She had not brought such a thing to him, let alone tried to poison him. Thurloe's demonstration was not, truth be told, for the two women but for himself. Thurloe had been struggling with the news that Susan carried his child, their child. His instinct was at odds with his intellect, his heart with his obligation. There was still a small but vocal part of him that wanted to spirit Susan away and keep her close that they might... the voice was drowned out by that of the goat. Thurloe watched as Mrs Chaffin looked at the flask and removed the cork. She smelt the liquid inside. By the look on her face Thurloe figured that she recognised the odour above the sharp taint of the now rather vinegary wine. She nodded at Mary, who took the goat by the head, stepping over it to hold its body with her thighs, and pulled its head backwards, opening its mouth as she did so. The goat struggled and kicked but to no avail.

'Angels of mercy both,' said Thurloe. 'It fairly warms the heart.'

Mrs Chaffin merely looked at him, and poured the contents of the flask down the goat's throat. 'There, it won't be long now.' Mary let the goat as free as its tether allowed and stood at the other end of the room.

'I trust you feel suitably guilty in taking its life this way?' said Thurloe. 'But it was what was planned for me. Miss Susan was intent on my destruction but she lost her nerve and warned me, thinking I did not know that it was she who had placed it in my cellar. She adds incompetence to her crimes.'

The goat's bleats began to change in their intensity, and its back legs began to wobble. 'There we go,' said Mrs Chaffin. 'So it begins.' The wobble turned into a collapse as the goat's back legs gave way, and its back began to twist. The bleats grew louder and more desperate as the goat fought hard, scrabbling with its front legs to escape the pain. But it was tethered and doomed. The front legs gave way at the same time as its bowels, filling the room with the putrid smell of dying goat. It writhed and thrashed on the floor, its bleats becoming fainter. As the goat slowly lost its battle, Thurloe looked at the women in front of him. They were scared witless. They feared their turn was yet to come.

'For the love of God, man,' Mrs Chaffin implored. 'Put the poor creature out of its misery.'

Thurloe just smiled. 'This is a misery that you caused, may I remind you,' he said. 'I wonder that you are happy to let another child of God suffer so, but you women are a breed apart. We wait until it has fully expired.'

29

Monday 21st April, 5pm
Nathaniel welcomes a visitor

Nathaniel had met the minister at the front gate and led him down through the labyrinth into the area that housed Susan. He was of average height, pale and clean shaven. His hair hung from his head in greasy curls like seaweed plastered to a rock at low tide.

'Is that your master I hear?' said the minister, in a soft Scottish accent.

'Merely a goat,' said Nathaniel, shaking his head. 'Though it is true to say that Master Secretary has been sporting a very particular beard of late.' Nathaniel wondered whether this might not make a useful rumour. He looked at the minister, who seemed to grow paler with every step he took. 'Don't worry, most people get an attack of nerves on their first time down here. Especially the prisoners.' He scrabbled with the lock and the door swung open. The minister hesitated. 'Go on, minister, your sinner awaits. I shall allow the woman some privacy.'

'Thank you,' said the minister, as he walked through the low doorway.

30

Monday 21st April, 5pm
Talbot takes a letter

Talbot felt his stomach muscles tighten as he entered Susan's cell, where the smell of piss, shit, blood and fear leaked from the very walls. Susan was thin, pale and wrapped in a filthy sheet. Only her proud belly showed any sign of health. 'My child,' he said. 'What have they done to you?'

'Everything that is indecorous,' she replied, in a whisper. 'Thank you for coming, Colonel Talbot, though you know it may well be your end.'

'Indecorous?' said Talbot, opening his Bible. 'I will not allow it while I live.'

'On that we are agreed. But I do not wish to hear from a man,' she said, shivering slightly in the cold, damp cell. She coughed. 'Take my testament.'

Talbot took out his chapbook and his ink, dipped his pen and held it, poised. 'Ready.'

Susan began to speak.

I am Susan Hyde.

Sister to Edward Hyde.

Sister of the Sisterhood.

Daughter of Ophelia.

Je suis la différence.

This is my testament. None may read it but she who holds the key to all hearts.

I was born a sister, then a daughter. I will never be a mother, though I have held that office by proxy.

I lie here, already in my burial shroud, and soon my sisters will lay me in the stream, where my sins will be washed away, and I may finally become forever faithful to the Sisterhood. Then this too sullied flesh will melt and I will join our eternal mother.

Though my sojourn on this spinning orb was short, in that time I have known love, laughter, misery, pain and more. I have been faithful even as I betrayed, I have been honest even as I have lied, and I have been true even as I proved false.

I am Susan Hyde. Je suis une fille d'Ophélie. Je suis une agente invisible. Je suis la première, la dernière.

I am Susan Hyde yet.

I see now all that I did, all that I said, all that I was is of no importance. As I await my death, like Cleopatra in her monument awaiting the figs in which her destiny slithered, I know that only those directly responsible for my end will mourn my passing. Those others who see it will curse their lack of agency, while to most all of the world, it will be of no import. It may change everything but no one will ever know.

And you, John, my darling John who is both love and hate to me, who is both life and death, who is both the pillar that holds up my world and the storm that destroys it, to you, John, I bequeath the knowledge that I gave you, the worst of men, the very best of me.

But I do not die for you, John, nor yet because of you. I die for something more beautiful than you can ever know.

I am Susan Hyde.

And I am ready.

With this last word she reached out to Talbot, who gave her chapbook and pen that she might sign her name. She did so shakily, and returned the chapbook to him. He sprinkled sand onto the inky pages, shook it off and cut the paper from its binding. He folded the sheet carefully, took a flask, uncorked it and took a good swig. He gasped as the alcohol drew a line of fire down his throat, then poured some of the spirit onto a wafer, placed it between the two loose flaps of the letter and pressed them hard together onto his Bible before stamping it with a signet he wore. He placed both letter and flask back into his bag. He opened his Bible.

'Take solace from the good book, my child,' he said, holding the open book in front of her. There was a small compartment hollowed out of the pages in which sat a locket and a vial. 'From Acts to the Epistles of John,' he whispered, smiling. 'No great loss.' Susan took the locket from its resting place and smiled back. Behind the locket and vial there were words. Susan read out loud.

'*And the seventh angel poured out his vial into the air; and there came a great voice out of the temple of heaven, from the throne.* The Revelation of St John the Divine. Sixteen seventeen. You have a poetic soul.' She kissed the locket. 'I am ready.'

'Then take your rest, my child.'

Susan then took the vial, which was sealed with the image of a nightingale. 'Thank you, Father. Go in peace.' Then she whispered the words 'Good luck.'

'May God forgive you,' said Talbot, and stood up. He rapped

out three solemn knocks on the heavy oak of the door. It opened and he walked through to where Nathaniel stood.

31

Monday 21st April, 5.30pm
Susan's final act

'She'll have none of it,' he said to Nathaniel. 'The bedswerver is damned, there is no doubt of that. Allow me to take my leave of this accursed place.'

'Follow me,' said Nathaniel, locking the door.

'Thank you, Nathaniel,' said Talbot.

Susan listened as the two men walked away. She waited a few minutes, and while she could still hear the plaintive but weakening cries of the goat, she fastened the locket around her neck, kissed it, and offered up a short prayer. Then she broke the seal on the vial and poured the contents into her mouth, throwing both vial and seal into a dark corner of the cell. 'It is done,' she said, and lay back on the floor and felt the darkness spread through her body until it claimed her, overwhelming the single light that burnt in her cell.

32

Monday 21st April, 5.30pm
Nathaniel's memory is stirred

As Susan waned unsuspected behind her cell door, the two men walked. But of a sudden Nathaniel held back slightly, then stopped altogether, allowing Talbot to take three paces further before speaking. 'Tell, me, Minister,' he said. 'How do you happen to know my name?' Talbot turned to face his questioner, his right hand reaching for the sword that wasn't there. 'You betray yourself now, Swordsman.' Nathaniel drew his blade.

Talbot threw down his Bible and opened his cloak. 'Queenborough. We fought there but you took me for a drunken adventurer. And also at Worcester,' he said. 'You were brave and strong but limited technically. I watched as one of my fellow men-at-arms had you at his mercy but dallied, fatally.'

'The one who quite lost his head. I see you now. You were bearded like to a man, but this clean chin suits your skulking boyness rather better. There will be no need for a third party to ensure that you and your head are to be rendered strangers evermore from this day.'

'If you say so,' said Talbot. 'On that day I admired the speed at which you learnt that your sword was a danger to you. I wonder has that wisdom deserted you? I watched you retreat against your next foe until ground rather more suitable presented itself. I would have followed but another called for my blade, and you were gone.'

'And now my sword is my advantage,' said Nathaniel. 'And I have a grudge to settle. I will first best you, then make you pay for poor Jonny. For shame, not even a man and you took him from behind like a coward.'

'Who? I know no such man but I can assure you I did no such thing. I may be your sworn enemy, but I am a man of my word and I likewise believe you honourable, after your own fashion. I never kill a man who runs, for his cowardice is enough, and I never kill a man who does not know I mean to strike.' Talbot's eyes met Nathaniel's and they held each other's gaze, each as implacable as the other. 'And I most certainly do not kill boys unless they threaten me directly. I swear to you that this death cannot have been at my hand.'

In the flickering shadow-light of the prison corridor Nathaniel summed up his opponent. They were enemies, yes, and they had each killed men the other called friend, but if they shared anything, it was the honour of a soldier. Nathaniel nodded at the Swordsman, whose escape route was blocked by a door to which he held not the key. 'I believe you speak truly. Yield. You cannot hope to win.'

'I never yield,' said Talbot. 'Unless ordered to. And there is no one here to give me such an order. You may find a dagger somewhat more dangerous in my hands than you think.' And with that Talbot threw his cloak at Nathaniel, following the feint with a thrust of his dagger, the blade penetrating the cloth but missing its mark. Nathaniel shook off the material and made a counter-thrust. Talbot parried. Nathaniel feinted, slashed and thrust once more, this time catching Talbot on the shoulder.

Talbot, however, in the same move sliced a line across Nathaniel's cheek.

'Impressive,' said Nathaniel. 'You have been practising. It is a pity you are doomed.' Another slashing attack from Nathaniel saw Talbot control the sword with his dagger and snap its blade with one movement before closing the distance between them. They each struggled to assert their dominance. 'If not you, then who killed Jonny? He had one wound, in the back of the neck. Precise. Fatal. Instant.' With this Nathaniel headbutted the Swordsman.

Talbot staggered backwards, his face covered in blood, his eyes closing from the impact. 'Diana,' he said. 'You'd do well to treat her with caution.'

'A woman?' said Nathaniel, as he punched the now unsighted Talbot. Nathaniel realised where he'd seen the woman watching Morland's house before.

'Yes,' said Talbot, as he made a final, instinctive thrust with his dagger. His aim was true, and its point penetrated Nathaniel's side. He felt the resistance and heard the shock of the victim and allowed himself a smile. It did not last long.

'Not,' said Nathaniel, grabbing Talbot's arm and twisting it so that he let go of the dagger, which remained in its new scabbard. 'Good,' he said, bringing his elbow down on the arm, snapping it. 'Enough,' he said as Talbot fell to the floor.

Talbot spat the blood from his mouth and levered himself to his knees with his remaining arm. Nathaniel held the newly sheared point of his sword to the man's breast.

'Yield,' said Nathaniel.

'I will not die in your master's chair,' said the Swordsman.

'I will not kill a man on his knees,' replied Nathaniel.

'Then I shall not remain so,' said Talbot. His dagger was still lodged in Nathaniel's side. 'And now we finish.'

With this, the Swordsman started to move upwards, forcing his limbs to obey through the pain.

'Stay down,' said Nathaniel.

'I will not die in bonds,' said Talbot, summoning one last effort.

As he stood, Nathaniel's sword pressed down. It pierced the Swordsman's breast, and found his heart. Talbot fell backwards, his bodyweight pulling itself from Nathaniel's now shortened sword.

'You fought well, and bravely,' said Nathaniel. 'You have earnt your rest. Farewell.' He then fell to the floor himself, breathing heavily. After a few moments, he stood, wincing as he did so. 'A worthy opponent.' He pulled the dagger from his side, and felt the wound. It was clean, and so far as he could tell, unthreatening. 'Now, to release Susan from her torment. I can blame the silent Scot as he cannot now gainsay me, so at least the apothecary will live.'

Nathaniel walked uncomfortably back to Susan's cell, his hand on the leather pouch on his belt, unlocked the door and walked in. He then walked straight out again.

33

Monday 21st April, 6pm
Thurloe denied

Mrs Chaffin and Mary could no longer look at the goat as it writhed in agony. It had been doing so for minutes. Thurloe saw that they could barely look at him, either.

'What is it you enjoy most, devil?' said Mary. 'The destruction of this poor creature or the fear you hope to instil in us?'

Before Thurloe could answer, Nathaniel burst into the room. 'Master Secretary,' he panted. 'It's the malignant. She's dead.'

'What?' cried Thurloe. 'And you bleed?'

'Yes. The minister was a Swordsman. One of the two arrested in Queenborough.'

'You told me they were drunken adventurers only, Nathaniel,' said Thurloe, as his anger grew. 'You begin to fail me.'

'That was all they appeared.'

'Appearances ought not be trusted, idiot,' said Thurloe. 'Bring him to me.'

'I cannot.'

'Cannot? For which side do you fight, Nathaniel?'

'I mean that there will be no third meeting,' he said. 'He was a ferocious man, highly skilled. A fine warrior who fought dagger against sword and came close to success, as my side gives testament.'

'You could not take him alive?'

'I almost perished. He would not yield.'

'And the whore?'

'I returned to her having taken my leave of the Swordsman, and she did not reply to my offer of water, so I entered the cell, and she had gone. I mean, passed.'

'How?' said Thurloe.

'It appears she had apoplexy of some sort,' he said, 'but she is gone, there is no doubt of that.'

Thurloe rushed out of the room towards Susan's cell, the door of which was wide open, pausing only at the bloodied mess that was the Swordsman. 'Search him,' he said, and carried onwards, the two women following. Thurloe looked at Susan as she lay to all the world a corpse. 'No, you do not thwart me now,' he shouted, slapping her around the face. 'You dare not! Wake up, witch!' He took out a dagger and held it to her left eye, the eyelid of which was open. It did not move even when its point touched, and then penetrated, the eyeball. 'Damn you, whore. How dare you die without my permission.'

'Good God, man,' said Mrs Chaffin. 'You are an abomination.' She spat at Thurloe, upon which he struck her with the back of his hand.

'Get out and take this filth with you,' he shouted at the two women. 'Before I hang you both,' he said. And was gone.

34

Monday 21st April, 6.30pm
The Sisters do their duty

The two women stood, dumbfounded. 'He is truly the devil,' said Mary. She looked closely at her sister, who bled slightly from her lip. 'Truly.'

'I will live, Mary,' said Mrs Chaffin. 'But let us begone with haste lest he change his mind and returns to violate the corpse.' They inspected Susan carefully, then exchanged a grave look. 'And it is a corpse. Diana and Molly failed.'

They wrapped Susan's body as quickly as they could, winding yards of linen around it, tying limb with limb, until it was covered from toe to crown. They muttered a prayer before each took one end of the body and carried it slowly and carefully up into the London evening. At the prison gate they commandeered a cart and pushed their burden to the main gate. There they were stopped by the guard.

'Idiot, am I?' he said, untying his mastiff. 'Let's see what you have here, then.'

'Just the corpse of our dearly departed mother,' said Mary.

'If she was your mother, she must have been an old bitch,' said the guard. 'Or maybe a slutty young bitch always on heat.' He pulled the mastiff towards him. 'Perhaps she'd care to meet my mother.' The mastiff walked onto the cart, squatted and pissed on the corpse's leg. The guard laughed. 'I trained her well. She always pisses on malignants.' He inspected the corpse, spat on it and waved them through. 'And don't come back.'

'First intelligent suggestion he's made all day,' said Mrs Chaffin.

With that the two women pushed their cart to the river and hailed the waiting boat. They expected to hear the tramp of boots and shouts of Thurloe's men but there was silence. Silence as the men they had hired lowered the corpse onto the boat. Silence as the two women stood by the body of their departed sister, Susan Hyde.

And they cast off and rowed towards the estuary where another boat waited to transfer them to Antwerp. In the darkness, the daughters of Ophelia stood watching as the dancing lights of the city gave way to the measured darkness of the estuary, and the coast of their country of birth vanished into the night.

Finally, they were going home.

35

Monday 21st April, 11pm

Nathaniel presents the evidence

Nathaniel hesitated for a second before entering the room in which Thurloe sat, brooding. It wasn't clear which aspect of the whole sorry tale had upset him the most, but it did seem unlikely that even a polite enquiry would yield a favourable response. It also crossed Nathaniel's mind, and not for the first time, that there might possibly be circumstances in which lying to his employer, or at least not being entirely truthful, would be the best course of action. Today, however, he did not have the luxury of discretion, though the feeling of the vial he had taken from Hinton's shop tapping against his leg in its leather purse told another story. He entered.

'Master Secretary.' He waited, hoping for an answer or even an acknowledgement, but as neither were forthcoming he steeled himself to deliver the information that he had stumbled upon. 'I have made a discovery, of sorts,' he said, and he placed three items onto the table in front of Thurloe along with Susan's testament.

'What are these trinkets?' said Thurloe, the distaste on his lips unhidden.

'The locket was found in his house by Samuel following Miss

Susan's transfer to Lambeth, though I'd lay money on his having stolen it from her. There was an almost identical one around her neck when she died. The vial was found in the corner of her cell. The letters were with the Swordsman.'

'Do not use that malignant's name in my presence again, Nathaniel. And a gentleman cannot steal from such a creature.'

Nathaniel simply nodded and as he did so felt a pang of sympathy for anyone who had the misfortune of being arrested and brought in front of the spymaster today. He could not explain why he did not believe Morland's claim that he had found the piece. Like many of Morland's statements, it tripped all too easily off the tongue. Nathaniel had long thought that Morland's immediate response to any question was designed primarily to absolve him of either responsibility or blame, and his explanation of the genesis of the silver locket that Thurloe was casually inspecting instead of the letters that were on the table in front of him was most definitely one such. He began again.

'The lockets are virtually identical, like I said.' He waited for Thurloe to respond. All that was forthcoming was a grunt of approval. 'And the vial that was found in her cell small enough to have been secreted about his person without fear of discovery.' Nathaniel placed his hand on the vial he carried. He purposed to keep it, even though he was not one for such methods.

'Forgive me, Nathaniel, but why do you think these items, or that dead... thing, ought interest me in the least?' said Thurloe, his voice betraying no hint of emotion.

'Well. Perhaps if you cast your eyes over them that question would answer itself.'

Thurloe raised his head slowly and stared at Nathaniel. It was a look he had seen directed at many prisoners before now, a slow smile utterly bereft of warmth. It didn't fill him with confidence. 'If you insist, Nathaniel,' he said, before picking up the locket and inspecting it carefully. 'No progress on Jonny?'

'No, Master Secretary. Field admitted detesting him but naturally denied any involvement. He said he'd considered getting someone to teach him a lesson but,' at this Nathaniel chuckled, 'he was rather wary of inviting my disapproval.'

'Not mine?' said Thurloe, raising an eyebrow.

'No. He was of the opinion that my interventions in such matters were likely to be rather more direct than yours. But it seems most likely that it was the Scot. And if so we may consider him avenged.' Some information was best kept to himself, Nathaniel reasoned, and for all his cold-hearted rationalism, Thurloe did not approve of his employees executing personal vendettas while on State business, even if he did approve of the diligence such vendettas lent to their work, as Isaac could testify. Diana could wait. Nathaniel had a long memory. And he had liked Jonny.

'Well, in that he may well consider that he made a wise choice in leaving Jonny alone,' said Thurloe. 'But this locket is interesting. You were right. *Ego avis enim cantans inaspecta.* Does this mean anything to you? And the twist of hair?'

'I have no clue as to its meaning. I do not even have pig Latin. Look at the vial.'

Thurloe picked up the small glass vial and inspected it carefully. 'Well now, that was most unexpected. I think we've been cozened, Nathaniel.'

'Indeed, Master Secretary, I think you're right. Though I'm not sure how, in what manner or by whom.'

Thurloe began to roll the motto around his mouth, as if tasting it. Though he had trained as a lawyer he had not worked as such in years, and his Latin had been poor to begin with. 'There's an I, and *cantans* might mean song. I think it does. *Inaspecta?* Not inspected? Not suspected? *Avis* must be bird. Bird singing unsuspected?' said Thurloe. 'We will have to follow the song, should we happen to hear it again.' He inspected the letters. One bore a single word by way of endorsement: *mother.* The other, thicker package was addressed to *The Lord Protector.* 'Well,' he said, and placed the letters in his bag. He said nothing more.

36

Tuesday, 22nd April, 3am
The Sisters cross the narrow sea

'Still no word from Diana,' said Mrs Chaffin to Mary, as they stared into the darkness at the sea they left behind them. 'Not that we are in need of it.'

'Indeed not,' said Mary. 'Have you experience of this, sister?'

'No,' said Mrs Chaffin. 'This is new territory for me, also. 'I wonder did they even try.' She paused and stared into the clear night sky. 'I never did trust that woman. Not for one moment.'

'Not a true Sister. Only one thing matters to women like that, and it isn't la différence. I thought she would at least try. Can't blame Molly.'

'But to see Miss Susan, so cold, so thin, so stark. So lifeless.'

'She died a martyr's death. And she will receive a martyr's reward. Of that we can be certain.'

They heard a muted cough, and turned around to look at their companions, to see what it was that they wanted. The two sailors on deck looked tense, one with his hand gripping the tiller as if the boat was trying to steer him, and not the other way around, while the other stood hard beside him, boathook in hand.

'Yes?' said Mary. There was no answer. 'What did you want to say? Is there a problem?' The sailors just stared at the bundle of linen that lay on the deck.

'The corpse, miss,' said the sailor with the boathook. 'It, it coughed.'

'Don't be stupid, man,' she said. 'Corpses don't cough.'

'Well it wasn't us. We don't like witchcraft on board,' said the other sailor. 'It's bad luck, it is. Bad enough having women sail with us.'

'Well, if you knew anything about witches you'd know that firstly it's good luck to have one on your side and secondly that they can't cross open water,' said Mrs Chaffin. 'And corpses don't cough.'

'You tell it that,' said the first sailor as what sounded very like a muffled cough came from beneath the linen.

'For heaven's sake,' said Mrs Chaffin, motioning to Mary and rushing to the corpse's side. 'You're right. Corpses don't cough.'

'So it's not a corpse,' said Mary, finishing off her sentence. The two women set about the bag in which Susan lay, slicing it open and rending the material apart. Her face was revealed first. The lips were blue and the left eye swollen. The four looked at Susan, who lay motionless.

'Corpse,' said the sailor.

At this Susan coughed again, but this time the cough was followed by an attempt at a deep breath. Hoarse. Urgent. Desperate. And another cough. The women tore off the remainder of Susan's wrappings and her chest began to heave.

'Apparently today is not Susan's day to die,' said Mary, with tears in her eyes. She knelt down and hugged her sister. 'Welcome back,' she whispered.

Mrs Chaffin poured some water onto a cloth and held it to Susan's desiccated lips. She washed her face. Susan's chest heaved once more and this time more air entered her body. She coughed and spluttered and tried to speak. Mrs Chaffin squeezed the cloth, wet it again and squeezed some more, and the drips of liquid began to find their way into Susan's mouth.

'So. Cold.' Susan's words were trapped, her throat too dry for her to push them out. With that, the two women began to rub her legs and arms. Slowly, as her blood began to circulate freely once more, the blue in her lips and fingertips started to fade. Susan was coming back to life.

'Where? Is this? Am I?' said Susan. 'Is this death?'

'You're on your way home, Susan,' said Mary. 'You're on your way home.'

'I can't feel my legs,' said Susan.

'It may take some time to recover their use,' said Mrs Chaffin, before turning to Mary. 'Diana and Molly made it!'

'And I'm cold,' said Susan. 'So very cold. Where am I? Diana? Diana is anathema.'

Mary and Mrs Chaffin exchanged glances. They were both thinking the same thing. Perhaps it was permanent. Perhaps the poison would only release some of her. She had appeared so much as if she were dead.

'Diana is finding her own way,' said Mary. 'And without her you would not be with us now. There's no need to worry.' They wrapped her in blankets and gave her brandy to drink and soon she was asleep.

As Mary sat by her, watching her chest rise and fall, and do so more easily, Mrs Chaffin stood up.

'Well, get on with it!' she said to the two sailors. 'She's neither corpse nor witch, so let's get this tub to Antwerp, shall we?' The two men simply stood staring until she clapped her hands. 'Hie thee, make haste!' she said, and they snapped into action.

'So,' said Mary. 'What are we to do?'

'We cannot take her home, she must take the convent,' said Mrs Chaffin. 'We must take her to Lady Knatchbull's.'

37

Wednesday 23rd April, 9am
Antwerp receives visitors

'Wake up, Susan,' whispered Mary as the sailors made fast the boat. 'It's time to go home.' Susan walked slowly down the gangplank and onto the Antwerp dockside, supported on either side by her sisters. Susan gripped her locket in her hand. There was a carriage waiting for them. The three women squeezed together inside.

'Well,' said Mrs Chaffin, 'when she says home, Mary does, of course, mean the convent.'

'Ghent?' said Susan.

'Yes,' replied Mrs Chaffin. 'Ghent. With Lady Knatchbull. Then a place will be found for you, naturally. One commensurate with your position, naturally, and your skills.'

Susan lifted her hand to her left eye and touched the bandage gently.

'Does it hurt?' said Mary.

'It is sore when the carriage hits a bump, for certain,' said Susan. 'But what happened? Why is it bandaged? Why am I here? How?'

'What do you remember?' asked Mrs Chaffin.

'I remember being in a cell, a minister coming with a Bible

containing a vial,' said Susan. 'I was reminded of St John. "Eat thou this scroll, and it will taste in your mouth like honey for sweetness, but will be bitter in thy belly." And I tasted the vial.'

'And then?' said Mary, as if she were expecting a ghost story.

'I remember my tongue going numb, and the next thing I knew I was barely able to cough,' said Susan. 'And the rest, well, the rest we were all there for.' She shook her head and the coach hit a stone big enough to rattle her teeth. 'Dammit, that hurt. I should be dead.' She paused. 'What went wrong?'

Mrs Chaffin shrugged. 'Nothing. We discovered your plan and made a substitution.'

'As simple as that?'

'As simple as that,' said Mrs Chaffin.

'Nothing is that simple,' said Susan. 'Nothing at all. And Diana?'

'What about Diana?'

'She betrayed the Sisterhood, she betrayed a Sister.'

'Without Diana you would not be here,' said Mrs Chaffin. 'You owe her your life.'

'But she is anathema,' repeated Susan. 'You know what has to be done.'

'She came to you in your hour of need,' said Mary. 'Yes, she will face the courts, but these last actions will stand her well, regardless of her previous misdemeanours.'

'And where is she now?' Mary and Mrs Chaffin looked at each other. Their hesitation extended itself into silence. 'Well?'

'We do not know, sister,' said Mary.

'She and Molly landed together,' added Mrs Chaffin.

'And?'

'That's all we know,' said Mary.

'Molly?' said Susan.

'Molly will be just fine, Susan.'

'And Edward?'

'So far as Edward knows, so far as anyone knows,' said Mary, once more looking at her companion, 'you are dead.'

Epilogue

May 1656

'Louise Hollandine,' said the woman, smiling. The easel she stood by supported a canvas from which the likeness of the abbess was slowly emerging as if she were pressing her way through a winter's morning mist. The woman was extremely well dressed, elegant and poised. A lock of hair wrapped in a silk ribbon hung from her left ear. She was visibly pregnant. 'Princess Palatine, for what it's worth.'

'Princess,' said Susan, falling into a deep curtsy. 'I had no idea...' The Princess Palatine was the daughter of the Sisterhood's grand mother, the Queen of Bohemia Elizabeth Stuart. Susan was not sure what surprised her most, her being pregnant or her being in the convent, like to a common sister. But then, all Sisters were equal in the eyes of God. Susan realised that her surprise was what surprised her most. She had spent too long in the company of people like Thurloe, people for whom life was conflict, people who strove to spread discord rather than harmony.

'You had no idea that I might have got myself into trouble, or that someone would dare force me?' said Louise. 'You must have guessed I was a Sister, however.'

'Yes,' said Susan. 'Well, no. Well, I didn't expect to find you here. What happened?'

'It matters not,' said Louise. 'All that matters is that we're Sisters. It just happens to be that we are so in more ways than one.' She paused and looked to her painting, before adding a sweep of black to the abbess's brow. She stood back to inspect her handiwork, and spoke without turning. 'Have you decided where you'll be going next?'

'Me?' said Susan. 'I hadn't really considered it.' She sat down beside Louise on a wooden stool and sighed. 'That's not even close to being true,' she added. 'I'm going back into the field.' If Susan had learnt one thing from this disastrous campaign, it was that fate did not speak with a clear voice. Now when she read Lilly's chart she saw the end predicted not as her end, but Susan's. Susan Hyde was no more.

'With the eye-patch? You'll end up like a character in one of those prose romances.'

'Well, I'm not going to be much use as a painter, am I?' She looked at the image that Louise was working on. 'It's very good. Reminds me of someone.'

'The subject or the style?' said Louise, laughing. 'Gerard von Honthorst, by any chance?'

'Yes,' said Susan. 'That's right.'

'He was my painting master. When I've finished the Abbess, I'll do one of you. As a pirate. Perhaps on the bridge of one of Rupert's ships.'

'How about you?'

'Oh, I'm taking the convent permanently.'

'Permanently?' said Susan, silently wondering which side would be the better when Louise was ready to take her portrait.

'Sister Louise, yes. My mother - our mother - is furious. I will officially go missing next year, when this child is born and I'm sure it's gone to a good home.'

'What of the child's confession?'

'It is more important to me that she has a good family,' said Louise. 'I want her to be well brought up.'

'Well,' said Susan. 'That's settled then.'

'Pardon?'

'Our daughters will be of very similar age, will they not?' said Susan.

'Virtually sisters,' said a third voice. The abbess had entered the room. 'Your children, and may God grant you both daughters, will be virtually sisters.'

'In that case, I will call mine Mary-Louise Hollandine,' said Susan.

Louise laughed. 'You do know that the *Hollandine* is worth £200 a year to me? The States of Holland bribed my parents to name me after their province by giving me a pension for life. Sadly I don't think they would let me transfer it. So be content with Mary-Louise, and I shall be content with naming mine Susan,' said Louise.

'You may place the two girls together, if you have a suitable home,' said the abbess.

'I do,' said Susan. 'Kate Ayliffe. She will happily take "twins", and is a good woman.'

'And what is your connection to her?' asked the abbess.

'She is the mother of my sister-in-law, Anne, who died in childbirth. She will consider it an honour and privilege to educate our daughters. Anne would have felt at home in the Sisterhood.'

'Then you ought name your daughters accordingly,' said the abbess. 'Or simply let Mrs Ayliffe name them as their temperaments dictate.'

'As you see fit, Reverend Mother,' said Louise.

'But we are ahead of ourselves, ladies,' said the abbess. 'Some months lie between us and when we must think of such things. In the meantime, you, Susan, have a visitor.'

With this, the abbess turned and left the room. Susan took her leave of Louise Hollandine and followed her hostess along the convent's corridors until they reached the main gate. The abbess pointed to a small door to the left that was ajar, and motioned for her to enter. 'Remember you are under the protection of the convent,' she said. Susan walked in.

'Good morning,' said the more elegantly dressed of the two men, choking slightly as he took in Susan's appearance.

'Well if it isn't the great Sir Samuel Morland,' said Susan, looking him up and down. 'It appears our situations have much changed since last we met.'

'Miss Susan, I am so very sorry,' said Morland, indicating his eye. 'Sorry for...' he stumbled over his words.

'Your master's delight in defiling me, as if he had not already tormented me enough?'

'As you know, Master Secretary Thurloe took your betrayal hard.'

'I do not doubt it. I took his piercing of my eye with his dagger hard.' She lifted the patch, revealing a milky white orb. 'I saw it, you know. Every second of it.'

'Now that is interesting,' said Morland, but Susan cut him off with a wave.

'What is it you want, sir? You have come a long way to meet a woman who does not wish to see your pasty face and over whom you have no power. You and your man cannot lay a finger upon me.'

'And why would Nathaniel and I wish that?' said Morland. 'We are ambassadors of a different nature.'

'And we'll find who told you of my whereabouts, and they will suffer.'

'Save your breath. I found you by mine own endeavour.'

'You? How?' Susan barely suppressed her laughter as she spoke.

'It wasn't hard,' said Morland. He then presented her with his hand, opening the fingers to reveal a silver locket lying on his palm. 'I believe this belongs to you.'

Susan stared at him before taking it from his hand. 'Thank you.'

'A fine piece, with a particularly interesting hinge. I believe there to be just the one maker in Antwerp capable of such delicate work. Goes by the name of Gordon, though it appears there is not a Scots bone in his body. He is a mischievous individual, ever keen to spread gossip if it works to his advantage, though only if it be truth. I would trust him with my last penny, though perhaps not yours. It just so happens that I commissioned him to make a smaller and more accurate version of the counting machine I showed you. While we discussed its inner workings I showed him the locket, your locket, and following some persuasion he informed me that he makes several every year. Always the same design, always for women.' He paused as he smiled at his own ability. 'The women are always different, and yet always already possess their own locket, so they plainly do not intend to wear it themselves. And I find this most interesting. Moreover, the bill is always settled from the same source. And when I trace the source, what should I find but a convent I recognise as one of the correspondence addresses of S.H.? And who should appear when I request an audience with Miss Susan but Susan Hyde, sister to Sir Edward?'

'Congratulations,' said Susan. 'Though I think you may find that no one will believe you, when you say you have found a dead woman.'

'There are at least two others aware of your Lazarine resurrection,' said Morland. 'Though I concur that they know not who you truly are.'

'Very impressive. And is your employer one of these individuals?'

'No. Master Secretary Thurloe has not the slightest inkling that you, and his child, are alive and well. He mourns, in his own way.'

'I can't say I care overmuch,' said Susan. 'Nor do I much care that you came all this way to tell me how clever you are.'

'Not exactly,' said Morland. 'We came here to lay our service at your feet. We came here because we wish to switch sides.'

Afterword

On 1st December, 1656, John Cosin wrote a letter to Edward Hyde. In it, he recounted a story told him by his daughter concerning 'ye Gentlewoman yt had so neere a relation to you, & so great a friendship for her'. The story was of the arrest, imprisonment and, ultimately, the tragic death of Susan Hyde, following which he notes that 'Mrs Chaffin got her burryed, but ye mayd knows not how.'

At the end of the letter, Cosin refers, it seems, to Hyde's pamphlet, when he says that he will 'number yor sister among them yt haue ye glory of Martyrs'.

Because of the unreliability of the postal service, especially to the continent, Hyde did not receive this letter until the following April. His response, assuming he penned one, is lost.

In *The History of the Rebellion*, written by Sir Edward Hyde, Earl of Clarendon, following the restoration of Charles II to the throne, no mention whatsoever is made of his sister, Susan.

As for Diana Jennings, time will tell.